By The Icehawk's
Feather

· · · • • ● • • · ·

Gisela Gibbon

ISBN: 9798674040422

Hello & Acknowledgements

IT'S BEEN QUITE an adventure writing my first novel, inspired by https://nanowrimo.org/. The idea is to write 50,000 words in November and then continue with your newly developed habit. I'd strongly recommend visiting the page if you fancy giving your writing a solid start.

My biggest thanks goes to my husband Howard Gibbon for coping with a very absent minded wife writing like a woman possessed, ignoring him, night in, night out, and having to read the whole thing twice, even though he's not a novel reader, at all.

A huge thank you, also, to Susan Bird, for proofreading the second draft of the book, with much patience and brilliant editing tips. And equally to Susan Cripps, for her invaluable advice during the third, or was it the fourth? And final draft - every writer needs the input of a retired English teacher. Fact.

The late Roy Carter in the book was our real life music teacher, with a history in Barbania much as described, and I'm pleased to say that he liked what I wrote about him, which I was able to show to him in the months before he passed away. Here's to you Roy.

Also the late Amy Hildreth Duncan, jazz pianist, composer and band leader in Rio de Janeiro, was an online friend of mine who was pleased when I told her she'd get a mention. Here's to you, Amy. All other characters are fictitious, or are they?

John Denver's song, 'The Eagle and Hawk', let it play through your mind while you're reading, and if this ever gets turned into a movie, it'll be the title song. The song, sung before the shed meeting is courtesy of Roy Heim, based on a poem by Star Stone.

Also, thank you to Donald Ellis, New York https://www.donaldellisgallery.com/ for his kind permission to use the image of Yup'ik Shamanic tool. I would love to visit this gallery!

Cover design by the brilliant Sam Aalam, thanks, Sam!

Thanks also to others who had a go at reading some or all of the first draft and giving valuable feedback during various stages, namely Janet Goring, Richard Kemerink op Schiphorst, Sophia Robson, Chris Edwards, Sally Brown and Chris Fairchild.

The locations themselves are pretty much accurate, so are the descriptions of Balderson's, https://www.visitthorntonledale.co.uk/local/baldersons-welcome-cafe and Wardill Bros. http://www.wardillbros.co.uk/ both of which I hope will still exist in 2033.

Since I'm no scientist and I've never been to Alaska in my life I couldn't have written this book without reference material and online research. No idea what the good people of Chignik will think of my imaginative take on their place, they will probably roll about laughing, but I hope some might enjoy the story and maybe even feel a bit flattered that someone in the UK fell in love with their life from afar.

http://www.alutiiqlanguage.org/

https://en.wikipedia.org/wiki/Chignik,_Alaska

https://en.wikipedia.org/wiki/Kenneth_B._Storey

https://en.wikipedia.org/wiki/Laura_Mersini-Houghton

Enjoy the book, thanks for buying it, folks!

Gisela www.giselagibbon.co.uk

· · · • ● ● ● • · ·

Contents

· · · • ● ● ● • · ·

Chapter 1
November 5th, 2033. Nina.

NINA DANIELS DIDN'T know about the crash. She was kicking pebbles at the deserted bus stop, waiting for the No.42 to take her home. She shouldn't have done it. It was stupid and flippant to mock the law, and now they had taken her car. They, who had no sense of humour about the obligatory satcam she'd covered up with a smiley sticker, apparently that wasn't funny. Nor that she didn't want to be spied on in her own car. At least she'd get it back once they fitted it with a new tamper proof one. She'd gotten off lightly, really, she shouldn't be moaning. Frowning at the grey North Yorkshire sky, Nina quickly analysed the clouds, willing them to bring snow. But no, no sign of it yet, too early in the season. Pity. Not too early for the newspapers, though, already screaming the winter warnings complete with the usual snowdrift images, dotted with stranded cars and old people struggling in heavy coats. It was the same story every year, playing on the great British fear of the snowflake. The very stuff she adored.

She'd felt slightly more in charge at the estate agent earlier. The night before her and Brent had been all excited about their joint decision to sell the house, to find new horizons and adventure in their lives, only to be rudely interrupted by the police knocking on their door to announce they would confiscate her car, with stern looks, unimpressed with her sticker idea. Not really the adventure they'd had in mind. The Law showing up like that had seriously freaked her out, but the next day, cheered on by the memory of Brent hugging her and laughing it all off with his usual lightheartedness, she had ventured out as planned, by bus instead, to find out how much their little cottage would be worth, and go from there.

After the discussion with the estate agent Clarice it would have been so much nicer to get back into her hatchback. Her 'Prof Dad', as she'd called her father affectionately, had bought the car for her just before his sudden death three years earlier, for her thirtieth birthday. Such a great memory, of the two of them venturing out together, visiting local car dealers, in total harmony. On a mission to find what had become a rarity, a truly spacious hatchback that wasn't one of the tiny self-driving things that would feel like a mobile birdcage taking over her life. Nina needed something to suit her independent spirit and her endless creative ventures, and most of all her one woman interior design business. Greg had agreed that she should be able to load it up with tools and paint and old bits of furniture to tart up. And there it had stood, that vision of metallic red in the far corner of the sales yard, the hatch open like an invitation, waiting for her in the sunshine. Perfect for advertising her 'Ninja Nina Interiors' business, making people laugh and remember her name. It was great to make people laugh, while remaining totally professional, turning even the smallest spaces into something special. And now this? She was cross with herself. She could have lost her license, with that little sticker stunt. Not clever, not clever at all.

Not that it wasn't justified, that satcam shouldn't be spying on her and everyone around her. On where she was going, when, how fast, how often. Mass surveillance just wasn't right, however much they kept going on about road safety. Who'd want to share their life with Big Brother anyhow? And now she'd have a remote alarmed 'grass-up' satcam invading her space. Nuisance. She could feel her shoulders itch with the irritation of it and reached for another chewy sweet in her pocket. Chewy sweets were cheery things. Clarice had watched Nina eating one after another in disbelief, not appreciating that today was obviously a comfort food day.

The bus was late. That didn't even make sense. Few people used it off season and the Kirbymoorside round was hardly London rush hour. Especially the only bus route to the old Ryedale Folk Museum, the nearest stop to her and Brent's home in Hutton-le-Hole. Almost entirely controlled by the head office, buses were never late. Nina swiped the iLink on her wrist across the stop scanner again, to make sure the Malton depot would know she was still waiting. The green in-service sign flashed dutifully, 'Viver's Place, Kirkbymoorside', but there was no reply, no notice of any delay or cancellation. Just too weird. The previous year it had been announced that bus drivers weren't needed any more, the new coaches could drive themselves, but local people had as much as boycotted automated busses, so Bill Stanley and a few other drivers got their jobs back in a surprise move, all within a month.

Nina smiled at the thought of her Mum Mary, who travelled on Bill's bus all the time, to do her shopping in the Malton Retail Park or to call in at Janet's Tea Rooms, loving every minute of her journey. Bill was really a friend, to everyone in the village, a big and comfy round bellied man with an unruly mop of fuzzy ginger and grey hair. He had a shiny pink faced big grin that only fell when he talked about driverless transport being forced on everyone. And that it was digital or virtual, D-screens or V-screens for every single thing, when you could just use your own eyes.

Everyone knew Bill liked her Mum, that he was being careful not to be too pushy seeing as she was a widow, but when he talked to his passengers about the stink of diesel with such fondness on almost every journey, her Mum would come home repeating it all with a cute subtle glow in her laughing eyes, the affection obviously mutual. Nina really only remembered petrol, LPG and electric cars, before solar energy plus hydrogen fuel became the standard, just as soon as someone had figured out how to store hydrogen cheaply enough locally, without it evaporating. She did remember service stations smelling horrible, probably because of that diesel Bill was still on about 15 years later.

Force of habit made Nina check out the purply grey cloud cover in the sky again, with hints of yellow in it, that would have to be that bit more mustardy, even greenish, to mean snow. Snow, and the longing for it, was in her blood, her Grandmother Nellie Saltwater was a born and bred Alutiiq in Chignik, Alaska, and still lived there.

When other kids talked about grandparents in Scarborough or holidays in Spain, Nina would talk about her Grandma and their holidays in Alaska. She loved to show off with that one, even now. Effective every time. She would tell stories about the bay sheltered by the snowy mountain range, of strong good humoured men and women working on their nets and fishing boats bobbing about in the icy Chignik waters. She'd laugh how when it was cold it was properly freezing, nothing like this tepid cold here. How the Alutiiqs were a hardy and beautiful people, Nellie, Mary and herself all sharing those same dark almond eyes, olive skin, shiny black hair like a mustang's. Her Mum and her stood out as being 'different' in North Yorkshire, but Nina was okay with that. Having been raised to be confident about her looks had helped against the odd racist remarks from other kids which thankfully never got out of hand. But visiting Chignik and looking like so many of the locals there really was just the best, it did feel like home. So very different than hanging about like this in Kirkby. It would be right to move, to new challenges, to a different life. It did feel stagnant now. Maybe she should suggest to Brent for them to move to Alaska? Why had she never thought of that before? Would she want to, would he? What was there for them? Her Dad had worked there on his science projects for weeks at a time, but Brent was an artistically minded carpenter, a proper old fashioned chippy, as he called himself. Would there be enough work for them? She remembered the mostly utilitarian houses and furniture, smart design meant useful there, not necessarily pleasing to the eye, however charming in a rustic sense. Alaskans made do, fixed old things up, got more excited about the latest snowmobile than house interiors, but even with her flair for design Nina loved the

Alaskan life, the air, the food, simple survival, unfussy, and often brutally honest.

The cutting sound of a car horn startled Nina back to that much less exciting bus stop. Her neighbour Sharon Gossling, aka Sharon Gossip, drove past her tooting the horn, at a ludicrous snail's pace in her silly little frog like self-drive car, no boot space whatsoever, and waved with a wide smile, or rather a showing of teeth, like an aggressive dog pretending to be harmless. She could have stopped to offer her a lift if she really was as friendly as she was making out to be, Nina realized crossly, seeing as she was on her way home from work, but then it would have been like climbing into a car with Jekyll and Hyde. You never knew when that bleached blonde smiley neighbour of theirs turned into some hormonal monster from hell, a sad fact often talked about amongst the other villagers who had been equally snarled at out of the blue. Her kids had been taught much the same ways, and the husband had finally legged it. And who could blame him? That woman needed a scan for sure, starting at the head, Nina grinned inwardly.

'Nowt so queer as folk' old Spencer from the village always said about Sharon, gruff but kind, salt of the earth Spencer. He popped round every so often, with the gift of the odd illegal bottle of his home brew hidden under his coat, knowing they wouldn't tell. There wasn't a lot left in life that wasn't illegal, that much everyone knew, all the best basic fun experiences and any idea of independent experimentation frowned upon by some grey people in grey suits in grey offices with grey lives who preferred robotic Serfs to talk to. AI woven into everything. Good job people knew how to have a laugh up here still.

Nina looked up over the rooftops and sniffed the air. The afternoon had brought out strong late autumn smells like an emerging perfume of dry leaves and old moss from somewhere. It would mean some more light showers within a day, followed by sunshine. She was still good at that, reading the colours of the clouds, and interpreting the smells of nature, fancying herself as an expert ever since Grandma Nellie had taught her. Nellie could smell exactly what type of rain or snow or wind was to come and from which direction, or even if there would be an ice fog, that covered everything in icicles, cruel and beautiful at once.

Iced over eyelashes were one of Nina's earliest Alaska memories, she was only four or so when it was her first time to experience what was routine for everyone else there. She had been so excited, running back into the warmth of the house, the 'Denali' as it was called, after the Great Mountain, to show everyone. By the time she got to the warm kitchen her eyelashes had melted and everyone had laughed at her when she was all excited about it. The other Elders would let her sit amongst them by the big old kitchen stove, wrapped in a thick red, blue, green and yellow patterned blanket, matching their brightly coloured waterproofs drying on the wooden pegs, and they'd all listen to the wind howling and the snow getting deeper outside, the sound of others' footsteps outside changing depending how deep the snow was. Nobody was scared of it, it was part of life there, so Nina wasn't scared either.

She'd curl her little hands round the mug of hot cider and have her sourdough bread with smoked herring and a bit of tinned pear and sit listening to them laugh and talk about the herring drying and the nets full of salmon and Alaskan char again after some crisis years back. She loved the way Grandma Nellie would do her hair and then plaited Nina's just like it, in the old Inuit way. Tiny Chignik was inhabited partly by Alutiiqs, making up over half of them at least, but there were a few families from all over the US, and those of Russian, Chinese, and Japanese heritage there, and one or two Europeans as well. It meant most of the classic features and colours of the world were seen in the small community of around three hundred people, all living together peacefully, at least that she knew of.

Grandma Nellie, her daughter Mary and Nina shared the same strong legs and shoulders, genes that had helped generations to cope with walking through deep snow, through rainy gales, or balancing themselves on boats and with carrying the meat cuts from the muskox hunts.

'And you three women are as stubborn as a stubborn hoofed moose.', Nellie's best friend Bob Tukatuk would say. He lived two houses down. The memory of Bob made Nina smile to herself, looking as he did, like a huge native American chief straight out of the movies, the only man there who had long black hair with chunky streaks of grey and white in it, and kind and humorous eyes. Nina nodded to herself, idly picking some loose paint off the old bus stop railing. She would call her Grandma, now probably the oldest Elder, when she got home, to tell her she remembered it all. It had been too long. And that sometimes she could see a bit of the green aurora from Yorkshire, which made her feel kind of homesick for Chignik. Nina missed the rainbow curtains in the skies above Alaska, even though she'd never really seen the most stunning ones, Chignik being too far south. But they had been good enough 'light dancers' as she called them, like fluorescent skirts and sails billowing in the wind, and that was better than enough for the memory and for a good story. She'd have to tell Nellie that Brent and her were planning to visit again, soon.

Where on earth was that bus? She checked her iLink again, 23 minutes late now, totally bizarre. It was three and half miles to get home. Walking wasn't really part of her exercise plan for today, but as there was only one bus every hour, it was a toss up between standing there and getting grumpy, standing there and turning the whole situation into some kind of meditation of surrender, or walking and feeling righteously worn out this evening. If she rang Brent now, her gorgeous funny ginger haired pale and freckly Brent, her "Carrot Face", he'd drop everything, probably shut up his workshop for the day and pick her up. That would be so weak, though. She should be able to get herself home, figure this out for herself. She could call a taxi, which would be the obvious solution. The taxicon on her iLink was all it would take, her location forwarded, a taxi sent, driverless or Serf driven, either would do. It always cost a small fortune though. No, the obvious solution would be for the bus to arrive as it was supposed to. She'd give it five more minutes, and then start walking. Anyway, never mind the cost, needing a taxi would be almost as pathetic as calling Brent.

The new solar foot and cycle paths feeding into the local grid were smooth and soft, easy to walk on, she'd only have to amble along the main road for a tiny bit and then turn north towards her village, in between the winter spelt and dormant rapeseed fields. With any luck she'd see some pheasants, wildlife was plentiful in North Yorkshire, nobody hunted or culled anything any more and it was all organic farming, too. Most of the Brits had joined in with the resistance against chemicals in food, against fracking industries polluting their water and trashing the countryside, and with Yorkshire having been especially successful, it was still beautiful here.

Yes! A long walk would do her good. She could think about their house move and surprise Brent at the workshop. A quick look on her body monitor in her iLink said she would need neither food, fluids, nor a bathroom break for another couple of hours, so that was ok, too. Nina set her trainer soles onto the walk mode setting, giving them more of a springy rebound. The next bus if that ever showed would probably pass her. If it was Bill at the wheel he'd stop for her anyhow. Her Mum might even be on that bus; that would be fun for both.

In the end Clarice had been positive enough about their chances of selling their traditional semi with the small south facing cottage garden at a decent price. Quite good not having kids, she thought, yes, sometimes she wished they had, but the freedom to go just anywhere, without having schools with their fixed child locality laws and ethnic balance regulations to worry about was pretty neat. Babies just never happened for them, and it was ok.

The village of Hutton-le-Hole was idyllic. Orange yellow sandstone houses, daffodils and bluebells in the spring, an oxygen filter stream. Mainly good people lived there, artists and musicians and retired teachers, Sharon being a bit of an exception. And there were picturesque places nearby, Kirkby itself wasn't bad and Thornton-le-Dale was so great, with her favourite 'bits and pieces' shop, owned by the now fifth generation of the Wardill Brothers' family. Sound people they were, and sold just about everything in that veritable Aladdin's cave of theirs. And then there was their favourite cafe and bakery, too, run by the Balderson's family since 1890, which was spacious and airy and served wonderful home made, traditional, 'proper' food. The cafe even still served real mashed potatoes and sausages on old fashioned plates, not on those depressing calorie measuring ones. There were a couple of decent pub restaurants and the cutest ever annual duck-race down the little stream passing by the historic thatched cottage with the front garden full of bright flowers. Nina and Brett could spend the day in York or Scarborough if they wanted to, or go up to Whitby. Being bored with such perfection was perhaps bordering on ungrateful, but they both agreed they needed something different to happen, some excitement, some new challenges they just weren't presented with here. Except for a perfectly controlled bus not turning up.

Turning off the main road into the field path her thoughts wandered back to Chignik. She wouldn't have such easy choices of luxury there. Those special childhood memories were all about being loved and cared for, about feeling safe and free. She felt safe with Brent, but both might get bored rigid living in some deserted place, with harsh winters, however much they'd be welcome there. Strange how she just needed to think of Nellie's house and could feel herself transported there almost immediately. Ah yes, the smell of the salmon jerky from Grandma Nellie's larder, and the hot apple cider with pumpkin pie vodka, the welcome drink they'd always get to make them strong against the cold, with a thin layer of cream on the top. Like pie in a glass it was.

Nina could still feel her red hot cheeks and tickly nose when the alcohol hit her, especially aged nine, when she'd had a sneaky extra sip from her mother's glass. Just one was enough to make her feel so comfy she wanted to stay forever.

The sound of the snow mobiles, the 'saniiks', a bit like quad bikes on skis, how fast they could fly over the snow, and the barks of a few sled dogs somewhere in the distance, with their sleds just waiting for her like a fun fair ride. The knowing that they'd go for a ride on them before long, and the grown-ups would let her practice the commands, shouting out "Mush, mush!" for "Go", or "Gee" for "right", and "Haw" for "left", which had made her feel like a real musher. And the mixed breed Alaskan huskies all being gentle and obedient with her but so powerful all the same. Her grandma just called them 'piugtas', 'dogs', so she did, too. Being allowed to try the pedalling, which meant pushing the sled with one foot while the other remained on the runner, was quite a skill she only got the hang of after she turned twelve or so. Also learning to keep the dogs from running off too soon, so eager they were, by using the snow hook as an anchor. Those were proper winters. Mild as far as Alaska was concerned, but just perfect to her mind.

The summers were never too hot, full of wild flowers and berries, and the fishing tourists always thought she was a local girl. She never put them right. And she'd casually on purpose pretend to ask for the visitors to hear if anyone was taking a boat out to Eagle Rock, the rocky island that looked so special she wanted to live there all by herself. Alaska was such a place of extremes, of hearty hospitality and ingenuity at one end and the hateful shooting of beautiful wolves, wolverines and bears for sport at the other. All right, begrudgingly she had to admit, sometimes for survival, too. But she'd never forget those bear heads on the walls staring at her, and the countless photos of grinning hunters, kneeling by the beautiful animals they had shot in such a cowardly way. As if it took any skill at all to hit such huge and innocent targets. It made her feel sick to the stomach and ashamed of being human. Unless the animals were killed for food of course, sustenance hunting was ok somehow. She'd had a bear burger once and didn't want to admit how much she had liked it.

Nina realized the walk was making her hungry. Another mile to go, she would raid Brent's not so secret cake stash at the workshop and they could chat about their future, surrounded by the smell of sawdust and coffee.

Chapter 2
The Bus - Mary, Damian, Bill, Karen and Kade

'THIS IS SUCH a fancy coach.' Mary thought, looking at her heavy bag of shopping with satisfaction. 'Glad to sit down now.' She liked the new solar buses they had introduced, quiet, clean, and with the antibacterial handles and seat coverings, the perfect air-conditioning and air disinfection systems. Not that she wouldn't much rather stick her head out of an open window sometimes, but those days were long gone. The toilets were still as claustrophobic as ever though, and the floor at the entrance doubling up as scales was ridiculous. So was the unfairness of the fare being calculated by weight.

Mary looked at Bill's face reflected in the mirror. Such a kind man. Some other drivers wouldn't even hold her shopping while she stood in the weighing area, saying the shopping had to be weighed, too. It was degrading and punitive, her daughter Nina was right about that, but she loved the journey all the same. The Yorkshire countryside timeless, green, with those ever changing skies and Bill chatting away was such good fun. In your own car nobody bothered you about what you weighed. But you never had anyone new to talk to, her own car would be more expensive in the long run, and there was no Bill to listen to either. She wouldn't be so lucky in London, she appreciated again for the umpteenth time. It was all driverless public transport there, hover trolleys linking up with hydrogen fuelled trains. The black cabs, too, all driverless or Serf robot driven.

At only sixty-one years old, she hadn't gotten round to getting her over 60s driver's license, when everyone had to take your test all over again, at the driving school in York. The testers put her off when she went to have a look at the place, a bunch of condescending twenty year olds talking to anyone with greying hair as if they were slow minded and hard of hearing. She had loved driving just as much as Nina did now, but it just wasn't the same anymore, not for her, she mused. In the old days she could just drive up at the pump, fill her tank and pay with real cash and then card, and then by the wrist scanner. But you somehow knew what you're putting in there, how it all worked. Now, however, it felt like driving a hydrogen bomb on wheels, even if those were puncture proof, which admittedly was pretty good. Nina always teased it was better than a petrol bomb on wheels, both of them having a good giggle about it, remembering the dog sleds in Alaska they always called the snow rockets.

'Ah, Alaska. Home.' Mary continued her reverie. Memories, of looking after the dogs every day before her father insisted she should go to a boarding college in Oregon to study for her teaching degree in Maths and English. Alaska was good for nobody, he always said. It was a compromise apparently, instead of being sent even further to New York and how lucky that her tall and wiry geeky Greg had made college more exciting than even the sled dogs. He adored her, worshipped the ground beneath her feet, thought that her dark Alaskan looks meant she was strong and exotic. She had been rather more conscious of her classic hook nose she thought was so ugly compared with the white American straight noses. She had the best white perfectly even teeth though, with no help from the dentist at all, which came in very useful to flash them American style when other girls bitched about her, calling her Eskimo trash and so on. Mary laughed just thinking about it. It all seemed a long time ago now.

Quiet gentle Greg. He had made her feel safe and valued and she in turn managed to bring him out of himself. He started to socialise more, got used to not always acting the quintessentially British intellectual, though to find things that would really amuse him had been hard going at first. Somehow they muddled through their differences, and eventually moved to North Yorkshire, his home county. He'd been glad to be back and she quite liked the place then as much as now, there was the same straightforward hospitality as the one she'd missed away from home. They got married and lived easily together, at a comfortable pace. Thankfully Yorkshire was far removed from the government in London. The capital historically classed the North as a second rate part of the country and pretty much ignored it. Mary considered this a bonus.

Then Nina came along and they both felt complete. For Mary to be able to give up teaching was a blessing, what with the ever growing maze of rules all schools were subjected to, none of which had anything to do with expanding young minds, nor with real life. They felt lucky and comfortable. Greg's status as a biophysicist had soon grown into the much respected name of Professor Gregory Hudson, with his breakthrough discoveries in molecular reactions within body cells. He had even overcome his shyness to become an international lecturer and writer and was involved in biodiversity research back in Oregon and all over Europe. He never seemed stressed, quite the opposite, he'd become increasingly excited about the idea of biological processes and other life forms in a quantum universe. Yes, she would listen, and would nod her head for so long, but someone in the family had to have their feet on the ground, she'd been the practical pragmatist. Being a mother, and having some success as a landscape artist and with her soapstone carvings, being in love with Greg, yes, she nodded to herself, that life should have gone on forever, much longer than it did anyhow.

Nina. Gorgeous little girl she was, happy as can be. A continually giggling whirlwind, with her mane of black hair and fast little legs running through the house and down the lane and back again, like an excited puppy. It wasn't long before they

13

nicknamed her 'Huskie', it stuck too, even Brent used it with her at times, Mary had noticed. And now she was an equally cheerful freelance interior designer, a very good one indeed. Mary took a deep breath to dissolve that familiar tightness in her chest, still fruitlessly angry with Greg for dying too soon. Sixty-three was just no age at all. If it wasn't for Nina she'd have probably gone back to Alaska by now, just to find her centre again, but, her life was here now, with Nina and Brent and her friends and with special people like Bill.

Damian Turner sat a couple of rows behind Mary, lost in his own thoughts. He was angry. At thirty-four years old, he'd basically been thrown on the trash heap. 'Sacked. Fired. Let go', kept repeating in his head. After nearly eighteen years! The last conversation he'd had at work, if you could call the female voice of the admin Serf a 'conversation' at all, was when she handed him the notice chip he was supposed to take to the employment distribution centre, the EDC. No warning, no notice, not even a human handshake. Replaced by AI, just like that. And there was nothing he could do about it. Workers rights? A thing of the past. He was so angry he could spit.

He'd been the head of the quality control department of the P&M Rubbers & Plastics Company, 'The Rubber Shop' as everyone called it. For eighteen years he had worked his way up from apprenticeship onwards, dutifully climbed the ladder and was good at the job. He had hoped he'd work there for life, there was nothing he didn't know about rubber. He seriously loved the stuff. He knew how it was supposed to smell, how the heat sealed seams were supposed to feel, how to squeeze dodgy ones to show the boss why they were faulty and would be an insurance risk eventually. He actually thought his boss liked him. What a fool he'd been.

That rubber, HIS rubber, was used in everything. In bikes and hover scooter handles, in bags and mattresses and armchairs, in 3D printed replacement limbs, in screens of all sizes, even the huge exterior ones in the cities, it really was everywhere, even in implants. Like the latest versions of the iLinks which were manufactured mixed with the wearer's stem cells. They grew into the skin as part of the person after a while, harmlessly, which made it much harder to lose them, but much harder to turn off as well. Damian was wearing one of the first ones that had started to grow into his skin, he'd even volunteered as a guinea pig for it, during some brainless ambitious moment. How easy it was to be turned into a sheep. He groaned at his own stupidity.

The government loved the grown-in idea. Nobody was supposed to switch anything off, nothing that could track every-one's movements anyhow. It wasn't quite compulsory yet, to wear the iLinks 24/7, officially it was 'strongly advised' but whenever he'd turned it off in the past, Damian had received strange home calls after a day or two. And he was certain that the street cam drones in towns like York and Scarborough, Malton even, followed him around until he switched them on again like a good boy. Everything was checked out and supervised all the time, mostly by Serfs. Damian laughed to himself at the irony. That admin one had even put her heated rubber AI hand on his shoulder as if to comfort him. He had probably helped make that hand.

The reality was, he went over it in his head, that unless someone stepped up and offered him a job on the way to the EDC, which realistically wasn't going to happen, he and every man and his dog knew what that chip would mean. Being sent to do SSJs, Supervised Social Jobs, for all the 'delicate commu-nication skills' the more sophisticated Serfs were too expensive and precious for, and not very good at still. He'd most likely have to make conversation with the pensioners in the assessment centres, who didn't understand why they had to be there at all. Some didn't understand very much at all any more. Long weakened by a system that put an unquestioning youth and the usefulness of obedient Serfs before anything or anyone.

He could just picture it. He'd be told to sit there with them, being served crap tea by crap Serfs, patronising the old folk he had been taught to respect. He'd be told to convince them that there were systems in place now, for their own protection, to help them forget the old, outdated ways and assimilate the new technologies available to them more easily. That they would be so much happier if they just trusted the programme, and no longer a burden. They wouldn't want to be a burden to anyone or society, would they. That it was all about social unity. And while they were there they could just as well have their free 'vaccinations' for their own good health. He'd have to pretend to agree with it all. There was just no way he'd cope with that. He'd be trapped there forever, too, as nobody decent employed anyone who had worked for such a contemptible place.

Damian punched the backrest in front of him in frustration, unaware of the dark stare from Bill who had caught the sudden move on his rear view monitor. He remembered his Mum crying in bitter outrage when she confided in him that she discovered, by some total fluke, that the sudden onset dementia so many were told about was deliberately engineered. As a nurse she'd chanced upon a secret memo she wasn't meant to read, - that the much advertised extra gentle flu vaccine for the elderly were actually injections to deliberately cause dementia. Easily done by a strong cocktail of amyloid and tau proteins, which basically destroy brain connections, to be given to a vast number of the over 70's, especially those who were on record to have had a bit of an anti-government past. Records they themselves had provided, conveniently, through social networking so popular until just a decade earlier. And how easy that was, a flu vaccination a perfect cover. And if they didn't volunteer for the jab a bit of 'gentle persuasion' from 'counsellors' would help things along. Like lambs to the slaughter, perfectly healthy and active pensioners would queue up and get their flu jabs and return home not remembering anything of any use within a couple of weeks or months. Not even their families. Clearly it wasn't the young the government were worried about, it was the older ones who still remembered real democracy, freedom of choice and movement, and voted accordingly. And who inspired the young to question the system and rebel, too. What better way to silence the population than literally dumb the old ones down?

It was an obvious sign of the government's insecurity, though, which in itself was enough to fuel the idea of a freedom revolution, the need for it growing all the time. Damian and his Mum had sat together, so angry about it, wondering what to do about any of it. Vaccinations weren't part of Yvonne's job any more, all done by Serfs with the vaccination gun, so it was frustratingly difficult for her to intervene without getting found out. She'd tried her damnedest to put off anyone in that age group from going, keeping her eyes and ears open for like-minded colleagues to help save the elderly.

Damian leaned back in his seat, and breathed hard, rubbing his dark curly hair with both his hands. He would love to get away, just for a while, the urge was almost overwhelming. His Mum and him had even talked about how he could start an undercover revolution, to turn it all round with like-minded good people, until there would be enough of them to be an undeniable force for liberty and justice. He'd be a revolutionary, a modern day hero, Robin Hood of the 2040s or something. An amusing fantasy, if nothing else, but slowly the idea had grown in his head that it might be possible - 'Freedom for the People!' He'd shout, followed by his Mum laughing and enthusiastically punching her fist in the air, calling him a 'wicked socialist', both of them laughing and fantasising about parallel universes where they could meet with like minded souls without arousing suspicion. Damian loved the way his Mum's eyes would light up, in hope and belief in him. As mothers went she was seriously cool. And the last person he'd want to let down.

Damian stared out the bus window. He felt different just thinking of it again, always had, felt there was something bigger out there for him, a more important destiny. If he could only reach the voice that kept telling him, hear It more clearly, enough to understand. He would have dreams, in which he'd know what to do, but every time he woke up he'd forget the details, left with the pain of knowing there was something that needed to be done, so frustrating it made his shoulders itch, as if he wanted to jump out of his skin. The world needed a change, so did he now, but first he had to get away, and think how. It wouldn't be easy, he couldn't use his bank funds to get away, all transactions would show exactly where he was, courtesy of a cashless society, every move on record, but he did have his little gold stash he could get to still, his Mum's wise investment for him when he was little. Gold was still good, plenty of people who'd accept it in exchange for helping him disappear and get him the gear he might need. He had also managed to steal a sample piece of the new contact rubber he wasn't supposed to know about, that could mess with electronic signals, blocking them completely. Duplicating that would be a priority. He just wasn't going to take it all lying down. But what could he do? How?

Staring glumly out the window Damian noticed a flock of seagulls swooping over the field they'd been feeding on. They could take off, just like that. Could go anywhere they pleased. Wouldn't it be great to just grow a pair of wings and fly away, just like them, unnoticed? And why was it suddenly so cold? Looking around to see if some window had opened he felt the shivers down his back and in his legs, like the ones you might get with a flu. Had he caught a bug of sorts? Great, that would round off the day just perfectly. Damian rubbed his thighs, looking at the others, nobody else seemed to feel it.

Bill was careful not to make it too obvious that he was still watching Damian on his monitor. He'd never seen him so agitated. He was a good lad, but his face was like thunder now, so unlike him. And lovely Mary Hudson. One of these days he'd have to ask her out. He only took the shopping bags off her when she stepped into his bus, so he could accidentally on purpose touch her hand, like some spotty teenage boy, he was quite smitten with her. Mary had this quick humour, a great laugh, and a shapely figure he wouldn't mind putting his arms round. Her hair was a salt and pepper chin length bob, with a striking white streak just off her forehead, and intelligent dark eyes but still somehow fragile, they made him want to protect her. Men weren't supposed to talk like that any more, wanting to protect women, it was supposed to be sexist, but heck, he was a man and a Yorkshire man at that. He liked that slight American twang in her voice, with her daughter the spitting image of her. He could listen to her for ages. Both Mary and Nina had taken it hard when Greg died so suddenly.

It had come as a shock to everyone, he'd been a friendly face around the village.

Greg had been a scientist of sorts, but it was all a bit too highbrow for most to really find out what exactly he specialised in. He had often locked himself away writing his academic books and preparing his lectures that made good money to help finance his frequent travels, including his Alaska work trips he was able to take Mary and Nina on to see family there. Bill remembered how Greg had helped Brent set up his carpentry workshop, too. Definitely a good sort. Not sure how he could compete with memories of someone like that, but there was something promising between him and Mary, so he wouldn't give up hope. In another life maybe he'd have been the one to snap her up first.

The little boy in the first row, with his neat short brown hair and even neater side parting, sitting with his Mum silently reading her book was getting on Bill's nerves, banging on his dividing screen with his drinks bottle.

"Will you give it a rest, lad? Try and break some glass somewhere else, enough already!"

The boy giggled and pointed at the satcam watching Bill and pronounced in a rather cocky five year old voice, knocking all the louder on the glass.

"My name is Kade, not 'lad', and you're not allowed to talk to me like that, you'll get the sack and get replaced by a robot!"

"Stop that, Kade, we agreed we mustn't talk like that to service people." His mother said through tight lips.

"What the hell?!" Bill shouted out, not in response to the woman and her kid, but at what he saw on the rear view screen just below the satcam, a dot meaning something coming up behind them, way too fast, at unreal speed! Too fast for even the override to take over! One look at his external mirror stopped any other expression in his throat, all he could do was to instinctively swerve to get out of the way of that thing as hard and fast as he could, steering the bus over the grass bank, over the solar footpath, losing control there, hitting the brakes and finally stopping. The left side tyres down in the muddy ditch he felt himself being thrown to the left, his temple hitting the window hard, and the seat constraint digging into his ribs. A freezing cold gust of wind blew in from somewhere and he could just hear Mary cry out in the back before he lost consciousness.

Chapter 3
The News, Brent and Connor

BRENT WAS IN his 'Brent Daniels, Carpentry and Bespoke Furniture' workshop sharpening his router bits with his laser set-up, uneasily keeping an eye on the cheerful wall clock Nina had bought him. His 'Cheer-o'clock Clock', she called it, so typical of her childlike enthusiasm for daft things. 3pm already. Through the dusty window he could see it was a bit dull outside, but no rain yet. The wind was just strong enough to turn the roof turbine that powered his smaller machinery. Right now the 3D printer, that fused left over wood shavings and resin to make little toys to his designs, was purring along quite y. Nina's clients liked them, they sold a lot of them to people who liked a special personal memento from their home designer when her work was done. Nina was late, not that unusual, but he was getting impatient to hear from her, and what the estate agent had said. He was feeling a bit uneasy, too. Jittery for some reason. He was wondering if she got into trouble about her satcam, they hadn't heard any more about it, no fine or anything. A mild slap on the wrist and a request for an alarmed refit seemed almost too easy. Brent had told her at the time that sticking a smiley sticker over the lens wasn't really such a good idea, however funny. He did agree with her reasons for it though. Nowhere seemed safe any more from prying eyes.

It had started so innocently, Brent knew from his parents and their contemporaries, how convenient it had all been. First the computers and smartphones with cameras, and then the location software that would help you find your lost or stolen property. The microchips for your pets, then the chipped toy watches and keyrings to track where your kids were. And next of course the medical e-bracelets, so you could be found in an emergency and so it went on. It had created so much fear, but of what exactly? And now everyone was trapped, all those communication and safety devices had become the balls and chains of convenience.

They'd had a family confab about it once, and decided to reduce their iLink use unless it was absolutely necessary. It was just better to actually meet up and talk face to face. There were still places where you could be pretty much yourself, if you put a bit of effort into it.

Scrap yards were safe, with so much metal and old plastics interfering with signals. Empty churches, too, they still stood but had largely fallen into disrepair, the stained glass windows and benches gone, stolen mainly, or more kindly, kept safe. Any public gatherings for any reason were a thing condemned to the past. First the pandemics put a stop to all group activities, even team sports, and then almost overnight all expressions, symbols, statues, songs and literature of all religious faiths had been destroyed and made illegal worldwide by the all encompassing New World Order that had been birthed to stop the threatening war between East and West. Adherence to international atheist law was immediately enforced by the NWO armies and spybots, denounced as outdated indoctrination that would only result in terrorism and extreme indoctrination. The irony hadn't been lost, of course, there was no talk of love and tolerance in the new order.

Some of the tiny deserted rural chapels were still romantic places to go to and to imagine what it must have been like when people could still come together in them to say prayers or give thanks to whatever god they pleased, without any fear. Brent and Nina would venture out to the ancient Rievaulx Abbey sometimes, another quiet un-surveilled spot, a favourite of Nina's Dad who had tested some strange equipment up there nobody understood.

There was a definite if low key anti-surveillance movement going on, people were just tired of it. The domestic Serfs didn't encourage a sense of privacy either, as useful as they were to have around. He and Nina enjoyed cooking for themselves most of the time, but if they didn't want to they could ask Jester, as they christened him, to throw them something together. He'd scan their iLinks and decide what was most nutritious for them there and then and usually came up with a decent dinner, he wasn't all bad really. He'd order what was needed to stock up the fridge if they asked him to, or put the shopping away if they got it themselves, all very comfortable and convenient. It was still a bit odd cuddling up with Nina on the sofa with this quiet humanoid robot around. Brent was uneasy about it but Nina was much more relaxed calling herself a closet exhibitionist as she laughingly flirted with Jester who literally never batted an eyelid. Brent just hoped that the few adjustments he had made to Jester's system preferences meant their privacy was guaranteed.

He was tempted to call Nina. He could tell her quite honestly that he'd been feeling uneasy all morning and that he couldn't wait for the estate agent news. The house looked good, but wasn't equipped with child safety in mind as they didn't have any. He wasn't sure how easy it would be to sell without the expense of the necessary alterations.

"Brent! Carrot face! Yoo-hoo!" Nina stuck her head through the door, all beaming grin and shiny eyes. "Surprise! Missed me?"

Brent spun round, with such a relieved smile on his face that it made her laugh, he was so cute, and how he dropped everything to rush towards her, with outstretched arms to sweep her into one of his gorgeous hugs.

"Sweetie, where have you been?! I was just about to give in and call you!"

"Ha, I've had an adventure! Would you believe the bus didn't show up? And I walked, really, I did, all the way from Vivers Place, isn't that good? I just can't believe the bus didn't show, has Mum been round? Phew, I'm puffed out! Shall we have a coffee here or go home? Have you got any cake? I'm dying for some cake!"

Brent looked at his wife, as she glowed and waved her arms about, chatting away about her hike from Kirkby and her walk setting on her new trainers being great, and that she'd tell him all about the estate agent once the coffee was made. She was like a whirlwind of enthusiasm and her brain all over the place, creative chaos she called her head. How sexy she looked, god, he fancied her. His soulmate. She was so seriously hot. They'd been together for 14 years and were still good together, in bed and out. His perfect woman, his best friend. He called the "Two lattes" command to the coffee machine, not being able to take his eyes off her. Her black shoulder length hair was windswept, her eyes with such thick black lashes that would never need mascara were dark and fiery and her smile with her perfect white teeth infectious. The dimples in her cheeks showed when she was at her happiest. Nina stopped talking, stopped waving her arm about, noticing that look in his eyes, recognizing her husband's mood she felt herself tingle and was just about to throw him a suitable come-on line to tease him right there in his sawdust covered workshop, when a voice called in from the gate.

"Brent, Nina, you guys in there?"

"God, I don't believe this." Brent said under his breath. "This will have to wait then, but not for long, Huskie, not for long." He squeezed her arm and walked out towards the familiar voice he couldn't quite place. It confused him. Nina loved it when he called her Huskie, her nickname since forever and he made it sound so sexy. Sighing at the interruption she walked over to pause the coffee machine and took a deep breath to settle herself into the welcoming smile she used with her clients, when she realised that voice must have been Connor's. Why did he sound so odd?

"Oh God, Nina, I'm so sorry." Brent turned round to her when he felt her approach, with Connor McLeigh, Brent's best friend who lived across the road at No 5, standing there, looking unusually pale and worried and shuffling his feet as if embarrassed, hands in his grey duffle coat pockets, with pulled up shoulders and rigid arms. Nina looked from one man to the other, both of them always jolly and up for a joke with each other, and now their faces looked so uncharacteristically serious. Something in her turned cold and she looked straight into her husband's eyes, to search what she could read. "What is it, Brent? What's happened?"

Brent turned round helplessly to Connor.

"Nina, there's been an accident." Connor puffed the words out as if he'd been holding his breath.

"I'm so sorry. Bill's bus. And your Mum was on it. She's in hospital. Bill, too. I don't know how bad it is. Someone saw it, and said some seriously weird things, that something flew into the back of the bus, but it made no sense what he said, about a lot of water or ice or something and all sorts. Want me to give you two guys a lift to the hospital, to save you having to fetch your car? I'd be happy to, really. I don't mind..." His voice failed, both Mary and Bill, and Brent and Nina were some of his favourite people of all time. He hated the idea of anything bad happening to any of them, ever.

Nina stood tall, she looked pale, mouth open in shock, her hand to her throat as if to protect it. Closely watched by Brent, and Connor could see it too, it was obvious she was steeling herself, her eyes fixed onto some distant spot. She made herself think positively. Controlling her voice she sounded strangely formal. "I would be grateful, Connor, thank you. Thanks for letting us know, too. My mother will be alright, I'd have felt it if there was anything really bad going on, let's just see what's what before we get all freaked out. I'll just go and get my bag."

Brent followed her in, knowing all too well that she could be strong one minute and go to pieces the next, and he had to turn off his machines anyhow, throw his clean sweater on and lock up. He hadn't told Nina what Connor had told him just a second before she joined him. That one of the passengers had disappeared, into thin air apparently, that it was their friend, Damian Turner, and all that was left of him were his iLink and all his IDs. Nor did either mention say that there were some large feathers stuck on the bus and some inside, too. Brent felt sick. The last time he'd seen one of those was on Greg's deathbed, he didn't understand it and didn't want Nina to hear about it either. "Are you ready?" She nodded, suppressed panic in her eyes.

The long drive to Scarborough Hospital was torture. Nina sat in the back seat, calling her Mum's iLink for the umpteenth time. She had to be alright, she just had to be, she'd have felt it otherwise, of that she was certain. But if she was, why didn't she answer? Bill didn't reply either. What a stupid, stupid situation it was in this day and age to have the hospital as far away as Scarborough. They weren't allowed to break the speed limit of fifty miles an hour, even though Connor and Bill had tinkered with both their cars to enable them to go faster, but on the main road it was just too dodgy, the last thing they needed was to get stopped by one of the police drones hovering in front of their windscreen until they stopped, and then wait for the police or an armed ticket Serf to arrive. She groaned out loud, Brent leaned back to squeeze her hand. They had called the hospital and tried to get some sense out of them, but got no information apart from standard replies and the confirmation at least that Mary and Bill were indeed there. Damn modern communication, Brent thought to himself, all this watching us, but when we need some help there is nothing, no give at all. He was frustrated and worried at the same time. It would be a 40 minute journey without any hold-ups to Scarborough. Also they had all these security checks in place, to check people coming into the town centre for the Guy Fawkes festival, after some youths thought to repeat a mini version of history the year before and tried to blow up the council offices.

"Everything will be alright, won't it?" Connor offered.

"Of course it will." Brent joined in. Nina didn't say anything at all.

Chapter 4
Now or never

DAMIAN GROANED, INSTINCTIVELY touching the top of his head. It felt very cold, and wet. He tried to get his bearings. Struggling to open his eyes he could see the inside of the bus he'd just been traveling in. He couldn't make sense of anything, there was ice and water everywhere, and feathers, large reddish brown and grey striped feathers. His head hurt. Was he hallucinating? Was he dead? No, dead people don't have sore heads, he reassured himself. Looking round he saw that Mary had sunk forward in her seat. Her seat constraints were hanging on to her, but her body looked odd, wrong somehow, and covered in ice. There were icicles everywhere, as if water had dripped off her shoulders, off her hair, off the seat handles, and frozen puddles on the floor. He couldn't see Bill properly, just the visible bit slumped towards the window. The woman with the annoying kid looked straight ahead, as if frozen in time, the kid bent forward with his head against the glass. Nobody was moving, there was no sound at all, why was it so bloody freezing? One window on the left was broken, it must have hit a post or something. Damian saw they were really deep in the ditch, at a slant. His work bag with his stuff was under the seat on the left, the shoulder strap caught around one of the legs.

The sight of his work bag brought it all back, he'd just been made redundant, replaced by Serfs, given his notice chip, oh and then there was the EDC, the job he definitely didn't want! Again his fury rose in him and he felt even colder than before, cold with anger. He looked at his iLink, it wasn't working, it was covered in a layer of frost, frozen into his wrist. He couldn't get his head round it, as a thought formed in his head with such urgency he couldn't ignore - he could get out of here! The broken window, the ditch, he could try! He had no idea what had happened, but he did know if he just left everything behind that could identify him and went to hide somewhere, maybe he could wait it out and remain hidden? For a while at least. Without a further thought he ripped at the grown-in iLink to get it off his arm, it hurt like hell despite the ice, made him bleed, but he continued ripping at it, didn't care, he'd heal, he just wanted rid of the thing. The satisfaction to get it off was way more powerful than the searing pain. His arteries looked intact, that was the main thing. He angled for his bag, the flap frozen, and fished for his IDs, throwing them and his bloodied iLink forward into the silent bus. He'd keep the contact rubber, and the apple and sweets he still had, he'd keep the bag, too, he didn't know what he would need and what not. He just needed to escape, that much he knew.

Damian's head was throbbing, all the more for being torn between making a run for it and checking if he could help the others. But really, what was there he could do? He didn't know if they were frozen, or dead, or what, and that shattered window pane, it was like a sign from the gods, he had to take advantage of it. It was a chance at least. He crawled over towards the window, over the frozen seat. The water had collected along the edges of the floor, partly frozen, his own trousers wet and icy, but he felt no pain apart from his wrist and head. He must have banged it somewhere, it didn't matter, he had to get out.

Damian couldn't see out, but when pushed, the soft broken safety glass gave way easily, and he felt the warm air outside almost tenderly stroke his face, a quick memory of coming home after playing outside in winter, when you opened the front door and the warmth of the house was so lovely and inviting. None of this made sense, but the earthy smell of the mud and grass in the ditch the bus had ended up in were positively welcoming. Looking back at the motionless others once more, Damian wriggled his slim frame through the window.

He tried to figure out which way would be better. Turn right and crawl along underneath the slanted bus, hidden out of sight, or turn left towards the back of the bus where he'd be out on the road in a jiffy, but would most likely be picked up immediately. The police and god knows who would be here soon, ambulances and nosey parkers, so best hide as long as he could. He decided to turn right, hoping the bus would just keep resting securely on the bank, rather than fall on him.

Damian shuffled along on his knees and elbows, couldn't figure out why the outside of the bus was still icy, but the air and earth was warm and normal as it should be, it hadn't been cold. His head was confused, but mainly occupied with trying to figure out how to hide as long as he could. It would be about 4pm, depending how long he'd been out, but it was still just light enough for him to see, even under the bus. He'd have an hour or so before it was properly dark. Would they leave the bus lying there like that long enough? And why was nobody here yet? He heard nothing, no police, no onlookers, no traffic, nobody. Everything was just strange beyond words. He carried on a bit further, spotting a bit of pale, milky grey round concrete sticking through the ground, and if he'd had the space his next thought would have been to punch the air in triumph. Of course!!! The field drains!! Round concrete pipes big enough for him to fit in, along with rats possibly and spiders and whatever muck collected in there, but he didn't care, this was perfect!

He peered into the damp darkness of the drain, it wasn't exactly inviting. Would it be better to go in head or feet first? There wouldn't be any snakes in there, would there? He told himself off for being a wuss, the odd grass snake, some adder maybe, or whatever they were, no more than an outside chance. And he'd never heard of anyone being bitten to death by anything in North Yorkshire, he'd be ok, but it was better going in feet first so he could look out and see what's happening. He decided to take his padded jacket off to maybe put it in front him, it was dark grey so probably not such a bad thing to hide behind in case someone thought to shine a torch in to look for him. He turned round to stick his feet into the pipe and push himself backwards like a scared mole just as he heard some voices, some commotion on the street side of the bus. He knew he had to hurry. He pushed himself further back into the slimy void as fast as he could, stuffed his coat in front of him and rested his bleeding hand and his face on his bag. He'd wait, wait it out as long as he could and try and figure out what to do next.

Chapter 5
Chignik, Alaska. The Icehawk.
Nellie and Bob.

CHIGNIK WAS IN shock. So the Icehawk had come. It really had come. The oldest prophecy ever told had finally happened, on a perfectly clear full moon November night. Perfect for the promised aurora borealis the community had come out to see. Normally not everyone would bother themselves to get out of their beds, auroras being common enough, but this time everyone had gathered, just in case there was some truth to the rumours. Crazy rumours which had started a couple of days earlier, of the first sightings of 'The Sign' by an old Shaman of the Cheeshna-Tribe. Discarded as the foolish vision of a senile old man at first, it was passed on all the same with a bemused frown, mostly. But then the next evening a few dozen people at Sand Point insisted they'd seen it in the distance. Then more news came from Bristol Bay, from the Port Heiden settlers, followed by the Perryville folk. Some of them, too, had seen a huge Redtail in the sky and not all of them were drunk either. The fabled 'Icehawk' had arrived, they were sure of it, the Giant of the First Age, the Angel Beast from the legends, a God of lesser gods.

As it is with unlikely rumours, nobody really believes them until they see for themselves. Naturally those who considered themselves sensible people put all that nonsense down to mass hypnosis, a self-generated hysteria after the shaman's stories. Logic could be stretched maybe to a UFO, or, most likely, to some covert air force exercise.

But now, on this full moon night, nobody in Chignik could deny it any longer. It was true, however bizarre, frightening and illogical, no matter how hard to even describe, the Icehawk really had come. It was just like the prophecy everyone in the usually calm and cheerful community knew about, and it had left them shaken, afraid and confused.

They had stood chatting in the moonlit night, about mundane things as they always did, the aurora doing its beautiful dance as ever, stunning, yes, but nothing new. They had joked about hysterical visions and people obviously drinking too much, when Ken from the store suddenly pointed to one particular shadowy silhouette in the sky that had appeared in the midst of the green light. Something odd was happening there, didn't quite look right.

Twinkling bursts of light, hardly bigger than the stars above at first, getting larger and brighter as they watched. Similar to ships' flares flashing up all at once, the lights sparked around a small black shadowy form that moved and changed its outline like black ink on oil. The Chignik folk had stood fixated, watching the closest green and purple aurora frills around it contracting, getting sucked into the black void like form, as if drawn in by a wormhole in the night sky. In one smooth easy movement the shadow gathered the rest of the aurora veils into its centre, all the while changing its shape until it looked very much like a large bird, or a pair of outstretched arms perhaps. All so fast and fluid it was hard to say, defined mainly by the sparkling flashes around it. And then it changed again as if charged up by the aurora it had absorbed, the shadow now turning into a glowing white form. This one looked like a bird without a doubt, emerging from its own shadow, turning ever whiter and brighter as it grew above them.

There was no noise that anyone could remember, all was silent. The bird resembled a huge glowing white dove or perhaps

32

a seagull at first, as if the whole metamorphosis had been orches-
trated by some clever stage lighting. The dimensions were
confusing. Too high up to really be that big, yet it was too easy
to see the details. It appeared like a hologram with unfathomable
depth. They pointed their fingers at it, gasped and murmured,
struggling to comprehend how it could possibly be that this dove
or whatever it was could carry on growing and changing. At the
height of its brightness, turning the night into spotlit day, just when
it was getting too painful to look at it any longer, it changed colour
very quickly. Softening the light and accompanied by a low-toned
hum it sounded oddly familiar. However illogical, it was a comfort
to recognize this metamorphosis into a now much loved and
familiar red-tailed hawk. Yes, it was still too big and was glowing
in this strange way, but at least they could make out that it was
a mature one. Its rust and pink coloured tail feathers had been
clearly visible, now looking bright maroon in the changing light.
And then the bird had screeched just like any ordinary Redtail,
it was like hearing the voice of an old friend. One man even
managed to laugh at that and to call 'Hey there!' in response. It
broke the tension for a few seconds at least.

If it had just carried on flying in circles above them nobody
would have thought much of it after a while. They would have
put the whole thing down to a strange atmospheric trick of the
light. They may even have thought that an adventurous Redtail
had visited their thin strip of land, invited by the unusually mild
November temperatures. It would have been good enough to
laugh it off and enjoy as a great story forever after. But nobody
had been prepared to see it grow as huge as it did above them,
the wingspan doubling about every ten seconds or so. It was
simply incomprehensible. As it circled lazily above them, the
hawk's size and very presence were overpowering. As if taking
over their usual breathing space with a totally different kind of
energy, so commanding it was.

Everyone there stood paralysed into motionless silence, in
awe as well as from confusion. Frightened yes, but with an even
greater sense of wonder. Not one of them, not even the children,
could even think of moving, or of running away. It would have

been useless anyhow. Instead, they just stood and stared, unable to understand how any of it could be possible. This was no longer just a bird, its wingtips close to touching both outcrops of Chignik Bay above which it seemed to come to rest, suspended, defying gravity. The hawk had hovered effortlessly in the air, not hurting anyone or anything, but looking down on them with the calm watchfulness of a far superior presence. And absolutely able to put an end to them all if it so chose.

If all that hadn't been enough, the hawk had then proceeded to change appearance again, it had taken a while to realise what was happening, but however much everyone had squinted their unbelieving eyes and shaken their heads, they could clearly see it beginning to ice over. First the tail feathers changed to a translucent white, then the wings, then the body. Its pale chest shimmered, as did the magnificent head and the keen eyes, all of it as if illuminated from within, freezing over in white light. Like a chiseled ice sculpture it had hovered motionless in mid air, a living frozen bird of prey above them, exuding immense power. Beautiful it was. Reflecting and absorbing the night sky in the most stunning way, it was now also truly frightening in its illogical, silent presence. If gravity had worked as expected the hawk would have fallen down on top of them, crushing them all under its icy weight or drowning them with the resulting tsunami from the Bay. There was nothing visible to stop either possibility, nothing that was holding up its immense mass. If anything, it had looked comfortable hovering in complete control.

Who or what was this apparently fully conscious creature, capable of defying the laws of physics? Even afterwards nobody could work out how it had been able to mirror the smooth transition of the aurora. Whether it had been something it could do itself or whether it had reflected the moonlight in some way. Was it even possible to give out the aurora energy it had absorbed from within? Nothing made sense, a miracle of sorts, surely. Or an alien spaceship. Either. As if to take pity on their shock and fatigue the hawk smoothly, almost kindly, changed from its enormous icy state back into a real enough bird. Rapidly thawing and shrinking at the same time, no more than a soft shower of sweet water droplets fell onto the crowd. The again reassuringly familiar Redtail had continued to watch them from above for a while, getting ever smaller as it circled them four or five times, closely above their heads. Lazily flapping its wings it released a few stray feathers like a parting gift and flew off into the night sky.

It had taken a long time before anyone had dared to move. Some had fallen to their knees, some in tears, some embracing each other. Nobody had known what to say, when to speak, when to go home. And nobody had dared to touch the feathers.

But they had all remembered the old legends and songs of the prophecy of the 'Icehawk'. It would come, bringing with it a great transformation on Earth as profound in meaning as the legend of the Phoenix. It was to herald the end, the end of the world as they knew it and the rebirth of a better, more conscious and more peaceful mankind.

Trying to recover, getting up off their knees and making sure everyone was all right, the Chignik community could think of nothing else to do but hug each other before stumbling back home, supporting each other the best they could. A few were helplessly looking to the Elders for some kind of advice, some reassuring wisdom to find comfort in. Nellie and Bob looked at each other and all Bob could come up with was, "Go home, everyone, get some sleep, it looks like the show is over. And tomorrow evening at 6pm we'll have a full meeting at the Shed, with everyone there, full council members, everyone, please, and we'll talk it over then." Bob had walked Nellie to her front door neither of them knowing what to say to each other but grateful to be able to walk together. Their mutual bond now more obvious to both of them than ever.

"Leave your lights on, everyone!" Ken had called out from his store. "It might make us feel safer!"

Everyone had nodded in agreement, wanting to be close to their loved ones but not lose sight of anyone else either. It would be a sleepless night for most.

"Morning Bob!" Nellie called out to her dear old friend the next day, watching him aimlessly wandering around, pretending to check the knots on the nets that didn't need checking. Bob Tukatuk walked across the wooden planks to her, with heavy feet matching his worried frown.

"Morning, Nellie, dear, have you had some rest? I can't say I have." He looked at her with worried eyes. "Right now I don't like what's happened one bit. Didn't think I'd live to see the day, really. What do you make of it all?"

Nellie walked out her door towards him and pulled gently at his arm. "Come in Bob, get warm, you shouldn't be out there in this, we're both too old and decrepit to get cold right through. I'll make us a strong sweet coffee, and we'll talk?"

"It'll be my third one this morning, dear, but yes, I'll join you. Let's put our heads together over this." He entered her familiar and welcoming kitchen and sat down on the old wooden chair with a heavy sigh, watching Nellie busy herself with the coffee.

The best thing about Chignik was that it hadn't changed, Bob thought, everything always stayed the same except for some newfangled machine at the canning plant and a seasonal workforce bringing new blood in. The tourists who came for the king salmon fishing in the summer had gone all modern. Ever more stuck up and showing off with ever fancier gear nobody here really wanted or needed. But the locals who lived in Chignik permanently were as good as they come, hardy and honest, fishing families mainly, or employed at the fish processing plant. He should have snapped Nellie up decades ago, maybe they should have an 85th birthday wedding, he could ask her. He even thought she'd say yes. She was the oldest woman in town, and fitter and brighter than the few 60 year olds left. Still quite tall and upright as well, refusing to hunch over. He liked that. People didn't live long in these parts, life was too cold and damp with none of the city comforts. Despite Ken's store being the only place to get groceries supplied by the supply ship every couple of months and having to rely on the medical drug delivery drones flying in for emergencies when the weather allowed, it was a good life. Scenic, simple, peaceful and humbling. You didn't forget that nature was boss here, as plentiful as it was. For whatever reason he and Nellie had managed to make it into their eighth decade without much of a fuss. He didn't think he'd see the Icehawk appear, ever. He trembled inwardly and not because of the cold.

Nellie was watching him quietly. He'd aged over night and she could see he was afraid. She wasn't sure what to think. Throughout her long life people had talked, sung and made art about the Icehawk for as long as she could remember. But, there were too many stories with too many different slants to know exactly who or what they were supposed to be. Just that one or more of them would come. Nellie respected her people's wisdom too much to think of it all as just some old superstition. Also she could hardly forget the case of her poor Mary's Greg, who had died in his hospital bed three years earlier. The doctors had said he'd caught a chill and then pneumonia. Having recognised him as a strong man behind his pale geeky looks Nellie knew that was hardly likely. When Mary had gone in to see him, with Nina and Brent closely behind her, they had all seen it, the feather, that's all it had been. They had told her all about it. How it looked somehow harmless, quite beautiful, large, hefty even, with a broad rounded tip and brown with bits of black, grey and white in it. How it had a kind of glow over it that made the nurses say it was an angel's feather, they didn't have to be white. Brent hadn't recognised it, but he knew enough to see it was a bird of prey of some kind which didn't sound as friendly as angels, so he'd made a joke of it. He'd told Nina and the nurse it must have been an angel in disguise. Nobody could think of any reason why there should be a feather like that in a Yorkshire hospital, let alone on Greg's chest. And Nellie hadn't said anything, she never told anyone that it made her think of the Icehawk legend.

Poor Mary. Poor Nina, too, Nellie thought to herself, taking her time making the coffee. Good job she had her Brent. A good soul, warm and dependable, he reminded her of Mary's father Chontook, long lost at sea, like so many others. Brent had talked with Nellie about the feather in detail once, when nobody was around to listen, and between them they figured out that it looked just like a Northern red-tailed hawk one, which made no sense whatsoever, as they were an American, not a British species.

Nellie couldn't think about it any more now, it was all too much. She sighed and carried the mugs of steaming coffee to the table.

"Here you are then, Bob. Get some of this down you. Are you ok?"

"Hm, not sure, Nellie. Not sure what wisdom they're expecting of us Elders, do you?"

"How much time do you think we have? The world, I mean?" Nellie asked him, with wide brown eyes, trying to sound relaxed about it.

"Well, it's all legend, isn't it." Bob pushed his hands through his long mane. It made him feel guilty saying it like that, disrespectful somehow. He so wanted to feel knowledgeable right now, he was all out of sorts, didn't know what to say. 'Pull yourself together' he thought to himself, 'She's waiting for a decent answer'. "Ok. I'll tell you what I think. My gut says we have time yet, a year maybe, or two? Or even longer? That's probably long enough to figure something out?" He smiled somewhat unsure of himself. "Then again we might be dead by then, you know. Never know anything about it."

Nellie reached out for his hand, fragile like a little girl. "I don't want to think it's going to end for everybody just because the world's made a mess of things, you know? All the young ones with their lives ahead of them, what did they do wrong? Will it be the apocalypse?" She squeezed her eyes shut her as if the pictures forming in her mind were too painful to visualize. "And I don't want to face it alone either."

Bob looked at her rarely seen fear, her eyes fixed on him again now, darker than ever, and fell for her, right there and then, more deeply and more intensely than ever. 'Damn old age', he thought. He'd want to be there to protect her, shield her from whatever was to come. He'd whisk her off to the bedroom right now, had they both been younger. "Nel, Nellie, dear." His voice was a bit croaky all of a sudden. "I've been thinking. And not just because of the meeting tonight. Well, I've been thinking..."

"What," Nellie replied, softly, searching his eyes. "What have you been thinking, Bob?"

He took a deep breath and returned her gaze. "I'm thinking of you and me getting married, at long last, you know? Nellie Saltwater, would you marry me, you young thing?" Bob smiled wide, the skin around the corners of his mouth crinkling like old boot leather. Nellie looked at him, taking in every inch of his face with its white stubble. She looked at his broad shoulders under the warm smell of his sweater. She trusted that smell of wool, man, sea, air and coffee. He watched her, both a little tearful now. She was just the sweetest woman ever. "I don't want you to start crying on me, Nel, you can say no, you know, if you want to."

"Don't be daft, Bob, of course I want to!" She really sobbed now, overwhelmed, and he got up, pulled her up gently from the wooden chair, and kissed her softly, and how wonderful it was that she kissed him back. He didn't feel old, not one bit. He held her like he'd been wanting to hold her since forever as she rested her head on his shoulder, crying quietly. They knew each other, been there for each other as the best of friends through thick and thin. He loved her. And she loved him. They'd have each other for however long there was left. The two Elders stood there for a long time, holding on to each other, like two gnarled old oaks finding each other, and giving each other strength.

There was no thought of going to work that morning in Chignik. Everyone was trying to make sense of the night. Nobody really knew whether the old legends were truly prophetic. Was what they had seen a sacred moment or foretelling a disastrous one to come? Was the Hawk really a sign from God, or of the return of the Son of God, or of many gods freeing the world from evil? Or, extra-terrestrial intelligence exploiting their superstitions, for better or worse? To save the planet? To colonise and take over our Earth, some asked in whispered dread, and those most scared said there would be hawk like aliens who would harvest their bodies, peck out their organs and eat them, experiment on them and torture them. Only some felt that perhaps it could possibly mean something good, though even they struggled to think how. Could it be an angel? A spirit? Would it maybe mean an ice age? The Icehawk hadn't looked exactly friendly, though not actually hostile or aggressive either. It had just been there, powerful and watchful somehow. Some who had the presence of mind to watch it disappear into the swirling green lit sky had fancied it changed back into a dove, a peace dove even, but couldn't be sure, blending as it did back into the restored aurora, its colours even more dazzling than before.

The questions on everyone's mind however were: Would the Icehawk come back? Would more of them come? Would they be attacked or crushed by it or them in their sleep? Would something or someone else appear? Would they die?

Chapter 6
Barbania, Italy, Marcus.

D R MARCUS CARTER sat in his small, but clean and typically Italian guest room above the Taverna in Barbania, a small village near Turin he knew so well. He loved the traditional dark furniture. The wooden shutters that let the winter sun stream in through the slats onto the salmon pinks and greens on the bed cover. The worn gold velvet covered armchair and the creaky black wooden wardrobe, both desperately ambitious to look like genuine rococo, totally over the top with ornate carvings every-where. The retro look the third time round, at least. He had just hung up his hastily collected clothes and put his suitcase under the bed, they should see him right for a week or two, he could always buy more at the market. Nobody but old friends here would bother to look at him twice. He thought not for the first time how handy it was to be small, at only five foot three he didn't stand out amongst the locals. Not that he had ever felt the need to hide before.

Marcus was well liked here, not because he had ever done anything of note, but because his late parents had lived in Barbania for years, a long time ago now, until his mother's ill health forced them to move back to England. His father Roy, who had continued to visit Barbania every summer to play with the concert band, even into his early eighties, and bright as a button till the end, had felt more at home here than in his Scarborough home. There were many stories about Roy, a free spirited, somewhat opinionated but good humoured soul who had worked all his adult life as a professional musician. How he could play the clarinet and the saxophone and the trombone better than most, could handle a flute, too, how he could compose complex pieces on the back of an envelope and how he was fully aware how good he really was. He had confidently stepped in to help that band make a name for themselves, winning competitions and gaining respect for the first time since they'd started as a little village concert band. Marcus thought back to his father forever going on about that playing any woodwind instrument was harder than brain surgery, harder than anything any scientist would ever be able to cope with. So it was kind of ironic that Marcus who couldn't play a note, not one that should be heard anyhow, had opted to study biophysics instead. Some summers he would come along with his father, for the holiday experience and for the Italian girls, despite feeling like a spare wheel most of the time, not being able to join in the band practice with the others. The music genes had clearly bypassed him and were bestowed upon Maxine's daughter, his wonderful 'little niece' Sabine instead. Not so little any more, rather a twenty-six year old who was both an accomplished musician and a chemical scientist. She would come to join him in a couple of days, help him work out how to proceed from there, what to do with his discovery.

Sabine, who was working at the York University laboratory knew just about everything there was to know about chemical reactions. She was an unassuming but naturally pretty young woman. Small, somewhat boyish with brown hair like him. She wore glasses rather than opting for laser surgery and just like him preferred working behind the scenes. They had a lot in common, got on easily and the conversation always just flowed. Every time she was in Italy she laughed that she might dye her hair black to turn into a raven haired Italian beauty overnight and capture every passing man's heart. He didn't doubt for a minute that she could if she'd set her mind to it, just as she was, as he always thought she was more attractive than she gave herself credit for. She just needed a good man to bring it out of her. He smirked at himself, that little knot in his stomach meant he was channeling the Italian uncle vibe about her. Overly protective and no doubt casting an analytical eye over any prospective boyfriend.

If only Greg was here. His old friend Greg, he still missed him, never more so than now, as a trusted colleague, but also as a friend who would listen and know what to do. Greg's theory he'd been working on, amongst others, was that across the globe there was an evolutionary process going on to generate a natural antifreeze within the human body. A quality much like the wood frog already had, a phenomenon that was discovered by Prof Kenneth Storey thirty years or so earlier. The frog was able to go through a freeze and thaw state naturally, to survive its habitats' rapidly changing temperatures, freezing and thawing along with all the plants around it, and thriving! The frogs' skin itself would freeze, and special proteins in their blood, called nucleating proteins, would then cause the water in the blood to freeze first. This freezing process, in turn, would suck most of the water out of the frog's cells. At the same time the frog's liver would start making large amounts of glucose, which would then pack into the cells and prop them up. Scientists had been able to utilise separating these proteins and mimicking them in organ transplants, meaning donated organs were better able to withstand the frozen state.

Greg had been curious how this could be utilised in general, at the very least as a tool for survival in extreme conditions, and had worked with scientists in Alaska to that end. Greg had insisted that in time, as organ recipients had children, that ability to freeze and antifreeze would be passed on and then inherited down the line. Surely it would eventually become a major part of human evolution to cope with survival in space even, but Greg had died too soon to be able to see if his theory would prove correct. And here he was, Marcus, with all the details of his own discovery on plain old fashioned paper in the false wall of his suitcase proving his friend's theory. You couldn't trust to save anything digitally, there was no such thing as digital privacy.

"You were right Greg, again." Marcus muttered to himself. Marcus had found the gene of the protective protein in a human tissue sample. The natural antifreeze, freezing and thawing ability of the living human had begun. It might even be widespread already. This was huge. If any government on the planet knew that he had not only proof, but had been able to isolate the gene, he'd probably be dead already, his discovery 'transferred' away, he was convinced of it. He wouldn't be the first scientist to disappear shortly after a meaningful breakthrough. Marcus wanted to make sure, just like Greg would have, that his project would be used to save lives, not to manufacture superior bioengineered armies that were kitted out invincibly enough already. It frightened him, that eagerness to not only increase the power of AI, but also to create a mixed species, bio engineered super humans, invincible forces to control ordinary humans, for ever more.

Marcus had no obvious reason to hide, as far as he knew his secret was still safe, but he needed time to think, and wanted to be out of circulation for now. Yes, he wanted to brainstorm with Sabine, as he wondered whether this protein molecule would be both safe and effective as a vaccine, or whether there might be any adverse reactions to be aware of. Bachelordom and his reputation as a bit of a ladies man had its advantages, he just mentioned in passing he was going on a 'interesting' holiday with a new lady friend who liked the geeky type. Nobody would even bother him, he wasn't the most popular of guys at work anyhow, arrogant as he was, or pretended to be, so he could work in peace.

Chapter 7
The Hospital

NINA BREATHED A sigh of relief, she felt she'd spent the whole journey simultaneously holding her breath and pushing down on an imaginary accelerator. It was a strain not to get irritated with Connor who was driving by the book, and Brent's face wasn't exactly reassuring either, he looked almost more worried than she was! Nothing was said except silly observations, like 'It's still really warm today', or 'Won't be long now', or 'She'll be alright". What had she been thinking even considering moving away from her Mum! Living more or less next door to her was perfect! They got on so well, she felt ashamed having taken it for granted, she'd never think of it again, she swore to herself. Just as long as her Mum would be alright, she just had to be.

Connor turned into the hospital car park, the display showing his numbers on the monitor, which meant his bank account would be charged the parking fees from that very second. How very ironic, Nina thought, to make money from others' misery. She'd have to remember to pay him later. Connor dropped them off at the main entrance to save time, promising he would wait for them or join them if they needed him. He patted his iLink, they'd find each other with the location finder they were programmed in as close friends.

Brent walked up to the registration window and politely and cheerfully as ever asked the welcoming Serf where he could find Mary Hudson and Bill Stanley, who must have been brought in together. He was immediately handed a printout of the hospital map, where Mary was shown as a red dot in the intensive care unit, and Bill, too, as a blue dot, also in the ICU, not far from each other at all. Nina and Brent looked at each other, horrified, intensive care really meant this was serious. They rushed onto the transporter belts, hurrying past the other visitors who looked at them with sympathetic alarm. People running in a hospital never meant good news.

"Nina Daniels, and Brent Daniels, for Mary Hudson!" The admission Serf sang out as they arrived, like some staged comedy reception. The door to the Intensive Care Unit slid open, and they rushed through the hall past windows looking at the faces of patients on the 3D-screens behind the glass, until Nina let out a little cry. There was her Mum, her dear Mum, looking so grey and white she was almost blue. She was wrapped in silver foil blankets and had some equipment around her that Nina didn't recognise, nor did she care. Seeing her mother look like that was just awful. How could a face change like that?

"Look, she's alive." Brent whispered senselessly to Nina, pointing to the vital signs monitor, and they both saw it. She was only just alive, though. From where they stood, they saw no outward sign of injury. "I'll see if I can find a nurse." Brent walked on past the other windows. There was a woman he didn't know, then a little boy he could hardly see under a heap of silver blankets, when he suddenly stopped and called out to Nina who stood looking at her Mum as if mesmerised. "Nina, Bill's here, look, he's the same!"

Nina felt a pang of guilt leaving her Mum's window, but hurried to join Brent, who looked equally shocked. "What's happened to them? What's wrong with them?"

"I'm afraid it's a very serious case of extreme hypothermia." The voice behind them said, making them spin round to see the petite ward nurse looking as serious as she sounded. It was

Yvonne, Damian's Mum, thank goodness, she was great, both Nina and Brent thought with united relief.

"Hi, Yvonne, good to see you. But I don't understand." Nina said, calming down a bit. "How can it be hypothermia? It must be at least eleven degrees out there! There must be a mistake, my Mum and Bill here were in a bus accident, not out at sea!"

"We don't understand it either." Yvonne shook her head. "They were brought in half frozen, literally, covered in ice as if they had been in arctic conditions. The other patients, too." She pointed towards the woman and the boy. "All the passengers in the bus, though one is believed to be missing, I don't know who. Luckily there were only a few of them, but we don't understand the severity of the cold. I believe Mr Marsden, the duty consultant, has messaged the weather station, to find out if there had been some freak ice storm we don't know about, but, like you, we're at a loss to understand how this can be. We have never had a case like this."

"Except when Dad died." Nina said under her breath, her head spinning.

"My father died of cold, too. Nobody understood that either. You can't let them die, please don't let them die..." She sobbed and ran back to her mother's window, her palms pressing against the glass to get as close to her as she could. Brent and the nurse saw Nina's shoulders shaking, both knowing she needed time alone.

"When will you know?"

"The next hours, even the next day will be critical. I don't pretend to have any experience with this severe type of hypothermia, so really we are all relying on the monitors to tell us more about what's going on, but we will let you know as soon as we can. Do we have your permission to access your iLink to contact you?"

"Of course, please do, just as soon as there is any change at all." Brent replied, only half realising what just happened. Yvonne had given away what had been denied in the media all along - that even a nurse could access everything about them, their whereabouts, even their physical and emotional state, without a police warrant. It wasn't like asking someone for their number, it was so much more than that. He suddenly felt tired. Just as long as they helped Mary and Bill and those two others, what did it matter? He walked across to Nina, knowing she needed him now.

Chapter 8
The Shed Meeting

IT HAD BEEN a strange day across Bristol Bay, disorientating. Nobody cried now, nobody even knew how to be. The online searches on the iLinks and computers focused on the scriptures and depictions of the hawk, of the totem poles and carvings, basically everything that had ever been told about them. It was hard to know what to believe, whether to follow cynical modern day logic over ingrained beliefs. There was so much information, but none of it felt as real as what they had seen. All the Elders of Bristol Bay would be there tonight, at the head table of the meeting Bob and Nellie had called. Not that anyone would stay away, or even cared where anyone would sit, but it was reassuring to have some order in place. There was still no police presence, hadn't been for decades. It just hadn't been needed.

Nellie and Bob sat together at her kitchen table, holding hands, still trying to digest all that had happened. They were both overwhelmed to think of living through this now at the end of their long lives. It was almost comical, exhilarating even, to think that life still held such a surprise for them, but deeply worrying for the young ones. Nellie had invited Bob into her bed the previous night, neither of them used to sharing the night with anyone any more, not for thirty years or more. It had been lovely, too, so very lovely, feeling each other close like that, skin to skin, old age had given them a gentle humour that was almost as fulfilling and somewhat more reassuring than youthful passions. They had held each other, laughed together and wept together. They had cried tears of love and joy, tears of fear, and tears of gratitude to have each other. And they had slept soundly next to each other. For all her strength of character and wisdom Nellie still felt embarrassed the next morning, and Bob looked a little awkward, too, until they both admitted that being eighty odd did nothing for confidence about their bodies the morning after. They had hugged each other and laughed that it was all right, and that best of all they wouldn't have to face what was to come on their own.

It was just before 5pm, and Chignik witnessed a very unusual sight for the second time in as many days, the sight of a five hundred strong crowd descending onto the Boat Shed like they would if there was a wedding or New Year party, but the mood so different, nobody knew how to behave. Those who were flippant and light hearted drew chastising looks from some, and those who looked like they were going to a funeral were told not to worry, nobody had died yet, it was just a sign. Then there was quiet again, best just to see what that meeting would bring, however doubtful the use of it was. Nobody really knew any more than they did, did they?

"What are we attracting, and why?" One woman asked.

"Haven't we always said that whatever happens to us is our responsibility?"

"Nonsense!"

"This doesn't apply here! This is bigger than us!"

A woman at the back began to sing, her voice reaching out across their heads, just loud enough to be heard, and for the song to be recognised, one of many that had passed through generations like an adult nursery rhyme, they all knew it. It was the Alutiiq rhythm of days long gone, translated many times from the ancient languages, but still in their blood, in their soul. This simple but empowering song, with many verses, not all repeated every time, and with breaks between each line filled with drums and humming, would have been sung around the fire or when doing crafts in the old days.

Her voice was clear and she sang with conviction:

"We Are ...

... Men who have re-wilded ourselves

... See us evolving women

... With the marks of our tribe

... Our songs

... The instruments we carry

... The glow of our aliveness

... Our skin revealing different parts

... Of our soul's journey

... See us

... With our faces full of red

... Tending fires all night long

... Sitting in contemplation and prayer

... Humbling ourselves ....

and the others joined in, so comforting it was, to sing something that made them all feel strong and together as one tribe full of hope...

"... Notice us

... The way we move

... Vibrating freedom and strength

... To everyone we meet

... Our strong hands that have made love

... Our strong hands that build things

... See us reading

... Scriptures and sacred texts

... Listening to our inner guidance

... Tasting our own Godliness

... Freeing our souls

... As we dance together

... Open and free

And then the chorus, sang higher and faster, oh how good that felt to them all, good enough to sing louder still:

... "We will heal this together

... We are Woman, we are Man,

... Awakened and ready

... For your power and strength" ......

The Shed was full to bursting point with a now much more positive crowd, looking like a mini United Nations gathering, cheered on by that simple song that reminded them of the challenges they had all faced, and always survived, of the human spirit that would survive this, too. The question now on every-one's mind was, what would the Elders have to say?

What Bob said made most sense, commanding instant respect. "I want to know what its weakness is, everything and everyone has a weakness, no exception."

"That's true." A woman called Grannie Martha said out loud. "Even Jesus got killed, and he was the son of God, wasn't he?"

People turned round at her with an uneasy shuffling of feet at the illegality of her remark, though people did nod, many of them having grown up with prayers at the table, giving thanks to the same God their parents or grandparents believed in, and many had prayed to Mother Earth, too, and still did, whatever the new law said. They just didn't really believe that it would help now, not really. This thing, whatever that Icehawk was, was something so out of the ordinary, it hadn't harmed them, though they were sure it could have if it had wanted to. Wasn't this supposed to be the beginning of the end of the World? Or what?

"Maybe it won't come back?" A little girl suggested. "Maybe it was just coming to visit and will go somewhere else?"

"Now there's a thought!" The people agreed hopefully, maybe the child had a point? It might be years before it showed again! Maybe it had showed up generations ago and that is where all the songs and stories had originated from? The world didn't end then, did it?

"We have to make sure of one thing." A stocky man at the back suggested. "We don't want no reporters crawling around here making up all sorts and creating some panic, and getting the army in, all that nonsense. That won't do anyone any good. Has anyone talked to anyone outside of Bristol Bay about this?" He looked around, people turning quiet and looking around, then shaking their heads and shrugging their shoulders.

"Nope, not here, no, me neither, no, nothing, wouldn't have known what to say."

It was true, who would have believed them? It was a bit like those endless UFO tales, how many of them had been about and mostly drawn ridicule? And still no aliens had landed, not so far, unless that hawk was one.. it was so confusing what to think. Nellie wished Mary and Nina were there, how would she be able to explain it all over the phone, especially as the message was to not talk about it as the calls were probably monitored anyhow?

"It probably isn't a good idea to even talk about it beyond the islands."

She had really talked to herself, but it was still loud enough for her people to hear. It was decided to shake hands on it, not to talk to anyone else, and try and go about their everyday life as always, unless something else happened.

"Well, this is as good a time as any then!" Bob said rather loudly and cheerfully. "Nellie and I have some news of a different kind!" He looked at Nellie who was glowing like a twenty year old shy thing, nodding at him cheerfully. "Well, last night I asked Nellie to marry me, we've decided to have a birthday wedding, in April, she'll only be eighty-three and I'll be eighty-five, best time to get married, if you ask me!"

The surprised roar of delight from their people was wonderful, a riot of whoops, laughter, clapping and shoulder slaps, hugs and kisses all round. What a night! If those two Elders planned ahead for a wedding, well, then surely there was no reason to be afraid of anything at all. The silent day they'd had suddenly seemed very inappropriate, they would celebrate this, oh yes, they would! To Nellie and Bob!

As the doors of the Boat Shed opened out into the night, Chignik was ready to face the future. Everyone felt it, or at least sensed it. They knew that somehow, they could be strong, and there was hope again, perhaps it wasn't over yet. They would reclaim their power and find a way to see clearly, know what to do, united.

Chapter 9
The Fugitive

IT WASN'T EXACTLY comfortable in that field drain. Damian started to shiver, his clothes wet, and lying in muddy darkness really wasn't his idea of fun. He'd been so confident of his idea to get away, to hide and start a freedom revolution, that he had never thought it through how to actually go about it when the time came. Now he felt like an idiot, like a toddler telling his parents he'd run away only to turn back twenty yards from the house, because he remembered he wasn't really quite grown up enough. What was he going to do?

He'd heard the ambulances arrive, the police sirens threatening to split his eardrums with the sound bouncing all around him, off the concrete walls, and then disappear into the distance again. He heard the bus being straightened and towed away, and the small crowd dispersing. Nobody seemed to look for him, no torchlight was directed into his tunnel. It was as much of a relief as a disappointment, he had secretly hoped for more attention, something at least to tell him he was missed.

Anyhow, what to do. He could hardly just show up now, he had no way of explaining where he'd been, why he'd left his IDs, and even what had happened. All he remembered was that Bill had shouted something, then the bus swerved, and when he came round everything was covered in ice and water and feathers. For crying out loud, feathers of all things! Strange that he was the only one able to move, apparently. He thought again. Was he really the only survivor, were they all dead, could he have saved them? That had been Nina's mother in there, he should have at least tried to help her. And Bill. All of them. But they'd be in hospital now, looked after. The drawback about getting rid of your iLink and other traceable gear was that he had no way of finding out what had happened to them. Was someone looking for him already? Was it safe for him to come out, seeing that it was dark now? And where would he go? Damian cupped his sore and bloody wrist with his right hand, and tried to think.

There was one special person he could trust, completely. Sabine. She was smart and fun and just beautiful in all ways. He'd met her when she was teaching health and safety at the factory, about rubber fumes mainly. She was the one he thought he might talk to about that stuff he'd nicked. He could tell her anything, he knew that, and he felt she'd be okay about it, discreet, and probably helpful if need be. He was amazed that they had hit it off so easily, she was so much smarter than him with her doctorate. He had no idea why she was even happy with her modest job at the university. She could work anywhere at all. She had told him he was the really smart one, dealing with actual products that would make people's lives easier, and improving things all the time. They had talked about the superconductive graphene, too, they both loved its possibilities in so many applications, and how its interfacial adhesive energy was slowly changing the energy industry.

Being able to create super-capacitors out of graphene had possibly been the most exciting step in electronic engineering in a very long time. While the development of electronic components had been progressing so fast over the previous twenty or so years, power storage solutions such as batteries and capacitors had been the primary limiting factor due to size, power capacity and efficiency. He remembered talking as technically as possible about it to impress her, in his own mind he'd just call the old batteries a bunch of crap, and was really excited when they started combining graphene with rubber in mind-control-lable limbs, the super thin and light graphene layers within the rubber transmitting warmth and energy much like a natural part of the body. It had felt so meaningful to be part of this new development, all hush hush still, and now? Now they've given me the sack, he thought bitterly. But he did have a bit of it in his bag, and the specs on paper, too, maybe Sabine could regenerate it or something, or her Uncle Marcus, another scientist, a good guy, if a bit arrogant maybe. Damian's mind was made up. He'd wait a little longer, until it was properly dark but not too late to show up at her place, knock at her door and just hope for the best. Cheered up, thinking of her made his hideout much more bearable.

Sabine looked around in her little flat above the bakery. It was colourful and cosy, a space all of her own, her music stand in the corner, with the flute and the clarinet standing to attention, waiting for more practice time before she'd dutifully pack them away, clean and dry, for the night. She loved her music, it had been her friend as long as she remembered. Life without music would be like having to do without your favourite foods for the rest of your days, or worse. Tonight though, she just couldn't get going, she'd picked up the flute, put it down, picked up the clarinet, put that down, too, not being able to tell what on earth was wrong with her. All she knew was that she had the feeling she was waiting for something, but didn't know what.

The news of the bus crash had unsettled her as well. She'd only heard a bit about it on the way back from work, too late to catch it all. The couple of people she'd bumped into outside her flat shook their heads, hadn't seen it, but already gossip seemed rife. The driver had been drunk, there was a pheasant on the road he had tried to avoid, there were pheasant feathers all over the place. The woman from the bakery said it was some fluke gust that blew the bus off the road, looking up at the sky with an exaggerated sigh, quite sure that global warming was going to get them all eventually. Irritating nonsense. Sabine didn't know who'd been on the bus, she just felt jumpy, uneasy. She sat down in her huge green and black armchair, a present from Uncle Marcus, it could be her cosy place, he'd said. Mug of hot chocolate in hand,

57

she decided to call Damian, he was always so easy to talk to, and made her laugh.

She swiped over his profile on her iLink and waited for him to answer.

"Damian Turner is no longer available." The iLink voice piped up.

"What?!" Sabine sat up with a start. "What do you mean he is no longer available?" She shouted at her iLink, alarmed. She had never even heard of such a reply before.

"I am sorry, I do not understand your question." The virtual assistant replied.

Sabine rephrased it, irritated. "Where is Damian Turner?"

"Damian Turner is no longer available."

This was ridiculous. She called his work, knowing full well that the place would be shut now, but she could leave a message with the reception Serf who was available 24/7. She called, and as she asked if she could leave a message for Damian Turner, the Serf, with her very friendly velvety AI voice gave an equally emotionless response. "I am sorry, but Damian Turner no longer works for us."

Sabine couldn't believe what she was hearing. They told each other everything, even if they weren't in touch every day, they were friends, weren't they? What on earth was going on? She sat down again, trying to settle herself. OK, she knew Damian, a bit rough at the edges somehow, swearing too much at times, but apart from that he was a solid diamond, something must have happened. Her blood ran cold, what if he'd been on that bus? Was he dead, was he in hospital? No... in either of those cases the iLink would have told her. There was an instant record if someone had died, or the assistant would have told her of his hospital location. It was impossible that 'he was no longer available'. That just didn't happen. She tried her virtual assistant again, only to get the same answer. This was just crazy! Maybe she should nip over to his place to make sure he was alright? She bit her bottom lip, she was tired, edgy, hadn't had a shower, was all out of sorts, not really the way she wanted Damian to see her, it was important to her what he thought of her. He was, well, special. She should turn on the CV, to take her mind off things and maybe there would be some proper information on that bus crash?

She was just about to call out 'CV on!' when she heard a faint knock at her door. His knock, the one he always used! Heart pounding, she ran downstairs rather than use the door buzzer and was met with a very wet, muddy, strangely smelly Damian, with some blood on his sleeve and white as a sheet, shivering.

"Oh Damian, where have you been?!" She ushered him in, quickly closing the door, somehow sensing he didn't want to be seen. "I was so worried, I tried to call you, and the assistant said you were no longer available, and I called your work and they said you don't work there anymore. Oh, come in, come in. Goodness! What's happened?"

He followed her up those ridiculously narrow stairs and they both fell into her cosy living room, Sabine quickly shutting the door behind them. He stood there, with a crooked tired smile, shivering.

"Sorry I'm in such a state, do you think I could use your shower? And maybe wash these clothes?" He was embarrassed looking down at his garb hanging off him as if he had rolled in mud all afternoon. Well, he had, hadn't he. Sabine saw his wrist, his bloodied empty wrist, and realised there was a lot going on here, first things first, the man needed to warm up. She went across to the cupboard to get some fresh towels for him, opened the bathroom door, and pointed out her dressing gown, a white robe with big bright flowers on, and laughed. "Help yourself to that after your shower, and throw me your clothes out on the floor, I'll put them in the washer, they'll be as good as new in a mo."

She wondered if his Mum knew where he was, should she call her? Yvonne Turner was great, she really liked her, a petite tomboyish woman with her short red pixie cut hair, always cheerful and a great nurse. Why hadn't Damian gone home instead? Sabine decided to wait for him to tell her everything, she'd get some food on the table first of all.

59

Damian nodded thankfully, he could have burst into tears there and then, the shock of the day getting to him now. It all seemed like some horrible dream, and he had no idea what to do next. He just knew that he should at least be presentable. A hot shower would be wonderful.

The hot soapy water stung his wrist, and his head hurt again. He felt for the bump, oh yes, right there under his wet hair, half a potato it was, at least, he must have really banged his head good and proper. He didn't feel sick or dizzy, but realised how hungry he was, so that was a good sign, he was alright. Lost and missing to all but himself and Sabine, but he was alright. He'd have to somehow let his Mum know he was ok, but didn't know how. There had always just been his Mum and him, yes, he'd had girlfriends, of course, and he wasn't a Mummy's boy by any means. He did care about her a great deal though, she'd brought him up by herself, taught him so much, and he simply wouldn't allow her to be worried about him. She was a rightly popular ward nurse at Scarborough Hospital, her job meant quite a commute for her but she loved living in the countryside, didn't like touristy Scarborough so much. She always joked she needed peace and quiet after work to cope with him until he'd give her grandchildren and had a good woman to take him off her hands. They both laughed, as she wasn't really the old fashioned kind, but working locally and with property a fortune and them getting on so well, it was just easy to share the house with her. He always made sure he contributed both to his share of the bills and the chores, he wasn't a bad cook either. She never talked about his Dad much, Damian just knew he was the much loved result of a passionate weekend with a handsome Frenchman he inherited his dark and somewhat brooding looks from, it was ok.

He suddenly remembered a little game his Mum and he used to play, where he pretended to be Winnetou, the Native American Apache Chief, and she pretended to be 'Old Shatterhand' his white Cowboy friend, and they'd have all sorts of imaginary adventures together, playing with a homemade bow and arrow in the garden, even though stuff like that was frowned on now, everyone seemed to be forever scared of hurting themselves. The light bulb went on in his head, his Mum would understand if he asked Sabine to send her a coded message! Energised again he hurried to finish his shower, smelling like freesias of Sabine's girly soap, and even had to laugh as he put on her flowery bathrobe, catching sight of himself in the mirror. He'd had better looking days and definitely more masculine ones.

He opened the bathroom door somewhat shyly, to see that Sabine had laid her small table, and made hot soup, with chunks of bread on the side, some fruit, some cold meats, some cheese, hot tea, it was wonderful. A candle was lit in the corner, and Sabine had changed from her work clothes into jeans and t-shirt, looking so pretty.

Again he could have cried, this day seemed to pack in at least a month's worth of experiences. He looked at her and saw she was trying not to laugh at the sight of him in her fluffy robe which was much too small for him. And at his embarrassed struggle to keep himself, well, covered up. It was such a relief to be able to burst out laughing in response, he sure was on an emotional rollercoaster.

"Come and have something to eat, Damian, please, I hope there's enough, I just put everything on the table I thought you might like, and I haven't eaten yet either. No cooking Serfs in my place, I'll have you know, so if you hate it, it's my fault." Quietly she was really excited to have him there with her, she figured out that something very unusual must have happened to him to say the least. Realizing he'd come to her first, she felt flattered and touched and excited about it all at once.

"Listen, Sabine, this is so wonderful, I don't know how to thank you, but before we start, would you mind texting my Mum, so that she knows I'm ok? I'm trying to disappear, and so far I've managed it, but don't want her worrying."

Sabine nodded, and waited for instructions, fingers over her iLink.

"Tell her, 'Winnetou is looking for Old Shatterhand'."

"What?? "What are you on about?"

"She'll understand, it's a game we used to play, did you never read those old classic books? Anyhow, she'll know I'm safe, and she told me to disappear ages ago...that's W-i-n-n-e-t-o-u." He shrugged his shoulders helplessly, knowing that had come out all wrong, relieved to see the message sent and received at his Mum's. His Mum's reply came immediately. "Make sure he's wearing his moccasins the right way round!"

It made him laugh, a private joke from his childhood days, it was so typical of her to remember to use it now, it was almost as good as a hug.

Sabine saw he was struggling and exhausted, and suggested they should just eat and he could tell her everything when he was good and ready. She could make up the sofa, he was welcome to stay in her flat as long as he liked, though she'd have to go to see her Uncle Marcus in Italy in a couple of days. 'Everyone seems to be up to something, what's going on?' she thought to herself, and went to the medicine cabinet to get Damian the antiseptic spray plaster for his poor wrist.

Chapter 10
The Mystery

THE PATIENTS WERE all stable, their monitors showing neither progress nor a worsening of their condition. The huge 3D screens above their beds showing their faces and vital signs were brutal, even as a nurse Yvonne Turner was still alarmed by that look of patients being close to death, projected cynically like holograms, with all their details spelled out above them. Hospital care had become so unkind and intrusive and not at all private. She straightened her white uniform, adjusted her medical record belt, checked the time, and set about doing the night rounds again. She preferred doing them herself, though she could have just sent the nurse Serfs around for basic check-ups and just kept staring at her office screens like some security guard in a block of flats. She still didn't like the digital age much, however useful, and thought patients deserved a real human to keep an eye on them, especially at night, when many were disoriented, in pain and lonely, or had fitful dreams. She'd swapped shifts with her colleague, Marcia, just so she could do the nightshift at the ICU, it would be quieter then. In reality, she wanted a closer look at those hyperthermia patients from that bus crash.

Yvonne had overheard on the grapevine when people had whispered behind her back, that Damian was supposed to have been on that bus. Someone even asked her, and she just laughed it off and said he was at work, that there must have been a mix-up. She wasn't a fool though, she knew her story wouldn't last long, and it was obvious to her that Damian had taken his chance to disappear, as they had talked about so often. She didn't want to call anyone to ask about him, didn't want to get him into any trouble, wanted to give him time to sort something out. He had a good head on his shoulders, and would somehow keep in touch. The message from Sabine a couple of hours earlier had been a huge relief nonetheless. Sabine was sound, Damian obviously agreed, too. All she had been able to figure out was that her son had been on that bus, though she had no idea why at that time of day, and that apparently everyone else had been admitted to the ward, half frozen to death. For whatever reason, he wasn't one of them.

She passed Mary Hudson and looked at the pale blue face, her condition stable. She was still unconscious, just like the others. Yvonne knew Mary quite well, what with Damian and Nina being just a few years apart age wise, and Mary living not far from her in Hutton-Le-Hole, where everybody knew each other anyhow. Of course, she remembered poor gentle intellectual Greg dying of this sudden pneumonia, brought on by cold, with the feather on his bed. Now this very strange accident with the bus where feathers had been seen again, of all things, well, it was too bizarre, creepy even. If Damian had been on that bus, had he managed to get off before the crash had happened? As she stood and puzzled an idea formed in her head, that there was something, something she ought to remember, that would help. It was frustrating she couldn't reach it, it was more a vague instinct as yet than anything else. Perhaps it would come to her. She went on to Bill's bed, same situation, same horrid facial colour. Neither of them were out of the woods yet. Karen Hills and her little boy Kade, she didn't know either of them, and nobody had enquired about them yet either. Kade was only 5 years old, according to his iLink, and the fact that no father was registered on either his or his mother's records saddened her, remembering only too well what it had been like bringing up Damian on her own. All the big occasions, when a dad should have been there, but wasn't. Ok, losing control that one fateful night at the Royal Free conference hadn't been one of her best decisions, but she didn't regret having Damian, she loved him and felt protective of him from the start. One glorious weekend with Jaques, French charm personified, and then he was gone. Some men, some fathers, just didn't give a damn, it was a sad fact of life. Perhaps it was the same for this woman and her boy.

There was the bell signal at the ward door, how odd, visitors weren't allowed in at night, and the admin Serf would have rejected anyone untoward. She went to have a look. It was the Police.

Two male officers, one female and one Serf, all four of them armed. Yvonne turned cold inside, only keeping up her fixed smile from years of patient care experience. "You're out late, how can I help you? I'm on duty, as you can see."

"Mrs Turner." The tallest officer spoke first. "We have reason to believe that your son Damian was involved in an accident while traveling on a bus, the same one that caused your patients in the units on ward C to be brought in. Have you spoken with him?"

It was pretty disconcerting to have cold pairs of stern eyes staring at her, with that Serf, his trigger hand at the ready. She had to explain her emotional state reader obviously flashing adrenaline activity. "You're scaring me, Officer! Goodness, no, I haven't heard from him, he's a thirty-four year old man so I'm not expecting him to call me every five minutes! But he isn't here, so I doubt very much he's been in any bus accident at all. I thought these were the only passengers?"

"You are trying to tell me that you haven't been told that he was on the bus?" The woman officer looked at her, part curious, part cynical.

"No, I haven't heard anything about Damian! I tried to call him earlier, as I do sometimes, but have had no reply, which is fine, and not that unusual. I was also told there was a dead pheasant on the bus, and how likely is that? People say all sorts!" Yvonne took a deep breath, knowing she had to sound strong. "Now, could I get back to my patients, please?"

"Did you know that your son lost his job at P&M?" The other officer asked her, ignoring her annoyance.

"He has what? That's impossible, he was the head of the department!" Yvonne shook her head, eyes wide, her genuine surprise obvious.

"Well, you see, Mrs Turner, we think there is a little more going on here than you're letting on. He was given his notice chip earlier today and was expected at the EDC this afternoon. We cannot trace him, but all his ID and his iLink have been found on the coach at the scene of the accident, so we can only assume that he removed them himself and made a run for it maybe? He doesn't like the idea of work much, does he?"

That last comment by the younger male officer really made Yvonne see red. How dare they. "I beg your pardon? He's been working at that factory since he was 16 years old and was well liked! You are telling me that my son might have been involved in an accident, possibly hurt, and you can't get hold of him? I'm thanking you for breaking the news to me so gently!" She said icily, before turning away to walk back to the ward office. She'd have about ten seconds before she'd burst out crying, she was sure.

"We'll be in touch, Mrs Turner!" One of them called after her and then there was silence.

She sank on her office chair and cried, her emotions tumbling all around her. And she totally understood why Damian had decided to leave when he could, the notice chip would have been the trigger. She was proud of him for that, desperately worried, grateful that they hadn't mentioned Sabine at all, and still couldn't understand why he hadn't been brought in half frozen like the others. She was afraid for him, she had always felt his passion as well as his capability, there was a drive in him, some kind of energy ready to burst out of him. Had that been obvious to someone at the factory? Had he knocked someone's nose out of joint with his rebellious attitude? Maybe that's why the police were after him?

Yvonne's head was swimming trying to make sense of it all. Whichever way she looked at it, all governments thrived on corruption still, cradled in the pockets of the few who managed to hang on to their privileges, holding the world to ransom with their disabling and disempowering laws. There had been a rush of optimism six years earlier, when most top bankers, media tycoons' and billionaires' businesses perished practically overnight, unprepared for the rise of AI taking over their accounts. It had been pretty hilarious, downright satisfying in fact, when it became apparent that the very robots developed for the physical and material security of the wealthiest few had ended up averaging accounts in favour of smaller, independent businesses, that's how the story went anyhow. The Serfs had outsmarted their programmers, even in the moral sense. A revolution run by AI in favour of the many. Who'd have thought it? But the results of the new state of affairs were less exciting. Ordinary people around the world were now living in a murky limbo state, stuck between paranoid governments with overzealous police forces, and seemingly more benign Serfs who the vast majority of the population were still afraid to trust. Damian would have to navigate those murky waters very carefully.

Nina and Brent lay in bed staring at the ceiling, unable to sleep. To see Mary and Bill like that had been dreadful. Also, Nina had heard the news about the feathers from somewhere, and that Damian had disappeared. It was all too much. Damian was one of the people they considered a like-minded friend in the village, who didn't like all the surveillance politics either. He was such a decent guy, pretending to be a bit tougher than he was, but he'd do anything for anyone. He'd been brilliant when Nina's Dad had died, supportive, helpful, a good guy all-round. Where was he? And what was that thing with the feathers all about? And ice? Where did it come from, and why? Was it the same thing that killed her Dad? And now her poor Mum, looking like nobody should look. And Bill. The always jolly Bill. And that young mother and her boy. Nina clenched her fists in frustration, helpless, life could be so unfair.

"Don't you want to turn on your sleep pulse for a bit, Nina?" Brent pointed to her iLink. A handy bit of kit that induced mild and natural sedation, working on the circadian rhythms in a similar way to acupuncture, non-addictive, just enough to drop off when needed. "It'll be a long day at the hospital tomorrow, I think we both need some kip."

Nina sighed and turned to rest her head on his shoulder. "I know. You're right. I feel I should be having an idea but it's not coming to me."

Brent held her tight in response, they both turned on their sleep-pulse and fell asleep in each other's arms. It was good to have each other.

Sabine was watching Damian stretched out on her sofa, fast asleep, looking pale and vulnerable. She wanted to go up and stroke his face, sit close to him, but she daren't, he needed to rest, and really, she needed sleep too. What a day he'd had. She'd listened to him tell her everything, that he got the boot at work, for no reason other than that basically Serfs were cheaper, and about the flu jabs for old people, causing dementia, she'd known nothing about that! How awful was that, and how weird was that bus crash, and the ice, and the feathers, and him deciding to disappear? Well, that was probably the most horrible and weirdest thing of all. She really, really didn't want him to disappear anywhere. Especially now she was supposed to go to Italy, her flight booked, Uncle Marcus waiting for her, needing to discuss something. She had been really looking forward to it, joining in with the band practice there. They'd have amazing food in the company of old friends, a chance to practice her Italian again and enjoy that bright Italian winter sunshine. It had sounded so perfect.

But what to do with Damian? He didn't have his car, and he'd probably be picked up in it straight away anyhow. Without his iLink she couldn't take him with her, never mind that *he* wouldn't be able to go anywhere, pay for anything, food, rent, anywhere.

Not without his passport he'd thrown into the bus, all of which, presumably, in police possession by now. His health records, his fingerprint records, his movements up to when he disappeared, they'd have everything, like an open book. Even his messages with her. Gawd. Most likely they'd be around before long to ask her whether she knew where he was. And where could he hide? If it wasn't for Uncle Marcus she'd actually feel quite tempted to up sticks with Damian when they were both ready, she could leave her ID's in the house and just walk out and keep on walking. Go on the run to nowhere, somehow meet others, start a movement. Damian said as much, that he'd like her with him, that he had a bit of gold that would see them right, and then bit his lip as if unsure whether he should have mentioned that. She could tell he'd been serious about wanting her to come along, and that at the same time he hadn't wanted to put pressure on her either, not wanting to freak her out, as he put it. Too late, she was freaked out, good and proper, she felt squeezed between the promise of a mad and romantic adventure and fear. The drawback was, she was a seriously hopeless liar. If the police were ever to question her about Damian, they wouldn't need to look at any emotional state meter to know she was hiding something.

His mum Yvonne would be good to talk to, but that was dodgy, and she couldn't ring Uncle Marcus for fear of being recorded. Not for the first time she realised how difficult it was to just be and live naturally, to go wherever and do whatever you wanted. Damian was right, society needed a revolution of some kind. She had seen the determination in his eyes, amazed that she had never picked up on how strongly he felt about everything. She had to admit, she liked that in him, a lot. It was 2am. Time she got some sleep herself. The sleep-pulse would come in handy.

Chapter 11
The Memory

YVONNE FELT WEARY. Her shift seemed to have gone on forever. The police visit had shaken her to the core, and, like Sabine, she was racking her brain with what to do. She figured Damian was with Sabine, so it would be no good going there in case she was followed, she would lead the police straight to him. Not that he'd committed any major crime, but leaving the scene of an accident, without helping anyone or calling an ambulance, and getting rid of his IDs, he'd be marked as a trouble-maker for sure. He'd have to go in for a social assessment in the crime prevention department, and who knew what they were doing with young people who didn't tow the line? Every now and then she'd heard stories, like everyone had, about police brutality towards people in custody, beatings and 'truth injections'. All of it sounded horrific, whether exaggerated or not. She was his mother, she would protect him in whichever way she could.

Yvonne thought back to an accident Damian had when he was a little boy. He had been playing on his bike, and fallen on some old wrought iron fence spike sticking up from the ground. It had gone straight into his thigh, injuring the main artery there; he'd nearly bled to death. He was only eight or so. Yvonne had been standing by the kitchen sink when, suddenly, she felt the most horrid falling sensation in her stomach. Strongly sensing that something had happened to him, she ran out onto the path winding along the fields where she knew he'd be; pulled by some unseen magnetic force towards her son. And there he lay, in a pool of blood, looking at her whispering: 'Sorry Mum, I made my clothes mucky'. In that moment she could have laughed and cried all at the same time for him to come out with something like that. She didn't care about the clothes, only about her boy hurting, and knew she'd have to get him to hospital, he'd lost so much blood! As a nurse she was aware she shouldn't remove the spike, he'd bleed even more, so there was nothing she could do but call the ambulance on her mobile, no iLinks in those days, and wait, the excruciating wait, for the paramedics to arrive all the way from Scarborough. It was just the most ridiculous thing ever; how long it took for help to arrive. He'd been given a blood transfusion while still in the ambulance; it had saved his life.

The blood transfusion! That was it!! Yvonne sat bolt upright in her office chair, she just knew she'd hit on something. That blood transfusion must have made some difference, possibly causing some change in his body chemistry! What had been in that blood to make him able to withstand the freezing temperature that the others on the bus had succumbed to?

She felt almost giddy with the realisation. It made sense, the pieces came together for her like an illuminated jigsaw puzzle. Since that day he had always been that bit warmer than everyone else, his base temperature a full degree higher than normal, and she had checked it, over and over again. At first she had suspected that perhaps he might have an underlying infection, but no check-up ever revealed anything. Even though he felt the cold, even the lightest draft acutely, he could just cope better. In the midst of winter, even when it snowed, he never needed gloves, rarely needed a sweater or none of the extra layers he'd have preferred before the transfusion. Instead of hot drinks he just wanted sweets more than anything, she'd tell him off for it, so many times. Eventually they had settled on hot chocolate which he would gulp down like there was no tomorrow. Then he'd run out to play in the snow again, without a coat!

Yvonne sank back down in the chair again, realising what this meant. It meant that the answer for the treatment of poor Mary, Bill, Karen and little Kade was likely to be found in a blood sample from her son. Damian, however, was in hiding. What rotten timing.

· · · • • ● • • · · ·

IT WAS AS if a soft blanket of recovery lay over Bristol Bay, soothing everyone. The initial shock and fearful discussions had smoothly made way for a very gentle state of mind, which was actually as baffling as everything else, but nobody questioned it. It felt like the calm after the storm, safe, comforting, and fresh.

The really great thing that had come from the evening of the meeting was that old Nellie and Bob were going to get married, and about time, too, most of them chuckled. Everyone had always known that those two belonged together, it was easy to be happy for them. The old couple walked hand in hand now, behaving like teenagers, as if to catch up for lost times. Bristol Bay's tiny international community felt more meaningful, they hadn't really given it that much thought until now. The wonderful mix of races from every corner of the world here felt inspiring again, encouraging peace and tolerance, a sense of all humanity being in this together. Of course, the ancient history of the Russians enslaving the Alaskans had always come up during the odd drunken fight, and probably would again, but the liberation and people intermarrying resulted in generations of offspring from various nationalities. Their community worked. Nobody really cared about where anyone came from, racism had become truly a thing of the past. Survival and working together was what counted in such isolated places under harsh conditions. Some fancied that perhaps the Icehawk was an angel after all, and it hadn't hurt them because at least they had peace amongst nations figured out. None of the tribes and rural communities were interested in war with anyone, that was the nonsense of city politicians. Whatever happened that night had passed, the song and the occasion had pulled them together even more, there was a lot of affection between everyone. Nobody felt like being in a bad mood, it was crystal clear how precious life was and how precious everyone around them was.

"Well, there are no reporters as yet, are there, Nellie?" Bob said to her over breakfast. "That's really something, nobody's blabbed, I didn't think that would be possible, did you?"

"No, me neither."

"What is it, Nel? You've got something you're chewing on, I know that face. Go on, spit it out."

"Well, I tried to call Mary, Bob, to tell her about the wedding, and I can't get through. I had it all worked out as well, what to say, without letting her know anything about the Icehawk. You know I'm still thinking about the parallels when her Greg died, thought of it when seeing those feathers left on the ground from the other night. But anyhow, I want to invite Mary, Nina and Brent for the wedding, they love Alaska in the spring, and I don't get why she hasn't replied, it's so unlike her. They are nine hours ahead of us, so it's not as if it was night time there. Maybe I should call Nina later, when she should be back from work?"

Bob sat back and watched her frown wrinkling her forehead and leant forward to kiss it and her worries away. "Hey, girl, don't you go all fretful on me now, you hear? She'll be fine, there will be an explanation, like no connection or something. Definitely, they should be here for the wedding. Everybody would love to see them again. So,.......I suppose you wearing a white wedding dress is out of the question?"

They both laughed, Nellie thinking how he could make her feel so much better, just by being there. He was right, everything would be perfect. If they both got to a hundred they'd still have a longer marriage than a lot of younger people. Time and age were really miraculous things, meaning something so different at different times and being oddly flexible. Today they'd go for a little walk, watch the birds over the bay maybe, she'd make some oat and coconut cookies, and think about her wedding and seeing Mary, Nina and Brent again in the spring. Life was good, creaking bones or not.

Chapter 12
New Friends

MARCUS DECIDED TO enjoy his time in Italy. He'd gone down for breakfast, like he always did, sitting in the same chair where his Dad would have spent the hottest time of the scorching summer days reading the Italian paper, not like himself who had just asked for the English one. Massimo who ran the Taverna was great, a proper cheerfully fiery Italian who laughed a lot and made a lot of noise, always talking and making the best pizzas. Nothing seemed too much trouble for him. Breakfast was a dream, with fantastic coffee and hazelnut pastries. Marcus had really got into the holiday spirit last night, but in the morning he had woken up with a sense of restlessness and a futility niggling at him, inner doubts increasing. What was he doing here anyhow? He'd called Sabine, too. Idiot. He should have talked to her in her little flat, taken her out for a pizza in Malton instead of going through all this cloak and dagger nonsense. At least Sabine was all for it, had some owed holidays she had to take before the end of the year. She was looking forward to playing with the band again and deserved a break. He, however, felt just as lost as what to do with himself, as he was when he'd been the non-musical spare wheel as a child.

His sister Maxine understood why he felt so at home in

Barbania now, but worried he was punishing himself with memories of musical inadequacy. But this was the place he felt closest to Roy, his stubborn, ornery, loveable Dad who point blank refused to cook, who usually had a derisive opinion about something or someone, but was solid as a rock and had a great sense of humour, mixed with his own brand of wisdom. If he'd say he'd do something he would, he'd even put a knot in his handker-chief so he wouldn't forget, and he always thought much more deeply about people and with more affection than he let on. He'd been a damn good father, too.

Thinking of Roy had calmed him down a bit, what would his Dad do if he'd come across something he wasn't sure what to do with? He'd simply sit on it until he knew what to do. 'Things will become clear eventually', that was his motto. It had seen him through all his travels and coping with people he shared his love for first class music with. Even when they didn't necessarily see eye to eye with him how it should be played, and about which members exactly would be right for the bands he'd formed over the years. Roy had been a patient man, and that was what Marcus needed to remember now, the patience to wait for things to become clear.

He licked the remaining crumbs of the hazelnut pastry off his finger and waved to Massimo for more coffee. The morning sun promised yet another beautiful bright November day, he would go for a walk and listen to the band practice in the band room adjacent to the Taverna, probably playing the tunes his Dad had written for them decades ago. He leaned back in the old leather covered dining chair, and picked up the refreshingly real paper version of the London rag, 'The UK Standard' Massimo had ordered for him, it was so much better than turning on a screen first thing in the morning.

And it was there on page 5, hitting him like the proverbial icepick between the eyes.

'Freak Ice Storm in a small Yorkshire Village. Four injured, one missing. Experts point to global warming and the threat of another Ice Age'.

Marcus read that it happened between Malton and Kirkbymoorside, that the bus had probably been turned over by strong winds, that the passengers were still in a serious but stable condition in Scarborough ICU, and that one local man, Damian Turner, had disappeared. The article reported that strangely, a pheasant or some bird of prey may have been caught in the storm, as both ice and large feathers, though no actual bird, had been found on the scene. The police were appealing for witnesses, and were asking for help about the missing man."

Marcus let out a pained groan, this wasn't possible! Not now! He'd have to ring Sabine, who he knew was friendly with Damian. She always talked fondly of him, he'd even met him briefly, though he'd never really spent enough time with him to be able to say he knew him well. And the cold, the feathers! Just like Greg! And he was sitting here in Italy eating pastries, for goodness sake! He really was useless. He swiped over Sabine's number to call her.

Sabine answered immediately. She sounded stressed and worried, telling him how everyone was shaken up about the accident, that her friend's Mum and the friendly bus driver Bill were half frozen in hospital, and a mother with her little lad, too.

"What about Damian? It says in the paper he's disappeared, have you heard from him?"

"No. No, I haven't."

He knew straight away she was lying. She couldn't hide a needle in a haystack, had always been like that. His mind was racing. So she knew where Damian was and didn't want to say over the phone. They were both silent, hearing each other breathe.

"Want me to put on the V-screen so we can see each other?"

"No, thanks, Uncle Marcus, I haven't got dressed yet, but I'm not sure I'm in the mood to go on holiday with you now, it doesn't feel right.."

Her voice trailed off a bit, and he could tell that she was telling him half truths. He saw it play out in his mind, she didn't want to put the V-screen on because Damian was there with her. And that's also why she didn't want to come to Italy; there was clearly some major stuff going on. He'd have to go back and help out. He'd made up his mind. "Listen, I'm going to catch the first flight back. I'm not enjoying my holiday that much either. Cancel the ticket, I'll reimburse you, don't worry about the money…I'll holiday in Yorkshire instead, ok? And trust me." He added quickly. Her reply told her what he needed to know.

"Oh great, Uncle Marcus, brilliant! Yes! I'll cancel my flight!" She added an equally quick 'Thank you', telling him she understood. They couldn't have been more in tune if she had been his own daughter. He'd let Massimo know and go upstairs to change his return flight online.

Damian had been watching Sabine and heard with relief she was going to stay. It was wonderful to wake up in her little flat, being made to feel so welcome. He still had no plan, but knew he was putting her at some risk if he stayed with her. Her Uncle Marcus was all right, he wouldn't drop him in it, with some people you just knew.

"What do you think I should do, Sabine? I'm really sorry I've put you in this position, hiding out with you like this. I'm just pretty clueless right now." He looked really embarrassed, and hopeful at the same time.

Sabine couldn't exactly claim she knew what he should do either. Him staying, even putting out a toothbrush for him, felt natural already. But no, he couldn't stay forever. People would notice eventually that she didn't live alone, and she could hardly lock him in the cupboard if someone was to come round. She thought of hiding him in the boot of her car and driving him somewhere in the middle of the night, but neither of them knew where, and it was November, too, not a good time to sleep in the woods or even in a cave anywhere along the Yorkshire coast.

"Maybe we should just wait until Uncle Marcus gets here tomorrow? He might have some ideas, and if I just do what I usually do, people seeing me out and about, as if nothing had happened, well, we should be ok? Actually, I was thinking of going to Scarborough Hospital to see if they are getting better, it's a good enough excuse, to visit people from here, and I might bump into your Mum, able to reassure her somehow? It gets dark around half four now, so if I'd leave now I should be back in time for it to be ok to have the lights on in the flat, you don't want to be sitting in the dark until people see me get back home? I could nip down to the bakery and get some stuff, make some small talk like I usually do?"

Damian looked at her, hardly knowing what to say. She'd thought about him, and about his Mum, too, that was special, seriously special. He stood right in front of her and just did it, leaned forward and kissed her right on the lips, without being able to pause and think about it. Oh my god, that felt so good. She kissed him back, and pulled herself a bit closer to him. He felt her back arch towards him, her breasts through her thin t-shirt, electricity surging through both of them.

"Woooah, Tiger! What brought this on?" She laughed as she pushed away against his shoulders a little, looking up at him, not looking the least bit angry.

"Must be the talk of the bakery." He kissed her again, both of them tasting each other, feeling each other, and it was so right.

"I've got to get going though. Otherwise you'll be sitting here in the dark all on your lonesome self, and we can't have that, can we!" She laughed and made herself turn away quickly to put her coat and shoes on, Damian watching her, feeling bereft. She was right, of course, but he really, really couldn't wait for her to get back. He'd wait forever if need be, and not just because he wanted to kiss her again.

Nina and Brent were getting ready to drive to the hospital, too. They'd had a rotten morning. Calls from the estate agent who seemed oblivious and totally insensitive to what had happened, and the two of them had argued about whether to ring Nellie to let her know about Mary. Brent reminded Nina that Nellie was a woman in her eighties and calling her in the middle of the night with bad news about her daughter really wouldn't be very kind. Nina was convinced that as her grandmother, Nellie should know immediately when something so important had happened, and that maybe living in Alaska she'd know of a more helpful treatment?

"People there must have hypothermia much more often and more severely than what's normal round here!" She was cross that Brent didn't see the urgency, that Nellie's knowledge might save everyone's life. They settled on calling Nellie when they got back from hospital with the most recent news, it would be lunchtime there by then. It was sensible enough, Nina conceded. Damian's Mum had messaged Brent's iLink that Mary and the others were still in a serious but stable condition, and that they were welcome to visit any time. It was the urge to be close rather than thinking her Mum would benefit from them being there that drew both Nina and Brent there. Poor Damian's Mum, too, with her son still missing, having to look after the others with so many questions of her own.

Connor was, as ever, a gem and offered to hold the fort in Brent's workshop for as long as necessary. Old Spencer came round immediately to bring a special bottle of homebrew 'for the nerves' and everyone in the village who had heard showed concern, even Sharon asked after Mary, even if in her usual nosy manner. There had been a bunch of theories about the feathers, that maybe a flock of birds or an unfortunate sparrowhawk had been caught up in a tornado-like ice storm. None of the theories so far felt right, but nobody could come up with anything better either.

Yvonne had been able to change her hours, working the day shift right after her previous night shift, ignoring her own exhaustion. Nobody questioned her about it, understanding that she was stressed and worried about her missing son, and probably wanting to be close to the people who had been on the same bus as him, even if they were still unconscious. The first couple of days were critical, everyone knew that. Yvonne was glad she didn't have to explain why she was really there. She was hoping Sabine might come to see her under the pretence of wanting to check on the other local patients, and perhaps give her a message from Damian. She also knew that they'd have to be very careful, she couldn't be sure she wasn't being recorded. Nor was she confident about what the police were capable of. Like Damian she didn't trust the authorities at all any more, especially not since she'd seen the memo about the dementia injections. Neither her, nor her son, nor the general public could move and do as they wanted. It all looked reasonable and peaceful on the surface, but real freedom of expression was fast becoming a thing of the past, like the right to protest, suddenly scrapped back in 2026. From one day to the next being a protester or a whistle blower could in effect mean the death penalty, also newly introduced, police serfs with guns didn't pause to ask questions. Again Yvonne found herself praying to God, in itself much more attractive since no-one was supposed to do that anymore either. She wondered how many still had their faith that surely couldn't just be switched off, still hoping for divine intervention to fix the mess the world was in. Oh yes, she supported her son for wanting to help turn things around, but as his mother she was also achingly afraid for him. The longer he'd be missing the more suspicious the police would become of his motives, every hour counting against him. Needing to have a look at his bloods only complicated matters further. More than anything Damian would want to help. Her job so far was to remain quiet and calm enough to be able to think.

Sabine meanwhile, nervous but determined, arrived at the hospital and let the reception Serf know she was visiting her friend Mary Hudson in ICU. There was no untoward reaction, she was handed the little map without any problems. Damian had warned her to be careful while talking to his Mum. He guessed she might be monitored, but he expected Yvonne would think the same way. Using Winnetou and Old Shatterhand again to let her know he was safe might be pushing it a bit. They decided that Sabine should just play it by ear, Damian was certain she and his Mum would figure things out between them. He had realised again how much he trusted Sabine, how their connection felt so reliable, easy and oddly familiar.

The Admission Serf to the ICU sang out her name, the door slid open and Sabine walked down the hall not quite sure what to expect, and not really knowing Mary Hudson. Considering she was the world's worst liar she'd have to learn fast. If Uncle Marcus had been with her she'd let him do the talking, so perhaps it was time she did things like that for herself, especially as she was half considering to disappear with Damian. If that wasn't a fantasy at all. The insecurity about what to do didn't help, she had to put it out of her mind for now.

"Miss Carter, hello! I believe you are here to see Mary Hudson? I'll show you the way." Yvonne spoke to her in her most professional voice, both understanding that that would be the least suspicious. Yvonne was so very glad that her instinct to wait for Sabine had paid off, but she had to be careful and play the game. She was experienced enough to continue making patient conversation. "I'm afraid there is nothing new to report as yet. All the patients are still in a serious but stable condition, their responses very much the same in all of them. I have to warn you it might upset you to see your friend like this. Here she is." Yvonne led Sabine gently to Mary's window, knowing full well that the patient's horrid complexion wouldn't be an easy thing for anyone to see.

As expected Sabine reeled, and cried out softly. "Oh my god... will she be all right?"

Yvonne laid her hand on Sabine's arm. "We very much hope so, Miss Carter, and we are doing all we can. I'm so sorry, this must come as a frightful shock. There is one avenue we are trying to pursue, which is finding records of hypothermia cases of people who had perhaps undergone a similar trauma but had not been so badly affected by it. We are hoping to find a better way of treating them, and a blood sample of those much luckier patients might really help us along."

It took Sabine a few seconds to understand what Yvonne and the slight deliberate edge in her voice meant, and daring to look into her eyes, Sabine saw the worry and conflict in a mother's eyes, which made her heart surge with affection and sympathy towards Yvonne. What the poor woman must have gone through over the past twenty-four hours, she could hardly bear to think about it.

"Oh, yes, I understand! That would make complete sense!" She couldn't quite believe how calm her voice sounded. "It's a great idea! I'm thinking, I work as a lab chemist at York Uni, I could ask around amongst the winter sports fanatics, maybe? I've heard of some students who seem to handle the cold better than others, perhaps they would volunteer some pin prick samples?"

Sabine looked into Yvonne's eyes with as much intensity as she could muster, hoping the meaning would be clear. "Would that be enough? Would it be at all helpful? I really think you might be onto something there!" She was getting seriously cool at this lying malarkey, she felt positively triumphant. Not even her emotional state meter picked up on anything much at all! Amazing. The relief on Yvonne's face was wonderful, however hard she tried to put on a poker face.

"That might just be extremely helpful, yes, Miss Carter, wonderful, thank you very much! Especially considering most of your students must be reasonably local, we could perhaps match them with the records we have?"

Sabine saw her chance to doubly reassure her about Damian and piped up, quite happily. "Oh yes, very local, you're right, the blood samples wouldn't spoil in the short transit time in the cooler bag. I am thinking of one young man in particular who is famous for running around in a T-shirt all through the winter, we keep telling him off for it! I wouldn't mind some of his blood myself, come to think of it!" She had even managed to come up with a natural sounding joke!

Yvonne's face went from delight to something close to ecstasy. If she had been in any doubt before, this definitely meant that Damian was well, that he must have told Sabine that he never felt the cold, or did they know each other more intimately than Yvonne had realised? Sabine resembled a glow-worm when she talked about him, however obscurely, and she would get a blood sample which would probably be all that was necessary to make some progress in treating the others. Yvonne could have burst into tears of joy, but knew she had to keep it together.

"Can I see the others?" Sabine asked bravely. She decided she needed to be able to tell Damian, and Uncle Marcus, too, as much detail as was possible to find out, though quite frankly those half frozen faces freaked her out. How was anyone able to be cold for so long and still be alive? Surely that wasn't normal with all the treatments they could have, the silver blankets and infusions? As if she had read her mind Yvonne explained that as the internal organs of the patients were so severely affected by the intense freeze, it would be very dangerous to warm them up too quickly, it was actually safer to let the body do the work itself, and provide a natural warmth instead, not higher than the normal body temperature, at the low end even. As if allowing them to thaw slowly.

Yvonne had to admit she wasn't sure herself how normal it was, to be unconscious for so long due to hypothermia. Not that anything at all about this case was normal. Sabine nodded, understanding what a miracle it must have been that Damian had not been affected. He did say that his iLink had been frozen solid to his wrist, not just partly grown in, so he'd been in the same ice storm as the others. And checking out his blood for answers made sense. He'd want to help, without a doubt.

It was time to leave. Sabine shook Yvonne's hand warmly in lieu of giving her a hug, and made her way back towards the exit, when she heard the Admission Serf call out 'Nina Daniels and Brent Daniels, for Mary Hudson!'

They were standing outside the glass doors waiting for it to slide open, showing the Serf Nina's bag for the security check. So that was Nina and Brent! She remembered Damian talking about them a lot over the time she'd known him, that they were kindred spirits as far as his dislike of big brother went, good people, he'd said. He had also told her that Nina lost her father in similarly odd circumstances, about cold and something about a feather. She couldn't remember anything else. 'And now her Mum.' Sabine just had time to think it when another thought crossed her mind.

Maybe they were worried about Damian, too? She couldn't say anything here, but she had to somehow let them know something so they could make the connection, Damian might need their help eventually, too. What could she do? Panic rose in her, she had to think of something in the next second or two!

"Excuse me, are you Brent Daniels?"

Brent looked at her confused and somewhat irritated. "Who wants to know?"

"Oh, it's just, it's just.." Sabine turned bright red, desperately trying to come up with some lie, and fished it out of thin air. "I've heard you're a bit of a bird expert, that's all, I wondered what you thought those feathers were they found near the bus in that accident." Shit, shit, that was so dumb, totally unhelpful.

"They were hawk feathers, probably." Brent replied, somewhat impatiently, aware that Nina had started walking ahead, just wanting to be with her Mum.

Sabine was desperate, and, rightly or wrongly, mouthed to Brent, silently,

"He's ok!"

Brent took a second or two to get it, she was trying to tell him someone was ok... Damian! It had to be Damian! And the cameras probably lipread what she just said, if anyone was watching.. "I don't think they ever found the bird itself, so I don't know if it's ok." He tried to sound convincing, looking at the uncertainty in her eyes, seeing that she tried equally hard to make this look and sound just like some inane small talk, neither of them used to this.

"Well, hawks are powerful, aren't they." Sabine replied, rather weakly. "He's probably ok somewhere, yes, I'm sure he is."

Probably the dumbest conversation ever, and she couldn't be sure, but hoped Brent had got it. This wasn't a good place to continue the conversation, they both knew it.

"I'll go and see my mother-in-law now, bye now." Brent was already rushing off, and she nodded in response, having to control herself not to run through the corridors to the outside as fast as she could. There was a lot she'd be able to tell Damian back home and she wished she'd done better with Brent. But she had tried her hardest, and with all the unexpressed adrenaline in her bloodstream, her irritation rose. After all, it hadn't been her idea that he should make a run for it and hide at her place. What had she let herself in for?

Nina and Brent stood at the window looking at Mary's face, pretending to themselves and each other that she was looking a little better already. Brent squeezed Nina's hand. "Remind me later to tell you about something!" He saw Yvonne approach, searching her face for her expression. Was he imagining it or did she have a bit of a spring in her step, her face looking so much more relaxed than yesterday? How frustrating he couldn't just ask her straight out about Damian... if she knew something from that woman who had talked to him, she wouldn't be able to say. But he could find out who the woman was, so asked her, casually. "You know the visitor we just passed on the way out, was she a friend of Mary's? She looked a bit familiar." He looked at her intently. Yvonne, recognizing the intent, mirrored his expression and replied carefully. "Her name is Sabine, and yes, I believe she's a friend of Mary's."

The glimmer of recognition in Brent's eyes confirmed it, Damian had talked to him about her, and his look of relief echoed her own. Damian was safe, and that was the Sabine he'd mentioned a few times, pretty smitten by the sounds of it. Nina and him had winked at each other more than once, and expected a romance in the making, so perhaps he was even with her? He'd heard the name in another context, too, but couldn't quite place it. He'd have to ask Nina later. For now they'd just stay around to be near Mary for a while, just in case she or any of the others woke up.

Chapter 13
Connections

NELLIE SAT DOWN at her kitchen table to call Nina, there had been no reply from Mary, and she was getting more and more worried. It was so unlike her daughter not to call her back, or at least message a quick reply. Nina felt the hum on her iLink immediately and one glance told her it was her grandma.

"Brent, it's my Grandma Nellie, I have to answer this, God, what can I tell her?"

"Just tell her the truth, gently."

"Hi Grandma! How are you?" After a brief pause to listen, Nina looked at Brent for reassurance and took a deep breath before she replied. "No, she isn't, I'm so sorry. I'm here at the hospital, in the ICU, something strange has happened...."

Brent watched her struggling to find non-sensationalist terms, but it was hard, repeating that kind of story sounded very theatrical, there was nothing normal about it. And the irony, that someone from Alaska should hear that their daughter was suffering from intense hypothermia in North Yorkshire. He shook his head. It was all too bizarre for words.

Nellie turned white as a sheet as she heard her granddaughter tell her the story of the bus accident, and gasped as she heard about the ice that was there, so illogically, and the feathers, oh goodness, the Icehawk, it must have been!

"The Icehawk!" Her voice muffled into her iLink in shock. "Why there? Why Mary?"

"Grandma, what are you talking about, what's the Icehawk? That is what you just said, isn't it? Tell me!!"

Nellie's head was swimming, and Bob who had just come through the door saw her pale and struggling to speak. He rushed to her, realised she was talking to Nina, and immediately concerned felt the need to take over.

"Let me talk to her, Nel."

Uncharacteristically without protest she weakly swiped the call over to his iLink, and heard him talk quietly to Nina, who repeated the nightmare tale to him. Nellie felt as if she had stepped out of a bad dream and right back into another, this time involving her own daughter, in a place so unlikely, so far away. Thinking of the Icehawk's size and power and unyielding iciness, that he may have attacked the bus her daughter was on, was just unthinkably frightening. Mary was in hospital, fighting for her life. Had she seen the Icehawk? Had he seen her? Was she a target? Were they, as a family?

Nellie felt responsible, the Icehawk had shown over Bristol Bay and then rather more theatrically in Chignik Bay, and now in a tiny place in North Yorkshire, surely it had to be Nellie herself who was the connection? What if it just wanted her? Had it even only turned up in the first place because of her, and was now after her daughter, too? But why? Why her? Why them? Nellie looked so pale, her hands trembling, Bob knew she needed some attention.

"Listen, Nina, it sounds like we'll have to talk some more soon. We have some news for you, too, but now is not the time. I think I need to look after your Grandma right now. Can we call you back later?"

After a short pause listening to Nina who was clearly upset and confused, Nellie heard Bob end the call with a warm 'Righto, try not to worry, I'm sure everyone will be alright, talk to you later, and say hi to Brent'. He sat down next to her with a heavy sigh.

"Well, we never expected that, did we. Can't make head or tail of it, can you?"

"It must be my fault Bob, I must be the link! What other reason can there be that the Icehawk shows here and then attacks my daughter? Oh and Greg! Greg died, cold, with a feather with him, remember? Is it about Greg? No, he isn't with us any more, so it can't be. I don't understand, what can I do? I need to find the connection to help Mary. Poor her, and those others, Lord have mercy! A young mother and her little boy, did she tell you? The Icehawk can't be a god, nor an angel, it must be evil, oh Bob.." She cried out in anguish.

Bob was struggling, too. He had managed not to tell what had happened in Alaska, as they'd all agreed, but nobody expected that anything like this had happened anywhere else. The Icehawk hadn't attacked them, but a bus? In rural England? And by the looks of it Mary's husband three years gone? That 'thing' had probably left its signature feathers around on purpose, like some cynical calling card, Bob thought, furious now. This was bullying of the highest order. If he hated anything with a passion it was bullying, but he had no idea what could be done about it. This wasn't something that could be fixed with a song. He guided Mary, who felt light and weak as a kitten on his arm, over to the armchair, and went to turn on the kettle to make her her favourite hot cloudberry concoction with a hefty shot of vodka. Comfort was needed now and answers, they needed answers. Would the Icehawk strike again? For what purpose? Nothing made any sense at all.

· · · • • ● • • · ·

DR MARCUS CARTER settled down in his seat, the 11am solar plane from Turin to Leeds was on time, one advantage of AI in the aviation industry, everything really worked like clockwork. The planes were wonderful, too, the noisy engines he remembered only too well were no longer around. Now these crafts were slick and silent affairs, powered entirely by solar power and ozone circulation. Serfs had largely replaced the onboard service crew, gliding about silently and efficiently. The papers in his false bottom case had not triggered any alarms, and why should they? The checks were all about security, not obscure scientific formulas on pieces of paper. Marcus ignored the celebrity magazines on the onboard smart screen and went straight to the 'Century Scientist', a magazine he'd been reading since he was a geeky boy, both intrigue and comfort zone in one. Global warming was as ever a much discussed subject, the arguments for and against a sure ice age in the making. Man made pollution had been much reduced over the last decade, but basically it was too little, too late. Marcus was convinced that his discovery could only mean that the human body was readying itself for an ice age, so to him that was telling in itself. There seemed to be a relatively fast evolutionary process going on behind the scenes to prepare perhaps all life on earth to become ever more adaptable. Was it wise to help speed that process up at all? Was he trying to mess with both natural order and selection?

Marcus decided to read the fringe science bit, sometimes amusing, sometimes with merit, and was just about to dig into some metaphysical ideas about human thought creation in alternate universes, when he stopped short. There, staring at him, was a full page article about strange happenings involving both icy currents and bird feathers all over the planet, not often reported apparently, but he knew the writer well, Paul Coll. Not personally, but he had been reading his articles for years, aware that he had worked closely with Greg for a while. From his photo he knew him as a dark haired, bright, somewhat odd looking young man with an exceptionally high forehead, and his writings had always been succinct and memorable. How exciting to come across this now!

Paul described the bizarre phenomena, admittedly based on anecdotal evidence, yet the reports had been consistent. They all described concentrated fluke ice storms, there was one in Mexico, a couple in India, two in Italy - Italy? He hadn't heard anything about it! - some in China, quite a few in China, actually, and one even in Australia. Paul's guess was that the ice storm perhaps behaved in a similar manner to ball lightning, concentrated energy, collecting more as it went along, just in this case it was cold energy, and that was the puzzle. How was it possible for extreme cold pockets, isolated as they were, to gain momentum in hot countries like India and Mexico? Especially in the height of summer? What all of the icy currents had in common was altogether more mysterious, and it was that that had caught the imagination of the writer - each of the storms seemed to leave a trail of hawk feathers in its wake, specifically red-tailed hawk feathers, no other species involved at all.

Marcus groaned inwardly. So it happened in other places, too and nobody was taking much notice of it! Why? Because a bit of freak weather, cold or ice, and a few dropped feathers weren't exactly headline material, were they? Especially in combination they sounded more like folklore. Even the odd ice storm by itself, no big deal, was it? Trust Paul Coll to pick it up, how on earth did he get his information? This must have been what had killed Greg. The article offered no explanation, it just reported that this thing was happening literally all over the world and nobody had joined the dots, until now. Paul had obviously written the article before he had heard that the same just happened in a sleepy village in North Yorkshire. He should send him a message, but wanted to know more from Sabine when he got there, and what the locals were saying.

Marcus could just imagine the reaction of his peers listening to him piping up with his fantastic new theory, that there was a murdering ice cold hawk on the loose that could strike randomly from anywhere and nowhere. Luckily he'd be able to speak with Sabine soon. He could be at her flat by early afternoon.

Chapter 14
Love Thy Neighbour

BRENT STOOD QUIETLY next to Nina, who was staring at her unconscious mother through the ward window. They'd been standing there for only a few minutes, but it felt like hours. It was torture, looking at her mother like that who didn't even know they were there, not being able to hold her hand or talk to her directly.

Nina couldn't get the conversation with her Grandma out of her mind, she had definitely heard her say 'the icehawk" and it was obvious Nellie had been really upset, differently than if it was purely about the news about her daughter. It was almost as if she had been dreading it, or something like that.

"What's an icehawk, Brent? Ever heard of them?"

"It's a sports team in the US, I think."

Brent replied absentmindedly.

"Why?"

"No, I don't mean as a name, I mean as a bird. Nellie mentioned it, it sounded like she knew what the bus thing with the ice and the feathers was all about. Any ideas?"

"Well, the ice and the feathers did remind me of how your Dad died, Nina."

Brent said it as gently as he could, knowing she had made the connection with the cold between her Dad and her Mum, but he didn't think she'd even thought of the feathers. And they had been hawk feathers, and only hawk feathers, specifically, so for Nellie to say something like that was really strange, from so far away.

"Is there some Native American tradition or legend or something to do with hawks, Nina, do you know? Could it be a curse of some sort?"

"You, believing in curses? No way!"

Nina almost laughed, was this really her no-nonsense husband talking?

"Well, I've been asking myself where hawk feathers or any feathers would have meaning, combined with cold or ice, and the only thing I could come up with were Native American stories, and their traditional dress, the feather headdress and all that, their customs and traditions, and, well, angels, they crossed my mind, too. Or shamanic stuff of sorts.."

He blushed slightly.

"I just don't know enough, buzzards are hawks, aren't they? I remember the harris and goshawks at the falconry centre, so I'm just trying to make sense of it. Maybe we should ask the centre if they know anything? Though they couldn't explain the ice, could they?"

Brent gazed sadly at the normally so strong and gregarious Mary, looking so fragile now. The white streak in her hair appeared almost luminous now, like half a halo framing her face. Halos were another of those old terms hardly anyone understood, just assumed energy or enlightenment itself, but there was so much old knowledge lost now, Brent pondered. He did have a sense that something magical was happening, was it black magic? It couldn't be anything good, not with two women, one man and a child fighting for their lives. And how come Damian had got away? Though he was always the one never needing a coat in winter, Brent thought back with amusement. He remembered having a snowball fight with him when Damian was in a T-shirt, not that long after he'd been found with that bit of metal in his leg. The 'Iron Man' he'd called him for a while after that. He was over the moon to think of Damian being all right, and couldn't wait to tell Nina when it was safe to talk. He was getting hungry, so decided to ask Nina if she was ready to leave, there was nothing much they could do here. She agreed, this was just hopeless, this standing there, unable to do anything useful.

Walking through the car park outside the hospital, Brent pointed to his and her iLink, to swipe them into the Deep Sea Dive mode, a neat privacy setting he'd figured out only a week or so earlier and said to Nina under his breath. "I think I know where Damian is."

"What? How? Tell me!"

He laughed at her typical impatience and seeing that both iLinks had clouded over as if underwater was fantastic, it really did work. He thought it was a fault in the set-up, or maybe a fluke when he'd found out that if you turned it onto the deep sea dive setting, the microphone would shut down, maybe because you couldn't talk under water anyhow, but he was pretty sure you couldn't be overheard either. The whole thing muted itself. He'd taken an old one to pieces, checked the software out and tested it. There were still ways to outfox the system, and that was just so satisfying. "I think he's with that Sabine. He mentioned her a few times, remember?"

"Wow, yes, I do! How?... Oh, wait, was it that young woman by the ICU entrance who was babbling a bit strangely? It was, wasn't it! Tell me everything! Yvonne said she was a friend of my Mum's, but I've never seen her, have you?"

"No, though she seems familiar in some ways, but I can't figure out where I've seen her face before. Anyhow, I think Damian's Mum and her just talked about your Mum as a cover, in case they were being listened to. That's why I couldn't tell you in the hospital, there must be cameras and mics in every corner. She was trying to tell me about Damian, that much I finally understood, but she was no good at pretending, she seemed really sweet actually. I could see her with Damian, I really could. Would be good to meet up with him, or her, or both, and find out what's been happening. I wish I could remember where I'd seen her before."

"I didn't really pay attention, sorry. But Sabine, it does ring a bell, it'll come to me. Or maybe we just search for her and see what comes up online? And I need to call my grandmother, to see if she's all right, and what she meant. I'd love to be able to tell her better news though."

Lost in thought they made their way out of the car park, heading home, looking forward to some quiet time just on their own, trying to forget the sadness. An early dinner, maybe chilling out with a movie later. Somehow they'd have to learn to relax despite everything. Both knew, however, they would search online for Sabine and what could be learned about hawks.

Neither Brent nor Nina had been in any way aware that part of their conversation in the car park had been overheard, not all of it, but enough. Not by anyone via their iLinks either, but by a bleached blonde woman sitting in a little frog-like car they'd walked past without noticing. It was Sharon, their tiresome neighbour, the corners of her mouth pulling into a slowly widening, sly and very satisfied grin.'Oh, now, this could be fun! Telling the police about the whereabouts of Damian'. She had never liked him, not since he got the job her son had applied for all those years ago. Stole that job he did, she was sure of it. He was edgy and rough and had something about him she didn't like. The police would find that Sabine. She decided to call that handsome officer Matt Collins at Kirkby Station there and then. He really was just her type. If she played her cards right she might even get him to ask her out to dinner. It was important to assist the police, you never knew what people who chose to disappear might be up to. She could tell her friend she had come to visit in hospital all about it, too. What an exciting day it had turned out to be.

Chapter 15
The Drone

DAMIAN WAS HAVING a look at the titles in Sabine's bookshelves. She was amazing. Her reading covered so many subjects, a lot of science, chemistry, medicine, metaphysical stuff, too. On another shelf there was a whole collection of natural world titles, some on growing your own food, even surviving in the woods. The fact that she still owned paper books was fantastic, they made her place feel cosy and learned. She'd have hundreds more ebooks, for sure. It was 3pm, he couldn't wait for her to get back. It was strange without his iLink, having to guess how the hospital visit had gone, or where she was and how soon she would be here. He was literally tiptoeing around her flat, not to be noticed. He didn't listen to any news or music, and didn't turn on the CV. A fine revolutionary he was, he laughed to himself, hiding in a ditch and then running to a pretty woman's flat and not daring to make a sound, never mind not having a plan either. Not exactly the stuff heroes were made of. He ran his finger over the V-screen album, feeling a bit guilty looking at her pictures and recordings but too curious to stop himself.

There were pictures of her with her Mum, with someone he assumed was her Dad and Grandparents when she was little, some of her playing her clarinet, and quite a few with her Uncle Marcus who seemed to have a different woman on his arm in every picture. Sabine in Italy, in her summer dresses and one in a bikini, too, well, for some reason he had to look at those images at least ten times, she looked gorgeous, and seriously sexy. Some pictures of her with her cat Domino, too, he remembered her mentioning it, a grey and white long haired characterful one she obviously adored. It had died a year or so back and she'd been so upset. Damian decided there and then to get her a kitten one day, imagining the look on her face when he gave it to her. Lucky kitten, he thought, spending its life with her. Pictures of her with a kitten, and then garden scenes with little children running about, a baby in her arms, and, well, him standing right there next to her. The scene played out like a happy families movie in his head, before he even realised it was happening. He didn't feel like fighting any of it either.

He'd go and make himself presentable before she got back, tidy the sofa up, maybe clean the bathroom. She'd be hungry, too, but he couldn't risk going shopping, so he'd have to wait until she got home. Maybe she could nip to the shop herself, but he'd cook for her. He was a decent cook after all, sometimes challenging their kitchen Serf at home, to come up with a better lasagne than his.

He was just folding the blanket and tidied it away on the chair in the corner when he heard footsteps coming up the stairs to Sabine's door, and not her light-footed run either, this was definitely a man's walk. Why hadn't he heard the downstairs door open? He was sure Sabine said she'd lock it, as well as her apartment door. Was it the police? Here? Already, onto him? It had only been a day, and he hadn't really done anything wrong apart from disappearing. His head raced into a whirlwind of possibilities, none of them reassuring. He threw the cushion on top of the blanket to make it look less like bedding and ran first towards the kitchen, then changed his mind. He could all but run into the bathroom, just before Sabine's door opened, and consider whether he should climb out the window and probably kill himself, when he heard a voice call out to Sabine.

"Hello, Sabine! I'm here! I've let myself in, hope you don't mind, can I use your bathroom?"

And there Damian stood, frozen to the spot, when Marcus entered the bathroom.

"What the..!" Marcus nearly jumped out of his skin, looking as shocked as Damian. The two men reeled and just stared into each other's eyes for a second, until it sunk in that they knew each other, and they both caught their breath. Marcus was just about to speak, when Damian quickly put his hands to his lips and pointed to Marcus's iLink, with a covering movement, just in case it was able to record. Marcus sensed that Damian was jumpy and desperate, yes, but also that he looked honest, decent behind the panic, and did as Damian suggested. Instinctively he even went further, he took his iLink off, put it in the bathroom cabinet, turned the bathroom tap on and pretended to chat to Sabine, just traveller small talk, as best he could. "I'm so glad I'm here, planes are such a pain! The traffic was easy, though, didn't take me long to get here at all! It's still mild out, isn't it!"

Damian quietly squeezed past him back out into the living room. Marcus ran the toilet flush, closed the door and joined him.

"What the hell is going on, Damian? Where is Sabine?" Noticing the angry inflamed looking scab, he kept his voice low. "And what's up with your wrist?"

Damian almost whispered his reply, somewhat embarrassed. "She's supposed to be back in an hour or so, she's gone to Scarborough hospital to let my mother know I'm ok. God, sorry Marcus, hello, sorry I made you jump. Basically, I survived that weird bus crash, the one you talked with Sabine about, and got my notice chip from work just before that. My car is in the garage, I can't even get that now! I don't want to end up working in the assessment centre, so when I came round on the bus I decided that it was my chance to get rid of my IDs, my iLink and disappear. I tore it off, it's the new implant type one. Doesn't look too good, does it. Then I hid in the field drain until I had no better idea than to turn up at Sabine's. I'm such a moron..." He looked down at his hands interlocking his fingers and unlocking them again.

"She's done everything, she took me in, she cooked me a meal, washed my clothes, let me shower, let me sleep on the sofa.. and now she's gone to the hospital to find out more and reassure my mother. She even cancelled her holiday with you. I'm so so sorry.. and the police are probably after me now for not showing up at the centre. I wanted to get away, to think. Shit. The last thing I want is to cause Sabine any trouble, she's so great, just great."

"I see." Marcus nodded calmly, having watched him closely, feeling the need to reassure the young man.

"Ok, we'll think of something. What do you remember about the accident? Is what was said about it in the paper true? That there was ice involved, and hawk feathers?"

"Not sure about what kind of feathers they were, they were big though, a bit like broad pheasant ones. But the ice, that was unreal. Yeah. Ice everywhere, and the others looked frozen, there were icicles inside the bus, and on the outside of the bus, too, but the ditch I crawled in was really warm, you know, and.."

"Shhhh!!" Marcus motioned him to stop talking. "I heard something! Yes.. I think someone is coming up.. go in the bathroom, quick.. no, here, go in there!" He shoved Damian towards the wall cupboard, opening it as quickly and quietly as he could. Damian heard it too, a faint noise just outside Sabine's door, there was no doubt, someone was there. He quickly crouched down in between Sabine's suitcases, shoes and fitness gear, careful not to make a noise. Marcus closed the door behind him leaving him in the dark like a trapped mouse. There was no knock on the flat door, but Damian could hear the hiss of the door lock as it opened, and Marcus calling out.

"What the hell is this?" Marcus seriously couldn't believe what was happening. He knew that this is how things worked, he'd seen it on CV, on the news and in movies, but it had never happened to him, so was completely taken by surprise. The door had opened, had been unlocked, and he was confronted by a white, red and yellow coloured police drone, hovering just inches away from his head. With its camera pointing directly at his face, it was talking to him, for god's sake, in a clipped digital male voice:

"This is an unarmed police surveillance drone. You are in no danger. This drone is employed to search for a local man, Mr Damian Turner. Believed unarmed. Wanted for enquiries. As a fugitive witness and for presentation at the employment distribution centre. Please step aside for face recognition surveillance."

Marcus was furious. This thing was buzzing around Sabine's flat, first through her living room, then into her bedroom, even hovering just above the carpet to search under her bed, just inside the bathroom door, into the kitchen and out the front door again, thankfully ignoring the cupboard. The drone even locked the door with that hiss, meaning it could just override the door lock. The search had taken no more than seconds, and the drone had left without any further comment, no apology, no good-bye, nothing. Unbelievable. No interest in who Marcus was, where Sabine was, just like some automated flying hunting dog sniffing for Damian, with no consideration whatsoever of the effect on him, or anyone else who might have been present. Incensed, Marcus opened the door again, ran down the stairs, out the front and just caught the drone flying back into the open door of a police van parked half way down the tiny street. With a real life officer sitting in it. Marcus didn't think, he just followed his instinct and fury and ran towards the van, before catching himself. Better calm down before he got shot on the street in so-called self-defence. He would say something though. That policeman was positively smug, and lazy with it, the van door half open, looking at Marcus cynically under his ridiculously unnecessary helmet.

"Can I help you?"

"Yes you can, Officer. Next time when you send your THING into my niece's flat looking for some random bloke you could at least show some courtesy and appear in person, if only to apologise for any upset! This is outrageous. This is a small village where everyone knows everyone, not some New York movie scene. My niece can invite anyone she likes into her flat and certainly wouldn't do anything illegal!"

"And your name is?"

"Dr Marcus Carter." Marcus replied curtly, making an obvious point of his title. He had noticed that Officer Matt Collins, according to his badge, was just that, a mere officer, hardly more than a traffic warden Serf. Sometimes it helped playing the superiority card with little upstarts like this badge flasher who obviously enjoyed playing with his little drone toy.

"Just doing my job, we had a witness report." The officer shrugged his shoulders with this really irritating satisfaction in his voice, patting the drone like a pet.

'Moron.' Marcus muttered under his breath turning away after saying 'Goodbye!' still furious. He made his way back up the stairs to Sabine's flat, but not before he turned round to see the police car leave round the corner. Good, he was gone, for now anyhow. Damian!! That poor man must be petrified still in the cupboard, he'd have to get him, get him into his car and out of Sabine's flat, he wasn't safe here. They could explain everything to Sabine later. He ran the last few steps up to her flat, quickly locking the door behind him and helped a confused Damian out of the cupboard, who ducked at first when the door opened, unsure what had happened exactly. Just that the police were looking for him. Again Damian felt like crying, partly out of fear and relief, and partly out of gratitude that Sabine hadn't been confronted by the drone. Marcus quickly explained his plans to get him out of there. He could drive his hatchback close to the front door, and open the doors as if to deliver some boxes. Damian could then climb into the back, hopefully hidden well enough from anyone's view, except for maybe a split second. They just had to chance it. Marcus would then drive him to his place just outside of York in the first instance, and put him up in the self-contained annexe behind his house. It had been his Dad's during his last few years and had been unoccupied since Roy had passed away. His room was pretty much untouched, still filled with sheet music, Roy's books and his collection of random electronics. It would make a good enough, and most of all, discreet guest accommodation, placed as it was at the back of Marcus's house. Damian nodded in overwhelmed agreement with everything. There was no way he'd want to put Sabine through what had just happened.

Hoping Sabine would understand that he was just borrowing her things, he picked up the toothbrush and towel she'd given him, wanting to take something of her with him. He missed her so much, worse than he had ever missed anyone before. Marcus and he had a quick look around the flat, made sure that he had all his clothes, his jacket and his bag, all clean and fresh thanks to Sabine's hospitality. As far as they could see there was no sign that he'd ever been in the place at all, it was good enough. Marcus backed his car as close to the front door as he could, whistling some cheerful tune as he pretended to unload something to her flat, and Damian slipped in the back just as easily as planned, and lay down as low as he could, his and Marcus's jackets over him.

Marcus let the doors lock behind him and they were on their way. It would be just under an hour's drive to his home, and it should be conveniently dark by the time they got there.

Marcus was driving along Helmsley Road, not wanting to speak in case he was being listened to on his iLink. He had no idea whether he put that copper's nose out of joint or put him off well enough, but the surveillance drone whirring inches away from his face had been horrible, he couldn't help but keep checking whether he was being followed. He decided to turn the music player on, just to lighten up the journey a bit for both of them. Poor sod, he thought, he has been through quite a trauma, in such a short time, too. It had only been a day since he got his notice chip, then the bus crash, deciding to run for it, with only a bit of a break at Sabine's before the drone showed up and now cowering in the back of his car with all that police business in his head. It was crazy. The whole situation was crazy. Marcus hadn't expected to come back to anything like this at all. He had assumed he'd be having dinner with Sabine and maybe Damian and had hoped for a proper chance to talk about the news, see how she was, all that. He was tired out now, just wanted to get home, unpack, have a shower, some food, recover from the journey and the madness and have an early night. He thought longingly of the gorgeous Italian cuisine he'd left behind, Massimo's disappointment to hear he was leaving, the concert band even more disappointed that Sabine wouldn't come and join them, she was so well liked.

He was just wondering whether he should call her with an innocent message that he'd arrived, not saying anything about Damian when his eye fell on his wrist - his iLink wasn't there!

"I don't believe this! Damian, I forgot my iLink in Sabine's bathroom cabinet, I put it there so we couldn't be overheard earlier! And you don't have yours. How on earth are we going to let her know about anything before she starts panicking about you? She'll probably be home by now, do you think?"

Damian was relieved that Marcus finally spoke to him, and wished he could sit up from under the coats, but that was just too risky. "Can you hear me ok from back here?"

"Yes, fine." Marcus was furious with himself. That drone had really shaken him up, he'd forgotten all about the iLink in the heat of the moment. "I've always refused to install the phone app in the sat cam. I just wanted some places in life where I could have some privacy still, you know? Usually I'd have my iLink if I ever needed it. Honestly, now, of all times!" One of those times when paranoia didn't serve you, he thought crossly. He could install the phone app easily enough, but it probably wasn't a good idea while Damian was in the back, he wasn't quite sure how much the mike would pick up on.

"I can't quite tell from back here, is it getting dark out there yet? Sabine and I agreed that she'd be home just before it got dark, she was worried about the lights coming on without her being home, with me inside, alerting the neighbours. She thought of everything."

Marcus nodded, yes, that was his 'little niece'. She had a very ordered head on her shoulders, a systematic way of thinking that was perfect for science and in an emergency, too. She could think on her feet and get things done. But he also knew that part of her was emotionally fragile, she had always needed a lot of reassurance. The idea she'd come back to her flat with Damian gone, and with the obvious chemistry going on between those two, well, he could imagine she would be very hurt and mystified about it and take it badly. He knew she would try and call him to see where he was, expecting him soon, not good. "She might try and call me and hear my iLink hum from her bathroom cabinet? It would be confusing, but at least she'd know that something had gone on while she was at the hospital, which may or may not help."

"Can we get in touch with her from your house?" Damian had never met anyone who had not used his sat-cam as a phone before. Which was so cool, definitely a fellow system rebel.

"Yes, that's not a problem, I'll talk to her from home. Don't worry, I'll figure out what to say. I'm just sorry I'm making her wait so long, she must be pretty confused with you not being there, and me not having been in touch yet. She has been expecting me, we have each other's access codes to our homes. Family, you see?" Marcus smiled.

"Oh, stupid me! I forgot, you've flown in from Italy today, haven't you! And then had to deal with me and all that police business, I'm really sorry, you must be shattered!"

"Well, Damian, I must admit, I've had easier days, but harder ones, too, so don't worry, please, Sabine's friends are my friends. That drone experience was horrible, I wouldn't want you to go through that again. Oh, I never answered properly, did I, yes, it's nearly dark now, and we should be at my place in twenty minutes at the most".

Chapter 16
Let Down

I T WAS NEARLY dark when Sabine arrived back home. How exciting it was to get out the car, look up at the windows of her flat and think of Damian waiting for her. She opened her front door and listened. No sound from her flat above. That was good. Damian was keeping really quiet, in which case the bakers wouldn't suspect anyone up there in her absence, wouldn't be asking questions about visitors just out of friendly curiosity. And, she wouldn't have to lie. Lying stressed her out, and that conversation, if you could call it that, with Damian's friend had been hard going, not so much lying but trying to say something behind a veil of sorts. How ever did spies manage? It had gone great with Yvonne though, and as Sabine ran up the stairs she couldn't wait to tell Damian all about it. Admittedly, she couldn't wait for him to hold her in his arms again either. She swiped her iLink over her door lock which opened with its faint hiss, walked into her living room, and there was - nobody.

Damian wasn't there. Confused, she looked in the bathroom, in the kitchen, in the bedroom, even in the store cupboard, none of his clothes were to be seen, nothing. No Damian. He had gone. Chosen to leave without her. It was as if someone had pulled the rug from under her feet, she felt sick, disorientated, weepy, punched in the stomach, though she didn't really know what that was like. She'd never been in a fight before. It couldn't be worse than this though, she was sure. She sat down on the sofa that showed no trace of Damian's overnight stay, the blanket folded neatly on a stool in the corner, the cushion plum and neat on top. He'd left without asking her if she wanted to join him, without even saying goodbye. Had he not cared about her one bit, not cared that she went to reassure his Mum, not cared that she'd had to lie, nor cared that she'd just spent close to two hours in the car to Scarborough and back. She was so disappointed she couldn't even cry. Suddenly very tired she dragged herself to the bathroom and noticed the toothbrush she had given him was gone, as well as the towel. Bastard. Bastard. Bastard. Had he gone to another willing female only too happy to put him up? Would he kiss her, too? With that the tears did come, and hanging onto the edge of the washbasin, she watched her face in the mirror contorting into her ugly crying face, looking like a monster. No wonder he didn't want to hang around, she was just really ugly. She was 26 years old and nobody loved her. Liked her well enough, but not love, oh no, she wasn't good enough for that, was she. Frustrated and furious, she threw her hairbrush across the bathroom and heard it land in the corner with a satisfying crash.

Then she remembered, she'd cancelled her flight to Italy for him! And Uncle Marcus who would probably be here any minute now, she hadn't even had a chance to ask him what time he'd arrive! She cried out in frustration again, felt a complete idiot, taken for a ride. She couldn't ring her Mum, she couldn't tell anyone, could she, not without dropping Damian in, and that didn't feel right either, however much she detested him now. She thought of poor Yvonne, doing her best in that hospital, god, how selfish of him, having her worried, too. How had he managed to get out unseen when it was still daylight? He must have really wanted to get away from her, she thought bitterly. Probably worst of all, she couldn't even get the blood sample of him. She'd let him know one day that he had probably been those patients' last hope and had let them down, which was even worse than leaving her like this.

Deflated, Sabine realised she should eat something, she felt ridiculously weak and plain awful. What she really wanted was to eat and sleep, sleep made everything better. But Uncle Marcus would be here soon, so that was no good, and he'd probably be hungry, best prepare something for both of them just in case. If only she hadn't used all her best stuff she'd had in last night, for her and Damian. It was all just too much effort, she couldn't face going to the shops right now. Weak and miserable she took a few bites of a banana and chewed half a biscuit, then lay down on her bed to nap. Just for five minutes. Uncle Marcus would let himself in, he had the code, she'd hear him. Exhausted, she dropped off to sleep, almost immediately.

Chapter 17
The Eagle and The Hawk song

NINA AND BRENT arrived back home just as it was getting dark. Jester, true to his programmed word, had the welcoming smell of perfectly timed fresh coffee hitting them as soon as they opened the door. It was good to be home, kick their shoes off, and wash the hospital air off their hands and face. If only it was so easy to wash it out of their minds. Just over a day had passed since the accident, but it seemed like an eternity already, so much had happened that was inexplicable which made everything all the more upsetting. Accidents were bad enough at any time, but in such bizarre circumstances, it was exhausting trying to make sense of it.

They drank their coffee silently, while turning on a soothing waterfall on their CV. It would be good to have a day out some time when all this was over, Nina contemplated, maybe a long autumn hike to Falling Foss. The real thing rather than watching a virtual tropical one splashing into their living room anyhow. The Cybervisions were so much better than the old TVs, what with their seamless 3D and holographic projections, but the smells, of earthy and muddy reality underfoot, and of the coffee and homemade scones sold at the waterfall, well, they had to be experienced for real. And not a Serf in sight. Nina hoped Jester couldn't read her mind. Good old Jester. He was almost part of the family by now, much like a clever pet, though not cuddly at all, which was probably just as well. Reality, what was that now anyhow? What would feel real when she would talk to her Grandma? About an event so far fetched, only proven by retro-spective facts. She was nervous. There was nothing new to tell, good or bad, but her Grandma's voice last time had disturbed her. It wasn't how the strong, cheerful, no-nonsense woman she knew normally sounded like.

Nina sighed, appreciating Brent's kind look and his warm hand on her arm before he got up to put the plates away, leaving her to make her call.

Nellie answered at first buzz, as if she'd been waiting. The connection was so quick that both women were at a loss as to what to say for a second. Feeling so close, seeing each other in their mind's eye, and both having the same thought that they wanted to see each other, they turned on their virtual screens at the same time, beaming up from their iLinks.

"Hi, Grandma!" Nina called out, taking in Nellie's familiar face. How old she looked, Nina thought, small and fragile, somewhat resembling her mother's face in hospital. Nellie in turn took in a sharp breath looking at Nina looking so much like Mary, her dear Mary.

"Hello, dear." Nellie replied, enlarging her V-screen, so Nina could see Bob sitting close by, too. How brilliant, Nina thought, Bob being there, he must be keeping an eye on Grandma, which was immediately reassuring. "So, tell me everything, Nina, tell me what's new?"

"I wish I could tell you more, Grandma, but Mum is still in hospital, so are the others, but one of the passengers has gone missing since the accident. He's a friend of ours, we don't know where he is, just that he isn't with the others in the ICU."

"Tell us again about the bus, Nina, if you don't mind?" Bob interrupted, kindly, but with an obvious sense of urgency.

"Well, it's all very strange. Bill the driver, everyone knows him round here, he's a friend of Mum's, and has been driving for decades. He must have had to swerve for whatever reason and drove the bus off the road. There was no other vehicle involved. The bus landed in a ditch, which is no big deal, but for some reason the inside and the outside of the bus was covered in ice, ice everywhere, so strange, because it's been such a mild season so far! It wasn't even raining that day! And the passengers, Mum, Bill, another woman and her little boy, well, they are almost frozen, and unconscious still. Intense hypothermia, stable though." Nina added quickly, as she was trying to interpret the expression on Nellie's and Bob's faces.

"We went to see Mum and the others in hospital, the ward nurse there is the mother of our friend who's disappeared, she knows Mum and Bill, too, and I know she's going to take good care of them. According to the local news the dashboard monitor recorded Bill seeing something come up from behind and swerve to get out of the way of whatever it was, but the recording just didn't show much detail, a dot on the screen, basically, so nobody is any the wiser."

"Didn't you mention feathers yesterday?"

"Oh yes, those weird feathers. People thought that maybe a pheasant got caught up in it all, but Brent recognised them as hawk feathers, and he said that the feather that Dad had had on his deathbed had been a hawk feather, too. Nobody seems to mention anything else but hawks now. I hate hawks. I don't understand what this all means, what it's about! Nothing makes sense at all. She hesitated a bit, searching Nellie's face for clues, and breathed deeply before she dared to ask.

"Tell me, Grandma, I heard you mention an 'icehawk', that's what you said, didn't you? What did you mean?"

Nellie looked at Bob, Bob looked back at her, calmly, he was not going to interfere in what would be said next. The community had decided not to talk about the Icehawk's appearance, but Nellie's daughter was fighting for her life in hospital, most likely because of it, there was no way he was going to stop her from saying anything at all.

"Oh, Nina, dear. It's very difficult to know what to say, and I think it's best if I keep it simple. The 'Icehawk' has been a figure of legend here in Alaska, in every tribe, for the longest time, in countless stories and songs, old and new, you might even remember a newer one I used to sing to you when you were little, 'The Eagle and the Hawk', do you remember? We always fancied it was partly written for us, the Old People." Nellie started singing a few lines to remind her, shakily, as she had sung it to Nina when she was little, who was now close to tears as the memories came flooding back. All those old songs and stories would have to be looked to again, Bob pondered. Would they give them any clues they were looking for now, that might help them?

"But, Grandma, I don't understand, what has that song got to do with Mum? I'm confused... I thought the Icehawk thing was just a story?"

"I thought so, too, it's just, and I'm not supposed to say, oh well, I have to risk it. The Icehawk appeared here, three nights ago, everyone here saw it. We were out watching the aurora as it was forecast to be more spectacular than usual as far south as Chignik, so we all went to look. It was like watching a dance, very intricate colour formations, right above the bay, but then the light changed into this truly gigantic hawk, it sounds ridiculous, I know. How could it? It even turned into ice, hovering above us all, just looking at us, not hurting anyone. It could have been like a spaceship, but it was alive, it was just like a Redtail, you know them, what can I say.. It sounds so silly, I know, and we were frightened, but we didn't panic, strangely. We all saw it, all of Bristol Bay had come out, there'd been rumours... Bob and me, too, we stood together, it was nearly big enough to reach right across the Bay. We didn't imagine it, we couldn't have, and now we're struggling to believe it even happened. It felt like a god. Or an alien, or a spaceship in the form of a super-sized Redtail, I don't know. We don't want the press all over this, as they wouldn't believe us anyhow, and none of us even know what to think. So we're all keeping quiet about it. But your story with the bus, and of your Dad's passing, too, involving a hawk feather, well, it made me wonder if it's something to do with me, or our family, and if it is, I'm so dreadfully sorry. So so sorry, and I've probably said too much already, I'm so sorry..." Her anguish showed in her old face so clearly, and for the first time in her life Nina saw that her Grandma was about to cry, she had never ever seen her cry, ever. That was almost worse than that icehawk story, it just sounded too unreal, too impossible, but Nellie and Bob? They were not people prone to fantasies. Brent came closer to the screen. "Bob, can I ask you, what do you make of it? What are your thoughts?"

"Hi, Brent. All I'm thinking right now is that if this hawk is flying around killing people we love, then we need to find out what its weakness is to defend ourselves. Everything and everyone has a weakness. But it hasn't been back, and perhaps I'm barking up the wrong tree. As yet I can't make head nor tail of it."

Nina interjected, more worried about Nellie than anything else. "Please don't cry, Grandma, please. It's not your fault, how could it be? It's probably happened at other places, too, and we just don't know about it. I think Mum will be alright, I really do. Deep down I do, you know? I'd have felt something otherwise, and I just didn't, didn't feel anything bad happening to her at all. I was waiting for that bus and cheerfully walked home when it didn't arrive! It's all really bizarre, but I really do believe she'll be alright. I love you, Grandma. Please don't upset yourself, you've got enough going on over there!"

Brent nodded with what she was saying. "Yes, I think she'll be alright, too." He wasn't so sure at all, but poor Nellie needed reassurance now.

"I'm glad you're keeping an eye on Nellie, Bob." He said with a warm and respectful smile. It was quite something talking to this amazing old Alutiiq Native, like talking to an old Native American Chief from the movies, what a striking character he was. Nellie, too, wonderful people.

"Well!" Bob drew a big breath. "There is something else we wanted to tell you, much less scary, I hope, Nina."

His grin was wide, waiting for her response. Nina and Brent both looked at each other, feeling the sudden happy change in the atmosphere.

"What, what?" Nina laughed.

"Well, I thought I'd ask your Grandma to marry me, Nina, I think it's about time, as she's the only woman left worth having round here." He laughed and rubbed his arm in response to Nellie giving him the best loving slap she could muster. It was wonderful, just wonderful, Nina shrieked with delight and Brent leaned back in his chair, laughing, and leant forward again, stretching his arms up in the air as if hugging them.

"Well, that is just the best! That's fantastic news! That's so unexpected, but, well done that, man, well done!!"

And Nina, too, she was so obviously over the moon, nobody quite knew who was happiest about this. And what a sensation, the heart opening in her chest that had been tight and worried.

"Oh, wait until I tell Mum about it, I'll tell her as soon as I can, she'll get better really quickly, I bet, you know? Oh, I'm thrilled! When is the wedding, can we come? We've been meaning to visit you anyhow!"

"I'm so pleased you're happy for us! We thought we'd have the wedding on my birthday, on April 4th, round the spring festival, or on Bob's, the 16th? Bob said it should be on mine, but I think any time when all the flowers come out would be quite wonderful, don't you think?"

"A spring wedding is just perfect for us two spring chickens!" Bob interrupted, and they all laughed, forgetting about the distance altogether, or even that they were talking via their V-screens, it didn't matter, the four hearts soared in unison. Everything changed in that moment, some magic, the magic that happens when love is taking centre stage. Bob and Nellie noticed it especially, as it was the second time that week. Love did replace fear with courage and optimism, it was quite extraordinary. They had never quite noticed it as much as that, at least not as consciously, in all their eighty plus years.

Nina and Brent promised to call them just as soon as there would be anything to report about Mary or the others. After warm and cheery good-byes they both fell back on the sofa looking at each other, with an excited smile in their eyes.

"That'll be so good, just think, in Alaska for the spring, going to Grandma's and Bob's wedding! How exciting is that! And that hawk! The Icehawk! And that tune, 'The Eagle and the Hawk'! I always thought it was just a song! Wow. We'll have to research hawk symbolism and stuff. Doesn't it sound huge? What a week..."

And then she remembered her Mum with instant anxiety. Fighting the lowering of her own mood Nina willed herself to think of her Mum getting better, how it would be a great story in a couple of months. She did tend to worry overmuch, and imagine the worst, she really ought to stop that. After all, her gut still said she'd be alright. "Let's find Damian!"

Brent laughed. "I'll have a look if I can find that Sabine online and see where she lives, maybe we could just go visit?" The result appeared almost instantly. "Sabine Carter, Kirkbymoorside! Look, her address is right here! It's just four and a half miles away! Shall we go? Can you cope with it now?" Brent was already jumping up, all bright eyed and enthusiastic. Nina laughed. "All right, why not, it's not far. Don't you think we should call her first?"

"Nope. She'd be surprised, not sure who we are, and probably say something wrong, let's just go see her. And maybe Damian is there, too?"

They said good-bye to Jester, a bit of a silly habit, considering he was just a Serf, but it was just easier and to be pleasant and not wonder about it, and walked to their car with a spring in their step, holding hands.

"Going out?"

A voice rang through the air. Ah yes, it was Sharon, just driving up to her house, waving exuberantly, clearly in a good mood. But then she always was that bit friendlier towards Brent, a source of amusement to them both, It was just a matter of keeping her own smile up, Nina thought to herself.

"Yes, we are." Nina replied politely. "It's a beautiful evening, isn't it?"

"You think so?" Sharon smirked, those teeth still showing, all gleaming white like a Serf on a wrong setting. "I'm surprised you're so cheerful with your Mum in hospital, poor thing. Still we have to do what we can to cope, haven't we!"

And with that she pulled into her drive. Brent and Nina stepped in through their sliding car doors, both breathing a sigh of relief once in the privacy of their seats.

"Honestly, that woman!" Brent almost spat the words out. "She really is the most toxic bitch I've ever known. What makes people turn out like that?"

"Who knows." Nina shook herself as if to shake off Sharon's vibes. "But aren't you glad she likes you especially?"

And they both laughed again, Brent shuddered, and then exclaimed, bashing the steering wheel. "I've got it!! I've just remembered where I know Sabine from, you know her, too!"

"I do?"

"You do! Her surname is Carter, does that ring any bells?"

"Carter.... you mean, as in.. MARCUS Carter? Oh my word, she's not... you think she is, oh wow, she's his niece, isn't she? You're right, I do know her! She was only little, maybe thirteen or so when I saw her last, she was with Marcus when he visited my Dad, they worked together sometimes! How do you know her then?"

"She's a teacher now, I think. Chemistry maybe? Not sure. She works at the college anyhow. I remember seeing her picture in the local news ages ago, something about her job, and her name rang a bell because of your Dad and Marcus, though I'd never properly met her until earlier at the hospital! I thought she looked familiar, but just couldn't place her! I'm sure she won't mind us visiting, with us being Damian's friends, and your connection to her uncle. He's over in York somewhere, isn't he?"

"I think so, yes." Nina shrugged her shoulders. She'd never seen him again after her Dad had died, her Mum had been a bit disappointed that most of Greg's colleagues didn't care enough to visit even once afterwards. "I'm not really bothered about him, but it'll be really good to talk with Sabine, hope she's there. And that Damian is there, too."

Brent nodded in agreement. He only remembered Marcus as a sort of geeky person, a bit arrogant, too. Possibly a decent enough guy, just not so great with his people skills. Greg had liked him a lot, though, so that had to mean something.

Chapter 18
Trust

SABINE WOKE UP on her bed, fully clothed, groggy, and instantly reminded of her horrible afternoon by her stinging eyes and swollen eyelids. She looked round at her iLink on her bedside table, next to the half eaten biscuit she'd left there. Seeing the time she realised she'd only slept half an hour or so, but she'd slept deeply, and definitely felt better for it. She'd dreamt of Damian and Uncle Marcus, all jumbled together somehow, and sighed heavily. Not having heard from either of them, she swung her legs over the edge of the bed, and sat, trying to think what to do next. 'I could be packing for Italy now' she mumbled crossy, looking at her clarinet, annoyed that she'd forgotten to practice. She'd have to call Massimo's brother, Claudio, the band leader, and apologise in person for not showing up as promised. Getting up somewhat wearily, she heard the downstairs front door bell. Immediately she jumped up. Was it Damian? She called into the speaker.

"Yes?"

"Hi, is that Sabine? It's Brent and Nina, could we come up?" The answer came back. Brent and Nina, Brent and Nina, Damian's friends, she clawed from her groggy mind.

"Oh, ok." She replied, before she had really thought it through and swiped her hand over the door release. Seeing her pale face and red eyes in the mirror, she groaned, what a state she looked. She had just enough time to run her fingers through her hair and straighten her clothes up a bit, when they came up the stairs. Her curiosity about their visit was stirred enough for her to decide to let them in, who cared what they thought of her.

Brent and Nina looked at her, taking in the fact that she must have been crying and immediately felt sorry for her. She looked like a really sweet woman, disheveled and vulnerable, and clearly upset. They closed the door behind them, swiped their iLinks to the dive setting and walked up to her, Nina instinctively stretching out her arms. "What's happened, is it Damian, Sabine?"

Sabine looked from one to the other, kind eyes, good people, and she dropped her shoulders a little, relaxed, checked to see that she didn't have her iLink on, and remembered it was still in her bedroom. She walked the few steps past Nina to close the bedroom door, squeezing her arm in appreciation for her gesture, and tried to think of what to say. These were Damian's friends, he had only ever said good things about them, and if they were here now they probably cared about him, and maybe even about her, too.

"Did he ever mention me to you?" She turned around to face them both square on and they both looked back at her, slightly surprised at her question, and replied, both at the same time.

"Yes! Lots!"

"He's got a huge crush on you, we thought!"

"To say the least!"

"We kind of expected him to turn up with you sooner or later, he mentioned you a lot!"

Sabine stared at them, not quite knowing what to think. "Well, he doesn't seem to care about me now." Looking down and feeling Nina's sympathy made her just want to burst into tears again. "I don't know where he is now, he was here, I did all this stuff for him, went to the hospital and everything, and now he's gone. Couldn't even leave a note, he let me arrive back at an empty flat, after promising he'd wait here for me." She swallowed hard, not wanting to cry. "Anyhow, I was expecting my Uncle Marcus, arriving from Italy, and he isn't here either. Seems I'm super popular, doesn't it."

"Awh, Sabine! I'm sure there is an explanation!" Nina exclaimed. "That doesn't sound like Damian, he doesn't let people down!"

"Could your uncle and Damian have gone somewhere together? Have you spoken with him? Marcus, I mean?" Brent ventured.

Sabine let that thought sink in, she hadn't considered that at all, Marcus could have let himself in, yes, while she was out, but surely he would have messaged her?

"No, I haven't, I just thought he'd just turn up, and then I fell asleep. Sorry, I know I look in a state." She added, somewhat embarrassed.

"Why don't you ring him now, Sabine, and just ask him where he is, and then you'll know. And afterwards maybe you could tell us about Damian? We don't know anything about what happened in the accident, with Nina's Mum in hospital..." Brent tried to sound reassuring. Something strange was going on, and Sabine looked exhausted. Sabine looked at Nina, who hadn't said a word, was just watching her, and with Brent mentioning her Mum Sabine realised how worried Nina was. She felt a kind of womanly solidarity with her.

"I'll call Uncle Marcus now." She walked into her bedroom, sat on the edge of her bed looking through the door at her visitors, and picked up her iLink. There was no harm in finding out where he was. Sabine swiped over the screen and tapped on his name to call him. There was a faint buzzing, and for a moment none of them understood. It wasn't possible, usually, to hear anyone else's iLink unless you were right there with them. But it was definitely buzzing, and then it stopped.

"No reply, right? Can you try again?" Nina asked, eyes wide.

There it was, and Nina, quite sure of the direction it came from, ran towards the bathroom, yes, it was getting louder. Sabine saw and jumped up to join her, Brent followed. Nina, feeling very much the visitor, let Sabine pass so that she'd be the one to go in first. There! The buzzing was coming from the bathroom cabinet! Sabine almost tore the door open and her Uncle Marcus's iLink was right there on the little shelf! She stared at it in disbelief, her mind racing to come up with an explanation. How long had it been there? Had he come in while she was asleep? Had it been there all along?

"It's Uncle Marcus's! I recognize it, it's that fancy extension strip he put in, didn't like it too tight, there, see?" She showed them both the iLink.

"Let's sit down and talk." Brent suggested, both women nodding in agreement. They seemed like old friends already, Sabine thought, and uplifted by the notion, she offered to make tea, which they both gratefully accepted.

"What time did you get back from the hospital? By the way, I got it when you tried to tell me that Damian was safe, thank you for that. I didn't recognise you, Sabine, I thought you were behaving a bit oddly, but I understand it now."

Nina agreed. "That was really good of you, thank you. You were there for his Mum, too, weren't you. Poor woman, she's great, you know, really good. So, what's happened to Damian?"

As the three new friends settled down with their steaming mugs of tea, Sabine's iLink buzzed on her bedside table. Sabine ran across to the other room. "It's Uncle Marcus! From his place!" She swiped across to reply as quickly as she could, and heard his voice immediately.

"Hello, cara mia!" It was his affectionate nickname for her he used when he was pleased about something. "I got back from Barbania earlier and called at your place but you weren't there. Some other stuff happened as well, but I'd rather tell you when I see you, I'm bushed. Fancy coming round, tonight or tomorrow?"

Sabine looked at Nina and Brent, questioningly, wondering if he meant he'd seen Damian, and Nina, more by instinct than anything else, whispered to her. "Let me talk to him."

Sabine held her wrist out so Nina could talk easily, and, taking a deep breath Nina spoke cheerfully. "Hello Marcus! It's Nina, Greg's daughter, remember me?"

"Oh hello, Nina!" There was some surprise in Marcus's voice, but he sounded warmer than she remembered him. "I didn't know Sabine and you knew each other?"

"Ah, we've only just met again after a long time, we're getting on like a house on fire, she was worried about you, and has had a bit of a confusing day. Brent is here, too, my husband, remember him?"

Marcus paused, and then continued in an equally chatty tone. "Hey, that's great! I've got a friend visiting here, he's about the same age as you young ones, do you three want to come round and get to know each other? Dying to see you, Sabine! I could kick back at last with a glass of wine, get my Serf to make us an Italian dinner, fancy it?" And then, after a little pause, "I don't want my little niece to think she's being left waiting over there, she's much missed!"

Sabine's eyes went larger and beamed at Nina and Brent, nodding vehemently, forgetting to speak, and Nina laughed into her iLink.

"I think that's a 'Yes', Marcus. We'll see you in an hour or so?"

"Perfect."

"Sorry it's a bit short notice, and late in the day, too, but I really can't face coming out again after the journey from Italy. It'll be fantastic to have you all here, in true Italian tradition. My buddy here is in total agreement, he's nodding in the background. See you later then, ciao!" He hung up before anyone could say anything else that might implicate them.

Brent, Nina and Sabine let out a long breath, it felt as if they'd been holding theirs throughout the conversation. Brent pointed at her iLink and asked, 'May I' and without any resistance Sabine handed it over, not even questioning what it might be for. Brent put his hands on his lips, to stop her from saying anything, showed her silently how to change the setting to 'Deep Sea Dive' and she watched in amazement how the start screen dulled over, with the microphone symbol turning to mute.

"Wow! does that mean what I think it means?"

"Yeah. Ours is done, I just did Marcus's, too. We can talk freely now, I'm pretty sure. I can't wait to show your uncle, it'll come in handy." Brent looked at Sabine, who still had eyes like a startled deer, and waited for her obvious question to burst out. It did, as expected.

"So, do you think the friend Uncle Marcus was talking about is Damian?"

Her heart was beating so loudly she thought everyone else could hear.

"Oh yes." Nina replied, with tenderness and with the power of her own conviction. "I'm pretty sure it's him. I can't swear to it, but I think he wanted us to come so soon for more than dinner, don't you? Not taking away from the fact that he obviously wants to see you, Sabine, but visitors, after a trip back from Italy? It's got to be important!"

Brent nodded, he thought so, too. He wondered what it all meant, why Marcus would be getting involved in it all? Was it just because of his niece, because of Damian, or did he know something they didn't? How mysterious it all was. He had to admit, he was tired, the idea of driving to York instead of curling up with Nina in front of a movie wasn't exactly the most appealing thought right now, but he knew he couldn't let Sabine go over there on her own, she looked as weak as a kitten, and Nina, clearly loving every minute of it, was as curious as he was, only a lot more energetic about it.

"Do you want to freshen up before we go, Sabine? All that stress has knocked you for six, hasn't it, but nothing that a quick splash of water, maybe a change of clothes and a bit of mascara couldn't fix."

Sabine immediately understood Nina's intention, she was right, there was no way she'd want Uncle Marcus and Damian, if he was there, to see that she'd been so upset. She still didn't get what had happened, but the hope that perhaps she hadn't been badly let down after all gave her a much needed boost. She did as suggested and reappeared in front of them looking like a new woman, with subtle make-up, fresh jeans and a beautifully fitted turquoise sweater, and a matching scarf that brought out the blue in her eyes and made her brushed hair look silky and wonderful.

"Thanks for making me look like an old hag now!" Nina laughed. "Let's go!"

Damian had hung onto every word Marcus had said to Sabine and Nina, trying to think if what had been said could possibly have been enough to let Sabine know he was right there with Marcus. Everyone had been so cautious trying to say a lot without saying anything at all, and to hear that Nina and Brent were with her was just the best news ever, he didn't understand how or why, but he remembered the conversations he'd had with them about Sabine several times over the last couple of years. If she did ask them whether he'd ever mentioned her they would say yes for sure, and probably that he liked her, too. He had seen the looks between them both every time he'd mention Sabine, and he'd pretended not to notice or had been too embarrassed to react. He hoped she'd understood why he wasn't there when she got back, and so hoped she didn't think he'd tried to run out on her. That would be horrible.

"Thanks for inviting them tonight, Marcus. And thanks for bringing me here and being so generous to put me up, too, I'm really grateful."

"Well, I couldn't cope with your belly aching all night and all tomorrow morning until you've had a chance to talk with my niece." Marcus laughed. "Let's get Robin to make us some spaghetti Bolognese.

"You call your Serf Robin?" Damian laughed. "I like that, Robin Hood in your kitchen, great idea. I don't mind cooking instead, you know, or is there anything I can do to make myself useful?"

"To be honest, Damian, I'm really more interested to hear more about why you think you weren't affected by the ice in the bus like the others. Any ideas?"

"I've been wondering about it, too. I was knocked out for a bit myself and don't know if the others were unconscious because of the crash or the icy cold. It was a cold like I've never felt before, even colder than what I'd imagine to feel in the arctic, not like our Yorkshire winters. But I don't really suffer from the cold like others do. Been like that since I was little, after I had a run-in with a metal spike in a field. It went right in my leg nipping my femoral artery, I needed a blood transfusion and stitches and masses of chocolate, and heaps of attention, too." Damian smiled. "Anyhow, since then cold just doesn't get to me like how I remember it did before then. Brent used to call me 'Iron man' for ages, he said some of the iron from that spike got into my blood, and all that. I pretended to be a kind of superhero for a while, and ran about in t-shirts in the winter, just to show off. Damp gets to me though, hiding in the drain was horrible, being wet through, I was really struggling then. So maybe I've lost my superpowers?" He smiled wryly.

"Hm, interesting." Marcus thought out loud, and then, making a decision, asked. "Listen, I know this might be unexpected, but do you think I could take a blood sample from you, just a finger prick should be enough to run some tests? What we find out might help the others, you know."

"Oh, you mean, the ones in hospital? Wow, my Mum would love that, she's really into research and stuff. She could take a whole lot of blood from me, if I knew where the heck I'm supposed to be going from here. If I show up in public now I'll have to answer all sorts of questions, probably implicating you and Sabine. Afterwards I'd still be allocated to some nightmare job I really don't want."

He fell silent, miserable. He wanted nothing more than everyone to be okay, have his job back, and be able to take Sabine out on a proper date, buy her flowers, and all that.

Damian looked around Marcus's living room, now this was a proper house. It even had an annex where someone else could stay. There were some more photos of Marcus with his sister Maxine and Sabine as a little girl on the bookshelves, and of her grandparents, her granddad Roy more often than not with a clarinet or a trombone in his hand. Music was obviously in the family. Marcus had pointed to some of those photos earlier, telling him that every time when Sabine came to visit him, she and his father would jam together, making their impromptu jazz session look and sound so easy, and how he had felt totally inadequate. Damian was surprised at that, he could see Marcus was all right, politically, too, but somehow he hadn't expected that a doctor of science might have insecurities like everyone else. Endearing, yes, but at the same time not exactly reassuring. He'd have no chance to ever impress Sabine in the long run, would he. Not with an uncle and a granddad like that. Yet she did like him now, so maybe he should just wait and see. He looked at himself in the wall mirror behind the armchair in which Marcus was sitting.

"Don't worry, you look fine." Marcus laughed, and laughed even more when Damian blushed. He liked Damian, and felt only too well how nervous he was. When was the last time he had felt like that about a woman? What happened to that head swimming, heart pounding, clammy palms rubbing, nervous kind of love? He was nearly sixty and hadn't found it yet, not for a long time, and for a moment he felt old, really old. "I'm sure we'll work something out, what to do with you." Marcus added, quietly, as if reading his mind. "And whatever happens, we'll get some blood out of you." He laughed, making a mental note to write to Paul Coll from the Century Scientist about any findings.

Chapter 19
Paul Coll

PAUL COLL SAT in his office in New York, enjoying his lunch break, treating himself to a super sized coffee he sorely needed.

'Burning the midnight oil is for the young ones', he sighed into the steaming cup, inhaling the promise of a caffeine hit. He'd had yet another sleepless night when his research brain wouldn't stop bugging him about those icy currents.

Stretched out flat in front of him, built into the top of his office desk, was his trusty interactive virtual cork board where his digital notes could be turned on and off and connected at will like a multi-level station map. It was so useful, his secret journalistic weapon. More often than not the algorithms in the software were capable of offering up the strangest parallels and connections between his notes, incidences around the world which didn't seem related at all at first glance.

What Paul really felt like doing was to talk things over with his late friend Greg, like he used to since their heady student days. They had both been smitten with the stunning Alaskan Mary, who had chosen Greg over him. Yes, it had taken a long time to stop smarting. Greg, however, had remained a friend and mentor, even across the Atlantic, Mary no more than friendly and polite, but she would always ask after him, how he was doing, noting that he was single again, before passing the conversation on to Greg far too quickly. Paul loved knowing both of them, they were like a distant family, taken for granted until it was too late. Greg used to come up with little statements which he found later were the making of his career, especially Greg's mantra. 'Everything is connected. Once you find the connections, science is easy.'

He wished Greg was here now, he would be able to make sense of his notes, flashing like lost searchlights on his desk, unwilling to come up with any kind of logic whatsoever. There was the article in the London paper that the irritating guy from the next office had passed on to him, with more than a hint of cynicism.

"Oh look, there's a bit of wind and ice in Yorkshire, England. Must be special! Why not call your project 'A bored mind looking for another headline in banalities?'"

Weren't supportive colleagues just the best. 'Freak Ice Storm in a small Yorkshire Village' it said on page 5 of the London based 'UK Standard'. Hurrah for them covering any other place than the city. It also mentioned those darned feathers again.

With a sweep of his hand, he added note 17 to his desk. Seventeen isolated, concentrated ice storms. They had hit mainly cars or lone pedestrians, much like the one that must have hit Greg on his daily walk back home. This time, a bus, a pretty much empty bus, but still.

India, Mexico, various places in Europe, the USA, Africa, Alaska, though Alaska could be doubtful as a point of interest. Ice wasn't a novelty there, neither were hawks, but there was a brief mention of an uninjured but very dead body in the ice with a single hawk feather on it. What was that all about? He tried to connect longitudes and latitudes, jet stream variations, global air circulation patterns, records of local weather warnings, anything he could think of, and found no common denominator at all. Nothing common about the people involved either, the youngest fatality a 12 year old girl, the oldest a Swedish woman, aged seventy-four, traveling through Canada at the time. Slightly more men than women, so far anyhow. All of different cultures, different conditioning, in the old days it would have been called different religions, now it was just 'conditioning'.

Paul couldn't find any similarities between any political involvements, nothing with regards to any common interest, education, nor state of health. No matches between any affiliations, nor personal or professional histories he could see, just seemingly random people. He wondered why the ice storm had struck a second time in North Yorkshire, assuming it was the same phenomenon. Poor Mary. Paul remembered her sending him a message about Greg's pneumonia, and then rang that he had died. It had all happened within hours. How upset she had been, and confused about the feather on him, she couldn't understand it, who would want to put it on Greg and why? Paul hadn't had the heart to tell her that he'd come across some stories like that, of the strange, sudden deaths, and the hawk feathers left at the scene. Greg's death had come as a huge shock. Paul's grief was to become the catalyst that had made him obsessed with researching any circumstances around similar events, working feverishly, late into countless nights. He was ashamed to think that he had never called Mary after the funeral where she had kept her distance. He was holding himself back too. He didn't know how to talk to her now, or how she felt about him, if anything, and had basically chickened out. He did know, however, how upsetting it would be for her to be reminded of the horrid scenario again so soon.

He stared at the current of the jet stream for the umpteenth time, correlating images and records. Just nothing. 'Nothing yet.' He could hear Greg's voice in his head. 'Find the connections.'

Paul decided to pluck up courage to give Mary a call later, to see if she knew any more about the bus incident over there. He'd ask gently, tell her that it made him think of her and Greg, and that he was sorry he hadn't called earlier. He looked out of his office window and wondered what it would be like to die. Did people really experience something beautiful? Greg had had a brilliant mind and a gentle soul. If there was an afterlife of sorts, his friend would surely be blessed with a heavenly one.

· · · • ● ● ● • · ·

NELLIE AND BOB were walking across to the only little store in Chignik. From the outside the decision to live life as usual was working, but the atmosphere had changed to a new sense of wonder, excitement mixed with fear. Time itself seemed to have taken on a different quality. Was it faster or slower? Both felt true, making life, the feeling of being present, more fluid somehow. Everyone would still have the usual concerns, food on the table, working heaters, fuel for the snowmobiles, food for the dogs, staying healthy, working, playing, computers, the tourist adverts, life had to go on. The Alaskans were proud of their stoic survival skills and rightly so, nothing was wasted, everything was looked after, and the reliance on Serfs or any AI for that matter frowned upon. It was a good life, a hard but hearty one, everyone was known and each had their place in the community, it still worked. They wanted to keep it that way.

Outside the store the kids were running about playing VeeCee, a wonderful toy, shaped like the old frisbees, but with a soft touch mirror surface that reflected the surroundings as it flew, rendering it almost invisible and very hard to catch. It was such good fun. You could only just see the outline, more or less of it depending on the angle of the disc, whizzing past. You learned to adjust your eyes, noticing it cut through the background view, much like a ripple in a pond.

"You've got to be pretty quick for these things!" Bob laughed, standing and watching with Nellie, pleased that their old eyes could still see it, too, though they doubted they'd be quick enough to catch it now.

Nellie was thoughtful watching it. "You know what it looks like, when it's whizzing past like that? It looks like a zip in the landscape, and that if it stayed in one place long enough, you could open it and step right through it. Remember what Greg used to say? That really, what we see is an illusion, but that it never feels like one, ever, because we're so used to it?"

"I see where you're coming from there, Nel. Though I never had the chance to really ask him what he was working on at the time. Did you know what he was really doing, and why he used to come up here, apart from bringing Mary and Nina to see you?"

"It was all a bit highbrow for me, Bob. But as I understood it, he researched how molecules interact, and how their behaviour affected living cells, and where the energy came from to turn molecules into a living cell in different temperatures. Mary said it was all about the relationship between biochemistry, epigenetics and molecular biology." Nellie smiled as she remembered Greg's enthusiasm. "He always said odd things, like 'Science is easy if you find the connections', without ever really saying what kind of connections he was looking for. But I guess that's scientists for you, they talk amongst themselves, and then it takes others who explain it all to normal people like us. I suppose the question, what makes or turns molecules into a living cell is THE question of all. I can't blame him for asking it, we all do."

"Food, I tell you!" Bob laughed. "I tell you, it's food! I'm starving. Let's go and see what the last delivery brought, maybe we'll get something new and exotic to cook for ourselves?"

The store, run by Ken's family who did surprise everyone every now and then with new and exciting stock smelled different to the usual sourdough and coffee mix. It smelled spicy and Eastern, and they laughed when they saw Ken bent over a yellow dust cloud of something or other in a large tub on the floor.

"Don't ask." Ken groaned straightening his back with a grimace. "This is turmeric, Bianca's bright idea of stuff that cost me a fortune. She said it'll help everyone's achy joints, and I'm left with the pleasure of filling these fiddly little bags with it, look at the state of me! You want some, don't you, admit it, this is what you've been looking for all your life, turmeric. From India, and the best, apparently."

"What do I do with it? Bathe in it? I'm hurting all over!" Bob laughed.

Nellie chuckled, thinking of him looking yellow all over. It was still new for her, seeing him naked, after so many years of just being close friends and neighbours. It had struck her that the beauty of an aged body of someone you loved was never written about, nowhere at all. The stories old bodies tell, like wrinkled faces so much more interesting than smooth ones, not prettier, but deeply beautiful all the same.

"I've got some magazines, too." Ken continued. "That science one you like every now and then, Nellie, and the bird and wildlife one you wanted, Bob. I didn't know you're into birdwatching? I guess the one we all saw, they don't come bigger than that, do they. I haven't recovered yet to be honest, wake up in a cold sweat, Bianca, too. Are you two all right, or ...?" He looked at them questioningly, not sure if he overstepped the mark somehow.

"We're ok, Ken, thanks." Bob looked serious. "I don't know if you remember what I said at the meeting, that even that gigantic bird, or whatever it was, must have a weakness. I'm still thinking about it, too, that's why I wanted the bird magazine. I've checked out redtails online, but wanted to see if maybe there were some new clues in there, just in case I stumble on something. I know it wasn't a hawk as we know it, but whatever it was, it chose to look like one, and if there is a likeness, perhaps there is a related weakness? Just poking about in the dark, really."

Bob shrugged his shoulders, feeling that frustration again. He was a man who liked to see what's in front of him so he could deal with it as necessary rather than some mystery he couldn't get to grips with. He didn't like the idea of anyone being afraid. Being the oldest amongst his people, still healthy, still strong, he had started to feel like an Elder, and liked it. It was up to him to make sure his community and his Nellie would be safe. He could feel his shoulders straighten again just thinking about it, a formidable figure still. Ken saw it, too, the old man's determination. It was good to have him and Nellie in the village. Somehow everything that was good about people was personified in them, they kept everyone together and without even trying to be, they were the glue of the community. He even heard one of the kids outside the store say to the others that he'd want to be like Bob when he was older, and the other kids had teased him. "What, wait till you're eighty before you get married?"

All of them had all laughed, but it was in a good hearted way. Nellie and Bob had the affection of everyone, and if Bob was thinking about the Icehawk's weakness that nobody else even dared to consider, well, it meant the community still had a leader. Ken smiled at the thought and got back to his task. He would have to ask Bianca to put some notes together about how to use turmeric properly.

Chapter 20
The Reunion

SABINE WAS TRYING to relax in the back of Brent's car before meeting up with Uncle Marcus, and, if they had guessed correctly, Damian, too. She had the strangest sensations in her stomach, all knotted up with butterflies, and her heart ached. She didn't want to miss Damian the way she did, and she wasn't even sure anymore whether she could trust him or not. She had no idea now how he felt about her, or what he was doing at Uncle Marcus's place, if it really was him there. She couldn't imagine Uncle Marcus inviting anyone as soon as he arrived from a trip away, he tended to keep himself to himself, so that was strange. He was nowhere near as warm towards anyone else as he was to her, she always felt privileged to know the real him better than most. Sabine loved how Marcus and her got on so well, they just had this easy rapport and he'd always been there for her, ever since she was little. He was her favourite relation of all, and very protective of her. If Damian was going to be horrible he'd know about it soon enough, Marcus would put him right. But then, and her heart did a little delighted jump at the thought, if Marcus didn't like him there was no way that he would have let Damian into his house at all. She couldn't wait to find out what had happened.

Brent and Nina in the front were lost in thought, too. The

conversation they'd had with Nellie and Bob, about a huge icy hawk that had appeared for all to see over Chignik, was almost too much. It hadn't hurt anyone, Nina conceded in her own mind, but again she was filled with hate, rage even, that this thing, this monster, had probably killed her Dad, and was apparently intent on taking her Mum from her, too. Why? What had they done that was so terrible? Or was it something she had done? Neither she nor Brent had dared to mention the Alaskan Icehawk sighting to Sabine. Nellie had made it quite obvious that Bristol Bay had decided to keep quiet about it and they had realized that she'd made an exception because of Mary. For now it didn't feel right to discuss it with anyone. Brent was thinking about Damian surviving this thing, whatever it was, and what it would mean for him, for Mary, Bob, and the other passengers, and in the end for Sabine, too, who looked anxious.

The three of them had talked about how good a blood sample from Damian would be, for Yvonne to have it analysed and hopefully something would show up that would help the others. The fact that he had chosen to disappear wasn't good, he must have been desperate to tear off his iLink ripping his flesh, as Sabine had described. The police wouldn't look kindly on that, he'd be considered a criminal, or at least suspicious. Brent shook his head. If he could afford to employ anyone in his carpentry workshop he'd offer Damian a job, so he could get around the notice chip procedures. That really was Damian's only chance to get away with it, to be employed by someone, so he could say he'd known he wouldn't have to hand the chip in. But who? Sabine worked at the school, Nina could barely manage to keep her own design business ticking over, and Brent himself, well, it wouldn't work, he just couldn't afford to employ anyone. If he could he'd want to offer it to Connor first anyhow. He had jumped in, without hesitation, to hold the fort at the workshop and Connor was reliable, very, very good with his hands, with no desire to disappear into thin air at all. 'Damn, Damian, you're not making life easy, are you,' he muttered to himself.

Nina looked at her husband, squeezing his thigh lightly to get his attention. "I hope Damian will be there." She said it under her breath so that only he could hear, with a quick look at the screen to check Sabine who still looked exhausted.

"So do I." Brent agreed, just mouthing the words. It had been a long day, the early November sunsets making it look much later. He almost regretted his earlier suggestion to drive to Sabine's. He could have just stayed put on the sofa relaxing with Nina, instead of all this going on. Still, they'd be there in half an hour, and then, at least, they would hopefully find some answers that would put them and Sabine out of their misery.

Wondering how he could lift the mood, Brent looked across to Nina, perhaps one of her favourite stories would be perfect right now?

"Why don't you tell Sabine a bit about what it was like in Alaska when you were little?"

Nina smiled, she knew what Brent was trying to do, it was too funny that he was practically sacrificing himself to hear it all for the hundredth time. So, only too willing, she turned to see whether Sabine fancied to hear more, who nodded with only the merest hint of curiosity. It didn't take any more encouragement than that.

"Those holidays were amazing." Nina began. "In all seasons! Well worth the long journey. I remember the ice cold wind stepping off the little sea plane, hanging on to my mother's thick winter gloves and trying to keep up with her determined long legged stride that all us women in the family have in common. And then the warm welcome, being enveloped, just like the mountains hugging Chignik Bay, by the biggest grandmotherly hug that made me feel instantly loved.

'Kiarwarluten, kiarwarluten!' My Grandma used to beam, still using some words of the old mysterious Inuit language. 'Come inside, come inside'. I tried to learn it." Nina laughed. "I repeated all her words to myself before I'd fall asleep in the little attic bedroom upstairs. I'd crawl under the heavy blankets, I can still smell the wool now! And the bed, it felt like my own little island! Huge to me then, surrounded by a proverbial museum of those old fashioned snowshoes, animal skins and fishing gear, bottles of vodka and canned goods for emergencies. All still there, can you imagine! Oh god, and there was that ancient carved wooden mask that kept staring at me, that was so scary! It had this prominent wedge-shaped nose, high forehead, heavy hanging eyebrows, and these v-shaped slits for the mouth. It took me three visits to build up courage to touch it and hide it away out of sight, it was way too creepy..."

As much as Sabine wanted to hear it all, it was tough to keep her eyes open now. Nina's recount was like a soothing bedtime story and very effective. She could relax now, they'd soon arrive in York. She could barely hear Nina's voice any more and was soon fast asleep, much to Brent's quiet amusement. He didn't stop Nina in her reverie, he could see the reminiscing was doing her good.

Marcus calmly crossed one leg over the other, folded his hands over his grumbling stomach, and took in the smell of the spaghetti bolognese Robin was preparing in the kitchen. 'Serfs do have their uses', he thought, lazily. He had asked Robin to make Damian's bed up earlier, lay out some toiletries and shaving gear in the bathroom, and to make sure that annexe was heated relative to Damian's own heat output. Again it was obvious that Damian's body heat was higher than his own. Robin had even suggested to turn the heating down in the living room, for Damian to be more comfortable.

Marcus sighed and settled on the mean difference between them. He felt sorry for Sabine, just thinking how she always felt the cold, and loved the heat of Italian summers. She'd have to overcome a few challenges if she decided to get together with Damian. Watching Damian talk about Sabine and everything else, Marcus got the distinct impression that Damian was very serious about Sabine, and that he was a thoroughly decent young man underneath the somewhat macho talk that slipped out every now and then, it sounded more like a habit than conviction. It was probably just factory floor talk, Marcus concluded, you had to be one of the guys to stand up to a bunch of human and robot workers, it was too easy to be seen as weak otherwise. The way he talked about his mother, too, was a measure of the man, full of affection, respect and appreciation, but not in a weak or dependent way as might have been the case considering he still lived with her. Damian had been very eager to explain that he was quite responsible for his own chores and upkeep, and that he'd never been spoilt. It had just been the two of them, there had been no father around. Marcus suspected that that was part of the reason for Damian's rougher edge. With an absent father, he may have well been given a hard time at school. Marcus quite surprised himself how much he had taken to Damian who seemed comfortable enough with him, too. Perhaps there was some pseudo father son thing going on that both of them enjoyed.

The doorbell rang. They were here. Damian was just about to run to the door, when Marcus warned him calmly but firmly to stay put. He'd make sure it was really them first, the memory of the drone crashing down on them both sobering the mood in an instant.

"Check who that is for me, Robin!" Marcus called out, and Robin, as ever on stand-by for any command whatsoever, dutifully turned the heat down on the panel stove and made his way to the door screen, that had already read the iLinks of the visitors.

"Sabine Carter, your niece, accompanied by Nina and Brent Daniels, from Hutton-le-Hole." He informed them in his best butler voice. "Would you like me to let them in, Marcus?"

"Yes, please do, Robin." Marcus replied, rushing to the door himself, but motioning to Damian he should stay put, he just wasn't sure enough about anything yet. As Sabine stepped through the door he saw her state of mind immediately, she looked very pretty, he thought, but goodness, the angst in her eyes, she needed reassuring, and quickly. His eyes took in Brent and Nina, not seen in years, Nina looking ever more like her mother, and Brent had filled out, more Scottish Highlander now than pale and lanky. They looked at him with a mixture of excitement and hesitation, they did remember him being rather aloof after all. "Cara mia!" Marcus turned to Sabine first, with a huge hug she received gratefully. "Poor love, come in, come in!" Turning to Brent and Nina he said warmly, "So good to see you both again, please, please, do come in, make yourselves comfortable, dinner will be ready soon!"

The three visitors looked at each other, this was just wonderful, such a kind welcome, the tension falling off them.

"I think someone is dying to see you, cara mia." Marcus smiled and pushed Sabine, tenderly but with determination into the living room, where Damian stood, beaming like a Christmas tree, if they had still been allowed. Sabine's face was a picture, all manner of questions written all over it, shiny eyes in contrast to her biting her lower lip the way she had done since she was a little girl, trying to see how Damian would react towards her. It was just the most touching thing to witness how he clearly couldn't stop himself any longer, rushing to her to envelop her in the biggest hug, then holding her head close to him, before stepping back, looking at her fully.

"I'm so so sorry we had to leave like that, Sabine, sweetheart, the police...god, I've missed you so much!"

"The police! Oh Damian, but how...?" She was trying to keep her knees from buckling, her mind filled with love, relief and worry in equal measure. "I thought you'd left without me, not wanting me with you anymore." She bit her lower lip again and looked searchingly into his eyes.

"Sabine, listen to me, I've not stopped thinking about you for a second, we'll tell you everything. Of course I wanted to stay with you, of course, come on, you know that really, don't you?"

Sabine nodded, her head and heart swimming, her eyes trying to focus as if on a fairground carousel. Letting herself lean against Damian who immediately closed his arms around her, she followed Damian's glance to see Marcus, Nina and Brett watching them intently, obviously enjoying every moment of the unfolding romance.

Damian laughed. "Ok, you guys, that's all you're going to get, for now anyhow!"

Sabine laughed along, feeling totally comfortable in Damian's embrace.

"Is that 'spag bol' I can smell, Uncle Marcus? My favourite?"

"It sure is, little niece! Prepared by Robin's own fair hands!"

The Serf somehow managed to look pleased behind his formal robot exterior. Marcus remembered what his father had told him years ago, that there were two things in life that brought people together: one was playing music together and the other was eating together. Roy had encouraged him to buy a round table, large enough to feed a group of friends, even though it seemed over the top in a bachelor's place. It did look good, all of them sitting together, enjoying the spaghetti which was perfectly *al dente*, and the delicious sauce Robin had conjured up from god knows what he'd found in the fridge.

"So, tell me everything." Sabine pleaded, while curling more pasta onto her fork. "But especially about the police!"

All of them listened agog and in disgust as Marcus and Daniel took it in turns, between mouthfuls, to describe the drone invading Sabine's home, about poor Damian hiding in the cupboard, and the smug copper in the police car down the road.

"How on earth did he know where to look?" Brent wondered. "I mean he isn't the brightest spark on the planet, is he? I had no idea they used drones like that in the villages. Cities, yes, I've seen it on CV, but this is horrible."

Damian nodded. "If you can make an ordinary person subject to such scrutiny just for losing a job and being in an accident, it shows what I've been feeling for ages. We are, slowly but surely, being made into less than Serfs. Slaves for all I know, underdogs with no freedom to create their own lives. I can feel it happening. Nobody can turn us on and off like Serfs, but they can work round our sensibilities by making us ever more fearful and therefore controllable." Damian paused and then laughed dryly, filled with self-cynicism. "I wanted to get away to start a freedom revolution. Instead, I hid in a drain and then ran to Sabine, and now I'm with the best people ever, eating spaghetti prepared by a robot. Some revolutionary hero I am!"

Nina had been unusually quiet, her mind partly on what was being said, but mainly preoccupied with her Mum, cold and lonely in that bed. She had to say something, shift the attention away from conspiracy talk to the main issue: Who or what had caused the accident? And why was Damian here happily chatting with them instead of being kept alive in a hospital ward in Scarborough?

"How come you're here, Damian? How come you're here when my Mum, Bill and the mother with her boy are in a coma in hospital? They were half frozen to death, by this THING, this ice thing!" She spat the word 'thing' out with as much contempt she could muster. "And you're sitting here, again in a t-shirt, when the rest of us are wearing jumpers or two layers at least. It's great you're here and safe, but I don't get it. Anyway, .."

"We need a sample of your blood, Damian." Sabine interrupted, rather forcefully. "Sorry, that came out wrong." She looked at Nina and Brent for confirmation. "Your Mum needs it, she's also figured it out, that there is a difference between how you and everyone else reacted. It might help her to save the others, you see? Think of poor Nina's Mum, we need to help all of them really."

"Remember me calling you Iron Man when we were little?" Brent smiled at Damian. "After you had that spike in your leg? Something happened after that, you didn't feel cold any more, did you? Just munching sweets like there was no tomorrow, really weird."

"Yeah." Damian replied, somewhat embarrassed. "Of course I remember. Yeah, it makes sense that my Mum would want to check out if there was anything useful to find. You can have my blood, Marcus wanted some, too, thinking along the same lines, weren't you, Marcus?"

"Yes, I was, Damian, and something just now, that Brent mentioned, what was that about the sweets?" Marcus looked keenly at both Damian and Brent.

"Well, it's just that when it's cold out, I get sugar cravings like crazy. Mum used to tell me off for it, wanted to get me something warm instead, so she gave me hot chocolate as a compromise. I don't like sugary stuff at all when it's warm outside, I don't know why. But it started with that spike in the leg."

"I'll be damned, that's it!!! You've got it! You've got the frog protein!" Marcus jumped up from his chair, shouting it out, making everyone jump, looking up at him in utter amazement.

"What?! What are you talking about?" Damian almost shouted back, not sure if he liked the sound of that. "I've got a frog what?"

"Uncle Marcus?" Sabine put her hand on Marcus's arm to get him to sit down again. "What are you saying?"

"Wait!" Brent interjected. "Nearly forgot!" He pointed to his iLink, and handed Marcus's over to him.

"I've turned ours and yours all off, Marcus, actually, more than that, I've turned them to the Deep Sea Diving mode, I'll show you. He swiped over it, tapping a couple of emblems as he did so, all the while making sure that Marcus could see what he did. Sure enough, the mute mic sign appeared and the start screen clouded over. Marcus couldn't believe it. That was such a brilliant and obvious idea because it blocked the microphone as well as the whole iLink from any kind of liquid ingress, even acids, salts and other aggressive materials, but he'd had no idea that the mike could be muted. He had always hoped that turning the whole thing off meant the mike was off, too, but was never quite sure enough to relax with the thought, basically hoping for the best. This was much better, at the very least muffling the sound making any recordings pretty much useless.

"Goodness, why oh why had I never thought of that?" Marcus shook his head. "This is brilliant. Do you use that all the time then when you need privacy? And it's honestly reliable?"

"I think it is. I checked out the software of an old one I butchered, and realised that it had to work. I tried to play back anything it captured in that mode, I couldn't hear anything of use. And if there should be a garbled low noise, there might be some de-garbling software eventually, but I don't think there is as yet. It's an overlooked glitch, cool, isn't it? Anyhow, I think we're good to talk. Is Robin safe?"

"Yes, he is. I made sure of that. Okay, back to calling you a frog, Damian, I'm not really, but this is the subject I had wanted to talk over with Sabine in Italy. It's all about the wood frog, native to Alaska, and how it survives in such harsh conditions. I believe that evolution is changing the human body, to prepare us all for the next ice age, making us frost proof, much like the wood frogs don't freeze to death.

Amazingly they can actually freeze and thaw, repeating the process over weeks and months and still thrive! Such incredible little creatures, they don't even need oxygen when frozen, they can just switch metabolic processes. They produce a protein that basically acts like an antifreeze, but for the whole thing to work it needs the liver to produce a lot of glucose, and I think, I really do think, that, maybe through the blood transfusion you got, you were somehow given that protein, and that it multiplied in your body. It's already being used to transport donor organs, suspended in blood serum, to make them more stable during the cold transport, see? Its use is relatively new, what if that was all the ambulance crew had available and used it hoping to save you?" Marcus was breathless with excitement now. "Which means you are probably ahead of evolution, by more than a touch, and your sugar cravings are because of your liver's need to produce glucose to fill your cells, just like the frog does, but as you're much bigger, well, you need masses of sugar. If you didn't produce enough the kidneys would jump in to try and release more, if you produced too much, your liver would know to store it as glycogen, but whatever scenario, you're uniquely equipped to cope in cold conditions for a long time, we would freeze well before you."

"A cryoprotectant! You've got your own cryoprotectant!" Sabine exclaimed. "It makes perfect sense! That's why you're here and well, and the others are suffering! Actually, several arctic amphibians and insects have that! Wow!"

"That's exactly right, Sabine. But, hang on." Marcus held up his hand to continue. "That's been my solitary work and I need to keep this between us for now. I've isolated the protein, simple enough, but more importantly the gene, too, which means, really, I have found a way to stop people from freezing, ahead of the natural evolution that might be taking place. I've been in a serious quandary about it, because I don't want this to be used as a military tool, for physically superior troops over ordinary people maybe, you see? We all know that becoming inferior is a real danger for all of us, within the next few generations anyhow. I want this to help everyone, not have it fall into the wrong hands."

Damian nodded darkly. "AI's are bad enough, but superhumans?"

Marcus sighed in agreement. It had weighed heavily on his mind, and now he'd told almost strangers about it, not clever perhaps, but it felt right, it felt safe. The others listened intently.

"The blood you received after your injury, Damian, might just as well have come from someone who might have had a blood transfusion of his or her own in the past, or perhaps from someone who had received a donor organ, that had retained some cryoprotectant. Whatever happened, your body managed to assimilate it and make use of it. You and who knows how many other people. It's possible that there is even a second generation of 'anti-freezers' already. For now, as far as I know, there isn't anyone looking out for the changes, as they are not really on the radar yet. A simple protein is one thing, but a gene, well, it's further reaching. What do I do with it? Is it just the protein that has changed your liver's capability, like a medicine of sorts, or has it changed your whole genetic balance? Would it be passed on to your children one day, for example?"

Damian and Sabine exchanged furtive glances while Marcus continued, unable to stop himself, his mind making new connections as he spoke.

"I just don't know. Right now it may help save Nina's Mum and the others retrospectively, and who knows how many populations in the future. But if I publish it, it might hurt millions of us at some point in time as well!" He shuddered. There was that horrible pressure building up inside of his head again, when he could clearly see that daunting futuristic possibility, he felt sick thinking he might contribute to it.

"I know what you mean." Damian nodded, glumly. "Let's face it, artificial limbs, eyes and even cochlear implants already work better than natural human body parts. With bio, stem cell and gene technology we see and hear better, and last longer. I know, because in the rubber industry, we got hundreds of spec sheets, showing the developing technology for all sorts of body parts, not just limbs. It was mind boggling. There are superhumans on the way, definitely. Even I am one already, to some extent, if I'm part frog." He winced thinking about it.

Nina had been listening, quietly, trying to find her centre as best as she could. She had just been thinking of one of the things her Dad had said, many many times, that the profit of the few must not be put above the profit of the many. She had always agreed with it, it was the basis of all her political and moral beliefs, but now, faced with perhaps saving her Mum, nothing was quite as clear any more. She knew she had to find her inner voice, Grandma Nellie was good at that, had taught her to step away from a situation until it could be seen more clearly, afresh, from a distance, but she was just too tired to make any decisions at all. Instinct was all she had left right now. "I might be delusional and I am very tired, it's been a couple of crazy days, but I still feel that my Mum will be alright, deep down. Yes...deep down, I don't feel she is in any danger. If it's helpful to get Damian's blood sample without it being harmful some time in the future, well, maybe, but it's not for me to decide - please don't make me." Nina felt herself becoming shaky and emotional now. It was one thing sensing her Mum would be all right, but quite another to feel responsible about some potential cure that might harm others in the end, she couldn't handle it. Suddenly it was there again. That inner voice coming to the fore, strongly, telling her to wait. "Actually, my instinct is getting really strong about this. My Mum is strong, so is Bill. They are older than the little lad and his Mum, they should be ok, too, shouldn't they? Let's wait and see what tomorrow brings. I'm really glad to be here right now, with all of you."

The warm smiles all around her confirmed that everyone felt much the same.

Chapter 21
Back to Life

AT THE HOSPITAL Yvonne and her colleague Luis were watching the monitors intently. There had been a change in brain activity in all four patients. The brain wave graphs of each of them moved almost ballet like in harmony, moving from Delta waves to Alpha waves and back again in complete synchronicity with each other. It meant they were already coming out of their comas, but the absolute match in timing was astonishing, more like a group communication rather than a personal struggle to wake up.

"Just look at it, look! I don't believe I'm seeing this! What's going on? Are they all coming round together?" Luis almost shouted it out.

Yvonne could only stare and nod her head, endeared by the impassioned response of the Spanish nurse she shared the shift with. Luis was great, she thought, not for the first time, of a slight built like a weasel and as quick on his feet as he was with his heart and mind. She was glad he was there with her. The brainwave activity was such a good development, she just knew it. In an individual it would be a good sign, but to see them synced like that felt magical, as if her and Luis were privy to watching something very special indeed. There was nothing to do but wait, no interference was allowed when the brain was trying to right itself, any external stimulus might be too much.

"The boy, too!" Luis whispered now, even though it wasn't really necessary. Kade's brainwaves were matching the others, showing a deep alpha state, a meditation in the awake state rather than a dream like one, well, it was simply astounding. They had expected Kade to be the first to come round, children were much better at surviving severe hypothermia, their organs generally less stressed than older patients. It didn't look like that now though.

Yvonne looked at jovial Bill, with his fuzzy grey mop surrounding his pale face, so different to his usual ruddy complexion. Looking closer though there was something changing behind that paleness, like a smile, or some pink maybe? He definitely looked more lively - fascinating. How many comatose patients had she watched over the years and never noticed that? The early change in appearance that probably couldn't be seen in a photograph. Luis watched her watching Bill, and expressed it calmly, confidently. "His energy is coming back. Good."

Yvonne was struck how profound that everyday term was. What was that energy, that life giving force? Watching it rise in Bill was humbling.

"Look, Karen, too!" Yvonne exclaimed. Sure enough, Karen's face had also begun to show that subtle glow, her rising energy like an underlying hum coming from her body. She exuded a vibration of sorts that was different to her earlier totally unconscious state. "She's a bit of an enigma, isn't she. Or is that just me? I've never even talked to her, but even in her coma she seems shut off somehow, her little boy, too, they seem of a different ilk to the others."

"Really? I don't really see any difference, I would just really like all of them to wake up and tell me what on earth happened on that bus. None of it makes any sense, does it?"

"No." Yvonne sighed, trying not to think of Damian and what a blood sample of his would show. She hadn't heard anything from Sabine, though it hadn't been long enough to really worry about it. Only, knowing her son wouldn't be there again when she'd get home after work felt dreadful. The house had felt cold and empty the previous night, it would take some getting used to. Not sharing breakfast, or at least seeing his breakfast plates in the sink, was depressing. Was this the famous empty nest syndrome? Whatever it was, she didn't like it one bit, especially as she'd had no chance to prepare for it.

Their brain waves synced back into the Alpha stage again. To all intents and purposes the patients were waking up, a cause for celebration, which was usually the time to ring the next of kin to let them know the good news. Still, neither Luis nor Yvonne felt like doing any such thing. These patients weren't in an average coma, if there was such a thing. The synchronised drifting in and out was so unusual that neither of them felt like predicting anything. Would they regress into unconsciousness, or come to properly under their watch?

"Look at Mary!" Luis touched Yvonne's arm. "She's glowing! And her hair, look at her hair!"

It was true, Mary's dark salt and pepper hair had turned almost completely black again, apart from the striking white streak on the side. It looked as if some very clever dye job had happened right in front of their eyes. The same was happening to Karen, too, her hair, a dull brown just a short while ago, was now closer to a shiny auburn. The woman was stunning. Yvonne's eyes fell on the V-screen showing Karen's son.

"Oh my goodness, Luis, look at Kade, he is smiling! What a dear little boy, look at his smile!"

Without a doubt, some kind of magical change was happening in all of them, even in Yvonne and Luis, too, though it took a while for both of them to realise what it was. It was the most overwhelming sense of love they had started to feel for these people, way beyond their usual professional caring as nurses.

"They've got to live, they've just got to!" Yvonne's heart felt close to bursting point, as if these patients were her own flesh and blood. "Come on Mary, come on back to us, life is so precious, there is so much out there for you still! For all of you!" Yvonne knew she wasn't behaving professionally, but she couldn't help her outburst.

"I dare say I am falling in love with these people." Luis followed suit. "I've either been a nurse for too long and am getting far too attached, or I haven't been a nurse long enough. This is amazing. They are all simply beautiful!"

Yvonne stood, close to tears, not understanding what was happening. Her emotions were all over the place. She sensed a familiarity with another feeling she couldn't even put into words, a sense of melancholy, a kind of longing she couldn't express. She knew, as did Luis, that they were witnessing something extraordinary. She decided to call Brent.

Marcus, Sabine, Damian, Nina and Brent had moved to the living room, stretching out their legs, trying to think what to do next. There was the issue of Damian who was, as far as the law would be concerned, on the run. The fact he'd got rid of all his IDs might be explained by the shock of the accident, but all in combination, being the only one to survive the crash unharmed, sounded odd enough to make his life very uncomfortable if he were to just appear again. At the same time Damian felt at a loss as to where his fantasies of revolution would take him. They had sounded great in principle, but having seized his chance spontaneously, without a proper plan, he had no idea what to do now.

Nina looked at him with some intensity. "What is it that you're really trying to do, Damian? What are you hoping to achieve?"

Brent watched his wife carefully, recognizing that she was trying very hard to keep herself thinking logically. As if allowing herself to get too emotional would bring the worry about her mother to the fore, and about what Nellie and Bob had told them about the Icehawk over Chignik.

Damian sighed, looking equally serious. "I always thought my job in the factory was really quite important, daft as it might sound, rubber is an amazing eco friendly material, with masses of potential still waiting to be developed. It might be the one material that will save us all from being watched and listened to and monitored, whatever we do. I guess my fantasies were to work in the factory, to get all the technical information necessary and get together with equally minded people to develop some kind of effective privacy protection for all ordinary people." He smiled, knowing that it might all sound silly, but he had been dreaming about it for years. "Initially, I imagined working completely in secret with trustworthy designers, manufacturers and scientists, much like yourself, Marcus, to help develop a cloaking material, shields in effect, as part of everyday clothing perhaps, to give everyone the chance to live normal, unmonitored lives. My mother and me included." Damian looked at Brent for reassurance. "I know that none of us are happy being watched all the time, Connor isn't either, is he, and even old Spencer isn't happy, and not just because of his home-brew he wants to peddle, I think there's a lot more to the man than he's letting on. I know I couldn't do it on my own, but that was the dream." He smirked bitterly. "And I was the only one dumb enough to actually agree to an ingrown iLink, hoping for a promotion at the time, how pathetic." He instinctively covered his wrist lightly that was still looking raw and a little inflamed under the spray plaster. "I know ripping the iLink off like that, so close to the arteries, was more risky and desperate than wise. But there you go, I did it, it must have been brewing in me for a while." He shrugged his shoulders. "Also, I knew that if I was to disappear I couldn't use my bank account, as any withdrawal would show where I was. Right now I have two things to my name, a bit of gold, yes really!" He laughed at his friends' surprise. "That's all down to my clever Mum's foresight. And a piece of still top secret rubber sheeting I stole from the factory when I was told to clear out my office. It's amazing stuff, it can scramble signals better than lead. Just think, you could include it in clothes, without anyone ever knowing! It could cover up iLinks when needed, or entire buildings, making monitoring probably not impossible, but definitely much more difficult, enough to get some kind of autonomy back. Being made largely of rubber it would, actually, be really hard to detect, before it'll be made illegal for public use anyhow."

Brent frowned. "A cloaking device for people. That's the stuff of movies, Damian. Whoaa! Off the radar, in more ways than one. Way too idealistic and far fetched for me."

Damian shrugged, disappointed. "Not sure what else I can do right now to convince you, but I've got the sample and I've got the spec sheets as well, to be able to reproduce it at any time. Abroad maybe? You might be convinced when you actually see it." He sighed again, feeling tired now. "Just days ago all I had to decide was, what to have for dinner, and how to get my Mum hitched up with a good man. Now she doesn't even know where I am, and I'm sitting here, snug as a bug with you all, next to this beautiful woman, with no idea what to do tomorrow. I know I can't have some drone arriving at any of you guys' places, it's also blooming cold outside, and I don't really know where to go." Damian looked downcast and clearly embarrassed.

"Alright then, let's join the dots and do the sums." Marcus felt he had to take charge, as obviously something had to be done, and a plan had been forming in his mind. He liked Damian, and could do with someone he could trust to help him with his research. Damian was in no way an academic, but it was clear that he was smart, a lateral thinker, who seemed dependable and determined. Marcus was sure he could trust him. "So, have I got this right, if someone offered you a job you wouldn't have to hand the notice chip in, and avoid all the horrid procedure at that EDC?"

"Yup." Damian nodded sadly, that knot forming in his stomach again. "And the longer I don't show or prove I have another job the worse it'll get. They'll talk about social duty avoidance and all sorts, and you know how heavy that's getting. I wouldn't mind doing any old job, but I do mind lying to innocent people, about flu vaccinations and such."

"Oh good grief, is that still going on? Really?" Marcus groaned. "That's horrendous. I had hoped they'd stopped that ages ago, that's truly depressing. How can they still get away with all that?" Marcus paused for a minute, looking at Sabine whose face was as glum as Damian's. "I might have an idea, of course I don't know whether you'll like it or not." Damian looked at him uncertainly, not sure what to expect.

Marcus smiled, though his eyes looked serious. "I might have a job for you, with me, in my lab, as a research assistant. I think I could get that passed. It might bore you to tears, but I need someone I can trust. I can afford to pay you well enough, and I could even offer you lodgings in Dad's annexe if the commute from Kirbymoorside was a problem, or until your car is fixed, whatever you want, really. It's been sitting empty for a while. I'm quite sure I could deal with any questions about bypassing interview procedures and such, and we'll think up some story with regards to the police. For all we know you could still be in shock. It's a bit sudden though, and I'm not sure if I'm just getting carried away with trying to help and see my little niece happy. Shall we'll agree on a six weeks trial for now, to see whether we can work together? Which would help me with the interview procedure, too, come to think of it. I could offer you a permanent position after a trial period more easily, make it official and above board then? And it would get you off the hook for now."

Marcus tried to work out Damian's facial expression, he resembled a startled deer. "It'll be a lot of computer work, online searches and collating material, nothing like in the factory, but, if you think you can cope or even fancy it, well, the offer is there. The advantage for me would be having you with your blood close by, to look at comparisons between the frog gene in the lab and in your blood, without making my findings public until I'm ready. It would have to be our little secret. And please, Damian, don't worry. I promise there would be no experiments on you apart from taking some blood samples here and there, to see when and why your sugar cravings kick in, that sort of thing."

There was a stunned silence in the room, before Brent spoke first. "Wow, that's a beauty of an offer."

Nina nodded, Sabine jumped up and to give Marcus a hug, whispering a 'Thank you!' in his ear.

She turned to look at Damian, as did everyone else, waiting for his reaction.

"Are you serious?" The startled deer finally spoke. "Do you really mean this?"

Marcus nodded, still watching him. "I don't know what to say, that's just amazingly generous. Not exactly a revolution, but probably a bit more sensible, eh?"

Sabine looked at Damian, with the widest grin across her face. "Ohhh, you know, that means we can see each other a lot, and you don't have to lie or hide at all. You'd be in the clear! And if Uncle Marcus could do with the help anyhow, it's a perfect solution!"

Damian looked at her gratefully, gently squeezing her hand, then turning to Marcus again. "With your research into the frog protein, do you think that between us we might be able to find out what hit the bus and made it so cold? I'd love to know. I can still see the ice on people's shoulders, and on their faces.. it was horrible." He fell silent, reliving for a moment all that had happened to him in such a short time. Now he was sitting here, being offered safety, friendship and a job. "I feel I've lived at least a year's worth of experiences since in such a short time.."

He felt close to tears again. Maybe he would wake up any minute now and realise it had all been a dream?

Suddenly, Brent's iLink was buzzing, making everyone jump. Nina held her fingers to her lips to stop the others talking while Brent unmuted it and answered it.

It was Yvonne. "Hello, Brent Daniels? It's Yvonne, the nurse from Scarborough hospital, we spoke earlier, if you remember?"

"Yes, of course, Yvonne, we've been hoping to hear from you. How are they?"

"I have good news! All the patients seem to be coming out of their comas, all at the same time, drifting in and out. We are very optimistic. They are all getting their colour back, and are looking very serene and very beautiful, actually. We're quite amazed at the change in them. Would you both like to come and see them tomorrow? I can't promise they will be alert by then, but it would be good for you to see what's happening to them, it's quite magical. Nina's mother looks incredible, glowing. They all look rejuvenated, I can't express it any other way. Anyhow, we're keeping a good eye on them, but as I said, I think it's safe to say it's good news." Yvonne's delight was obvious.

Damian fixed his eyes on Brent, both of them trying to think how they could tell her he was right there.

"That's wonderful, Yvonne, thank you very much for letting us know. I'll pass it on to Nina, and to, uhm, our mutual friends, who are saying hello and are also very grateful." Brent willed Yvonne to pick up on what he was trying to say. "Is your son alright?" Brent asked, when there was no reaction. That was probably risky, or was it?

Yvonne paused, not sure what to say. "I hope so, I haven't heard from him. I am worried, as you can imagine. The police came in to work to ask me about him, too."

"Oh, no, I'm sorry, that must have been so frightening, Yvonne! Are you ok? But you know, I'm sure he'll be fine, we didn't call him the ironman for nothing, did we!"

Would the mention of the memory and the smile in his voice be enough to reassure her? It sounded as if Yvonne had understood. There was a tiny gasp before she replied with obvious relief in her voice,

"How lovely you remember the old days, Brent! I best go, please give Nina and.. your friends.. my regards. See you tomorrow, take care."

She rang off. Brent set the iLink back to the diving mode, and everyone breathed out, laughing, whooping at the good news.

"Oh wow!" Nina exclaimed. "They're all coming round, and it sounds good, doesn't it? I knew my Mum would be all right, I just knew it!"

Everyone nodded eagerly. It was as if some invisible thread connected them to Yvonne and even Nina's Mum filling them with relief and joy. Damian was convinced that his Mum was reassured. Oh, yes, she knew. He hugged Sabine, and laughed as Marcus shook his head in amazement and said, with feeling, "What a day! I'm too old for all this! I had breakfast in Italy this morning!"

Sabine smiled. "We really should go, it's getting late anyhow.

152

I still have a few days off, since I'm not going to Italy now, which means I can even sleep in, how good! And you'll be safe and comfortable here, Damian."

"Yes, I'll be fine, better than fine. And thanks a million, Nina, Brent, for bringing Sabine here, and doing all you've done, and you Sabine, thank you so much for everything. And again, I can't tell you how sorry I am about the disappearing act in your flat. I so wish you could stay, but I'm not going to push it!" He laughed, feeling ever more relaxed and happy.

"Steady on, young man!" Marcus put on his sternest Italian uncle face, and Sabine gave him a kiss on his cheek in response. "I've got a protective uncle, how good is that? One who's offered my boyfriend a job! I love it!"

Nina and Brent laughed in unison how thrilled Damian looked being called her boyfriend. Everything had been just awful only hours ago, and now it all felt like an exciting adventure.

Chapter 22
The Feathers

YVONNE WALKED BY the windows of the ICU ward, barely able to control herself not to break out into an overly delighted grin. Damian was safe and well, and obviously in touch with Brent and Nina, Brent wouldn't have mentioned some friends and the ironman story otherwise, she was convinced of it. Were they all at Brent and Nina's home when they talked? She hadn't thought to swipe to the location finder during the call, she was just happy to be able to give them the good news, and in return she'd been reassured herself. Again she felt sheer joy and yes, love for these good people and her patients drifting, peacefully it seemed, in and out of consciousness, still in perfect harmony. Like synchronised swimmers they went through various stages of awareness, but there wasn't a hint of stress on the monitors, no panic, no gasping for breath, no intense dream state, no adrenaline surges.

She opened the door to Bill's room and nearly cried out loud in surprise, and yes, with the shock of it. There on Bill's bed, right on his chest, was a feather just like there had been on Greg's deathbed. She let out a pained gurgle of despair, immediately checking his monitors. No. There was no indication he was in trouble at all. Yvonne was reeling, her eyes fixed on the feather she associated with death, then deciding to check Bill's pulse herself, to reassure herself that the monitors weren't lying, she needed to feel the life in him. It was there, strong 68 beats per minute. Good. Her shoulders sank in relief, then unable to stop herself, she ran to Karen's room, then Kade's, then finally Mary's. Same again - a striped rusty brown feather had just appeared right on top of each of their chests, almost reaching their chins, and all were somehow mirroring the subtle glow the large feathers exuded.

There was absolutely no doubt, the feathers had appeared from nowhere. One on each bed, casually laid there, but with a kind of neatness in that all of them were placed across the heart of each patient in exactly the same position. Yvonne looked again, her logic trying to make sense of it, wondering whether she may have lost her mind.

Nothing appears from nowhere, but nobody had entered the wards. She'd been here the whole time, there were no visitors now, Luis had gone to get them both a coffee as always before heading home. Right now it was just her looking after these four patients, and both her and Luis would have to leave this mystery to the nurses on the next shift. What on earth could she say? What would they say? Would they all think it was some elaborate joke? Would they think she had done this? The patients looked fantastic, more post holiday rather than post hypothermic coma, and a feather on each of the beds, well, that was clearly against all health and safety rules. It didn't bear thinking about how to explain that one.

What should she do with them? Leave them where they were, remove them, or what? They did make them all look so well, she was convinced. Well, almost. And the stats on the monitors spoke volumes. Bill's cholesterol was perfect for starters, Mary's low blood sugar had levelled out, the little boy's histamine levels had also normalised, and his mother's creatinine levels showed that her kidneys were now functioning absolutely fine. Under any other circumstances she would have come to the conclusion that the body, needing to warm itself up, would have created such a powerful self-healing surge, instinctively that made sense to her. But the feathers made it obvious that something very different was happening, something that even felt familiar, but that she still couldn't put into words. Was it some magic, shamanism, witchcraft, or guardian angels? None of that fitted, not that she would have known for sure in any case. In all her years as a nurse she had only come across one similar scenario once before, and that was witnessing that feather on Mary's husband's deathbed, and how upset Mary had been, immediately running out of the room in distress. That had definitely looked like a recognition of something, was it some Alaskan Native knowledge she had and nobody else around here knew about? It would be good to speak to Nina, maybe she knew something as well? Perhaps her mother had talked about it to her in the past? But that wouldn't solve her dilemma now, what to do with the feathers before she left at 9pm. Luis's voice startled her as he came up behind her.

"Want your coffee left on the desk?" He looked over her shoulder at Mary and saw what she saw, and called out, equally shocked and taken aback. "What the hell? What did you do, Yvonne? Did you put that there?"

"I certainly did not!" Yvonne replied firmly, cross at the accusation. "I just saw it myself. They've each got one." She turned and looked at him, as he stared transfixed at the feather lifting and sinking with Mary's breath, fluttering slightly with the draft.

"Seriously? The others, too?" He put the coffees down, turned, followed closely by Yvonne, to take a closer look for himself, checking little Kade's pulse, just as Yvonne had needed to reassure herself, then Karen's, then Bill's.

"He looks as strong as an ox, I don't get this!" Luis turned to Yvonne again. "We can't leave the feathers here, we'd get lynched, breaking every ICU standard ever! Shall we pick them up, or what?"

Yvonne looked at him, his eyes darting from the monitor to Mary's face, with a strikingly beautiful olive complexion and her now glossy raven black hair still with that white streak, and then to the feather, she could swear it was radiating something. Luis was obviously trying to make sense of it all just as she was.

"Do you see that glow around the feather, too, Luis, or is that just me and my eyes playing tricks?"

"No, not just you, Yvonne, it's emitting something, isn't it. I don't think we should remove it, but I don't want to risk them being removed while we're not here, either." He needed to think, come up with something.

"I know!" Yvonne pulled on his sleeve with sudden excitement. "Shall we just place the feathers under their gowns, still on their chests? And tuck the blankets in very neatly, to make it all look tidy? With any luck they won't be disturbed for the next few hours, and might still be there when we get back in the morning? Well, and fingers crossed no-one will look at the recordings from when we were here, but then at least they'll know that neither of us put them there?"

"The recording!" Luis exclaimed, maybe the cameras will tell us what happened? I wish we had more time now, but we can't do it now, not before the night staff comes in. Maybe tomorrow? With Mary's daughter here even, we could all look together?"

"We've got to hurry now, Luis, will you do Karen's and Kade's, and I do Mary's and Bill's? We'll just put them in the exact same position on their chests, and cover it loosely with their gown, and then with the sheet. Let's not squash it, still give it air room, but make it look super tidy, ok?"

With that she lifted Mary's blanket and placed the feather that felt surprisingly good and safe to touch, onto Mary's warm chest, and gently covered it as planned. There was no reaction from Mary, her sleep uninterrupted, her smile still in place. Luis did the same, ever so carefully, looking down on Karen and Kade as he did as agreed, it felt good, felt like a caring thing to do. He would have liked to hold onto the feather a little longer, it felt like something special. Yvonne couldn't be sure if Bill's smile grew even wider momentarily as she placed the feather onto his huge chest, feeling a rush of affection, perhaps he felt being cared for on some level?

'What a lovely man.' Yvonne thought, 'even asleep he looks like a good man, kind'. Closing the doors quietly they went back to grab their coats and coffees just as the night staff arrived to take over, the monitors showing nothing mysterious at all.

· · • • ● ● ● • · ·

IT WAS JUST past lunchtime in Chignik when Nina rang. Nellie swiped up the V screen immediately, they both did.

"Hello, my dear dear girl, how are you? Any news?"

Nina looked good. Tired, but clearly cheerful and before she could even answer, Nellie knew.

"Oh, you have good news, don't you, I can tell by your face! Is Mary all right? Bob, quick, come, it's Nina!"

"Mum's waking up, Grandma!" Nina replied with a broad smile across her face. "I knew it, you know, I knew I'd have felt it if she was in real trouble, she'll be alright, the others, too, by what the nurse said. She rang earlier and sounded really positive! We're going to see her and the others tomorrow morning, at the hospital. How are you and Bob? Everything ok over there?"

"Yes, yes, we're all fine, Nina, oh, that's wonderful to hear, isn't it Bob?"

"Well, tell your mother to hurry up with the waking up so we can invite her to the wedding ourselves!" Bob called into the V screen, equally relieved. It was fantastic seeing Nina laugh like that, and how clever that was, being able to see each other across continents. It had been thirty years since Skype had been invented, Bob remembered his first video call, and how the whole village had been excited to reach friends and relations all over the world. It had been a huge thing back then, and still felt really special. But now, the holographic 3D V-Screens? Unbelievably good. Just a shame that privacy was a thing of the past. Bob would have loved to talk more with Nina about the Icehawk, but it just didn't feel safe. She could tell.

"We'll talk more when we can, Grandma, Bob, but right now

we've had a bit of a long day, and to be honest, I need a long hot bath and a good night's sleep, so I'll say bye-bye for now and will ring you back after I've seen Mum and the others tomorrow. Try and relax now, everything will be alright, and we'll see you at the wedding!"

Her and Nellie blew each other a kiss and the V-screens shrunk back into their iLinks.

Nellie looked up at Bob, obviously relieved, she had that little girl look about her again.

"Well well, she's strong like her mother, your Mary." Bob held her hand, and saw the tears of relief in Nellie's eyes.

"There, there, Nel." He got up and took her into his arms. "See? Nina said so, too. Everything will be just fine. And the Icehawk, if it comes back, well, it didn't hurt us, and it looks like it didn't kill Mary either. We still need answers but so far everything really dreadful has only happened in our imagination. Let's have another coffee, to take us through the afternoon, eh?"

Just as soon as they had walked into the kitchen, there was a faint knock on the door.

"Come in!" Nellie called out, as it was custom, everybody knew everybody, and was welcome everywhere, there was no-one to fear. The door opened somewhat shyly, and little Sophie from a few doors down, with her school bag over her shoulder, poked her head through the door.

"Excuse me, Grandmother Nellie, Grandfather Bob." She addressed them with their usual Elder title. "I've been sent by Miss Kelly to talk to you. We've been wanting your advice on something, is it alright if I come in?"

"Miss Kelly, your English teacher, Sophie? But of course, come in, sit down, what can we help you with?" Nellie immediately replied, with her customary warmth she was famous for. Bob came across, putting the two cups of coffee down and asked the girl kindly. "Would you like a drink, too, Sophie? Oh look, your glasses are all steamed up, let me get you a towel."

Little Sophie looked cute with her brown ponytail and big

blue eyes, looking even bigger due to the thick glasses she was wearing. She was a smart, sensible and sensitive girl, and had just turned ten before the Icehawk appeared.

"I'd love some cloudberry juice, Grandfather Bob, if that's ok?" Sophie shuffled her feet in a mixture of nerves and excitement trying to ask her question. "I've asked Miss Kelly, and she told me to ask you, because you would know. Anyway, it was my birthday the other day and my brother Stefan went to find some of the feathers the Icehawk had left behind, to give to me as a late present, he was really brave about it, even touching them in the first place! He got a bunch of them, there are still more about, but I don't think anyone else has gone to pick them up. But something happened to him when he touched them, and he told me about it, and now it's happened to me, too!"

"Well!" Nellie tried to slow down the flow of words tumbling out of the girl.

"What is it, Sophie, what happened to the two of you? You don't look very scared, it wasn't anything bad then, I hope?"

Bob stood, with the glass of juice in his hand, amazed. He'd been wondering if he should go and look for the feathers himself, and had talked himself out of it with all sorts of excuses, but basically, he'd been afraid to. And now there was this little short sighted strip of a girl and little Stefan who'd just gone and done it.

"I'll be damned." He smiled. "That was a mighty brave thing for Stefan to do. Is he still at school?"

"Yes, he is, Grandfather, Miss Kelly thought one of us leaving class was quite enough, but she wants me to come back after I've talked with you, so she can talk with us about it. I'm quite good at English, that's why she said it was okay for me to go. I think Stefan's a bit grumpy about it, really. So are the others, too, who want to have a go, but Miss Kelly said only after you said it was ok. And I am the older one." Sophie added, proudly.

"That you are, but make sure to tell Stefan that we think he was really brave to go and pick them up, and really generous, too, to give them to you as a present. So, what happened to you two then, with the feathers?" Nellie asked kindly.

"Well, it was amazing!" Sophie exclaimed. "First, when Stefan gave me the feather, he looked really sweet, much sweeter than he usually does, and then I took it. I was a bit scared, but it felt really, really nice, like a pet, soft, a bit like it was alive. So I sniffed it to see what it smelled like, and then it happened!"

"What happened, what?"

"Well, I saw everybody, even myself, too! It was like I was going into a dream, but really quickly, everybody was there, me, and Stefan, our Mum and Dad, and Miss Kelly, and all the kids from school, and you and Grandfather Bob and your daughter Mary, and your Granddaughter Nina too, and her husband and loads of people I didn't know. And you know what, the place was really good, like a nature park you see in the city. There was a really beautiful icy castle, too, but I didn't see the Icehawk, but I think it was his world. It was amaaaaaziiiiiiiiiiing!"

She drew out the word amazing with a big circular movement of her little arms, clearly looking entranced. "And then my brother did it, sniffing the feather I mean, and then he was standing right next to me, we were like visitors, seeing ourselves and everybody else in this other place. It was a really good place! I think we're all better there, you two looked really young!" She stopped, suddenly embarrassed. "I don't mean you look old or anything!"

Bob laughed out loud.

"But you just looked young and everybody was just really strong and happy, nobody was grumpy. Then a man came up to me, I didn't know him, and said his name was Paul and to tell Mary to remember that the feather is the key and the connection, and somehow I thought it's time to go, so I held Stefan's hand and suddenly we were just standing like we were before, right in front of our house where we were in the first place!" Sophie stopped and looked at the two Elders who stared at her in amazement. Bob sat down, looking at the girl intently. She wasn't lying, or even exaggerating, that much he knew. What was it she had seen? It sounded like the accounts of near death experiences, and what people imagined heaven would look like, but it could all be a really powerful hallucination, too, like an LSD type drug effect.

He remembered only too well how real they used to be, his own dabbling in his youth hadn't been forgotten.

"Sophie, dear, what did that man look like, the one you didn't know?" Nellie asked, hoping against hope it might be Greg.

"He had nearly black hair, and a sort of egg shaped head, like a clever professor, you know, where the hair starts really high up on the head, he looked friendly, just a bit weird with his high forehead. Clever people have high foreheads, don't they?"

All of them laughed as they instinctively felt their own foreheads to see if they were high enough to be classed as clever, though Nellie did so mainly to hide her disappointment that it wasn't Greg. She didn't know anyone who looked like that, not as far as she remembered anyhow, although if he knew Mary he might be a friend of hers. Nellie shook herself, there she was, seriously considering the truth of this, what? Dream? Psychedelic trip? Was there a strange effect to be had from sniffing hawk feathers?

"Sorry, I'm thinking, Sophie, that's quite some experience you've had there. And what is your question again, why has Miss Kelly sent you?"

"It's just that there are seven feathers, and our friends want to have a go, you know, sniff it and see what happens. I think Miss Kelly would like to as well, even though she's not really admitting it, but she says you might remember things about Shamanic traditions that she's too young to know about?"

"Bob?" Nellie turned to him. "Do you know anything about the use of feathers on Shamanic journeys?"

"Well, I remember Shamanic journeying, of course, induced with rhythmic drumming until we were in a trance, and some Shamans used substances, special mushrooms and herbs, to go into a deeper trance, and feathers, like other animal totems, bones and skulls and such, are used traditionally, yes. Come to think of it, the red-tailed hawk had the meaning of the messenger, of truth and being decisive, and probably more I can't think of right now, but they were all good and helpful qualities." Bob thought some more, and felt a sense of unexpected irritation. He just didn't believe any of it had anything to do with Shamanic journeying. Everyone had seen the hawk those feathers had come from, there had been a full moon but there had been no traditional dances or drumming or even singing, just looking out for the aurora, with everyday matters on their minds. "I don't think this has anything to do with Shamanic anything, we all saw the Icehawk, didn't we? And he looked the same to every one of us, unless I'm mistaken? What did your brother say, Sophie, did he see the same place as you? Or did he see something else?"

"I think Stefan saw everything the same as me, we were there together, but I don't know what he saw when he tried it the first time, I didn't listen well enough, sorry." She looked downcast at not having thought of that herself, to really check if her brother had seen the same as her, she had simply taken it for granted. It was pretty frustrating being ten sometimes, she thought.

Picking up on her embarrassment Nellie said kindly, "Well, I don't think I would have thought of comparing anything either. I suppose you want to know if Grandfather Bob and I think it's safe for all of you to sniff those feathers? That's a big question, isn't it? I think we should think about this a little bit, before we can give you an answer. But until then, Bob, do you agree? I'd say for now don't touch the feathers at all, and please don't let anyone sniff them, until we know what it all means?"

"Yes, I agree, Nellie. You and the others being safe is really important, so we have to think a little bit, not rush it, and you have to go back to school. Is that alright with you?"

"Okay, Grandfather Bob, Grandmother Nellie, but can you look after the feathers for me? I've got them here, all seven of them, it's just I didn't know where to put them to keep them safe, but you'll look after them, won't you?"

Nellie's eyes opened wide as she saw the girl take the bundle of feathers out of her school bag, she could swear they were glowing, subtly, but definitely glowing. "Oh my, they are beautiful, aren't they!" Looking at Bob she could tell he'd seen it, too.

"Please look after them really well, and thanks." Sophie said, as she placed the feathers gently into Nellie's hands.

Nellie felt it immediately. The warmth, the comfort, the joy. It was love, yes, she felt love. "Extraordinary!" She whispered, and both Bob and Sophie saw her transformation, just a glow about her somehow, a loving softness, a new shine in her dark eyes which only served to underline her usual sparkly expression.

"You look beautiful, Nel!" Bob gasped, and Sophie couldn't help herself but step up to her to give her a hug.

"You can feel it, too, can't you, Grandmother, I can see you can!"

"I dare say I can, Sophie, yes, there is something special in those feathers, isn't there. We have to be gentle with them, they are not toys, are they. So, Grandfather Bob and I will think and I promise we'll look after your feathers really well. Tell Miss Kelly thank you for sending you. You're a super girl."

Nellie stroked the shiny eyed girl's forehead, what a pure little soul she was. Sophie hugged her again, hugged Bob, and gently closed the door as she went out, leaving the two Elders somewhat speechless.

"Can I hold them?" Bob asked, not taking his eyes off Nellie, who was still staring at the feathers in her hand. They weren't particularly pretty, and it wasn't the first time she had seen or touched a hawk or any other feather in her life. She couldn't work it out what it was that made those feel so special.

"I was just wondering if I should try to sniff them, or if we should do it together." Nellie looked at Bob as she was handing them over.

"I don't feel anything special?" Bob just got out before his look changed, from somewhat disappointed to opening his eyes wide in surprise. "Oh my.." He stood there, like a child holding his first bunch of flowers. "I feel... wonderful!"

Nellie watched him, the effect of the feathers, now no longer in her hands, wearing off for her. As she watched, his face seemed to rejuvenate, as if his younger face and his old face were super-imposed on each other, not quite real, very attractive, very happy, but a bit disconcerting, too, definitely not quite real. She didn't even know whether she liked what was happening. The feathers had filled her with love and joy, but seeing that change in Bob, however endearing that was, was somehow too much. It was like trickery, she didn't like not knowing what she was dealing with. She felt a fear grip her. Was it something evil in the guise of something beautiful?

She jumped up and pulled the feathers out of Bob's hand, and almost threw them on the table, where they lay, softly glowing. Bob looked startled, taken aback by her change of demeanour. "What are you doing, Nel? What's wrong?"

"There is something not quite right here, Bob, I saw your face change, like your younger one and your face now, both together but separate, I don't like this, I don't know what to think of it? Did you change? What did you feel?"

"Well, I felt great, warm, energised, and yes, younger, I guess! I didn't feel it was doing me any harm?" Bob felt somewhat defensive and cross now, Nel had been able to feel the feathers much longer, and little Stefan and Sophie both had held them without being harmed. "I don't think you let me hold them long enough, Nel, ripping them out my hand like that. I'm going to hold them again, as long as you have had them for, let me know what you see this time."

Nellie couldn't have stopped him even if she wanted to, and so watched him, first fearfully and then stunned, as he changed again. It was as if a screen of his former younger self settled on him before being absorbed by him. Standing in front of her was her Bob, but a younger, stronger look emanated from him. She didn't know what to think, it was definitely him, this revitalised version of Bob, and he looked at her with the same love as he always did, just doubled up somehow. She was watching as the transformation came to an end settling into something altogether more normal looking. It wouldn't take more than a few minutes to forget what he looked like before, Nellie realized. Now that was worrying all the more and very confusing.

"Can I talk to you?" She looked at Bob, not quite sure if he really was her Bob now. She thought of old Sci-fi movies where people were taken over by aliens, they were pretty convincing.

"You've never asked me before, Nel, something must be troubling you, I'll put the feathers back on the table now and we'll see what happens, ok?"

"Ok." Nellie wasn't quite sure whether to be relieved or sorry for spoiling some fun. Bob leaned forward, easily, swiftly, moving in a more youthful way than she had seen him move for many years, and placed the feathers down, with an exaggerated flourish, as if to mock her. Again Nellie came to the conclusion she didn't like any of this. She witnessed the change back to the old Bob in his face as he seemed to calm down and sat down next to her, putting his hand on top of hers. The feathers lay there, as if watching them to see what they would do next.

"Better?" Bob asked, gently. "Well, this is puzzling. What do you make of it?"

"I liked the feeling of them." Nellie admitted. "And Sophie and Stefan are obviously all right, but it scares me, I watched your face change, Bob, as if there was another younger one of you, and then fusing into one. It's creepy. And you mocked me, putting the feathers down like that. You've never mocked me before, ever. What if it's some alien thing, like that really old movie, 'The Invaders', was it? You know, taking us over, and nobody realized because everyone looks the same, just behaved a bit oddly? I feel like crying, but like laughing, too, how can something feel like a good thing, but be a bad thing?"

"Drugs can do that, that's why they're drugs, aren't they, that's why people like their feel-good kicks, even alcohol is like that. Do you think there's something like that going on? I must admit, I rather liked it." Bob cast a longing eye back to the feathers. "Dammit, this is silly, it's just a bunch of feathers. Or is it a Shamanic blessing after all? I didn't think it was, but I've never come across anything like this. What do you think would happen if we sniffed them, like the kids did? It's the answer Miss Kelly is waiting for, too. We can't really comment unless we try ourselves, can we. But should we? I don't know if you have to be young and strong to survive whatever the place was Sophie and Stefan went to. Our brains might not be able to compute any of it? Maybe it's just a really strong hallucinogenic? We've tried those before, haven't we." Bob laughed, remembering his dabbles with an LSD microdot, a black little pill, tiny, and he'd spent eight hours laid on a bed, conjuring up all sorts he never quite dared confessing to, but boy, it had been good. Nellie, too, there weren't many of their age who hadn't had a go, and she remembered the light streaming in waves through the window shutters, and hitting her body like butterflies, and the delicious sensations that went with that.

"Oh, blasted memories, that was special, wasn't it." She smiled.

"Yes, maybe it's something like that? I'm all for trying it again then!"

She giggled. "But I'm really not sure what to say about that in front of Miss Kelly and the children!"

Bob and her burst out laughing at the very thought of it, some things really were best kept quiet.

"I'll tell you what though." Bob mused. "I don't feel I've come down in a bad way, not like after drugs where you feel like death warmed up afterwards. I feel more like I've had a good sleep, a good rest, you know? How about you, Sweetheart? Are you feeling ok?"

"Yes, fine, like you, I think? And, you're right, I feel like I've had a rest, too, like a really good nap, I don't suppose it can be that harmful?"

Bob and Nellie stared at the feathers, less than an arm's length away.

"I haven't got a whiff of any smell from them, have you? Maybe they have been out there on the ground for too long?" Nellie asked, and Bob shook his head, deep in thought.

"Do you think that was the real reason why our ancestors wore them, not just for decoration, but to be transported to another place, perhaps a happier one?"

Nellie had to concede the idea was possible, making it more tempting to experiment further. Her resistance was softening. They were both over eighty years old, could they really leave it up to the young ones to step into a new unknown, something they didn't have the courage to do themselves? It felt pathetic to think that they were sitting there dithering, when a little boy had just gone to pick them up, and both he and his sister had sniffed them, instinctively, without fear before or after.

"I think we should do it," Nellie said, firmly now, surprising Bob. "I might be many things, but I'm not a coward. If I don't do this I'd feel like one, compared with Sophie and Stefan anyhow. And if we die, it would be a real shame, before we even got married, but at least we'll die together. That is, if you want us to do this together? Do you want to? Or would you rather not, Bob?"

"Well, I was just thinking, that I should go first, and let you see what happens to me, and if it's dangerous, at least you won't have been harmed? And then you could probably call a doctor or a drug counsellor or something?" Bob laughed, watching her reaction, secretly amused as he already knew her answer.

"What? No chance, my dear, there is no way you'll leave me here all sober and make me watch you see all sorts and me not being there! We'll either do it together or not at all. Agreed?"

Bob nodded, suddenly feeling nervous. Nellie, too, both looking at each other not knowing what to say at all now. This was probably a really important occasion, and potentially dangerous, were they ready for something like that? Should they tell someone first? Nellie looked at the feathers and listened to her inner core, a pretty reliable voice when her emotions or logic threatened to overtake her instincts. It felt alright, she nodded to herself, actually, the urge was growing stronger, into a conviction that told her it was necessary even, important, the right time.

"I feel it needs to be done, Bob, my gut says it's ok. Let's just do this. If anything bad happens and anyone finds us, Sophie or Kelly will know not to let anyone sniff the feathers."

"Ok, here goes then." Bob said quietly, less convinced but trusting Nellie's almost always accurate instincts. In unspoken agreement they picked up one feather each, held it up to their nose and breathed in deeply. The transformation from fear to excitement once the feather was in their hands had happened almost instantly, the idea of actually smelling the feather already more exciting than any fearful hesitation.

As their eyes locked onto each other, they both felt it at the same time. They were being pulled away in a swirling circular flying motion through an icy cold vortex of images. Familiar and unfamiliar faces and places were rushing past, with dizzying speed, while both of them were still fully aware that physically neither of them had moved away from their warm kitchen at all. It was their suddenly liberated minds, feeling free and light in their non-physical bodies, flying together, as if to another planet, with such an unstoppable force, that Nellie let out a small cry. Before Bob could even react, the whirling sensation stopped to an abrupt and complete standstill and there before them, was the most incredible sight.

Still holding hands, still aware of sitting at the kitchen table, Nellie and Bob found themselves standing in warm sunshine in front of the school, with the children assembled, everyone chatting excitedly. It was a spring day, April blossoms everywhere, under a cloudless blue sky. Just as Nellie was catching her breath, the school door opened and out walked her daughter Mary, laughing happily, holding a tray of drinks for the children, turning back to look at Nina, who followed her with a second tray. Nina was cheerfully calling to the boys and girls that their drinks were coming up. Nellie noticed that the girls had beads and pretty little feathers in their hair, and that everyone was in their best outfits. There was a table laden with gifts, all the Chignik villagers were crowding around it. The doors of the adjacent village hall, the Boat Shed, were wide open, the inside decked out with garlands and lanterns, mellow jazz filling the air. It was an utterly beautiful and joyous scene. It was Chignik, but wasn't, everything just slightly different, the window shutters were blue rather than the usual brown, Ken and Bianca from the store both sporting different haircuts, little Sophie standing by the table waving to them, not wearing her glasses, and the plain white plastic school mugs were replaced by brightly coloured paper cups. It wasn't so much better, depending on how you looked at it, just different, fresher, more vibrant.

"I feel like a visitor in my own body, what's going on?" Bob whispered to Nellie.

"I think we're at our spring wedding in April!" Nellie spoke as she realised it, looking down at herself she saw that she was wearing the light blue suede dress she'd been planning to wear, and Bob had his best shirt on, too, he'd even had had a haircut, and had a feather stuck in the lapel of the fine wool suit jacket he was wearing. "Look at your jacket! You're wearing a suit! It looks familiar, but I haven't seen it, have I?"

"Well, I'll be damned!" Bob looked down at his sleeves and the shiny buttons in amazement. "I asked Ken to get me a good suit for the wedding, but it hadn't arrived yet! Do you like it?"

"I do, you look very smart, Bob, but what's going on? I can feel we're still sitting in the kitchen as well, can't you? As if there were two of me, and two of you?"

"Same here, but I don't understand it." Bob shook his head, trying to figure out which one was the real him, the one standing at his own wedding or the one he equally and clearly felt was still sitting in the kitchen.

"Are we having some major trip, or did we actually travel somewhere?"

"Is this the future? Did we just time travel?" Nellie whispered.

"I could do with a sit down and a stiff drink, Nel, I'm not sure what's real and what's not now. I'm not sure if it's the future, somehow people look, well, healthier, brighter, don't they? I can't put my finger on what the difference is. It all just looks newer, fresher, warmer. How odd."

He took a step forward to see if he could walk, see what the ground beneath his feet would feel like, still holding on to Nellie's hand. Everything was just as it should be, yes, he could feel the ground as much as the chair he was still sitting on. It just depended which one he focused on more, the chair and the kitchen still there by feel, though he couldn't see them, yet he could see, feel and hear all of their future, or present wedding, depending how he looked at it. It was getting seriously confusing.

He turned to Nel, who saw the same alarm in his eyes that she had begun to feel herself. The wedding scene was just how she imagined it would be, but she didn't plan on not being able to remember how she got there, and flying through space, or whatever that was, hadn't been the plan either. Bob took a sharp in-breath as he looked around, and Nel, following his gaze, turned to see a fair haired man carrying a box of gifts, chatting easily to a tall man, with a high forehead and receding black hair, carrying some chairs, both were approaching the gifts table. They'd be walking right past them, any second now.

"It's Greg! It's Greg! It really is Greg!" Nellie whispered, her heart in her mouth, her mind struggling to understand any of it. Greg died, three years ago, did that mean...

"Bob, I think we've died. We must have. We can see dead people. We can see Greg. Oh goodness..." Her words failed her, is this really what death was all about?"

"No. Nel, stop it. Right now. We are not dead. I am perfectly alive, and so are you. Squeeze my hand, go on, squeeze it, hard."

Nellie did as she was told, squeezing his hand with all her might, as if she could squeeze herself back to life. She felt the calluses on his knuckles. Were you supposed to feel them, when you're dead?

"I can feel you, I can feel your calluses there, Bob. Is that normal?"

"Of course it's normal, woman, I'm telling you, we're not dead!"

"No, you're not dead."

The voice behind them was familiar. They turned around, and there was Greg laughing warmly at them, his friend next to him.

"You're the man who talked to Sophie!" Nellie pointed her finger at Greg's companion in amazement. "Who are you? Where are we?"

"Hey, hi there, Nellie, hi there, Bob!" Greg said it with his typically warm and cheerful demeanor they remembered so well. "So, you've made it. I can see you've realised that the feathers are the connection. Or rather, sniffing them is. Or rather, what goes up your nose when you do sniff them."

"Hi there, Greg." Bob interrupted rather more sharply than he had intended. "What the hell is going on? I'm wrong footed here, one minute Nel and I are sitting in our kitchen, the next we're months ahead at our own wedding, and now you show up and you're supposed to be dead. And your friend, who is he?"

"My name is Paul, Paul Coll, I'm a friend and colleague of Greg's, he told me lots of good things about you. I'm a friend of Mary's, too, I remember her well, from college. She rang me when Greg died over at your place, or rather Base Earth as we call it, and I should have rung her back, I had been meaning to."

"That was subtle, Paul, thanks for coming right out with it all." Greg looked at him crossly. "I'm really sorry, and I'm not sure how easy you find this to follow, Bob, Nel, but basically, what Paul said is true. You are neither dead nor hallucinating, nor are you on drugs, which, I guess, had probably already crossed your minds. Quite the opposite, you're seeing more clearly now than ever. Welcome to your parallel life, on a parallel earth, one of many, but one will do for now. You're on Earth 4 right now, the one where I arrived, too, after I made a couple of mistakes experimenting with the idea of reaching alternate universes. Parallel earths have been around all along, almost as long as the Base Earth you are used to." Greg paused, trying to judge by the look in Bob's and Nellie's eyes if it was safe to continue. They gave nothing away, just looked totally puzzled, so he continued anyway. "So, to recap, you're not dead at all, but with the help of the feathers you just travelled from Base Earth to come here. Quantum hopped, in effect. Base Earth is the physical reality we all know, and were born into, the place we chose to be rooted in before birth. The planet we all know as home. We all make a choice where we want to be. I had always sensed that was the case, I think most of us wonder about it at some point in our lives, don't we? Anyhow, I digress, but with all the research and experiments carried out, not just by myself, I must add, nobody ever figured out how to actually *see* the other universes that, as quantum physics tells us, are there! Let alone move from one to the other, consciously, at will!"

"Consciously!" Nellie interrupted. "So you're saying we're doing it all the time, but unconsciously?"

Greg nodded enthusiastically. He'd known she'd get it, she'd always been eager to understand what he was talking about, however modest she'd been about it.

"Yes! We do, all the time! I'll tell you more why you're both here in a moment, please bear with me? So, consciously moving between universes and staying alive in the process, needs preparation, physical, mental and emotional preparation, evolutionary preparation even. I was neither strong enough physically nor was I psychologically prepared enough in any way, I couldn't even cope with the intense cold you felt in part just now coming here. Did you feel it?"

Bob and Nellie shrugged their shoulders, but didn't reply.

"Well, I guess you must have felt at least some of it. We need the cold for our energetic structure to remain stable and true to who we are, not dissipate with heat and get lost. Moving our energies at quantum speed in a cryogenic state. But then those of us trying to help did figure it out, how to consciously travel and even how we can help prepare others on Base Earth." Greg suddenly got the distinct feeling he was going on too much, exhausting the two Elders. What he said was too profound to take in all at once, even Paul shuffled about uncomfortably now. Universe hopping and talking to him, he was supposed to be dead after all, might contradict every belief the two of them had lived by all their lives.

As if on cue Bob glared at him, spitting his words out through clenched teeth. "For God's sake, Greg, couldn't you have chosen to tell us that at any other time instead of at our wedding? And what about poor Mary and Nina, still grieving for you? They buried you, for heaven's sake, and you've been playing spaceman?" Bob was fuming. "Tell me then, what did you do, tweaked a few feathers and called us up here, like puppets on strings? And what about Mary now, in hospital, half frozen to death, is she one of your experiments, too? You're having a laugh, Greg? And you,

Paul, whoever you are, you stay the hell away from little Sophie and the kids! I can't believe I'm standing here as if I was in some pathetic computer game. Virtual reality, for all I know. Well, thanks a million for ruining our wedding. You weren't invited in the first place, were you!"

Nellie had never ever seen Bob furious like that. She wanted to agree with him, but seeing Nina and her Mary around the children, everyone happy, she couldn't find any anger within herself, it was beautiful. Everyone was together, just as she had always dreamt it.

"Bob, I'm not sure they called us, we decided to sniff the feathers, nobody made us, remember? I don't think it's virtual, I think it's real. I feel it is. Let's just calm down, I need to understand this. I'm really tired..so tired.."

Bob looked at her, shocked to see how pale she was. Gone had her youthful look of just minutes earlier, she looked terrible. Greg rushed to put a supportive arm around his mother-in-law.

"No, Bob, that's not how it works at all, nobody called you, and it is real, but I understand that it might look all wrong. I felt like you did when I first got here, I thought I'd died, but the thing is, I actually did. You and Nellie didn't. It's not a game, it's just waking up to another reality that's always been there. Actually, you're making Nellie ill, your anger is weakening her. Please, let's all sit down, let's have some food, too, and we can talk. We didn't choose your wedding for you to learn about all this, the combined dreams of the two of you made that choice. Nobody is being harmed. Let's sit, please."

Chapter 23
Levels

PAUL COLL WAS drumming the table in his New York office with his fingertips, impatient and restless. He'd tried to call Mary over the past two days, leaving a couple of messages, but got no reply. Only the automated message that she could not be reached. Where was she? He cursed himself for not being in touch with her for such a long time. As Paul stabbed his electronic notes with his fingers, the retro LED display responded with a brightly coloured, oily smooth visual. He was thinking of Greg as well. What would he do? He'd just laugh and tell him that Mary would pick up on his thoughts eventually, he should just keep on talking to her in his mind, and would then go on about everything and everyone being connected across universes.

Paul laughed to himself, Greg did go on a bit. Paul had so wanted to understand more. He'd yearned to be part of Greg's brainstorming circle. And who wouldn't want to be working with someone who had been so close to cracking the multiverse code? But, Paul was lagging behind all the time, bluffing, basically, even now. More often than not he had pretended he understood, but these days, when faced with all the calculations and notes Greg had left behind, it was clear he hadn't understood anything at all. The explanations had been way over his head, and had become no more than a theoretical fantasy. It had been Greg who made it all sound and look so simple and logical, obviously feeling the truth of it. It was Greg who had held his hand through the complex mathematics, and it was him who had kept talking about connections, tools, keys, and the power of the creative mind. How deeply attractive it had been, addictive even, the notion that in reality, the human mind could create and control at will, build universe after universe, and live in them all at once. It had made Paul feel powerful, dreamy, but also insane and afraid in equal measure. It had cost him many relationships, both personal and professional. Yes, he was respected as a scientific writer, as an analyst, as a reporter and as a researcher, but without Greg he was hopelessly inadequate as any kind of pioneer.

It was awful when Greg was killed. He had been in Alaska not long before, on one of his work trips, taking Mary and Nina along, he'd even sent him a cryptic message about the cryoprotectant in Alaskan amphibians, promising to tell him all about it soon. He'd been so excited, he'd talked about it being another piece to the puzzle, asked him not to mention it. Another mystery from the man, who seemed to think Paul would understand immediately, but of course he didn't. Frogs and insects didn't freeze to death, that was old news, but then what?

He swiped over his desk to get to the cryoprotectant notes, left there years ago, forgotten since, underneath the hawk incidents ones, on top of the multiverse ones, some other of Greg's bits and pieces, quotes and jokes, but basically layers upon layers of dead ends and frustrations. Had he, Paul, ever actually had a single original idea of his own? Every single thing on his desk was connected to Greg, every bit of research fuelled by borrowed curiosity, to impress, if all else failed. Paul groaned to himself, swiping across the desk to make it black again, as if throwing the notes off the table, knowing full well they were still there. He looked glumly at the desk. Yep! Still there.

Yes! They were still there! That was it!! They were still there!! Paul jumped out of his chair, swiping across the desk, the notes appeared, swiping across again, the next layer and the next, and yes, he could drag and mix the layers, however feverishly, with both hands, faster and faster! It worked, had always worked! And he could make them appear and disappear, make them visible and invisible, yet they were still there! They were intact, unchanging, safe in their set perimeters within the desk software.

"Oh holy moly!" He muttered to himself, is that how it worked? Had he just got it, what Greg had been talking about? He, himself, nobody else had decided to 'open' the layers, close them, mix the notes up in between, close them again, open them, move them, shift them, one handed, two handed, he could do it all, with the decision of his mind, moving his hand, and all it took were a few bits of tiny electronic components to respond to his touch. It took nothing, so little energy, and they were still there! Paul could not believe what was happening in his mind, he saw it all so clearly! Even, he realized, even if I disconnect the power, and kill off the desk, even if I smash the screen, it's all still there, invisible, maybe, yes, but all it takes is putting the power back on, repair the screen, whatever the case may be, and all the notes would be back again, still there. Paul sat down again, shaking inwardly. His brain waves in overdrive, he was quite sure of it, he realised for the first time in his life he got it, he truly got that this just had to be how multiple universes worked. A new note, a new thought, a new imprint, a new timeline for that one thought, intermingling with other timelines, connecting, and making up new thoughts, new decisions, new consequences, each swiped away and resurrected again within split seconds, every one immortal, their essence there forever. Immortal! Paul stood up again, pacing the floor in his office, overlooking the thousands upon thousands of windows in New York, seeing in his mind's eye the individual universes each person created behind each window, continuously creating with every thought, with every idea. They would be there somewhere, out there, living lives of their own, growing, new scenes being played out every single moment of every single day.

"Oh my god." Paul sat down again, feeling the sweat under his shirt, he's still alive, everyone is still alive, somewhere. "Greg, you're still there, aren't you, I can just tell, that's how I can hear you in my head still. Talk to me dammit, tell me I'm on the button here! And how many of me are there? Do I already know all this in some other universe?"

And there it was, Greg's confirmation in the very core of his being. He was on the right track, and spent the next hour doing nothing but swiping his screen, and the notes, on and off, staring at it all like a man possessed. There was a flow between his intention, his decision, to his fingers, to the screen, to the appearance and movement and disappearance of the notes, in this case, just a bit of energy, a current of the right frequency. All that had to be figured out was the right frequency, the correct wavelength, the precise conditions needed, and he would have the key into the other universes. Most of all, which part of the brain or body was clever enough to filter out the frequency, to isolate the wavelength to use it purposefully just like the connection between his skin, the touchpad and the screen? This was exactly what Greg had tried to find out, and now that he, Paul, got it, he would find out, oh yes, he'd find out. He was certain of it. Again that definite and reassuring feeling of confirmation, he could almost hear Greg's laugh, of pleased amusement, mixed in with a universal applause of his eureka moment.

· · • ● ● ● • · ·

MARCUS AND DAMIAN were relaxing back in the living room, comfortable enough in each other's company to sit quietly now, both busy with their own thoughts. Robin had done the perfect job clearing away the dishes. The smell of dinner hung in the air still, as much as the warmth of the visitors. It had been wonderful getting to know each other better, Damian and Marcus, who liked each other more than ever now, Sabine, Nina and Brent clearly got on well, too. Marcus had lost his reputation of aloofness, at least in that little group of 'conspirators'. That's how they saw themselves now, 'one gang, one voice', Brent had laughed, all intent on trying to figure things out.

What was the bus accident all about? How to outwit the

authorities? How to live a less monitored life, and what to do about the promise of the frog gene? And of course there was that article by Paul Coll, who probably knew more than anyone about the hawk feathers, considering he had managed to join enough dots to write an article about them. Marcus debated whether to give him a call straight away, as it was obviously a good sociable day, or to wait until he had more news about how the patients were recovering. What an interesting time this turned out to be.

"How quickly everything can change, eh?"

Damian nodded, feeling much the same, overwhelmed with gratitude and plain exhaustion. "If it's ok with you, I could really do with some kip, Marcus, unless you want me to keep you company for a while longer?"

Marcus laughed, the rough edges had already fallen off the young man, right in front of everyone's eyes, even his new title 'Research Assistant to Dr Marcus Carter' seemed to alter his self-image before he had even set foot in Marcus's lab.

"So, I see you're quite taken with my little niece, Damian." Marcus grinned. "Remember, I'll keep my eye on you! You make sure to treat her well, she is very precious to me."

"I understand, Marcus, don't worry, we've just got together, it's early days, but I'll be good to her, you have my word. She is special, isn't she. And clever. And beautiful."

Marcus smiled and nodded, already moving on past the subject, ready to call Paul Coll after all, he wanted to do this one more thing before bedtime.

"I'll see you in the morning then, Damian, make yourself at home, you know where everything is, and sleep well. Try and relax now, you're safe enough working for me. I've got some calls to make yet."

Damian would have been quite happy to hug him, but decided on patting his shoulder instead as Marcus was obviously thinking about something else already.

Marcus pulled up the details of the Century Scientist on his screen, with the contact details of their writers, and looked at the picture of Paul Coll, trying to figure out how to best approach him. What could he say to him? He'd just play it by ear, see what kind of reception he'd get. It'd be late afternoon in New York now, probably as good a time as any.

Paul Coll answered immediately, though his voice was breathless, Marcus noticed, rushed maybe?

"I hope I'm not calling at an inconvenient time, is this Paul Coll? I am Dr Marcus Carter, from North Yorkshire in the UK."

The voice at the end of the line sounded odd, Marcus had no idea what to make of it.

"Uhm, yes, so you are. How can I help you?"

Marcus took a deep breath, this wasn't the eloquent reply he had expected from such a fluent writer. Still, Paul was the man to talk to.

"Paul, I read your article on the fluke ice storms that have been appearing around the world, where hawk feathers had been found, and realised that you've obviously joined a few dots. There was no mention of the one here in North Yorkshire, I assume it occurred after you published your article. Have you heard about it at all?"

Again another deep breath, and another. What was wrong with the guy?

"I'm quite happy to call back another time, would that be more convenient?" Marcus was beginning to wonder if he was talking to the right man.

"No, no, forgive me." Paul replied hastily, aware of how strange he must be sounding. "I just had some major breakthroughs, and am a little preoccupied. Funnily enough Yorkshire has been on my mind. I have friends there, how is that for coincidence!" Paul paused, sensing that this conversation might be an important one after all. If this Marcus was a Dr, perhaps he might have known or worked with Greg? A long shot maybe, but, still, a possibility.

"Oh, you have? Wonderful. Good people here. I've travelled all over the world but keep coming back. So, with regards to the ice storm, I don't know if you heard, it hit a bus here. There were casualties, all still in hospital, but by the sounds of it, hopefully coming out of their comas now." Marcus thought it best not to mention Damian, especially over the iLink, not until his new position with him had been made official. "And, the main reason I'm calling is, that basically I was hoping we could put our heads together and see if between us we can get to the bottom of it all? Unless of course I'd be stepping onto your territory there, and you're quite happy with the progress of your research?"

"Well, you might just be the next step on the ladder, Dr Carter, what's your speciality?"

"Biophysics. Would that suit?"

"That would suit indeed."

That laboured breathing of Paul's was starting to get irritating.

"Are your friends in the science field, Paul?"

"I've just spotted your location, Dr Carter, you're in York, not far from my friends, so you may know them? I used to be close friends with the late Professor Gregory Hudson and his wife Mary, I don't know if you have heard of them at all? I used to work with Greg. Actually, it was his death that prompted me to research further into the ice storms I had heard about previously." It was Paul's turn to be surprised at the sharp intake of breath he could hear from Marcus.

"Oh goodness, I had no idea, yes, I knew Greg very well. We worked together sporadically and I am friends with his daughter Nina and her husband, Brent. It's Greg's widow, Mary, who was on the bus, she's been in a coma for the past couple of days, along with the other passengers. She's said to be regaining consciousness, I just heard tonight, and am hoping for more good news tomorrow. Nina and Brent will go and see her, of course. All the passengers are still in intensive care."

"Mary!" Paul was shocked. "I have been trying to contact her! Lord, I can hardly believe it! She just has to recover! She's one special lady! I'll have to come visit all of you folks over there." Paul desperately tried to keep his composure, looking for help in the article in the London Standard on his screen. "It says a Damian Turner has disappeared, any news about him?"

"I'll let you know of any news as soon as I hear." Marcus answered quickly. "The main thing is that Mary and the others will recover well. Of course I hope that they'll be able to tell us more. It's been a long day, shall I ring you again tomorrow or when I have news? It's very good to hear you and the Hudsons were friends. If you like I could mention you to Mary? Hopefully I'll be able to talk to her soon. Only if you'd feel that would be appropriate of course?"

Another intake of breath, the man was clearly under stress.

"Yes, please." Paul's voice almost puffed into the phone.

"Please do, and thank you for getting in touch, Dr Carter."

"Marcus, Paul, please call me Marcus. We'll talk again soon."

Both men swiped the call off their iLinks, both somewhat perturbed by each other.

Chapter 24
The Drawer

NINA AND BRENT woke up with a start, just before the alarm went off at 8am. They had fallen into bed exhausted, after leaving a beaming, but equally worn out Sabine at her flat, promising to be in touch just as soon as they had seen Mary and the others.

"I need coffee, I seriously need coffee!" Brent groaned as he leaned over to give Nina a good morning kiss, forcing himself to ignore her warm arms instantly wrapped around his neck, her soft skin. There was no invitation for any morning love making in her eyes, she was just naturally delicious. He sighed, glancing at the iLink. They had an hour to get ready, have breakfast, call in at the workshop to check all was well there and that Connor could still handle it on his own. Then a quick knock on old Spencer's door, he'd left an old fashioned handwritten note through their letterbox asking to let him know of any news. Brent was grateful for good people, last night had been an inspiration, too. The fact that Marcus had offered Damian a job, after only knowing him for five minutes, was just brilliant, salt of the earth behaviour, and totally unexpected.

"Just goes to show!" He called over to Nina over her humming toothbrush. "I always thought Marcus was quite stuck up, but wasn't he great? The way he was with Damian, and Sabine, that was stunning, wasn't it? And Sabine is great!"

"She is! And I never knew there were people from around here playing in a concert band in Italy, that must be so exciting, being properly immersed in the culture like that. I should have kept up the piano, I just know it. I fancied myself as a jazz pianist, that would have been so cool. Remember when Mum used to listen to the Amy Duncan tracks my Dad introduced her to? Their courting music, he used to laugh, oh, it was great!"

Brent paused what he was doing, he was astonished. He'd never known anything about that Nina had ever even played the piano, or that Mary and Greg had listened to jazz, he'd missed that completely, never had a clue. "You? Piano? Why didn't you ever say, Huskie? You should take it up again! We can get you one, can't we? Might be just the right thing to destress you after work, and your Mum would probably be really pleased! We could tell her when she's awake enough?"

Nina laughed at her husband, he was all over the place again, but he was right about the piano. She did quite fancy it. She only played until she was about twelve. Work! She had forgotten all about work, and everything else. "The estate agent! I completely forgot about that, I think I was supposed to ring her, but she was totally snooty. She can wait. We don't want to move now anyhow, do we? Do we?"

She looked at Brent tying his shoelaces while secretly watching Jester make their favourite breakfast: boiled eggs, salmon and avocado, a multivitamin and mineral smoothie alongside, the one that Jester just couldn't get right. It was always turning out lumpy, not smooth at all, a total fail. "You could just make it yourself, you know." Nina laughed, realising how good they both felt, with an undeniable sense of optimism as if sent by her mother herself. The morning had a kind of party atmosphere about it, life was good. "Oh, shall we go round Mum's to pick up some fresh clothes for her, reading matter, and so on? We don't know how long she'll need to stay in, do we, and maybe we should think of taking Bill something, too? What does he like?"

"Old Spencer will know. Those two talk a lot, don't they? We'll ask him."

Brent added it to his to do list.

Nina looked up at the sky, ignoring what the clouds would bring, just glad to breathe in the new day. Today was the day she'd be able to talk to her Mum, however briefly, of that she was sure, her heart filled with the joy of expectation, a kind of certainty. She'd take her favourite nighty and soaps to her and the natural alder tree perfume she loved. There is nothing like a favourite smell when in hospital, it can change everything, from the sterile surroundings to feeling at home and somehow human again. She remembered her Mum talking about that when she had been making some knitted dice on a loop, filled with cotton wool, infused with different essential oils, for her friend Janet during a stint in hospital. Oils of lemon, orange and spearmint, even some coffee essence, each aroma to pick and choose from, to savour, as she fancied, at any given time. A thoughtful gift, so typical of her Mum. Nina remembered how delighted Janet had been to be able to smell her favourite things right there in the hospital bed. She always said it made her recover faster.

Spencer opened the door immediately, as if he'd been waiting for them, and almost pulled them inside, looking eager to see them.

"We can't stay long, Spencer, we've got to pick up some things for Mum and go by the workshop, too, before going to the hospital." Nina said quickly, not having the time nor peace of mind to sit and chat with him for ages.

"I know, I know." Spencer replied, nodding in agreement. "It's just I need to show you something. And I hope you won't be upset. Actually, I hope you'll find it as interesting as I did then, and it's cropped up again now."

"What are you talking about, pal?" Brent asked, curious, as Spencer was usually a bit on the lazy side, and a little mischievous, but never quite as animated as now.

"Well, it's like this." Spencer got up to walk over to his old wooden cabinet to open a drawer. "I have had this for three years now, and have never had the heart to tell you, though I have been meaning to, for sure. I've been looking after this, from when your Dad passed away, Nina."

And there it was, the very feather that had laid on Greg's chest, right under his nose in hospital, that had upset Mary so much at the time. Nina gasped, she had often wondered what had happened to it, hating it more than anything. To her, it had seemed like some cynical souvenir, left by someone, or, something that had taken her Dad away.

"How on earth?" Nina glared at him, not quite sure what to think, clenching her fist.

"Well, when we all went to see your father, Nina, I was the last one to visit, remember? I came in late? I asked the nurse, at the time, what would happen with the feather. And, as she didn't seem very keen to touch it, I decided to take it. I thought that maybe I could figure it out, where it came from or something." The old man shuffled about a bit, looking at his feet, not sure how to come out with it. "Actually, I've become really quite attached to it, and didn't want to give it up after that. Really, I think it's a bit magical."

Nina couldn't believe what she was hearing. She hated that feather. It brought back all the memories of losing her Dad so unexpectedly, seeing him lying there like that, he who had never hurt a soul in his life. And Old Spencer called that thing magical? "Well, you're welcome to it, I don't want to come near it. And I have no idea what you should find magical about it."

Brent had been watching the old man, who had obviously been expecting all this. He was curious. "Why are you telling us about it now, Spencer? Just when we're about to leave for the hospital?"

"It seems a bit tasteless, doesn't it." Old Spencer replied now very quietly. But I think it's important. You see, I went to the bus crash site, too, and collected all the feathers I could find there. I found five of them. All are the same, and all do the same. I thought they might help your Mum and the others, maybe? They make me feel good, give me energy, I don't know how they do it, but they do, though I handle them as little as possible, their effect is very strong." Again he shuffled from one foot to the other, knowing full well that it all sounded very strange, and probably very ironic, too.

"They didn't make my Dad feel better, did they!" Nina spat out.

"Hang on a sec, calm down, Huskie, Spencer wouldn't just talk rubbish, would he? He's a friend. Give him a chance, eh?" Brent looked at her with that gentle focus in his voice Nina liked so much, it made her listen, made her feel his sincerity. And of course he was right, Spencer was a good man, trying to help somehow.

"All right." She sighed. "I'm sorry for snapping at you, Spencer, it's just, I don't understand. How do you mean, they make you feel good?"

"Well, if you'd like to just touch it, this is your Dad's. At first I thought it had to do with him, that somehow it had taken on something of your Dad, you know I always liked him. Anyway, that's what I thought, but it was more than that. I've only ever touched it really gently, not to rub off whatever is on it, perhaps your Dad's DNA or whatever, and have just been keeping it in the drawer, and I've got the others in this one." Spencer pointed to the drawer next to the open one. "I didn't want to mix them up, but, the thing is, they feel the same. Like a really good shot of great coffee, but better."

"Can you see what I see, Nina?" Brent had been staring at Old Spencer holding that feather, and Nina, following Brent's eyes on the old man's face, looked again. He looked incredible. He was still wrinkled, but the greyness had gone from his skin, the slightly red bulbous nose from too much drink and a bit of heart trouble seemed to look more normal, and there was a more youthful look to his eyes, the white age rings almost disappeared. He looked happy, if somewhat embarrassed.

"How is this possible?" Nina whispered.

"Wow, Spenc, you look amazing! Can I hold it? One of the other feathers maybe, rather than Greg's? Watch if something happens to me, Nina?"

Old Spencer opened the drawer, took another feather, let the other one go quickly, almost as if holding them both would be too much. He handed a slightly larger feather to Brent, watching him very carefully as he took it, holding it gingerly at just one end, not quite sure if he should dare. It was the strangest thing Nina had ever seen. As Brent's eyes lit up, in an expression of pure pleasure, she looked at Spencer to see if he was witnessing it, too, only to see him reverting back to being just the Old Spencer they knew. Looking back at Brent, however, he looked stronger, more substantial, as if he had been on holiday, maybe working out a lot, looking well and healthy, and very confident, happy somehow.

"How are you feeling, Carrot Face?"

"Great!" Brent beamed at her. "I feel like after the best sex ever! Sorry!"

He laughed, looking pretty pleased with himself rather than apologetic. "But boy, I feel hot! This is great stuff!"

Nina saw Spencer nodding knowingly, was it some man thing then, some testosterone kick of some sort? "Let me have a go, see if this is just something for the boys."

Brent didn't look in any mood to give his feather up.

"Seems like we need another one for me, Spencer, can I have one?"

"Be careful, don't sniff it!" Spencer warned. "It gets a bit trippy, I've tried it. Got a bit scary, though I was a bit drunk at the time, but I wouldn't advise it anyhow, not before seeing your Mum. But you'll probably see why I thought it might help her get better? Maybe it was there to help your Dad get better but was all too late? I don't know, been thinking all sorts, really."

Nina took the feather, still afraid of it, it had meant heartache until now, but she'd never forgive herself if she didn't look to see what would happen either. And it was there. The surge of love traveling through her arm, up her shoulders, into her neck, chest and face. "Oh god, Brent, you're right, this is totally orgasmic, wow!" She laughed and felt her blood circulate through her veins as if it had been made fresh, it felt incredibly good! Unbelievably fabulous! "What is this! Oh wow!"

Brent and Spencer both laughed, this was almost too intimate to share, definitely some great druggy trip this was, but how could it be? How could touching a feather feel that good?

"I'm going to give mine back." Brent said. "We'll never get to your Mum's otherwise, and we've got to drop by to see Connor yet."

"Let me pack these four feathers up for you, to take to the patients, if you agree. If this doesn't help them, I don't know what would." Spencer suggested helpfully.

"I'm not sure about this at all!" Nina exclaimed. "It may kill them, like it did my Dad!" With that she threw the feather back at Spencer, almost immediately feeling the effects leave her own body. Old Spencer understood, after all the feathers had freaked him out too, at first, until he got used to just touching them, and hanging onto them whenever he needed a little boost of energy, or a large boost, depending. All in all he felt they had been pretty good to him, and he learned as much as he could about hawks, without being able to make any kind of meaningful connection.

"I'm not sure." Brent thought out loud. "Depending on what we find when we get to the hospital, you might regret not having them? Get a bag or some paper to wrap them in, Spencer, that way we won't touch them unless we think it might help someone there?"

Nina conceded he had a point, and Spencer was already looking for a paper bag for them.

"Oh, and Spence, got anything we could take along for Bill, any book you'd think he'd like?"

Spencer nodded, pleased to be asked, and took an old car magazine from a shelf. "Here, take him this, he'll love it. And I'll tell you more what I found out about hawks when you have time to drop by again maybe? I saved some notes about them, it's kind of interesting, not that I have figured out anything important yet." He paused, looking at Nina who was obviously struggling a bit. "All the best for your Mum and Bill, too, and sorry I've been keeping this quiet, I didn't really know what to do for the best. Let me know if I can do anything?" Spencer held Nina's hand to comfort her, feeling her shake a little, and who could blame her.

"Hey, you two! How are you coping?" Connor at the workshop was happy to see them. It had been a little lonely at work without Brent there, all the other times they'd been crafting alongside each other, easy in each other's company. But just being there on his own, finishing off a table top and continuing with the toys and some bird tables in preparation for the winter sale offers, well, it wasn't the same. "I've heard nothing more about the accident, how is your Mum, Nina? It's really boring here without you, Brent."

Nina laughed at his frown, and his sawdust covered face. "We are just on our way to see her, stopped by old Spencer, as he was asking about Mum, too." Nina wondered if she should mention what they had experienced just now at the old man's place.

"How are you coping with the orders, Connor?" Brent asked quickly, picking up on her conflict, deciding it might be best not to mention anything at all.

"It's ok, there is one new order, that's just come in for a storage bench I think you might like, I told them you'd get in touch within a couple of days. Apart from that I've just carried on with that lot over there." He pointed at the works in progress. I'll be okay for the day, if you're going to go to the hospital, just hoping you'll come back soon, I don't think I'm cut out for working in solitude. Maybe I should ask Old Spencer for some of his magic stuff, that would speed things up a bit, did he tell you about it?"

Nina and Brent looked at each other. Had Connor known all along? "Go on then, out with it, what has Spencer told you?" Brent looked half joking, half serious, making Connor wish he hadn't said anything. He blushed and felt it, and could tell that they both saw it. Nina, as ever, felt compelled to jump to the rescue, she hated seeing people feel uncomfortable. "You are talking about the feathers, aren't you, Con?"

She said it evenly, upon which Connor let out a sigh of relief and smiled at her. "Yeah, I am, Old Spencer showed me your

Dad's a couple of years back, and every now and then when I go over to see him for some of his home brew we sit holding onto the feather for a bit, gently like, getting into it." We both felt bad not telling you about it, honestly, kept thinking we should, but didn't want to upset you, seeing there is a connection with your Dad and all."

"Yes, Spencer showed us, earlier, and we both felt it. He told us that we mustn't sniff it..... Have you ever? Holding it felt pretty good, blew me away. Fancy you going to Old Spencer's for your kicks, you sad git!"

"So, who else knows about this? Anyone??" Nina asked, a thought forming in her mind.

"Well, not sure really, but I know Bill does, he was there sometimes, so he knows about it. He never told Mary, felt bad about that, too, but it was a bit of a guy's secret I guess, trying not to upset anyone because of what happened." Connor looked abashed again. "There were a few times when you were a bit worn out, Brent, and worrying about the shop when I thought, you could do with a boost. I thought I should just bring it along, but I never did. It's never done Spencer, Bill or me any harm though, and, as none of us got a woman in our lives, well, the feather fix has been pretty much the only excitement round here, see? Nothing much happens here, does it? Well, not until the accident anyhow. Sorry, that sounds all wrong. I wish I'd have thought of picking up the feathers off the road like Spence, that old dog. I've been kicking myself, I have. No idea how they work though, and I've never dared sniffing them, just didn't feel right. Spence was pretty out of it, by the sound of it when he did. He said he saw himself and others and all sorts, was hallucinating, I think."

"So, Bill knew. Bill knew, and you knew, but it was Bill's bus that got hit by this ice storm and feathers, but you and Spencer, you've been alright? Yes? No funny freak ice storms, no feeling ill, no blacking out, nothing like that?"

"Nope, nothing like that, Nina, it's just like a bit of a tonic, a really good trip, and I've never felt any side effects, none of us have, just feeling good, and smarter, more awake, and more decisive, have better ideas, and all that."

"And feeling hornier!" Brent laughed, winking at Nina, both amusing themselves as Connor turned bright red. "We've got to go now, sorry, and thanks for holding the fort here, mate. We've got to pick up some stuff for Mary from her place, but we'll talk more and try and figure out what's with those feathers. Don't you get high on the job, though, please, be safe with the tools and stuff, alright?"

Connor nodded and waved, with a similar look on his face as Old Spencer had when they left, relieved that they knew now.

Nina had found all her Mum's favourite things easily, knowing her habits well, and as always admired the organisation in her Mum's bathroom cabinet. Every single little tub of cream and bottle of oil of mainly natural products were standing to attention, like dominoes in a row. She thought how often she had copied that organised look in her interior design work, with her Mum's liking for orderliness in her mind, copying it rather than feeling it herself. Tidy rooms, gleaming worktops, symmetrical arrangements looked great in magazines, but, for the life of her, she could never understand how her artistic mother had ended up being so ridiculously tidy, when her home in Alaska had been infused with a practical working chaos. A hotchpotch of colours and styles, with evidence of all sorts of cultural influences, wonderful, yes, but not a home that would make anyone organize miniature bottles of stuff in neat little rows. Even her carvings adorned the shelves in perfect order, her paints neatly stored in see-through tubs on the glass work space. The same in her wardrobe, everything ordered in perfect symmetry, ironed by her Serf Tinkerbell, which stood passively in the corner, automatically set on stand-by after two hours of non-activity. Serfs were great for checking if anyone had been to the house, inside or out, and Nina remembered to check so she could reassure her mother that her home had not been touched. Tinkerbell's silver eyes opened to present a range of colours, scanning her memory banks, before calculating the information and relaying it to Nina. "No-one entered this house.

My face recognition system detected Sharon Gossling looking through the kitchen and dining room windows on three separate occasions over the past 48 hours, would you like me to inform you of the times? No attempt of forced entry has been made."

"Sharon! Again? Seriously?" Nina turned cold with anger. That woman really was too much. How dare she spy around her Mum's place while she lay unconscious in hospital?

"Well, well, we're going to have to ask Mrs Gossling what the hell she was doing here." Brent smirked in the car, as Nina was trying to calm down about it. "Don't mention it to your Mum if she's awake, that cow on her mind is the last thing she needs. It's not even 10:30, and already we've had all these new developments! What's going on? I thought it would be more restful today, after the crazy day yesterday? All I want now is your Mum and everyone to recover, get back to give Connor a hand at least, have dinner and sleep. I'm worn out, aren't you? No more crazy news, please?"

Nina nodded quietly, trying to digest yet more information. What did Sharon want at her Mum's place? She'll have some excuse for it, too, as usual. And that fifty mile an hour speed limit really sucked.

Damian stretched out on his bed in Marcus's wonderful annexe, waking up after a wonderful, deep and restful sleep. With the tastefully decorated creamy coffee coloured walls, with a suede like finish, some beautifully framed stunning black and white photographs, showing scenes of Italy, the room was classy and relaxing.

Pictures of the Barbania band again, Roy amongst them, some close-ups of the instruments in the sun, casting long shadows, and Sabine was there, too, in a short black dress, with a flower garland around her slender neck, playing the flute. In another she was laughing with her grandfather and some others, all sitting around a table, a summer evening, lanterns lit, wine glasses raised. There was still not a single restriction on alcohol in Italy, the Italians point blank refusing to give up on one of their main industries. How good it would be, just to sit with Sabine and Marcus and share a bottle of wine. Damian thought he could almost taste it, feel the hot summer nights, his mind moving onto making love to Sabine on some deserted beach, under the starry sky, with no spy-cam in sight. He could still see that look in her eyes, feel her response to their kiss at her flat. She was gorgeous. He groaned, pained. He'd love to get away, part of him had been looking forward to it, to the romantic notion of being a Robin Hood with his maid Marian in the woods. And now?

He had just tied himself into a job with Marcus that looked like such a great idea yesterday, basically because he didn't know how else to go about his great escape. He leaned back again and felt the familiar greyness press down on his chest, that itch in his shoulders. So that's what a golden cage was all about, an okay job, a decent boss, the love of a good woman. All good just as long he toed the line. He'd be given another iLink after a ticking off of sorts, and then he would be a research assistant to a scientist who might despair eventually at his less than academic brain. Sabine would pick up on it and get bored with him, and then what? It didn't even look like they needed his blood to save Mary and the others now, only wanted it for curiosity about why he was half frog. Ok, that was exaggerated, but still.

He'd been genuinely happy about it all last night, he brooded. What was real here? Should he be content and stop expecting more, or was he looking through some pretend screen like he always accused everyone else of? What was there, between opting out completely and conforming? The balancing act of sticking in the middle was really hard work, surely that wasn't what life was all about? Spencer did that, didn't he? Just escaped into his home brew every now and then, glad when others wanted some, to feel kind of rebellious and valued all the same. Was that the best everyone could do? And was that any better than being completely blind to the traps, and at least having the peace of mind of not seeing them? Maybe even the accident had been a sort of trap, some part of an experiment by unknown agencies out there. What else would cause freak ice storms?

It wasn't natural, for sure. It was engineered, wasn't it.

Probably to get to him, or to any of the others, maybe Bill. Who knew anything about Bill anyhow, over and above the jovial chap in the bus? Or maybe Nina's mother, having been married to a scientist, maybe she knew something and had to be gotten rid of like her husband? If it was something like that, nobody would care about a little lad getting caught up in it. It could even be the boy's Mum, nobody knew anything about her, she may have been targeted? And the thing with the feathers. What the hell was that all about? It had to be a red herring of sorts, to side track people's suspicions, maybe? He needed to get up. See what Marcus thought about everything the morning after. More than likely he'd be having seconds thoughts about his offer already anyhow. There it was again, his shoulder blades itching like mad, he couldn't help but use the doorframe as a scratching post.

Marcus looked at the message from Paul that had landed in his inbox in the morning. His writing was a lot less stressed than he had sounded on the phone. Still, he wanted to fly over from New York and speak to Marcus in person. Now that was unexpected. On the quiet Marcus had expected it to be the other way round, that it would be up to him to arrange a meeting over there to put their heads together, but this would be ideal! There was much to look into, to find a pattern in the ice storms and feathers, to find out whether Paul thought there was a connection between them and possible early signs of an ice age. Was the frog protein gene preparing humans for such a time when they needed to adjust to a different way of life? Was nature giving them hints of sorts, behaving unusually, because something was changing, but nobody was really taking any notice? How much of it was created by man, forgetting for a minute the habitual naysayers to progress that blamed every single natural disaster on pollution? Dinosaurs got wiped out without human interference, perhaps humans were no more than a passing phase, dinosaurs of the future, and Earth would someday go back to the amphibian stage? Plastic eating amphibians could survive for another eternity, there was enough of it about. The frog gene, was that the first sign of it? Being able to survive longer on land, ice and in water, maybe? Without food for months, even. Marcus felt fully awake and alert now, like he had hit onto something. Were they going back to becoming pond life, in the truest rather than the most insulting sense of the word? The feathers made no sense whatsoever, they were a serious irritation, but the ice storms and the antifreeze gene, yes, for sure, it was too much of a coincidence for them not to be connected. Nature always adjusted, or rather, evolution adjusted to nature. It would be good to have Damian there, being able to watch him as it would get colder in December. The whole sense of family he felt yesterday, being in the company of those four who seemed to like him even though he was quite a bit older than them, well, it was heartwarming. It stirred a sense of wanting to belong within him, creating the same kind of family or community spirit that he admired in Italy. Sabine would like that, too, and Damian obviously cared for her a great deal, he could be like a father figure. Marcus shook himself out of his musings, he was getting carried away, Damian might not be anywhere near as keen to work with him once he saw how boring research could be, or spend any time with him at all. For now he'd have to make sure that Damian could relax with regards to the police, which meant the best idea for now would be to drive to Kirkbymoorside straight after breakfast and present themselves at the little police station there, get it over and done with. Shame they'd be likely to be faced with that moron officer, Matt Collins. His speaker engagement suit would come in handy, made him look like the boss, as Sabine always laughed.

"Morning." Damian's voice coming from the hall sounded rather flat and cautious.

"Good morning, Damian! You're not a morning person then, I take it?" Marcus laughed at Damian approaching, looking so uptight it was almost funny. "What's up?"

"Not sure." Damian looked at him uneasily. "I woke up thinking that this wasn't what my plan was supposed to be about. Not to walk into another job I just got handed, without any effort on my part, get a new iLink that'll probably track me even more, and that you'd probably get fed up with me working with you anyhow, don't know really. And Sabine might get fed up with me, too, seeing she's used to surrounding herself with smarter people than me."

The young man's worries were written all over his face. Marcus could see what he was saying. All those things were true. He'd probably jumped the gun in his optimism, trying to help, or was it more like interfering, meddling even?

"Ok, I get you. But the fact is, Damian, you need help right now, before you slip unprepared into some rebellious but futile outlaw existence that would be very difficult to come back from. What would you do now? Hide in more drains like a gutter rat, through the winter? You'd be found and locked into a kind of 'community service' of the very nature you're trying to avoid. Not good. And Sabine, well, that's between the two of you, ... but right now the offer of a job is there, because I really do need someone, and I really want to find out more about you, and how you deal with dropping temperatures. You'd actually help me more than you might think. I just got a message from a science researcher who wants to come and help, from New York, that could be really interesting, for you, too. Let's stick to the trial period, remember, I'm not trying to tie you into anything you don't want. Hell, I don't like being tied down myself, why do you think I never got married?"

Damian stared at him, surprised at what sounded a bit like an outburst of sorts. "You're feeling strongly about this then? You're not regretting offering me the job?"

"No! No, I don't, Damian, and I truly enjoyed yesterday, Nina and Brent looking after Sabine, how everyone slotted together, that to me is more of a true rebellion against Big Brother than anything else. People helping each other by coming together, working with each other, that is what works best, you know, not hiding like some criminal. You have done nothing wrong, you're not on the run because of some crime you've committed, are you, you're on the run to avoid being part of the hated machine. I tell you, there are worse places to run to." Marcus took a deep breath, surprised to hear himself talk like that. "Now have some breakfast, and let's get you presentable enough and get you sorted at the Kirkby police station. I'll send Sabine a message to put the kettle on for afterwards, she'll understand. Unless, of course, you don't want to see Sabine?"

Damian's changing facial expressions were hilarious. That lad really couldn't hide anything at all, he'd make a useless outlaw of the type he fancied himself to be, he was far too transparent.

Sabine had slept like a baby and woke up grateful and excited about everything. She clearly had the best uncle with the very best ideas! And new friends! And being with Damian was so exciting! It felt so right, they laughed at the same jokes and made each other laugh, and the electricity of just touching him was out of this world.

'Put the kettle on.' Marcus had told her. So they'd be coming round, after the police station no doubt, and then Damian should be able to relax about being seen again. Poor him, tagged again no doubt, like they all were, whether they considered their iLinks as such or not. It was ridiculous, the notion that, really, everyone was beholden to some aloof authorities somewhere down in London, people who never bothered to see what was happening in the real world. Certainly there had been no obvious sign from any grey suit even looking into an ice storm that could throw a bus off the road, or whatever had happened. The notice chip was a totally disgusting process as well. It had happened to a teacher friend, she'd been given the chip when they combined the science departments, and she was still working with old people and the disabled. Not that there was anything wrong with that, but she loved teaching children! She never looked happy anymore when she called in at the school to see if there was a job going, any job at all. She'd even work as a dinner lady she said, if that role hadn't been taken by the Serfs. The health and safety laws had gotten ever more ridiculous as well. Humans were considered a poor choice to prepare the children's food now, in case one had a cold, passed it on to a child and the parents would then sue the school.

All complete nonsense, fears stoked up after the successive pandemic years, neatly falling into line with politics of fear. Vaccines or not, nobody really knew what a rational concern was anymore. What was really dangerous now? Traveling on a partly remote controlled bus wasn't classed as risky for sure, yet, what had just happened was freaky, certainly the way Damian had described it, anyhow. Damian. Even his name felt exciting.

·   ·   ·   •   ●   ●   ●   •   •   ·   ·

THE WEDDING PARTY was in full swing, in Chignik terms. Nellie and Bob sat, smiling, being congratulated, torn between enjoying the scene and not. Remembering that really, they somehow had jumped time and realities, and that they weren't ready. Greg was there, very much alive and well, which was wonderful, but still a shock, and his friend Paul, both of them understanding how disorientated Nellie and Bob were feeling. Nellie was trying to hang on to what Greg kept repeating, over and over, like a broken record. That they would soon get used to it, jumping between different lives, at will, eventually, and that it was already happening to everyone all the time anyhow, just unbeknown to most. That only now had the time come to become aware of it, that her and Bob were one of the first lucky ones to be conscious of it. They were to be pioneers within the evolution leading into universe hopping. How lucky it was that they were so in tune as a couple, that they could experience it together, with one vision.

Bob, however, wasn't convinced at all. It didn't feel lucky. Not only did Greg go on and on too much for his liking, he was also upset to see those window shutters had been painted by someone else, it had been his job for the past few years. He was still fixing things around Chignik, not just the nets, and was appreciated for it by the village. He liked that, he liked to be useful. Now, it looked like he'd been made to sit on the sidelines like a guest, like a spectator in a world where he didn't belong. He longed to get back home, back to the kitchen table with Nellie, to be needed by little Sophie and the children. He wanted to look forward to their wedding and enjoy taking part in all the preparations, not just arrive in this ready made place.

"But, Bob, it only feels ready made because you've only just arrived, a little ahead of time at that!" Greg tried to reassure him.

"You have been through the wedding preparations here, like you will on Base Earth, but you haven't been aware of it, that's why it feels wrong right now. And remember the only reason why you're experiencing your wedding now is because it's so important to you. You have moved forward to the right here and now as this is the place you thought of the most. It was a subconscious destination you both tuned into, as a safe and happy place, when you sniffed the feather. And then you both rode together, and how awesome is that, on the particular energetic frequency of the feather!"

"The wedding, yes, it would be safe and happy, yes." Nellie nodded, but she was exhausted. She really wished Greg would just stop talking for a while. She didn't remember him talking quite so much. Even Bob's hand felt weak on hers. She squeezed his fingertips, he squeezed back with a sigh that Greg was oblivious to.

"The frequency hits the nose." Greg continued. "Like any other scent, and gets picked up on by the brain. Just in this case it doesn't take you back into a place in your memory bank, like certain smells do, rather this particular frequency opens your brain up to consciously travel to different dimensions and universes, where you already are. Our ability to exist in different universes has always been there, but has remained unconscious, we just needed waking up, like smells can awaken memories."

Paul, who had been listening, nodded enthusiastically and interjected to help. "Like Greg said, you've always travelled, everyone has, just not consciously, not purposely. With the feather as a tool you are learning to do it consciously, and travel physically, too. That's the gift from the Icehawks, and that's what you need the cold for, but maybe that can wait for another time."

"Like a magic wand! Abracadabra! 'By the Icehawk's feather'! We shall jump universes!" Greg laughed, delighted with his own joke. Joking had never been his strong point. "Please trust me, you're not in a pretend world, you're in a quantum world that runs alongside Base Earth and many many others, all according to what people create with their imaginations, thoughts and decisions.

Just think what it means to be able to travel between universes. It means gathering strength when you need it, getting help, getting support, getting ideas, getting to meet lost loved ones in places where they aren't lost. You get what you imagine, no exception."

"Too much, too much, stop now, Greg, please!" Nellie was close to tears with utter exhaustion now, she just wanted to know one thing now. "Why did you die, leave Mary and Nina all alone, Greg? Did you have a choice in that, too? Did you use the feather as your ticket to here?" Nellie didn't care whether she was being polite or not, he was getting on her nerves, and she remembered only too well how her daughter and granddaughter had struggled to come to terms with his sudden death. They all had. "Why could you not just imagine yourself alive, recovering? Why are you alive here, when it doesn't help them in their lives?"

Greg nodded sadly. "I know, it looks bad, and I'm so sorry about that, I know what you've been going through, what everyone still alive on Base Earth is going through and it's so much easier on us than on you. We have become used to traveling between universes now, so we're not as stuck in one reality any more, you see?" Greg looked warmly at Nellie.

"That's the biggest load of heartless and arrogant garbage I've ever heard!" Bob was seething. "That doesn't explain anything at all! Mary has been heartbroken with grief, Nina, too, they miss you, and they are being played with, for what? We've been pretty upset, too, good people have been grieving for you! If you are so good at universe hopping, why didn't you just hop right back to Earth, our Earth, Base, or whatever you call it?"

Greg remained calm, which didn't make it any easier to listen to him. "Bear with me, please, Bob. I couldn't make myself immortal, however much I'd want to! There wouldn't be enough space for everyone to carry on living, immortality doesn't work on a single planet, but it does across millions of alternate reality ones. Look Bob, you've got to trust me. Please. You two are both here because your help is needed to speed up the awakening process on Base Earth. We need you. We do!" Greg and Paul both nodded vehemently as Bob lifted his eyebrows, torn between doubt and hope. Paul spoke again. "The parallel universes that man's imagination have been creating all along have outgrown Base Earth. They are happier, more peaceful, healthier. Nobody ever expected this to happen. Greg died, he couldn't stop that, and I am still alive in both places, it works, it's just the way it is."

Greg laughed at Nellie's frown that hadn't left her face, but the idea that they were needed had obviously cheered both of them up. "I am only alive here, doing what I'm doing, because of my overriding desire to help save Base Earth. I died because my earthly body was weaker than I thought." Greg patted his belly and laughed. "This body here is just as expected, just better, an improved energetic copy, a perfectly healthy pain free quantum clone. Anyhow, here we can all see the unnecessary suffering on Base Earth, and it's getting dangerous. Humanity and the planet are in trouble, endangering all the lives created in all the other universes, all the varieties of life we all want to experience!

That's why we needed to utilize every creative thought between us all to open the channels of communication." He sighed, struggling to explain. "Without Base Earth we wouldn't exist, this Earth 4 wouldn't exist. There would be no foundation for all the lives in other universes, it's the ground all the others are built on. So, we need to help teach, that on Base Earth everything we concentrate on comes to fruition, that we are co-creators. But most Base Earth citizens are rejecting that idea still, stopping the solution, and getting more afraid instead! Mary!" Greg waved to Mary, who had been mingling with the children. Nellie's eyes were burning with tears as she watched her daughter approach them, looking alive and vibrant, her hair black with that stunning white streak, looking youthful, well, and happy.

"Hey, Mum, it's a wonderful wedding, isn't it? Everyone is so happy for you two! And you look gorgeous, look at you!" Noticing Nellie's tears and Bob's serious face she stopped in mid track. "Are you crying? Oh Mum, what's up?" She looked from her mother to Bob, to Greg, confused. "Greg?"

"Mary, listen, Nellie and Bob just got here, from Base Earth. It's all new to them. They jumped about 5 months ahead and are in shock. I've tried to explain everything, but I don't think they remember their time here right now, just Base Time. We need to send them back with instructions, for themselves and the others. And I'm doing their head in trying to explain it all in time!"

"Oh Mum, you must have really wanted to be here, oh my sweet Mum!" Mary cried out, rushing to hug her. "And both of you are feeling the same?"

Bob nodded, feeling quite close to tears himself. He was too old and tired for all this. But, he did get that apparently they were all right, and they had a purpose back home, and were going to have their wedding there, and everyone would be there, just like now. Except for Greg. He shook his head. "Yes, we are, but this is quite a trip for us, Mary." Bob swallowed hard. "Greg just said something that stopped me from wanting to punch him. He said we're needed. Right, Greg? That is what you said? We have a purpose still, beyond fixing stuff and being the token Elders?" Bob's voice quivered, he had never admitted his biggest fear before, not even to himself. He absolutely detested the idea of being old, useless, and ineffective. And now a good, if somewhat irritating man he had thought dead and nodded enthusiastically in response had changed everything. He felt Nellie's hand in his, warm and safe, and looked at her. "Well, young lady, shall we go back and save Base Earth?"

Nellie smiled at him through her fatigue, relieved. "We might as well. I've still got a question though. What do the feathers do, and why that feeling of love and energy with them, and who or what is the Icehawk? What do we tell the others and how can we make them believe any of this?"

Mary squeezed Nellie's hand. "Mum, would you have believed any of this if you weren't experiencing this now? Probably not, so don't expect too much. I've helped my other self on Base Earth get angry with Greg, to help me with the grief, I've been mad at Greg there for three years, which is preferable to being heartbroken, and I've allowed myself to get close to Bill, and, in another universe, Bill and I are together already, and very happy, too. Sounds crazy, doesn't it? In yet another universe you're a

Great Grandma, talking with Nina's and Brent's children they don't have on Base Earth but dreamt about, a boy and a girl, they are 15 and 16 and are typical teenagers. Both teenagers on Base Earth wishing for lovely parents like them. Here on Earth 4 they just have Kade, just like they've decided on Base Earth, at least that's straight forward." Mary laughed. "It took me a bit to get used to it all, too, but the feather helps. Bit like channel hopping, just life hopping. Different tabs open. It's neat, it really is! "

"So, what is the feather? I still don't get that either." Bob asked, getting excited now, getting to grips with things. This was fantastic!

Paul was trying to steady him. "Simply speaking they are an energetic medium to help us all fly, in all ways, soar above the ordinary. And to connect our various selves, make them conscious. It's a very spiritual experience for those so inclined, but not for everyone. But, if we explained every detail now it would only be rejected as a fabrication when you pass it on. More people than you two will have to go through some trials first to be ready for both the explanation, and the experience. I am actually one of those people still not ready there, still grappling to understand, I can't believe how slow I have been on Base Earth to get what Greg had been talking about!"

Greg laughed. "Bob, as said, you and Nellie are very unusual to be experiencing two universes consciously together, by sheer intention, and Sophie, Stefan and Miss Kelly all got the message, subconsciously as it may be, to make sure to come to see you, and only for you two to decide about the feathers. They sensed that through both of you, our voices can be heard more clearly, via your immediate network of people, via all of us, and via intended occurrences that always look like coincidence, synchronicity."

Greg's words suddenly seemed far away. Nellie felt strange, she was wondering if she was dropping off, nodding off maybe? Bob did, too, felt vague, not quite there, and he still wanted his answer, so asked, as if from far away. "So, who or what is the Icehawk? And what about that ice castle over there?" Bob turned to look at the castle he had seen earlier. It wasn't there. All he saw was the clock above the kitchen sink.

Chapter 25
The Police Station

DAMIAN WAS QUIET in the car, he felt like a lamb driven to slaughter. He'd done all this hiding, running, and now this man who talked nothing but sense and showed nothing but decency, was driving him back to be tagged again. That's how it felt anyhow. "I'm really struggling with this, Marcus, you taking me back, handing me in, in a way. What if they don't let me go? What if they arrest you for hiding me?"

Marcus nodded. "I've just been going over the story I think we should stick to. Not that we should be required to say where you've been at all, you haven't committed any crime, have you. If we have to say anything, I can say that I saw you sitting on the pavement, that you looked distressed, and you seemed in shock after the accident, that's why I took you back to my place last night. It's as close to the truth as we can get without implicating Sabine. If they ask what happened to your iLink you can say, also pretty truthfully, that it seemed to freeze to your skin, so you got rid of it, and then you can't remember anything after that. How does that sound?" Marcus smiled. "And that I've decided to give you a job, that you're just the man I've been looking for."

Damian laughed. "You got yourself a bargain then, getting a brain like mine to work with you. But thank you. I guess I'll feel better when we've got that show behind us. I'm not feeling too comfortable right now, but you're right, I'm not a criminal on the run at all, am I? I keep having to thank you, I'd be well lost now, if it wasn't for you."

"No worries, Damian, we'll go and see Sabine afterwards, that should cheer you up. And tomorrow we should start to get to work, there are a few things I want to prepare. Remember Paul Coll, the guy from New York I've mentioned before? He's interested in the ice storm phenomena and he's an old friend of Nina's parents, what a surprise that was! So there will be a lot of putting our heads together, and having someone there who was actually in the accident and awake, well yes, like I said, you could be pretty useful."

Officer Matt Collins was brooding in his office, still smarting from the biggest telling off by his superior the day before. Searching the flat of a young single woman, who had no criminal record whatsoever, using the drone without permission, and giving the appearance of looking for a criminal when it was just a man without ID involved in an accident, had been completely over the top, waste of funds, as tight as they were, and really not very helpful as far as public relations were concerned. Another stunt like that and he'd be doing nothing but traffic duty alongside the Serfs, he was told. 'It's all that stupid cow's fault!' Matt had argued, and that hadn't been the right choice of words, either, apparently. It was true though, it was that Gossling woman's fault, telling him she'd overheard that Damian was in that flat, when it was just her uncle, a doctor, of all things, that just made it worse. She had looked as if she was after some reward of sorts, and he had been showing off to her, picking up that she wanted to be taken out for dinner. He'd fallen for it, too. He'd felt flattered by a nosey, interfering biddy. He had a good mind to go to her place and tell her what he thought, but then she'd probably complain to someone about that, too. Boy, she'd played him, good and proper. Bitch. The buzzer rang, the Serf's voice saying two unarmed residents were waiting at reception. Matt sighed, more village nonsense about some pigeon poop no doubt. Which, when he saw Marcus with a young man standing there he recognised as

Damian immediately, would have been his preferred option. Shit. They probably came to complain. He'd have to behave, Dr Carter looked like someone used to being in charge. And that Damian didn't look at all like he'd imagined. He had pictured a rough run-away, dirty and unshaven, but he was just an ordinary bloke. How could he have been so stupid?

"We're here to let you know that Damian has been found, luckily, pretty shook up and in shock after the accident, but recovering now, as my guest. He'd very much like his ID's back that got lost. I'm quite sure they must be with you?" Marcus looked at Matt as icily as he could, though he was really tempted to burst out laughing, that guy had humble pie written all over him. This would be a lot easier than expected. Damian was amazed. He had worked in a male environment long enough to realise what the score was here, that Matt wasn't a happy chappy, looked like he was scared of losing his job rather than wanting to give him a hard time. Cool. And Marcus, looking like the boss for sure.

"What happened to your iLink, Mr Turner?" Matt asked, pretending to feel at least a modicum of authority, hoping against hope that this man would identify himself as a terrorist sympathiser of sorts.

"It got frozen onto my wrist, it had half grown in, I thought I was going to lose my hand, I panicked and ripped it off, couldn't feel it with the ice. Don't really remember what happened after that.." Damian stopped as he felt the ever so slight but meaningful pressure of Marcus's elbow against his. 'Time to shut up, no rambling yourself into trouble', that meant.

"I see." Matt wasn't sure whether there was more to this, but there had been no crime, those two could be secret lovers for all he cared, but he had to be careful what he was saying, his neck was on the line. "We were told you had been given a notice chip to hand in, we found it on the bus along with your iLink, too, is there anything you'd like to tell us about that, Mr Turner?"

"I got the notice chip from my old job, yes, but there's no need for it now as I've got another job already." Damian felt he was getting his composure back, seeing that officer struggle, and

Marcus nodding in agreement, looking all relaxed now, as if he was having a chat over the neighbour's fence. God, he was good. "That's it really, if you would just pass me my ID and whatever else you found of mine, we'll be on our way. If you don't mind?" Damian was probably pushing it, but he was controlling himself pretty well considering he wanted to punch that officer's lights out.

"You're very lucky not to be in hospital like the others I've heard about." Matt said, not looking too pleased about it at all. "We are obviously trying to understand what happened with that bus. Do you remember anything at all?"

"Just that that kid was banging his drink bottle on the glass division behind the driver, and then something seemed to hit us from behind, and it got really cold, like from one second to the next, a woman screamed, and that's all I remember, I blacked out then, I guess?" Damian replied, feeling Marcus tensing up again.

"I see. And now you are staying with Professor Carter? What a coincidence, after our, uhm, meeting yesterday."

"Officer, I'm surprised you didn't see Damian half unconscious on the pavement as I did, seeing we must have passed the same stretch of road within minutes of each other? Perhaps you should use your drone more wisely next time? The ID's, please?"

'Shit.' So the Professor had found Damian, something he should have gotten credit for. Matt felt crushed. He probably would have found him if that stupid Sharon hadn't told him the guy was in that woman's flat. He might have had praise and promotion instead of all that heartache in the boss's office.

Matt got out the ID's and Damian's iLink that was in a dirty pink puddle of water in a sealed plastic bag and handed it over, acutely aware how bad it looked. He could have cleaned it up, or at least taken some DNA from it or something, instead of dreaming in his chair about drones and bedding that woman.

"Thanks a bunch for looking after it so well for me." It was Damian's turn to do the icy part now, he hadn't expected it to be handed back in such a state.

"That's outrageous." Marcus felt like rubbing it in for good measure. "Isn't there anything you can get right here? How long has Damian's iLink been lying in that distasteful mess?"

"Since, ehm, since we found it, I'm afraid, we've had no reason to look at it more closely since, seeing that, actually, Mr Turner hadn't committed any crime as such." Matt turned bright red.

"Good day, Officer." Marcus gave Matt a withering look and, closely followed by Damian, turned on his heels to get out as fast as he could, deliriously happy. That DNA was untouched, even with the melted ice water in a sealed plastic bag! Pure gold! Even more exciting than seeing that officer whimper in his boots.

"That went ok then, didn't it?" Damian tried to catch up with him. "I can't believe they've given me my iLink back in such a state!"

"Don't touch it!" Marcus almost shouted at him, seeing Damian fiddle with it. "It's got the water from that ice storm and your blood in it! We can see what stories that'll tell us, don't open the bag, please, it needs to go in the lab. I can't believe that moron's done us a favour like that, god, he really is beyond dense. Sabine will be delighted!"

"And my mother, too, remember, she wanted my blood as well. Maybe you two can compare lab results or something? You have my permission to share this attractive little bag with her." Damian grinned happily, this was great, and even greater if Marcus and his Mum would hit it off, they'd suit each other. "Maybe we can go visit Nina's and my Mum in hospital, with Sabine? See Bill, too? I don't have to hide now, and that deep sea dive setting is a bit cool, easier than ripping the iLink out of my flesh." Damian rubbed his wrist. He was worn out again, on an emotional rollercoaster, but still wanted some privacy with Sabine. Going to her flat felt like going home already.

Chapter 26
Two Worlds

YVONNE AND LUIS felt like conspirators, both arriving together for their morning shift, and rushing to look if there had been any mention about the feathers left on the chests of the patients. There was nothing. The patients were still breathing by themselves, the sheets looked untouched. They looked peaceful and stable again, with less of a smile though, looking less fresh and alive than they had the night before. Yvonne had talked to Nina who was on her way, told her that there was no change as such, that it would be good to see her, and to see if her voice was registering on her Mum's monitors. It was really a matter of waiting again, which made the appearance of those feathers even more puzzling, and most of all what they should do with them.

It was Luis who came up with the best suggestion. "What if we put the feathers onto the blankets again, not have them covered up? Maybe it's some pheromones they are emitting, that helped them last night? What you think?"

"It's not a bad idea, makes sense really. The aromatherapy approach."

Yvonne replied in agreement. "I think we should wait for Nina though, tell her how the feathers had appeared seemingly out of nowhere, and then she can be here to witness if anything should happen. Should we also wait to do this when the doctor is doing the rounds, as we're probably in enough trouble as it is for not mentioning any of this?"

"Gosh, Yvonne, no, no way! What if he insists they have to be removed?" Luis felt an immediate sense of panic at the very thought, he just knew the patients needed those feathers! He had experienced intense love touching them, as if in the presence of angelic beings. He even told his husband Ian about it, swearing him to secrecy, in the early hours, and they had both tried to work out logically what it could be. That was one thing he loved most about Ian. In all the years they had been together he had been as supportive and encouraging of his thoughts as Luis was of his. It had been such a relief being able to talk things over with him. Unlike Yvonne, who only had an empty house to go to, her son missing, no partner to share things with. "Ah, look, there is Mary's daughter and her husband! Perfect timing!"

"Hi!" Nina called out to them, looking just as pleased to see them, which was nice. Brent even looked like he was going to give Yvonne a hug, and then held back, not sure if that would be unprofessional, but the friendly air was obvious, and Luis was pleased to be part of what was to come.

Yvonne took a deep breath, deciding to just come out with it. "So, the news we have is that the monitors show that your Mum and the others are coming round, as said, and you are both allowed to talk to them, but gently please, and not for too long. And, there is something else. Both Luis and I think it's good news, however strange, but we want you to witness something we witnessed yesterday. Would you hear me out and then see if you agree?"

"Of course!" Nina exclaimed, delighted and Brent nodded, just as keen, with a sense of positive expectation that hung in the air. They listened in amazement as Yvonne and Luis were telling them about the feathers on each patient. Nina and Brent could both tell they weren't exaggerating.

Brent said what Nina thought. "Well, there is no time like

the present. We, too, have learned a bit about the feathers this morning, they seem to be the theme of today. Did you know there is even a song about them?"

"What song?" Luis asked, curious.

"It's a folk song about the hawk with blood on his feathers bringing freedom, my Grandmother used to sing it, it fits in with a lot of indigenous Alaskan traditions. So who knows?" Nina blushed a little. "I'm getting a bit freaked out to think they appeared out from nowhere inside a hospital, again." Nina shook her head as if to shake off the memory of the feather on her father's chest. "But if they do help my Mum and the others and not hurt them like I thought it did my Dad.."

Her voice trailed off, no longer able to express how mixed up she felt. Brent held onto her hand, trying to pass some of his own positivity about it onto her. The feathers were there to help, he was sure of it.

Luis and Yvonne walked ahead, into Mary's room first, Nina and Brent following close behind. Mary's previously grey complexion had improved somewhat, but wasn't as glowing as last night. Luis went to the far side of the bed to lift the covers so that all three of them could see what was underneath. There was the feather, moving slightly with the draft and Mary's breath. It was truly extraordinary. It was as if there was a barely visible thread, rather like a stream of blue light building up from the tip of the feather reaching out towards Mary's nostrils. So faint was the stream, they couldn't be sure if they imagined it, and as Mary breathed in the transformation was astounding. Nina watched her mother breathe in again, and again, as quickly and deeply as she seemed able, as if she knew what to do, in her sleeping state. Like someone breathing fresh air for the first time in a long long time. She breathed and breathed some more, so hungrily, that Nina felt close to tears, that ability to breathe life, how meaningful and profound that was. As if witnessing a baby take its first breath, the miracle of it. Brent squeezed her hand, he, too, had a lump in his throat. Luis and Yvonne stared at Mary's face as if transfixed, it was as if the years were dropping off her, not disappearing, but melting in with newer, more vital skin tones.

"Look at her hair!" Yvonne whispered, it was shiny and glossy, getting blacker with every passing second, the white streak untouched, still white, but the contrast, stronger now than ever, was stunning. Her high cheekbones were more defined again, the skin firmer, as if being photoshopped in front of their eyes. Nina saw her mother again as she remembered her from childhood. Back when she looked more Alaskan than in her later years, after somehow taking on a paler, more Yorkshire look.

"Oh, Mum, what's happening to you, can you hear me?" Nina called out softly. She instinctively put her left hand towards her mother, her right still hanging onto Brent, and without thinking touched the feather on her Mum's chest. Feeling her mother's strong heartbeat under her sternum just before she was hit by the effect of the feather, a sensation of pure and utter love. Nina gasped, this time the effect was different than at Spencer's earlier. It was like being bathed in pink light, and as she looked round to look at the others, they, too, looked beautiful, glowing. As she stood, she felt her legs strong, connected to the ward floor and touching Mary's bed, Brent's hand warm and definite in hers, but the walls of the ward were no more, and as she looked down at her mother, her mother wasn't there at all. Instead she looked down at a table, full of Alaskan party foods she recognised immediately. Smoothly, without any resistance in her mind, she was at Nellie's and Bob's wedding, and somehow she wasn't surprised, hadn't she known, on some level, about this already? Her mother was there, stacking up the empty plates, watching the children play around the Shed's entrance door, where the decorations were dancing in the breeze. Paul and her Dad were talking to Nellie, who looked like she was ready for a nap, Bob was next to her, looking very tired as well. The wedding day probably proved more exhausting than the two elders would care to admit. Her Dad!

It was then that Nellie realised that something very strange was going on, she was sure her Dad had died, was that just a dream, or was she dreaming now? She looked down at her legs, they felt odd, moving but not moving and she fancied she just saw a glimpse of a white tiled floor.

"The hospital!" She said to herself, then, "What hospital?" Followed by a cry, "Mum!"

Mary heard and looked round at Nina's sudden anguished outcry. "What is it, Huskie? What's wrong?"

The sensation of standing on a hospital floor wouldn't leave Nina alone, though when she looked she stood on the green and muddy grass of Alaskan springtime. "Oh my God, Mum, you're in hospital!"

She cried out again, causing Mary to set down her tray and to rush to her, and guide her to a nearby chair. "Sit down, Huskie, Sweetheart, I think a bit of you has just arrived, your Base Earth bit, am I right?"

"Is that what it is? Oh Mum, how can that be?"

"Stay there, I'll go and get your father, don't worry, there must be a reason." Mary rushed towards Greg, who sat looking perplexed. As odd as Paul next to him, she thought.

"Greg, darling, Nina just arrived from Base Earth, I think, just like Mum and Bob, and she's struggling, would you come over and talk to her? And what's up with you all, Mum and Bob, you look like you need a rest, and Greg, cat's got your tongue? What's up?"

"Mary, listen. Nellie and Bob just left, headed back to Base Earth, but I don't think they meant to, not that quickly. Do you understand that? Look at them, they're really disorientated now."

"That's way too advanced, for their first time! Were they ok?" Mary looked at her mother and Bob who looked a little bewildered. He moved his hand to scratch his chin and run his fingers over his head through his hair, as if to assure himself he was there still. "Well, I'll be damned, I dare say something strange is going on. Did we have a nap? Or was there something funny in our drinks?"

Greg stood up, after all Nina needed him. "Will you explain everything to them, Paul, while I go and check on Nina, please?"

"Of course, you go." Paul nodded and moved to sit closer to Nellie, who looked pale and shaky. "This wedding seems a powerful date, doesn't it? All three of you in one day? Things are moving fast!" He put his arm around the old woman's shoulder, concerned, realising that she had exhausted herself. Moving from one universe to another was exhausting and especially the splitting back again, taxing enough on younger folk never mind on this wonderful Elder. Paul was amazed they could even cope with it, considering Greg had died in the process on Base Earth.

"Nellie, Bob, you are both here because this wedding has been created in your minds for a long time, but you've done a bit of time and universe travel, your Base Earth selves just visited, and then left again, that's why you're exhausted.

"You know, I had more or less forgotten about my Base Earth self." Bob shook his head, patting Nellie's hand.

"But you're right, we all know about it, don't we, that we come from another place. I guess I must be getting old. You ok, Nel? Shall we go for a nap and leave those young ones for a while, and come back later for our dance in the Shed?"

Nellie got up heavily, she was exhausted. Instinctively she knew that the best way to look after her Base Earth self was to sleep. Joining energies with all of her selves in all the universes, weather aware of them or not, that was what she needed now. She looked around at her daughter and granddaughter who were being hugged by Greg, Nina looking a bit like she felt. Having a foot each in two universes was hard work, that much was clear, but that was the new task now, Base Earth needed the information. She would sleep and tell her Base Earth self not to worry and to enjoy the ride.

· · · • ● ● ● • · ·

YVONNE, LUIS AND Brent stared at Nina, unable to fathom what was happening to her. Her face was alternating between delight and confusion within seconds. She looked amazing, similarly transformed like Mary, but she also appeared anxious, desperate even. Brent instinctively reached forward to remove Nina's hand from Mary's chest, who was sleeping soundly, completely untroubled by it all, her monitors showing no change at all. The touch of his hand seemed to shake Nina out of her trance-like state, but she refused to move her hand from her mother's chest, still holding tightly onto the feather under her fingertips. Glaring at Brent with unexpected irritation, she shouted out. "No! I'm talking to my Dad! Leave me alone!"

"Nina, Darling? Huskie? What's happening?" Brent searched for recognition in Nina's eyes, but there was none. Even though she stood right there with them, her mind was somewhere else completely.

"Is she in shock?" He asked Yvonne, who looked at Luis, he shook his head. Neither of them knew what the matter was. Somehow though it didn't feel safe to forcibly remove Nina from touching her mother or the feather.

"I really don't know, Brent." Yvonne whispered. "But I don't think we should interfere right now, I think this is something bigger than us."

Luis nodded in agreement. "I wish we could measure what's coming out of that feather, look, Mary is still breathing it in, but I can't tell if Nina is just tuning in with her mother or if it's the feather doing something to her? Perhaps Mary is visiting with her late husband, and Nina is telepathically drawn in? They are very close, aren't they, probably able to tune in with each other?"

Brent looked at him, and if he hadn't been so aware that an argument was the last thing Nina or her mother needed right now, he would be making a fuss about the crazy talk Luis was spouting. Nina was sensitive, yes, he knew that well enough, but she wouldn't be talking to dead people with her unconscious mother, would she? And why was he feeling so angry all of a sudden? "I don't like this, I really really don't like this!" Brent shouted out.

"What's wrong, Brent? Did Luis say something wrong? For what it's worth, I agree with him, he could be right!" Yvonne couldn't believe the change in his demeanor.

"This isn't right, I feel like I'm losing both of them now! We don't know what the hell this feather is, and remember, it caused an accident, it didn't do Mary and the others any good, did it, and now my wife can't even look at me? Sorry for swearing, but this doesn't feel right to me, at all. Nina! Stop it! Nina, wake up, come back!" Usually calm and cheerful, Brent was outraged. His wife had never looked through him like that, uncaring, from some place so far away. He hated it. He wanted everything to go back to normal, for Mary to wake up, and Nina to be alright. He was feeling hysterical now, he felt overtaken by something dark and horrible, and he shook her hand furiously. Nina ignored him. Yvonne had had enough. She put her hand on Brent's arm, and spoke sternly, summoning all her authority as a nurse. "Let go of Nina, Brent, immediately! You are disturbing her. You are not behaving appropriately. We don't know how she is communicating or with whom, but it's not our place to disturb something which could be a very special and important experience."

Brent released his grip on Nina, who relaxed immediately and carried on looking at her mother, gently stroking her chest, while the feather was quivering in tandem, turning under her fingers. Noticing the feather responding, Nina continued, swivelling it between her mother's gown and her hand, staring at it, transfixed as if taught what to do by the feather itself. Its tip started glowing in its own blue light, its stream to Mary's nose getting brighter and stronger, and Mary's eyelids were fluttering, the monitors started kicking into action to let the nurses know she was waking up.

Yvonne, Luis and Brent looked at each other, aghast, their panic replaced by relief and a sudden sense of optimism. Whatever Nina was doing was working. Nobody would want to interrupt now. Or so they thought.

The ear piercing screech that had come from near the office window was so unexpected that for a moment it didn't seem real. A noise like they had never heard before. Luis was the first to run out the ward door towards the office to stop whatever was happening, but too late to stop the hawk swooping over his head into Mary's room, its wings skillfully avoiding the doorframe. It flew past stunned Yvonne and Brent, then Nina, almost touching her head and settled swiftly on Mary's headboard. It smelled wild, and cold, as if it had come from icy woody heights.

What a stunning creature it was, looking at them through piercing, regal eyes. This was no lost bird, trapped in the building by mistake. This was a bird on a mission.

"It's a Redtail!" Luis whispered. Sure enough, there were the telltale rust coloured tail feathers, the tips of its wings covered in ice, its eyes bright and clear. It ruffled its feathers, sending a shower of sparkling droplets into the room and then looked down at Mary who was slowly opening her eyes, locking them onto Nina in front of her.

"There you are, are we back?" Mary then turned her face upwards to the hawk, whispered a weak 'Thank you', and Nina, beaming, turned to the others, her smile wide, she began. "I know what we have to do now! Dad told me." With that Nina let go of the feather and her mother, and stepped to reach the hawk and stroked its neck, while it stared at her, as if tame, and as if they were old friends. Mary lay, looking around with a smile, winking at the startled Brent to reassure him, and nodded towards Nina. She looked utterly happy and at peace. Nina turned round and laughed, in that joyful way Brent always loved so much and said,

"We better go and wake the others, I know what to do." She leant forward to kiss her mother on her forehead. "Hi Mum, welcome back to Base Earth, I'll go and wake the others, just like Dad told me to. I'll be right back, ok? That was some wedding, wasn't it?"

"Nina, what's going on?" Luis asked. "And what's with this magnificent hawk? I've stopped the Serf from raising the alarm, how did it even get in here? And now what?"

"Bear with me, please, let's wake the others, it's time." Nina replied calmly. "We'll explain everything afterwards." She left the room to go to Bill and wake him. The hawk, however, didn't follow her.

"I don't know what to do, do you want to go with her while I stay with Mary?" Yvonne asked Luis, who looked at Brent.

"I'll go with Nina, if that's ok, Mary?" Brent replied, then turned to Luis.

"Want to come with me? I wouldn't know what to do if something goes wrong."

The two men got to Bill's room just in time to see Nina lift the covers as Luis had done with her mother and started swivelling the feather on his chest.

"I really hope this isn't some crazy witchcraft." Brent muttered, again not very keen on seeing his wife with her hand on Bill's chest, this time fully aware though, not in a trance now.

"Wait." Nina told him. "Don't touch my hand this time, you're not meant to. I'll explain later, it's time for Bill to wake up, but I don't know where he's been."

Luis shrugged his shoulders. Neither he nor Brent had any idea what Nina was talking about, and nor did they want to interfere with what was happening. Just as Bill's eyes began to flicker, the hawk flew in, circling over the visitors and then settled down on Bill's headboard, looking at Nina again.

"Look!" Luis whispered to Brent, pointing to the hawk feathers, its wing tips were even icier than before, as if glazed, They both could see the change but it made no sense at all, considering how warm the wards were.

"Maybe that's why Nina has to hurry? To stop it from freezing over before she's done?" Brent whispered to Luis, who nodded, trying his hardest to figure out what was going on. Soon the doctor would be doing his rounds and if they were found next to some wild bird of prey, fiddling about with feathers on patients' chests, they would all be in serious trouble.

"What took you so blooming long?" Bill's voice boomed through the room, half with annoyance, and half with affection, as he took Nina's hand and pushed it away.

"That'll do now. Am I back? Yeah, I must be back, those walls are grotty Scarborough hospital walls, aren't they, holy mackerel, is that the best they can do? And where is that crazy bird, I want a word with him!"

Nina laughed. "Careful, he's right behind you, ready to peck your eyes out if you don't watch it, Bill. Oh, and Mum is back, too, in the other room."

Bill's eyes lit up. "Splendid news, and you," He turned his eyes up to the hawk looking down at him, "You've got some explaining to do, haven't you. You better hurry before you get stuck here, we wouldn't want that, would we!"

"Hi, Bill, welcome back, pal, but what on earth are you all talking about?" Brent frowned at him, relieved to see his strong and cheerful self, but not liking one bit that everyone seemed to know what was going on except for him, and Luis of course.

"It'll wait, son, it'll wait, let me wake up first, it's been a bit of a night on the tiles! Go, Nina, go, wake Karen up and little Kade, and tell him if he ever talks to me like that again I'll send him to Earth 8. Ha."

"Earth 8? What??" Nina stared at him. "What are you talking about?"

"Ah, they didn't tell you about that place, did they, but that'll have to wait, too, just go wake them up before it's too late for our friend here." He looked at the hawk, with a hint of worry in his voice.

"Bossy as ever!" Nina laughed, blew him a kiss and walked onto Karen's room to fold back her covers. There was no feather. Karen lay white and still.

"Luis!" Nina called out to Luis who had stayed behind to check Bill's monitors, to make sure all was well. Brent ran into the room behind her, followed by Luis, who took one look at Karen's face, then one at the monitors which hadn't sounded the alarm, to alert of the patients distress. The screen showed that it had been twelve minutes since her last heart beat. Karen was dead.

"Oh my god, Kade!" Nina ran into the next room. The boy lay

there, pale, his lips that shade of blue. Yvonne rushed in, pushing her aside. She took one look at the monitors, flicked a few switches and pulled the covers off him. "Come on, Kade, you can do this, don't leave us now! Did you take his feather away, Nina?"

"No, you ran past me, I hadn't got to him, had I." Nina shook her head. She stood with Brent, watching this young life battling to stay, and Yvonne who, now helped by Luis, was trying to revive him, to no avail. He was leaving them. He had decided to go.

"How could he!" Nina cried. "It's not possible, I just talked to him! At the wedding! He needs the feather!" With that she ran to Bill's bed, called to him. "Can I borrow yours?" Without waiting for a reply she grabbed Bill's feather, and ran back to place it onto Kade's chest. "Come on, Kade, don't you dare die on me!" She shouted at him, and Luis and Yvonne giving way to her, she started turning the feather, right under the boy's nose, touching his lips with it, his nostrils, willing him to live. Brent, Luis and Yvonne stood in silence as the drama unfolded before their eyes, looking at this little boy, his mother dead.

"Maybe he wants to stay with his mother?" Yvonne laid her hand on Nina's arm, upon which Nina shook her head vehemently. "I know he has a job to do here, he will come round, he just has to remember. Come on, Kade, Base Earth, you're here, come on, school time!"

And with that the hawk flew in and settled onto Kade's headboard, looked down at him and the boy took a deep breath, breathing in the blue energy of the feather, again and again, gasping for its energy. The vibrant colour returned quickly, making the little lad almost glow, although he still refused to open his eyes.

"Kade! I won't say it again, it's school time! Wake up!" Nina kept her focus on him and then thought to touch the hawk, with half his wings now iced over, and simultaneously putting her other hand over Kade's heart, with utmost love and tenderness, still keeping Bill's feather which looked far too big for him on his chest beneath his chin, so he could still breathe it in more easily. The energy flow worked, the bird emitting real cold now was willing

221

and calm. At last Kade opened his eyes, which filled with tears as soon as he saw Nina. "I had to say bye bye to my Mum, she said she couldn't stay with me, but we're together on Earth Three, she told me not to forget, but she couldn't stay, she couldn't stay."

Kade cried and turned away from them, pulling his knees close to his chest. He knew that on Base Earth he was a five year old boy who had just lost his Mum.

"We'll look after you, Kade, don't worry, you're safe with us here." Brent heard himself say, surprising himself as much as Nina who turned to look at him, astonished, not sure whether to believe him or not. Brent shrugged his shoulders. "I don't know if there is a Dad or next of kin, and I don't understand what the hell is going on here, but it's way worse for Kade, isn't it, we can't just leave him to the authorities, can we? Assuming they let us look after him? Raise him?"

It felt so good and right to say those words, and mean them. Here was the purpose he'd been hoping to find. Brent realised he'd rather take a strange kid into his home and do a damn fine job raising him than feel inconsequential, not understanding what Nina knew, or what was going on. What he did know for certain was that Kade was on his own now and needed help, and he was there and able. And so was Nina, he could see it in her eyes. They were going to be parents. This boy's parents. He was as sure of it as if it had been written. His eyes locked with Nina's, in total communication and in agreement.

"Bye-bye, Mr Icehawk, say hello to my Mum!" Kade broke the silence, calling loudly, through his tears. As Nina and Brent turned to look they saw the now completely icy, almost transparent bird take off. With one flap of its heavy wings it circled over them showering them with soft droplets and then disappeared into thin air just before it got to the door. It had left as mysteriously as it had arrived.

Chapter 27
New Choices

"**L**OOK AT THAT, Nel." Bob looked at the clock above the kitchen sink that said 3:48pm. Hardly any time had passed at all. Nellie nodded quietly, only then did he realise how pale she was again. "Hey girl, we've just been somewhere together, haven't we?" Bob's warm voice was soothing, reassuring Nellie that he was still with her.

"I don't know where I am, I'm confused." Nellie whispered. "Where am I? Did I dream that we had our wedding? Where are we, Bob?"

"Well, darling dear, we're back home in your kitchen, remember? It's where we lived before we sniffed those feathers Sophie brought in. It's our home, Nel. You do remember now, don't you? Please say you do, Nel?"

There was a pause that lasted much too long for his liking, with Nellie's eyes flitting back and forth searching for recognition in her own home. "Ah yes, that's what Greg called Base Earth, didn't he. I had already forgotten. Where is Greg? And Mary? Are they here?"

"No, my love, we jumped ahead a little bit, to our wedding, on Earth 4, as they called it, and Greg is still there, remember? Why don't you have a lay down and just sleep, I'll do the same, I think we need it."

With that he gently helped her out of the chair and led her to the bedroom, lifted her feet up on the bed and took her boots off. He then covered her with the old multi-coloured blanket she loved so much before settling down on the armchair opposite her. He wanted to give her space, but keep an eye on her all the same. Within seconds the two Elders were fast asleep.

· · · • • ● • • · ·

SABINE WAS PICKING up the cushions on her sofa only to put them down again, this way and that. She turned the CV on, then off, and decided to put a coffee on so the flat would smell really welcoming. Damian and Uncle Marcus would be arriving any minute now, she couldn't wait to see them both, she really had the best uncle, and she had a boyfriend! She had been dancing about like a teenage girl, singing 'I've got a boyfriend, someone who la-la-la-la loves me', feeling deliriously happy. She glanced at her iLink and realised she still had it on the Deep Sea Dive setting, had forgotten all about it, and obviously nobody had tried to call her. Being able to choose not to be overheard anymore, was so cool and deliciously rebellious.

Marcus, pulling up to park next to Sabine's car, had to laugh at Damian, who, overly keen to undo the seatbelt way before stopping, had triggered the car's interior alarm.

"Steady on, boy!" Marcus laughed. "Don't worry, she'll be up there waiting for you." He watched Damian as he impatiently waited for Sabine to hit the buzzer to open the door, then disappeared up the stairwell to run up to the flat. 'Ah, youth, and being in love," Marcus thought to himself yet again. Why couldn't he find anyone he was so impatient to see? Those two were positively crazy about each other. If they got married, it would be him giving Sabine away, and he'd probably have to foot the bill for the wedding, too. He felt like an Italian Papa following Damian up the steps, and suddenly wondered if he should be there at all. He was an accidental chaperon. But if everything went well today, Nina would call them to say it was ok to come and visit, they could soon be on their way to the hospital. He'd probably have to fight Damian's mother for half of the watery blood sample in the iLink bag that was still in the cooler compartment in his car.

"Wow, Sabine! You look great! Missed me?" Damian laughed as Sabine threw her arms round his neck, which felt wonderful. He was going to hang on to this girl.

"I did, and I'm not going to let you go, ever, you know!" She laughed.

"Snap! I was just thinking the same about you! We're so in tune, haha, great!"

"Now, now, put her down." Marcus growled from the door, seeing this delirious scene, he had definitely missed out on something special in his life. "Have you heard from Nina yet? We haven't had a peep!"

"Nope." Sabine shook her head. "Maybe it's still a bit early? You know, they won't be thinking of ringing while they are visiting. We're not family, are we, just Damian and his Mum there. I hope everyone will be alright."

Marcus hung his coat up, the cupboard door in front of him a reminder of when Damian hid in there, it seemed such a long time ago already. He turned to the two who had no eyes for anything or anyone else but each other. "I don't suppose you'll be hiding in the cupboard any more then." He chuckled as Damian shook his head vehemently. "Not unless Sabine is going to make that my naughty corner!"

Both were in fits of giggles on the sofa.

"God, you two are going to be excruciating. I can smell coffee, is that just for effect or are you going to offer us some, cara mia?"

"Alright, alright, Uncle Marcus, god, he's such a slave driver, isn't he? Are you sure you want to work for him?"

Marcus's iLink buzzed, it was Brent. "I'll put you on speaker, Brent. Damian and Sabine are here, all loved up, so they can listen as well. How's it going over there?"

Sabine came closer so she could hear, too.

"Well, it's been a bit mad. I think it would be good if you could come over, Yvonne wants to see Damian, I think she needs to give him a hug. Mary, Bill, and little Kade are awake, but his Mum Karen, it's a tragedy. She died, it's such a shock, so much more going on I can't all cover now. But listen, I want Nina and me to look after little Kade permanently, he needs someone now, and we hoped you might be able to put a word in for us? The Social Services are supposed to arrive within the hour or so, so it'd be so great if you could come now, straight away if possible, to get here before them? It's all happening so fast! The other reason why it would be good for you to come now is to catch Yvonne and her colleague Luis while they are still here. I think they might be able to help with some research we were talking about yesterday, some bizarre stuff going on. Short notice, I know, but please, can you come?"

Marcus looked at Sabine and Damian who nodded in unison, and smiled into the iLink. "Of course, Brent, we'd better set off straight away to get there in time, we'll see you in a little while."

"Oh my God, the poor little boy!" Sabine held her hand to her mouth. "He's only little, isn't he? Isn't he only five years old? We've got to help Brent and Nina look after him, if that's what they want to do. Wow! That's so great of them! And yes, you in your posh suit and being a doctor and all might just help, I can see what he's saying. What a thing, that's huge, isn't it?" Her voice trailed off while looking in Damian's eyes, both of them already imagining what it would be like to have a child of their own.

"Okay!" Marcus exclaimed. "I'll have a quick swig of that coffee you made, I could have done with a chill-out really, but we can't be late. Are you ready, Sabine? We'll tell you what happened at the police station on the way, so chop chop, let's get going!"

Just then his iLink buzzed again. It was Paul from New York. "Hi Marcus, just wanted to check, would it be ok if I booked the flight for November 10th? I found a great last minute deal, and if you could find some accommodation near you that would be fantastic, just somewhere clean and simple and convenient will do?"

"Absolutely, Paul, yes, the 10th is fine, there is a fair bit going on here, too, I expect your input will be useful. I'm in a rush here, so let's talk before then, ok?"

"Deal. Talk soon." Paul smiled, he had the feeling they would get on just fine, and he might get to see Mary again, in fact, he was counting on it. What would she make of it, that he was convinced that Greg was still around, in at least one parallel universe? Would it upset her? Or would she understand? She must have been familiar with Greg's beliefs and theories, probably more so than him, and likely she knew all this already? He couldn't wait to talk to her, there weren't many he could talk to about things like that. And that Marcus, yes, he was open to things, he could tell. He had contacted him, hadn't he, it was like a stage play of fortunate coincidences, if there was such a thing. Or was it more a deliberate shuffling and moving of notes like on his desktop, by someone, by some intelligent entity? One click on the screen confirmed the flight. He was an old hand at travel now, but at no time did he expect that looking for the reasons behind those feathery ice storms would take him to see Mary again. He needed a haircut, and his casual winter clothes for Yorkshire instead of his New York suits, and remembered again that, even in his head, he always pronounced that place wrongly. It wasn't 'Shire' at all, it was 'Sh'r', as Greg had told him over and over again. He still hadn't learned. Much like the multiverse theory, or, rather, fact, infact. He really was very slow on the uptake.

Chapter 28
Learning to Juggle

NELLIE WEPT IN her dream, Bob heard it clearly, just before he opened his eyes and looked over to her from the now very uncomfortable armchair. It had seemed cosy enough when he first settled into it. He'd had a deep and dreamless sleep. Seeing her lie there, tears glistening on her beloved old cheeks, he wondered if he could do the task justice, the one he had set himself at the wedding on Earth 4. How could he possibly let people know about the existence of their lives in so many universes, and that their imaginings on Base Earth were vital to everyone? What could he do, an old man in his eighties, from a tiny community in the wilderness of Alaska? The Inuit wisdom ran deep and wide, and he looked the part, that alone would give his words meaning and authenticity, he knew that. Someone had suggested in the past that he should have his photo taken and sell it to publishers, as he apparently had one of those great faces the likes of which could be seen on posters and cards, with wise quotes, whether authentic or not. He fancied that it would take more than a sentence and one's face on a poster to influence the world in any way, to think otherwise would be vain and ridiculous. He smiled at the thought.

He didn't want to disturb Nellie, but it was hard seeing her upset even in her sleep. He had never seen her so fragile. She looked frail, despite her tall strong frame. Bob looked past her through the door and into the kitchen. The feathers were still on the table where they had left them. Would it help her, to be near them at least? They had felt so good touching them. Maybe it would make her stronger, just having one close? The temptation was strong. But what if it was dangerous, draining them again in some mysterious way? The journey to the other Earth had obviously drained Nellie too much. Or was it the shock of seeing Greg, believed dead? It was a little disconcerting to say the least to talk to dead people, who would believe them? And he never got the answer about the hawk, nor that frozen castle. What good was an ice castle to anyone? Was there such a thing as a god living in one? No, that sounded much too far fetched, he didn't really believe in gods, let alone that there was one living on one version of the Earth but not on another. He could make no sense of it.

Nellie stirred a little, pulling the blanket closer to her chin like a little girl, exposing her socked feet. He would have to go and turn the heating up, and really, make some food, it was a bit tricky to know when they had last eaten, considering they had been time traveling. Bob heaved his large frame out of the chair, he was stiff and ached all over. It was troublesome getting his legs working properly. A bit of a feather kick wouldn't do him any harm, that much he knew, and Paul had said that tuning in would invite the energy of all his multiverse selves, doubling, at least, his own energy, it was just a matter of being open to it. That Paul was a funny fish, but okay though, Bob thought. If that's how it worked, and he had no reason to doubt it, he'd just hang on to the feather while he was turning the heating up, and put the kettle on, he would see if the smell of some hot cloudberry juice with cinnamon would cheer Nellie up as she was about to wake up. Maybe he should add that shot of Vodka, too, to warm her up a bit. He'd have a coffee and a shot of Brandy in it, that and a feather fix would see him right. Bob chuckled, it had been a long time, since the 60s, that he thought of getting a fix of anything other than caffeine. He'd never heard of a feather doing anything at all, hawk or otherwise.

There was a knock on the door. A polite little knock, coming from little knuckles, Bob recognised it immediately. It was Sophie, coming to see what their answer would be, whether they'd say it was all right for all of them to touch the feathers at school, including Miss Kelly. 'Now what.' Bob was scratching his chin, with a sense of total confusion, something akin to panic. He could really do with Nel now to talk it over.

"Is that little Sophie?" Nellie's call, far too weak for his liking, came through from the bedroom.

"Yes, Darling, it will be. What do you want me to say?"

"Tell her we're going to have an assembly in the Shed, we'll let everyone know the time and day, but not to do anything before then. We will keep hold of the feathers for now, and if they find any more to bring them here straight away, not let anyone sniff them. And tell her I'm resting." She sounded weak, then strong and firm and now weak again, as if this announcement had cost her all the strength she could muster, while Bob opened the door to let Sophie in. It was blowing a gale out there, and the girl was shivering.

"Come in, little one. I'm just making Grandmother Nellie some hot cloudberry juice, would you like some?"

"No, thanks, Grandfather Bob." Sophie was a little embarrassed, she had just caught Nellie's voice and how weak she sounded. She had never heard her like that before. It was suddenly a bit scary to be in the company of old age, as if they were of some place she didn't know about yet, and didn't really want to know either.

"Don't worry, Sophie, Nellie is just a little tired, she'll be alright. Just to make sure you understood, I'll just tell you again what she said, and you make sure Miss Kelly and everyone at class hears about it, all right? And don't you and Stefan go out there on your own now, it's blowing a gale anyhow, and the forecast isn't good. Say hello to your parents from me and mind how you go." Bob smiled at her again, and she nodded politely in response, but she could tell he was preoccupied and worried. She didn't think she'd really known him before, now he was easy to read, like family, like a familiar really old uncle.

She didn't want to be that old, she decided. No, she wanted to be young and strong but also she knew she wanted to be a leader. She had felt it strongly ever since she had sniffed the feather and seen the other place with that icy castle. It was that kind of world she wanted to be in, suddenly she could see it so clearly. She was going to be a just and generous Queen one day, yes, that was it.

"I'm going to be a Queen, Grandfather Bob, I'm going to make everything better." As soon as she said it she covered her mouth with her hands, shocked at what she had just admitted to. It didn't sound like her at all, but she had meant it! Bob looked at her in amazement. A Queen? Where would she get such an idea from? The few Queens still in existence in various countries around the world had little influence, neither had any Kings.

"Well, well, Sophie, where did that come from? How extraordinary! I had no idea! It's a good thing to have a dream and go for it, you know."

Sophie was relieved, he hadn't made fun of her. "Thanks, Grandfather Bob. For not laughing at me and being so nice about it. I don't think I should tell anyone else yet though, should I. Maybe you and Grandmother Nellie know things nobody else does and could help me?"

She saw herself as a Queen, strong and straight, walking past sad people then touching them with her sceptre, making them happy, giving them ideas, endless ideas. They would be free to do what they wanted to do and not be sad anymore, and really like what they were doing. "Ideas are the real wealth, Grandfather Bob, I want to help people have ideas, and they will listen to me if I'm a Queen, won't they?"

"I expect they will, Sophie, hang on to that thought, it's a good one, and a very grown up one, too. You'll make a wonderful Queen!" Bob was smiling now, he understood what was happening. It was the increase in imagination that they were told Base Earth needed. Maybe the feather and seeing another universe had freed that little girl's mind? "Did you hear that, Nel? What she said, that she wanted to be Queen?"

"I did, Bob, I did, isn't it wonderful? It's happening, isn't it?" Nellie sounded better again, and looked up from under the blanket when Bob came in with their drinks, his brandy smelling strong enough for her to know she'd have her little shot of vodka, too. He knew what she needed. He sat down on the edge of the bed, helped her sit up, putting the pillows behind her back and looked at her. "How are you feeling, my love? You got me a bit worried before. You looked upset, what upset you?"

"You don't know? Bob, really, you don't know?"

"I have no idea, Nel, what made you sad enough to cry into your pillow in your sleep?"

"Oh, you know.. that we're in two universes and only just now got together, in both places! We've been so stupid, we could have been together all these years and travel to England together to visit Mary and Greg and Nina and could have done all these things together, and I never thought of it! I just enjoyed having you around, but we missed out on so much!"

Bob was dumbfounded. Not for one second had it ever occurred to him that she should feel that way. Not for one single second. But now he saw it, it was so obvious. Yes, they both wished they had been braver, that was true all right. He'd been slow and stupid not to ask her decades ago. All those times when she had been on her own, worried about traveling alone to England to see Mary, Greg and Nina, they could have gone together. They could have traveled through Europe, through Africa or India even. They could have done anything. He could have built her a better house than this old place. What a fool he'd been. "Oh my Nellie, forgive me, I'm so sorry." Bob shook his head sadly, and kissed her hands, over and over again. "You're right, you're so right, we were lacking the imagination, weren't we, and now we know, it's so obvious."

"Do you think we may have known better on any of the other Earths?" Nellie smiled, already feeling better at the thought, just knowing that Bob understood, and felt the same. "You know, that would make sense, wouldn't it. Just think, we might be celebrating our 30th anniversary or something somewhere, how good is that?"

"Maybe, just maybe we really can be anything we like, somewhere? It really is the thought that turns into reality, isn't it. On this Earth as much as anywhere else. It shows how important it really is to make sure to think right then, isn't it, Nel. We can't think of regrets now, can we? And we can't think of getting too old."

Nellie nodded, looking eager again. "You're right, Bob, yes, you are. I felt everything was too late and thought I was going to die, all of a sudden, but if we are supposed to teach that to the others, well, we need to be around a while yet, don't we. And we have the feathers to help. That's it, isn't it! To use the feather with the right intention, to double up what is right for all the different planes you're living on! That is true freedom, isn't it!" Nellie was now moving her hands about, shiny eyed, her previous tiredness gone. Bob couldn't help but laugh at her, she was really the most wonderful woman.

"And maybe, really, the feathers aren't necessary at all, once that is really understood? Oh Bob, just think, Greg knows all that, and Mary doesn't know anything about any of this, not consciously yet anyhow. We'll have to ring Nina and ask her, how Mary and the others are, and maybe to look for some feathers over there? Maybe it's even a sign from Greg? I don't know, but can I have another drink, just the same? And then I'll get up and we'll have some dinner, shall we?"

Bob hugged her, and felt sudden positive stirrings that in no way meant he was old at all. He had definitely missed out on years of passion with this woman. But life could still be good, the only secret was not to give up on it, that's all any of this meant, really. So astonishingly simple.

Mary looked around in her hospital bed, she couldn't believe that this sad place was the reality she had come back to. So, she was in a hospital somewhere, it looked like Scarborough, and

Nina had been there, and Brent, too. But no Greg. Greg wouldn't be here, he was at the other place. She had talked to him, just minutes before, about how hard it must have been for Nellie and Bob to learn of the existence of multi-universes. And now she was back here she wondered who on earth, or rather who on Base Earth she could mention this to, surely everyone would just assume that she had had dreams, or a near death experience. Was it a near death experience? Is this what that meant, making yourself open to one's other planes of existence, no matter what the body was doing? Was that even possible? The body was after all just a temporary shell to experience a physical life. How did she even get here, what had happened? She tried hard to remember, the last thing she could think of was being in the bus, Bill being annoyed with the bored little boy bashing his bottle about while his mother ignored him.

Oh, and feeling very cold, so cold. And then the sensation of being thrown forward, as if hit from behind. So was that how stepping into another world was done, making it look like some sort of collision or accident? Could she even move her body? Mary tried to wriggle her toes, and much to her relief she could feel her toes scraping against the top sheet. She could feel her feet and hands, she tried them, all good, she could wiggle her fingers, though it was somewhat difficult to move her arms, they felt a little heavy. How long had her body been asleep? She tried to lift her legs and felt the catheter. She groaned, that wasn't fun at all. Mary turned her head, seeing the monitors, BP 95/70, 'not bad', so far so good. I can move my legs and turn my head and now my arms are obeying, where was the button to call the nurse?'

The monitor kicked into action, picking up on the brain activity of her question and duly sounded the alarm.

"Oh, hello, Mary!" Yvonne called out with a smile as she rushed into the room and to Mary's bed. "Welcome back! How are you feeling?"

"Oh, it's you, Yvonne, how nice to see you! How long have

I been out? Am I hurt? Has my body reassembled ok? And the others?"

Mary's eyes were full of questions that needed to be answered gently, one by one, Yvonne knew. Noticing Mary's unusual way of asking, she considered all that hawk business and what had been going on. How much of it would Mary remember? The monitors showed no undue stress, which was good, actually, all the signs were that Mary was doing extremely well.

"No, not hurt, Mary, you were all hit by some icy current and got very cold but it all looks fine, and no bones are broken. Nina is here, too, she just went into Bill's room, he's just come round, too. Shall I go fetch her? And we'll get you free of all the tubes very soon, I'm just pleased you're back with us. I'll get you a drink, you might manage some water or some sweet tea perhaps?"

Mary nodded gratefully, what a kind woman that Yvonne was, she was the mother of Damian who had also been in the bus, she hadn't mentioned him. Was he still asleep? She hadn't seen him on Earth 4, or 10, or 16, for that matter, the only places she had had the chance to visit consciously. And she doubted very much he'd have been invited to the Intergalactic Council Hall of Ice, ICHI for short, that wonderful ice castle that was perfectly designed to host select members of the various galactic councils who supported humans in their development towards the 4th, 5th and further dimensions. It took some very special individuals to be awake enough to be invited to it. Had Damian already moved to the 7th, the non-physical dimension of the greater infinite? She would have to ask. It was hard to remember what people on Base Earth actually knew, she'd have to tread carefully, play it safe for now. Mary reached up feeling the familiar tickle on her chest, good, the feather was still there, she would need it to travel, and show others the way. Being able to touch it with her fingertips was so comforting, she hadn't imagined or dreamt any of it, she had just learned a whole lot of the secrets of life, what a clever thing that was to cloak it all as some kind of accident. She laughed to herself, remembering Bill's relief on his face when he could finally tell her how he felt about her on Earth 16, how royally fed up he was playing second fiddle to Greg in the other places. And how Greg had teased them on Earth 10 that they'd have his blessing on Base Earth, seeing he was so busy and their Base Earth life needed a bit of excitement. Did people on Base Earth know that? Mary tried to think, the fact that anyone you wanted a relationship with, sincerely, you'd be with them somewhere. Was that even talked about yet or not? It would be very tricky to remember to think within the narrow framework of just one Earth, one life, that would take some getting used to, especially as she fully intended to visit Greg again at the earliest opportunity. And the self healing, that was so good, just tuning into your healthy selves on other Earths, well, that's all it took, so easy. Had she not known that before? To find yourself in a hospital bed when she had just been dancing on Nellie's and Bob's wedding, that was just silly. But perfectly all right at the same time.

Nina rushed in closely followed by Brent, clearly relieved to see her, giving her a kiss on the cheek and a gentle hug.

"Hello, Huskie." Mary smiled. "So here you are. We did a great job between us at Grandma's and Bob's wedding, didn't we! The buffet went down a treat! And we stopped Kade from eating *all* the desserts. Does that boy ever stop eating? How do you feed him? Still got your feathers?"

Brent couldn't believe what he was hearing. How did Mary know about Kade? Had she somehow seen the future, was that possible, in a coma? And what did she know about the feathers?

"Sorry to interrupt." Luis stuck his head through the door. "But Social Services are here already for Kade, checking his mother's monitors to confirm her passing. If you want to talk to them, Nina and Brent, best do it now. Oh hello, Mary, welcome! Glad to have you back with us!" Luis sounded cheerful, but the stress of what had been happening, and, not knowing what to do for the best now, had started showing in his face.

Mary tried to sit up, with now eager eyes. "Nina, is that about taking care of Kade? Adopting him? I can help, I talked with Karen just earlier, she knows you two are meant to look after him here, you have her blessings."

"Mum, I don't know really how you know all this stuff, are you sure? I'm confused, a lot has happened, hasn't it, but it's all too fast and blurry. You're not going to mess up anything? Sorry, but you're sounding pretty out of it." Nina bit her bottom lip, and wrung her hands in front of her chest, feeling tight as a bow. Just moments before she had been certain about so many things, but now she could barely remember anything, she felt as if she was losing her mind. She and Brent hadn't really had a chance to think or talk about anything properly, but if they didn't speak up now, Social Services would surely take little Kade as soon as the doctors would release him. Her heart would break, she was sure. Kade was hers, she felt it, with all of her being. It was the only thing she was sure of now, everything else fading fast, like a disappearing dream.

"Trust me, Sweetheart." Mary patted Nina's hand. "Get Kade in here with us and Yvonne, get Social Services to come in here, so we're all together. As a group we'll be fine, it's how it works. Are you supporting Nina and Brent in this, Yvonne and Luis?"

"Yes, of course, I do!" Yvonne explained, feeling the magic of the moment, and Luis nodded his head in agreement, aware that he had to hurry to wheel the boy into Mary's room. Considering it was supposed to be an intensive care ward this was highly irregular, a wheelchair rather than the bed would probably be acceptable. "I'll be right back!" Already halfway out the door, heading for the nearest wheelchair, he grabbed it and ran into Kade's room as fast as he could, half expecting the hawk to be there again. It wasn't, but its very presence still seemed to linger, as if it was partaking in the proceedings. Luis knelt down in front of the boy. "Kade, the monitors show that you're okay to leave the hospital if the doctor agrees it's safe to, and you do look fine to me. But I have to make sure of something. Do you know about Nina and Brent looking after you? Have you been told that this is going to happen, and how do you feel about this? We have to hurry a little bit, as some people are here, government people, and they might not agree with it at all, if they asked you who you want to stay with, well, what would you say to them?"

Kade looked at him, with an oddly resigned expression in his eyes, as if he was surprised to be asked. "That Nina and Brent are my new Mummy and Daddy and that my Mum wanted them to be, that she told me so."

Luis looked at this boy who had spoken his truth sadly but calmly, not overly upset, as if he had been expecting it all along. What had been going on? Where had all these people been in their comatose state? "Come on then little man, let me take you to the other room where Nina and Brent and Mary are, and maybe you can tell the people from the social services the same thing? I think you're being very brave about everything, little soldier." With that Luis lifted the little boy into the wheelchair that was far too big for him and pushed him towards Mary's room.

"I'm not going to be a soldier, I'm going to be on the Ice Hall Council." Kade replied, again totally calm and Luis saw that this five year old had his strange sounding future very clearly mapped out. "Grandma Mary, oh, Grandma Mary, you are here, too? I didn't know!" little Kade cried out as he saw Mary sat up in her bed, supported by cushions, not looking too tired at all, and nearly climbed onto her bed if Yvonne hadn't stopped him jumping off his chair before he could hurt her. Instead he took both Nina's and Brent's hand on either side of him and said, loudly and strongly.

"These are my new Mummy and Daddy now, aren't they, Grandma Mary!" He looked up at Nina and Brent looking down at him in total amazement just as the suited man and woman from Social Services walked in, to witness the scene just at the right time.

"Yes, my little darling, just like your mother wanted, she asked me to make sure Nina will be your new Mummy and Brent your new Daddy. She was very clever, your Mum, wasn't she, she knew just what would be best for you." Mary had spoken without a hint of pretence, and there could be no doubt that there was the most convincing air of family love in the room for even the most hardened of Social Services officers to pick up on.

"This is all very unusual." The woman said, surveying the room, seeing nothing but a boy hanging onto a couple's hands who looked at him adoringly, and a grandmother who looked like a slightly weak but feisty enough matriarch in control of it all.

"We are simply following the mother's wishes, and only have Kade's best interest at heart." Brent replied, looking quite like the protective father already. "If we could sign the release papers for Kade that would really help things along."

"Where is the biological father of the boy?" The officer asked, looking through his record screen. "I can't see the name on Kade's entries?"

The silence amongst the grown-ups was deafening, this wasn't good, not to know.

"My Mum told me he'd gone to heaven, that he went to heaven before I was born." Kade broke the silence, causing an embarrassed shuffling of feet by everyone in the room. Nobody had known, and everyone felt they should have, for some reason. The woman officer knelt down in front of Kade, searched into his eyes with hers, warmly. "My name is Katherine, I know what it's like when a Daddy's gone to heaven, mine did, too. And you want to stay with Mr and Mrs Daniels here, do you?"

"Yes, they are my new Mum and Dad now, it's what I want, and they are going to teach me to be a good Ice Hall Councillor."

Katherine looked up at her colleague, now a little uneasy, who shrugged his shoulders, clearly putting it down to some fantasy.

"Well, I think, being an Ice Hall Councillor is a jolly good thing to be."

He laughed. "My name is Colin, and maybe you can teach me to become one, too?"

"I don't think so, you have to be chosen." Kade replied so seriously that the grown-ups couldn't help but laugh, except Mary, who nodded slowly in agreement. Nina put her arm around his shoulders, overcome by overwhelming love. She had never been a mother, but she would learn, and her Mum would help her. And Brent already looked like a wonderful father. They'd work it out, somehow.

Chapter 29
The Unexpected

DAMIAN HAD VOLUNTEERED to sit in the back with Sabine, with much giggling and teasing, Marcus grumbling that they were beyond nauseating, and of course, felt envious as can be. "What happened to your rough edge, I thought you were a man's man, Damian, not all sloppy like that?"

Damian laughed, he was far too happy to bite. It was true though, he had changed a lot, it did occur to him, too, but there again, he felt better than he had ever felt. The factory seemed a long time ago, now he couldn't wait to see his mother and just get on with his life with Sabine, depression was a thing of the past, he was sure of it. "It's all a choice, isn't it, Marcus, to reinvent ourselves. I've just reinvented myself to be a happy man, and Sabine is doing wonders for the cause. It'll be good to work with you, find out what's going on, and interesting for you to meet up with that Paul, won't it? Are you wanting me out of your Dad's space so you can put him up? I don't want to impose you know. I can commute when my car's fixed, whatever it takes, I'll be reliable, don't worry, I'll be at work in time. How many more days off have you got?"

"Well, it's good of you to think of it all, Damian, Sabine and I would have got back from Italy the day after tomorrow, and I was purposely vague about my return, which means nobody is expecting me just yet. With regards to Paul, I don't feel it's appropriate to invite him to stay with me, seeing as I don't really know him, and he might feel very uncomfortable, too. And, as to you, yes, fix your car up, definitely, but depending on your blood results I wouldn't mind keeping an eye on you, see how you change as the weather gets colder, but we've talked about that before, and we can be flexible. Won't you be missing your usual life with your mother? She'll need some quality time with you now! You moving out would be a big change for her."

"You know, Marcus, we have a really good thing going, her and me, she isn't like some mother hen, it was just a really good arrangement living together. It worked well, I lived close to work and we shared the chores, but I don't think Mum expected me to live at home forever. She'll probably be happy to see me go, it's more natural, isn't it. I'm no mummy's boy, but I do like her a lot, I am really proud of her actually. She's very together, very sound, a brilliant nurse, and hasn't sold out. You'll like her, too, you'll see." Damian just stopped himself from saying any more, playing matchmaker was just the worst, and tacky, but he could see them together, it was the oddest thing, his mother and Marcus, yes, somehow it was a given. Just like him and Sabine being meant for each other. Marcus was right, he was getting totally sloppy.

"Do you think your mother will be able to get part of your blood sample to the lab straight away? And keep some back for me?"

"I wouldn't mind some myself." Sabine laughed. "I might have different testing substances in the school lab, that might help find out more. I can tap you for some blood any time, Damian, but that melt water, wow, I'm really curious to look at that."

"All you guys want me for is my blood." Damian grumbled. "And there I was hoping it was love".

"You said the L-word." Sabine whispered and cuddled up to him, happily oblivious to Marcus rolling his eyes. He'd lost all their attention again.

"Damian! There you are, let me take a look at you, are you

all right?" Yvonne rushed up to her son, overjoyed to see him. "It seems ages since you disappeared, are you hurt anywhere?" Yvonne breathed his smell, there was nothing better than the smell of one's own child. No matter how old they were, it was like a time warp looking glass, breathing in memories of the most important person in life, it was wonderful to feel his strong arms around her. He looked good, softer than expected, without the growl she had seen him with recently. Yvonne smiled as he let her go and turned to pull Sabine closer who had watched the affection between them, and decided it was a good sign, a man who treats his mother well would treat all women well, she was pretty sure of that.

"And here's Sabine, Mum, maybe you can guess, we're a bit of an item now. Just think, I've got myself a girlfriend. Isn't she just wonderful?"

Yvonne and Sabine gave each other an almost sisterly hug.

"It's good to see you again, Sabine." Yvonne smiled. "And who is this?" She looked over Sabine's shoulder to take in Marcus, who was smallish, like her, but looked totally in charge, quite the authority.

"Dr Marcus Carter, biophysicist and more importantly, my uncle." Sabine turned and still holding on to Yvonne's elbow pulled her uncle closer, so the two of them could shake hands. It was like some slow motion scene that seemed straight out of some corny romantic movie, Yvonne and Marcus locking eyes, then almost automatically shaking hands, and desperately trying to sound normal.

'Unreal!' Damian thought. 'I just knew it, those two are meant for each other.' Sabine saw it, too. Their attraction hung in the air like a foregone conclusion, the electricity was palpable.

"Wow." Sabine mouthed to Damian. "Did you see that?"

Damian nodded, amazed, at his mother who was always in control of herself, now stumbling over her own words, looking somewhat flushed. As for Marcus, well, that was positively hilarious, no clue how to chat up a woman.

"We mustn't forget about the sample, Uncle Marcus!" Sabine tried as smoothly as she could to somehow bring the conversation back to some kind of normality. It was almost disconcerting to see her uncle struggle like that, he who could be the smoothest character ever! Yvonne breathed out, nervously laughing now, relieved to be helped by Sabine with something to talk about. What was wrong with her? She had made a complete fool of herself, couldn't even remember what she had said. But, oh how she felt drawn to this man, he was utterly fascinating, captivating even. She had to pull herself together.

"...I don't really want to lose it now, or contaminate it in any way. It's too good an opportunity to miss..."

She heard Marcus say, and realised she had no clue what he was talking about. Damian and Sabine both looked at her, and only then she saw that Damian had somehow produced a sealed clear pouch with an iLink suspended in its pinkish watery fluid.

"Sorry, I missed half of that, thinking of Nina and Brent down the hall, would you mind repeating all this again?" Yvonne looked at Marcus who seemed disappointed she hadn't listened properly.

"Would you mind just removing a bit of that sample, which is part Damian blood and part of the melted ice from the accident and let me and Sabine have the rest for further checks?"

This time Yvonne did understand, and nodded enthusiastically. "There is a lot about this accident you don't know yet, but this isn't the time or place to talk." She paused before deciding to continue. "Would you all fancy coming to our house for dinner some time next week to talk everything over? And I think inviting Nina and Brent and little Kade would be just right, too. If that's alright with you, Damian?" She looked at her son who looked as surprised as she was to hear her utter this invitation, hearing the words tumble from her mouth like that.

"Invite us for what?" Brent asked from the door, followed by Nina, with little Kade still in his wheelchair, holding tightly onto her hand.

"Nina, I think you all know each other?" Yvonne continued. "I'm thinking that we could meet at my house sometime next week for a bit of a gettogether, maybe compare what we all know? Especially if we have the lab results back then? What do you think? I'm in desperate need of sleep, what with all the extra shifts I've done, and I'm a bit befuddled, I'm hoping that I'm making sense? And I'd love to be able to just relax and chat normally!"

"Yvonne, that would be great!" Nina exclaimed. "It makes perfect sense! We need a bit of space to get Kade used to living with us, probably need to check out how to update the house for the child safety regs we never thought we'd need!"

"Bloody hell, Brent! What's going on?" Damian interrupted, much more his rough edged self again.

"Well, it's a long story, but it looks like we are adopting little Kade here who has just lost his mother. He seems to know more about what's been going on than anyone else. Apart from Mary that is, she knows everything about everything, too." Brent had shaken his head as he spoke, as if he couldn't quite believe what's been happening himself.

"You're the kid from the bus!" Damian exclaimed. "The one who was annoying Bill with your drink bottle! You were bashing it about and the next thing I knew we had an accident! Did you distract the driver?"

"Damian!" Sabine interrupted sharply. "Stop it, you're scaring him!"

"No, I'm not scared, but Damian is wrong, I didn't cause anything, and he knows this himself. He taught me so in the Ice Council Hall." Kade answered in a voice that was almost freakishly mature. "In the other Earth, not this place. Don't you remember ANYthing, Damian?"

Damian just stared at him, acutely aware that everyone else was staring at him, too.

"I'll remind you." Kade grabbed Damian's hand, while looking him firmly in the eye. "Close your eyes, you'll see."

Damian, despite wanting nothing more than to tell the kid off for his bottle stunts, did as he was told, and closed his eyes, only to be flooded by visions of himself sitting at an enormous carved table made of smooth and gleaming ice. He was surrounded by a group of beings of every imaginable colour and shape. He was as much part of them as they were a part of him, and it wasn't a memory. It was happening right now. Damian felt faint, weak as if he had been hit in the stomach, and just managed to hear little Kade tell him to open his eyes again, while pulling on his hand as hard as he could. "You can't go there now, we have a job to do here, you said. Mary will know, she'll tell you, too!"

"Well, I never." Marcus interrupted the shocked silence of the others. "It looks like Damian disappeared somewhere after all, but probably not as he intended? What's going on, Damian?"

"I'm not sure." Damian mumbled, looking helpless. "But when I closed my eyes just now I just saw things I didn't know about, but I recognised I was part of it.. I don't get it." Damian looked at Sabine who stared at him with big eyes, having instinctively folded her arms. "Sabine, I swear I don't know what's going on! I haven't been hiding anything from you."

Sabine looked at Marcus for reassurance, who in turn looked at Yvonne.

"Yvonne?" He asked gently, with the utmost tenderness. "Do you understand any of this?"

Yvonne looked at him, just as confused. "I don't know what you are talking about, Damian, but I can tell you're not making this up. We can't talk anymore about anything here though. Luis is still looking after the others, and we are coming to the end of our shift, soon, anyway. I'll take a bit of that sample in a syringe and reseal the pouch, you can have the rest, Marcus. Maybe it will give us all some answers." Yvonne turned to Sabine who looked pale and uncomfortable, reassuringly touching her arm. "Don't worry, we'll figure this out, what Kade said there matches what Mary told us when she came out of her coma. They must have gone on quite some trip. And Nina seemed to experience something very similar when she was holding her Mum's hand, we lost her for a bit, too. Whatever happened, my son is a good sort, Sabine."

"They are talking about what my father had talked about all the time while I was growing up." Nina's voice sounded strangely clipped, as if trying to control herself, stop herself from crying. "All the other Earths and living different lives at the same time, I think this is exactly what he was talking about, and it looks like Kade is proof of that. Maybe my Dad had been preparing me for all this?"

"Huskie?" Brent looked at her, puzzled. "What do you mean?"

Nina looked at him, then at all the others, and lastly down at Kade, before she replied. "My Dad said that we would be able to move between parallel universes, in a multiverse, in my lifetime, and that there were vital connections between everyone and everything. That it was just a matter of finding the relevant keys. I think it's starting. He was never afraid of it, he said it would save the world some day. So, I'm not saying I understand, but I am saying that my Dad understood things hardly anyone ever did, and I am his daughter, so, I'm going to decide not to be afraid either".

"Yvonne, while I remember, could I take my part of the sample back with me today?" Marcus looked at her, struggling to think what else he could say to her, she really got to him somehow, very strange. "I have a scientist friend of Nina's parents arriving in a couple of days, you may remember him, Nina? Paul Coll? It might be good if he was around when we all meet at Yvonne's?"

"Wow, yes, I remember Paul! He hasn't been in touch for ages, I didn't know you knew him? And that he's coming?"

"Long story." Marcus waved his hand. "And not important now, but I think it's time to leave Yvonne to finish her shift here. Can we pop in and see Mary to say goodbye or is it all too much now?"

Just then Luis popped his head through the door. "If you wouldn't mind keeping it short though, no more than five minutes? I think they need to rest but I am sure they'd like to say goodbye to you all anyhow, until tomorrow maybe?"

Sabine wasn't the only one who felt how much they all looked like one family as they popped their heads in the door to see Mary whom she had never even met and who looked so much like Nina. She had seen Bill once or twice in the bus, but had never really spoken to him, so she stayed in the background observing the affection between everyone, and how comfortable

Damian felt with them all. She couldn't help noticing, however, how he was also trying to hide his shock after seeing whatever it was when Kade had held his hand, all very mysterious. It was as if Damian wanted to be close to the little boy, but at the same time daren't come too close to him either, smoothly avoiding any accidental touch between them. Bill also looked conflicted about Kade, but very sorry to hear that he had lost his Mum. There was a lot to digest by everyone, that much was obvious, but the best thing was how well the three survivors looked, which made Karen's death all the harder to understand and accept.

"Mum, I'll go past our house to pick up some clothes and things. I'd like to stay with Marcus for now, seeing as I'm invited and as I'm going to work for him. Are you ok with that? It's all a bit sudden, I know." Damian had nearly forgotten, and felt ashamed that he couldn't think of a better way to break the news to her than this.

"Yes, I know all about it, Damian." Yvonne answered cheer-fully. "Nina and Brent sort of forewarned me, it's all ok, I shall miss you, of course, but it's all turning out well, I'm pleased for you. Just don't clear out the kitchen, please?" She laughed. Marcus could see that she was trying hard not to show that however pleased she was she was also upset, and felt his heart swell for her. She must have been besides herself with worry when her son disappeared, and now he was leaving again, without much of a warning.

He decided to ask her. "Would you like to come visit my home, soon, Yvonne? As soon as you like? It's not far, just outside York, and it'll be good to get to know each other better, wouldn't it. I'll be very grateful to have Damian's help with my projects, and perhaps we can put our heads together? Your nursing experience will be invaluable. If you can spare the time that is, or even like the idea. I don't want to be pushy at all."

Yvonne looked at him, and only after what seemed like an eternity she nodded and smiled. "Alright, Marcus, yes. I think I'd like that very much."

"So that's why you were going on so much about your Mum

earlier!" Sabine whispered to Damian on their way out of the hospital, leaving Marcus to amble behind.

"Yep, I just knew, how weird is that? I could see them together as soon as I clapped eyes on Marcus in your flat. It's all coming together, isn't it, and I really like that you like my friends. Nina and Brent are great, aren't they?"

"They are. And Mary seems so cool, too. Her and Nina look a lot like each other, don't they? And little Kade! What a thing, losing his Mum like this and just kind of going along with living with Nina and Brent? He didn't even look very upset, did he! I'd have thought he'd be in shock or something."

"Well, I'm not sure what to think." Damian frowned. "He is either one very clued up boy, or a way out creepy one. But he's only five, isn't he? I'm still getting over what happened earlier, I was afraid to touch him again after that, but Nina and Brent have been holding his hand all this time and look absolutely fine, they have really taken to him, haven't they. All very strange. And Social Services not making a fuss? How crazy is that? Since when can a kid just be handed over like that? What do you think, Marcus?"

Damian and Sabine turned round to Marcus who had caught up with them and smiled, "Well, maybe it's a magical day, where things just work out somehow?"

Sabine laughed. "Who are you and what have you done with my uncle? The one who doesn't believe in magic, only hard science?"

"And the Marcus I know called me sloppy and never blushed!" Damian joined in, thoroughly enjoying being the one to make the jokes for a change. "But I'm going to have fresh clothes again, aren't you all pleased? And I'm very happy to wait for my new iLink, it feels good being free from it. Take all the time you need with that precious pouch, Marcus."

Chapter 30
Welcome

NINA AND BRENT walked into their home, looking around as if seeing it for the first time. Kade looked smaller than he had in the hospital, more like an overwhelmed little boy now rather than some mini-master. Which, frankly, was a bit of a relief. But the house was totally unprepared for a child. None of the child safety installations were in place, not even Jester was programmed to respond to anyone other than his two owners. The only thing to do was to switch him over to the guest setting for now, so he wouldn't set off the intruder alarm. The CV had no parental controls, none of the hot water taps and eco heaters had temperature controls. And, of course, there was no dedicated children's room, no toys or games to play with, just a very classy grown up king size guest bed in a room with muted coloured walls. There was soft lighting, an empty and shiny desk, one armchair and a wardrobe, all very slick and terribly tasteful, and now suddenly awfully boring.

"We'll have to get your toys, and your clothes, Kade, and make this room into something you'll like. It'll just take a little bit of time, but we'll get it done, and you can help us by telling us what you like, is that ok?" Nina held onto the little hand and wondered what on earth had possessed them taking on a strange child without even sleeping on it.

"It feels right, Nina, let's just go with it." Brent whispered in her ear, picking up on her thoughts.

"Yes, I'll help." Kade said with a tiny but nevertheless determined voice.

"It's not your fault, and thank you for having me. Can I have a bath?"

"All right, Nina will run your bath for you and I'll drive to Kirkby and buy you some clothes and stuff to tie you over until we get your things from your old home. Does that sound all right?"

Kade nodded, Nina blew him a kiss, and Brent felt quite the father already. And he liked it. A lot.

"And when you get back it should be just about the right time to ring Grandma to let her know about Mum. They should be up by then."

"Oh, can I talk to your Grandma Nellie?" Kade piped up, shiny eyed and clearly enthusiastic.

"Grandma Nellie?" Nina asked, shocked.

"How do you know Grandma Nellie, son?" Brent asked gently.

"What do you mean, how do I know her?" Kade looked very confused.

"We all know her, and her and Grandfather Bob only just got married, too, and we were all there, don't you remember? Why does nobody remember anything? Not even Damian, and he's on the Council! Grown ups are such a pain, never remember anything at all. Can I have my bath now?"

Nina and Brent looked at each other, part amused part terrified. "So we have volunteered to be the parents of a boy who knows more than us, about something. Maybe about everything. This is going to be fun." Brent laughed.

"Of course you can talk with my Grandma, Kade, though she is quite old and might not remember everything either, so don't be upset, please? And don't upset her either, ok? We just want to reassure her that my Mum is okay." Nina winked at Brent to go. "Let me run your bath, I'm afraid I only have a very girly smelling bubble bath, but it'll get the hospital smell off you. Do you want me to help you get undressed or can you manage by yourself?"

"I can manage, thank you, Mummy Nina, and I'll call you before I step in the bath, like my Mum always made me."

"Sounds like a very sensible plan, I'll wait right outside then!" Nina gave him the thumbs up and smiled. She felt nervous, she had never been in charge of a child before, had only ever been a cheery face visiting other families with children. Kade would depend on her and Brent, and they had never even expected to be in this situation. And now here he was in their bathroom. It felt like the start of the most amazing journey, but a bit like a sentence of sorts, too.

'Best get on with it then.' Nina sighed, just as Kade called that he was ready. She'd have to get him a rubber duck and a teddy. New toys for his new life.

Brent felt a bit of a fool looking for kids clothes in the one and only children's clothes shop in Kirbymoorside, he had never given them the slightest thought and had no idea what was supposed to be cheap or expensive, good or bad. Even whether Kade was of average size for a five year old. Was he? He was a little person, talked like a grown up, and he didn't even know how tall he was exactly, he reached up to his waist, roughly? Scratching his head he was trying to explain just that to the shop assistant who was sure he had never set foot in her shop before. She knew Brent from his workshop though, and of the little printed toys he made, she had even considered stocking some. And now he and his wife had adopted a little orphan boy, how sweet! She would try her best to help. Between them they put a suitable outfit together to fit a five to six year old and she threw a free teddy in for good measure. It was a start.

· · • ● ● ● ● • • ·

DAMIAN UNLOCKED THE front door and stood for a moment, taken aback. The house still looked like home, but didn't quite feel like his home anymore. How could everything have changed so fast? Had any of it been of his choosing? Losing his job hadn't been his decision, nor the accident, only his decision to take his chance to run, that had been under his control. And then it had been on a super-fast slide of no return into the welcome of a great woman, of a new friend, a new job, a new place to stay. It had never been more obvious to him than standing right here, in the living room of the familiar home he and his Mum had shared for so long. Something had shifted, something had made those changes happen. What did that Kade kid know? Why was the talk of the Council in the Hall of Ice so familiar? Damian caught his face in the mirror above the shoe cupboard. He looked like he always did, yet different somehow. Just like the house, the walls, the pictures, as if it was all some kind of pretence, wanting him to believe that this was all there was.

"Are you ok, Damian?" Sabine had watched him stand there, not moving, looking bewildered. "Are you having second thoughts about moving out? I couldn't blame you! It's a beautiful home, warm and welcoming. Great art, too."

Again Damian looked in the mirror. If he turned a little to the side he could see Sabine standing behind him, looking concerned. Damian's head was swimming, somehow his and her reflection looked more real than when he looked down at his own arm. He finally turned to ask Sabine, his voice shaky. "Is all this real, Sabine? Or am I in some sort of dream? How do we know what's real?"

Sabine's face said it all, he was scaring her again, she had looked like that after Kade had come out with all this stuff at the hospital. So she didn't know, couldn't possibly have any answers. And he scared her, which she didn't deserve. It wasn't her fault that he had this odd sensation, like drifting away somehow. He'd have to think of something, to reassure her. "Oh dear, I think I need some food, I think my blood sugar levels are low, my Mum always knew when that was happening. I'll just go and see what's there to eat in the kitchen and then I'll get my stuff together. Do you want to call Marcus up, so he doesn't have to wait in the car?" Damian saw Sabine's relief on her face, the low blood sugar thing had made sense to her, even if it didn't really to him, but who knew what his iLink would have picked up on? What kind of state was he really in? He couldn't tell whether he was happy or sad or what, but what he did know was that he didn't feel he was in the here and now. It was as if there was a calling, inside of him, to be present somewhere else, but he couldn't reach it and didn't know what to do with it.

Marcus came into the kitchen to see Damian staring into space. "You okay there young man? You're not going to faint on us, are you?"

"I'll be fine, thanks." Damian replied, aware that it probably wasn't a good idea to look half cooked to his new employer, let alone his new girlfriend's favourite relation. He felt the need to explain his own uneasiness away. "I get that when I haven't eaten for a while, maybe it's to do with it getting colder? I'm always starving then, remember?"

"Ah, interesting, yes." Marcus remembered. "If your frog protein is kicking in let's get your carbohydrates up then. Got any porridge oats? I wouldn't mind some myself. Oh, and who is that woman who was hanging about outside, do you know her?"

"What woman?"

"Blonde woman, stocky, middle aged? She seemed to want to go up to your house and then stopped when she saw me sitting in the car, and walked down the road a bit when Sabine came outside to call me in. Friend of your mother's maybe?"

Damian walked over to the window. "Oh gawd, no, it's that gossip Sharon! I can see her! Nina and Brent can't stand her, she's a neighbour of theirs, forever sticking her nose in other people's business. Wonder what she wants here? I'll go ask her, watch what happens? Pick me up if I black out out there. Kidding, only kidding." Suddenly energized Damian grabbed the key and ran out towards the front door. Sabine and Marcus peered out from behind the curtains, it really was very odd how the woman was behaving. She had turned round from where Marcus had seen her last and was half sneaking, half ambling back towards the house.

"Who does she think she is?" Sabine whispered to Marcus.

"Maybe she fancies herself as a bit of a spy or something?" Marcus laughed. "Why are we whispering? She can't hear us."

"It's fun though, isn't it!" Sabine was still whispering. "Oh look, there's Damian now!"

It was quite impressive how quickly Damian hat reached Sharon, before she could even think of backing off, planting himself in front of her.

"What do you want, Sharon? What are you hanging around outside my house for? Don't even think of denying it, we watched you."

"What do you mean, Damian? It is Damian, isn't it! I don't know what you're talking about!" Sharon had said that a bit too loud, a bit too defensively. "And how do you even know my name?"

"Everyone knows your name around here, Sharon Gossip. So what is it you want, and how do you even know MY name, more to the point?"

Damian stood in front of her, fuming, half feeling sorry for the pathetic woman.

"Well, you shouldn't be surprised, Damian, as the police are looking for you, aren't they. I have a good mind to call them again, now that I've seen you."

"I see. 'Again', did you say? Ah yes, it all makes sense now." Damian glared at her. "So it was you who got Officer Matt Collins into serious trouble at work and got him to frighten the life out of friends of mine? I'm sure the officer would absolutely love to see you again, you might just be his least favourite person in the world right now. Be my guest. We had a good chat with him this morning, maybe you should check things out properly before you go snooping into other people's affairs?"

"But, I was only trying to help!" Sharon stuttered, bright red now.

"Oh really. And how exactly did you mean to help?"

"Well, you were lost after the accident, anything might have happened to you, you might have laid injured somewhere with nobody looking for you, I was only worried, that's all!"

"Spare me your lame excuses, Sharon, go home and have a good long hard look in the mirror. And if I ever catch you snooping around my or my friends' homes again I'll report you for harassment, I'm sure Matt Collins will bend over backwards to please." Oh, that felt so good. Damian felt his own triumphant smile all the way down to his stomach. She'd leave everyone alone from now on. Especially Mary and little Kade didn't need some nosey parker around now. Poor little Kade. He was unusual, if anything, he needed protection. With relief Damian found that his opinion of Kade had softened. There was more to life than met the eye, and if the little lad understood that, then his rather brutal exchange with Sharon just now had simply done him a favour and reminded him, too, what limited minds some people still had. Yes, people who could see further needed to stick together. Perhaps they were all finding their tribes. He'd have to call the Hawks in.

The thought had crashed into his conscience, startling him like an unexpected guest. What did that even mean? 'To call the Hawks in'? He knew what he meant when he thought it. Damian left Sharon where she was, not worrying anymore where she would go from there, he had said what needed to be said. It would take about twenty yards back into the house, and about as many steps. Ten seconds maybe. What could he tell Marcus and Sabine watching from above? That he had nearly forgotten already what he had just said to Sharon? That what she did didn't matter at all? And that he knew something about the Hawks, but didn't know what? He needed some space, some solitude, to figure everything out, he'd been with company almost continuously since the crash. Damian walked back through the door, with Marcus and Sabine laughing, they had been entertained, not being able to hear what he'd said to Sharon, but by her body language, and his, it had been obvious who had been in control. Sharon had walked some way down the road and had unlocked her car, to drive off, home probably, for a much needed cup of coffee.

"Looked good, did you have fun?" Sabine laughed, looking forward to him telling them all about it.

"Well, I just said what was necessary, I think she got the message. Let me get my stuff together, have some porridge and then maybe we should go? I'm pretty worn out for some reason, I know, it's early still, but.." He stopped talking, looking helplessly at Marcus who looked concerned, and Sabine, who looked disappointed.

"Let's get some food down you, young man. Tell your Serf to make you some porridge, enough for all of us, if that's ok, and then we can decide how to best deal with your watery blood sample, considering Sabine would like some, too. I guess the sooner we can have it analysed the better."

Sabine was watching Damian. "Something has changed since you talked to Sharon, did she say something to upset you?"

"Eh? No, not really, can hardly remember what she said, it doesn't matter.. I had a thought, but that doesn't matter now either, I've lost the thread, it might come back to me." Damian replied as honestly as he could. He didn't want to start pretending anything to Sabine, but he felt as if he was losing it, which was pretty scary. Losing it and feeling more powerful than ever, all at once. Power to do what?

"I think I need some time to digest everything, what Kade said to me, things going on in my head. Forgive me if I'm being a bit weird, Sweetie, ok?"

Sabine nodded, but didn't really feel like it, she felt as if he wasn't seeing her at all.

"Food, now!" Marcus put his foot down, he could see Damian's thoughts drifting all over the place and Sabine feeling rejected, taking it personally. He'd have to be gentle with the young man, he was probably a lot more sensitive than anyone thought. A change of subject was in order. "So, Paul is going to arrive from New York the day after tomorrow. In preparation I'm trying to sort out what we know, what we can figure out before he comes, and what we want to achieve or whatever else is useful. Ready to recap a bit? Anyone willing to go first?"

Damian and Sabine who looked at him like a teacher who had just set them some homework they weren't sure they were able to do, let alone wanted to. Damian sighed. "Sounds like Kade and Mary know more than me, and my Mum and possibly Luis, know more than you two. What are you getting at?"

"Humour me, you two. The others will have their own story to tell, show different aspects of what's been happening, which will be new to us. But each one of us will have thought or experienced something unique, adding another piece to the puzzle. So, let's start the jigsaw, get it in place before getting others to add to it. We don't know where and how our pieces will fit, but we know they will be useful. What exactly do you know? What have you figured out, what conclusions have you come to so far? Sabine? Want to go first?"

"Me? What do I know? I've just been reacting to what has been happening, but I don't understand any of it, Uncle Marcus, not one thing in fact! What's been going on is nuts!"

"Tell me anyhow, what are your thoughts about what's been going on? Please? Your ideas? There are no wrong answers, remember? Not even any wrong questions."

Sabine felt uneasy, put on the spot, she had tried to make sense of the past few days and hadn't grasped any of it, and she hated feeling inferior to Marcus's sharp mind. And to Damian who had had direct experiences of stuff she had only heard about.

"I saw what state Damian was in when he arrived at my flat, he was chilled through, filthy, wet, angry and desperate and confused. And he hasn't been able to pay for anything as yet as he couldn't access his bank account, could he!" She hadn't meant it to come out like that, but the fact that he had been eating her food, her uncle's food, getting free transport and was now raiding his mother's kitchen without contributing anything at all suddenly really annoyed her. It wasn't his fault, but.."

"Sabine, I'm so sorry. I know. Right now I'm not looking too good, am I." Damian felt both embarrassed and chastised, he had been aware of the very issue only too well without needing to be reminded. "I'll get my iLink back on as soon as I'm allowed to clean it up, or get a new one and pay my way again, don't worry."

"Don't even bother about that now, you'll have your iLink back tomorrow, we'll let Sabine take her sample at her place later." Marcus looked pointedly at Sabine, irritated at her outburst. "That is not what's being discussed now, though, granted, Damian, your situation explains perfectly the snags in the financial system we're tied into, involuntarily. It's something to look at some other time, but for now we have to figure out what's going on, what causes the accidents in the first place, and what can be done about it to avoid them. Anything else you thought of, Sabine?"

"That it's all a bit strange, Kade's mother dying and the little boy just walking out of the hospital with Nina and Brent straight after? And it being allowed? It's as if, as if...."

"As if what, Sabine?" Marcus asked, keenly. He had been puzzling about that, too.

"Ok, it's all a bit too smooth, as if it was, well, engineered somehow. As if everyone was reading from some script or something. And the hawk story is just too crazy to even think about. All the rubbish about feathers, I don't know what to believe about it and what not. There, I said it." Sabine looked at Damian with her chin jutted forward, she could feel he didn't like her saying anything negative about the feathers at all, but he didn't know anything either, did he, nobody did.

"It's not rubbish, Sabine, you don't know what you're talking about, not rubbish at all. The Icehawks are our friends, and the feathers are tools, there to help us. Like it or not."

"What are you talking about, they are our friends?" Marcus asked Damian, who looked just as perplexed about what he had just said.

"I just know. It doesn't look like that, with them causing the bus crash and all this confusion, but I feel that on some level I understand it, like Kade, I just can't reach that understanding yet. And a lot of good has come from that crash. Sabine and I got together, I've got a new job with you that might help you, too, you and my Mum have met, Nina and Brent are parents."

"And the mother of a little boy is dead, and Mary and Bill have been in a coma freaking everyone out! How can you possibly say that's good?" Sabine raised her voice, she knew she was being obstinate, but Damian sounded like a stranger to her now, not the man she'd been madly in love with just this morning. She'd prefer it if he started swearing, or be clumsy in expressing himself as she had known him, not this stuck up mysterious guy.

"I told you, I don't know, Sabine, but I don't need you talking to me like that, I'm trying my best here, ok?" Damian had raised his voice himself, startling Sabine.

"Kids, kids, please!" Marcus interrupted them, amazed at the change in them. "We've all been through a fair bit, Damian probably more than anyone, don't you think, Sabine? Let's just run with it, calmly. So Damian, you think the hawk or the hawks, plural, you said, are a force for good?"

As soon as Marcus had posed the question, the atmosphere in the room seemed to change. It became lighter, more loving again, kinder. It was obvious to all three of them, making Damian feel instinctively validated. "Yes!" His eyes shone, and he looked more attractive again to Sabine already. "I do! I really do! I feel the hawks and I have a connection. And, though I didn't tell anyone earlier, something happened when Kade asked me to close my eyes, in the hospital, to help me 'remember' he said."

"What? Damian, what did you see?" Sabine actually felt herself getting curious. Where had that come from?

"I saw myself, sitting at this massive table made of ice, with what I could only describe as aliens, intelligent, well-meaning extraterrestrials. I know, I know, it sounds mad, like out of some sci-fi movie, but I knew them, and we were discussing what was best for Base Earth."

"Base Earth? Wow, Damian.. then what?" Marcus was transfixed, so this was what Nina had hinted to, and Damian had had an experience Marcus himself had been wanting all his life, but which had eluded him so far.

"Then nothing, it was like a moment only, but it felt very, very familiar, as real as all this.." Damian swept his hand across the room. "As real as me sitting here. A different table, a different discussion, but still, me."

"Was I there?" Sabine asked, feeling left out again.

"I don't know, Sweetie, it was too quick. I really don't know." Damian looked at her, fully aware that it wasn't what she had wanted to hear. "If it makes you feel any better, I didn't know anyone there I know here."

"How do you feel now?" Marcus asked. "The need for food earlier, that was just an excuse, wasn't it? The blood sugar thing? You needed to figure out what's real and that's why you looked so out of it? Is that right?"

"Yes." Damian answered quietly. "I've been feeling like I've suddenly got a foot in two worlds at the same time, and I'm struggling to get a handle on it. It's all happening so fast. Sorry." He shrugged his shoulders, looking like the loveable awkward Damian Sabine had so taken into her heart.

"I'm sorry I shouted at you, I didn't mean to, it's just you've changed so much in just a couple of days, it's a bit hard to follow. But I understand a bit better now." Sabine squeezed Damian's hand and got a grateful squeeze in reply.

"Wow." Marcus breathed out hard. "I'm so glad I asked. Nina was right. Greg always said this would happen. The conscious switching between universes. And you, young man, seem to be right there. Damn, I had always hoped I'd be one of the first. What does it take?" Marcus looked at Damian, trying to figure out how this average kind of guy could step into a living awareness of something that he himself had always expected would be a top scientist's privilege. All this studying and research, and no joy, and then this ordinary Joe Bloggs just jumps on a bus. "I'll be damned.."

"I don't know, I didn't do anything special, not that I know of anyhow?" Damian wondered himself. And got the answer in his head immediately. Because he had wished for it, pictured himself, visualised it, over and over again. THAT would be his revolution, not hidden in some cave in the forest. He would help change this world from the plane of another, a parallel universe, with a different hierarchy, advanced possibilities, and the Hawks would help him. "I'm one of the Hawk Masters, Kade knows it, that's what my task is. The Hawks did what I asked, be there when I wanted out. Along with the others who benefitted from that accident as well. And now I have to figure out what else I need to do. Where, and why, and how." Damian paused, before continuing quietly, talking to himself, just loud enough for Sabine and Marcus to hear. His eyes closed, his body leaning slightly forward, he gave his inner voice his full attention. He was talking to someone else entirely. "Imagination is the key, and we are losing positive creative imagination. No, I don't know. Or do I?" Damian paused and nodded, looking stressed. "Yes, of course, I need your help, that's what this meeting is about! I know." Damian opened his eyes, staring blankly into his hands, as if reading from them.

"Blimey, Damian, I'll have some of what you're having." Marcus leaned back and sighed. What on earth was he going to do with any of that? He laughed to himself, 'what on earth', that was a good one. Maybe he should ask somewhere else.

Chapter 31
New Norms

NELLIE AND BOB walked out into crisp sunshine. What a beautiful morning it was. They had slept well, awoke refreshed, were still alive, so far so good.

"So, you're going to make an announcement at the Shed some time soon. Must say, I didn't expect that, Nel. What are you going to say?" Bob looked at Nellie, she was back at her old strong self, but he couldn't think of what on earth they were supposed to do next. Nellie shrugged her shoulders, and smiled, not because she felt like smiling, but because she really didn't know what kind of expression fitted the turmoil inside of her. "Actually, I haven't the faintest idea, Bob, it kind of fell out my mouth. But I'm trusting I'll know what to say when the time comes. I don't even know whether I should be scared or excited or what. Do you?"

Bob shook his head, and his stomach tensed at the question that had been growing in his mind.

"What is it, Bob, what aren't you telling me?"

"Well, apart from us, Sophie and little Stefan, the only unusual thing people here have seen is the hawk, and some feathers. They don't know anything at all about what happened to us, do they. And right now I don't feel up to the task of being useful at all, not like I did in the other earth place. I haven't a clue what to do with this. I hate feeling like this, you know I do."

"Yes, I do, Bob. We're just taking it in turns to trust it, like we always take turns in everything. I'm going to wait until Nina rings me with news about Mary, maybe that will give us something helpful to work with? I don't know, I just have a feeling it might."

Nina and Brent were watching Kade sleeping in that huge grown up bed. He'd said goodnight without any protest, had eaten some toast and jam, and agreed he probably still needed a bit more sleep. He could get up again later for a bit, maybe watch some cartoons, and then they would make some plans to drive down to his old home to pick up his things.

Nina and Brent settled on the sofa, talking quietly amongst themselves, wondering what would happen next. Would the police and whoever else involve them at all in Karen's funeral arrangements? Was there a will? Who would give them the key to get Kade's things, and were there any friends or relatives of Kade's who should know what had happened and where he would be living now? There was so much to think about, all totally new, and they had no idea what the normal proceedings were in such a case. Kade had shaken his head about any other family, siblings, father, uncles, aunts or otherwise. There didn't seem to be any grandparents even, as if he and his Mum had dropped in from outer space and into their lives. He didn't mention any friends, had shrugged his shoulders about his school or teachers or favourite things to do, the only thing he was clear about was that he was going to be Councillor in the Hall of Ice, whatever that meant, and that Damian would remember and help him. And that Nina and Brent were his new parents.

"He doesn't even look scared, or too sad about his poor Mum. That's a bit creepy, if you ask me." Brent whispered.

"Maybe he's in shock? Or maybe he's one of those geniuses with a massive IQ who aren't worried about relating to people very much? Maybe he is autistic? Or both?"

Brent nodded, that would make sense. "All I know is that I feel really protective about him, don't you? We'll just do the best we can, eh?"

"I don't know, I suddenly felt out of my depth when I gave him a bath. His little body and such a busy little head, and then all this grown-up talk, I guess we have to learn as we go along. I'll go and ask Jester to order some child friendly foods and drinks and download some kiddies' recipes. And let us know about how to enrol him in school and all that. I really haven't a clue." Nina breathed in deeply. "All of a sudden we're parents. How did that happen?"

There were some great cartoons on, Brent was having quite a good time flicking through the channels to come up with something suitable. The news was dire, definitely not child friendly. The New World Order didn't look so orderly, split as ever before. Everyone was cursing the cashless system, people were trying to buy gold again as the go to currency, its value going through the roof. Damian had been right with his gold then, but how did anyone even use it? Brent shook his head, he really knew nothing much about anything, except how to make great furniture, and he'd have to go back in tomorrow and take over from Connor. He was missing Kade already just thinking about leaving him for most of the day, but they had to earn a crust, now even more so. Nina could carry on with most of her work from home, and time client visits to fit in with school hours, so far so optimistic anyhow.

Nina sat down next to him when Kade came in, holding on to his new teddy and without a word wriggled himself between the two of them, leaning his head against both of them in turns, and then asked for food, he was starving, he told them. He had obviously had a good nap and looked comfortable enough, not asking any questions, just wanting more food and thankfully liked the cartoons. His hair all fluffed up and shiny eyes, his trusting cuddles meant that Nina's and Brent's latent parental instincts were in overdrive. With her head and heart full, Nina took a deep breath. "I'll call Grandma, it should be a good time now, let her know the good news about Mum and everything. I could do with her wisdom".

It wasn't quite as straightforward as that though, Brent knew they were both thinking the same. How would she explain that Mary had woken up, talked about seeing Greg and the future wedding, oh, and that there was a little boy living with them now, just like that. Nina scratched her head and sighed.

"Just do it, Huskie, it'll come out right. Put the V-screen up from the off, so that Kade, your Grandma and Bob can see each other straight away, it might just be easiest that way?"

Nellie's iLink buzzed. "It's Nina!"

Bob rushed to her, drying his hands on the towel, to sit by her so they could both see and be seen on the V-screen. The sight they were presented with made both of them gasp, there was the little boy they had just seen running around the wedding table, it didn't make sense! "So, who do we have here then?" Bob managed to get out, hoping he sounded something like normal.

"Hi, Bob, hi Grandma! Well, first things first, Mum is okay, she's come out of the coma, she's fine. And this little boy, well, he was with her in the same accident, sadly his mother didn't make it, and now we're his guardians, well, his new parents now. But we'll tell you more about it some other time. Both, say hi to Kade? He's five years old and a brilliant little boy."

"Grandma Nellie and Grandfather Bob, I've just been to your wedding, haven't I! And Mary and Greg, too, and Nina and Brent, but they don't remember, you remember, don't you!" Kade's little voice rang across the V-screen, with Nellie and Bob reacting in the most unexpected way.

"Oh my goodness, I thought it was you! Of course you were at our wedding! And now you're on Base Earth? Well, of course you are! Silly us! Well, that's wonderful!"

As if to confirm the absolute delightful absurdity of the moment Nellie clasped her scarf in the most dramatic fashion and Bob burst out laughing, a big throaty, deep, delighted laugh. Nina and Brent stared at them, speechless. Had everyone lost it completely? Base Earth? Wasn't that the word Mary had used earlier in the hospital? Or had it been someone else?

"Okayyyy, Grandma, you two are losing me, big time. What's going on, what are you saying? Kade has been talking about things we don't understand, and even Mum talked like you two just now, and I had a strange experience I can hardly remember now. Can someone help us out here? And there was a hawk, right in the hospital, if that helps at all, oh, and it turned into ice right in front of our very eyes. But, it saved Kade's life."

Nina took a deep breath, Brent was still lost for words, and Kade bounced up and down in his seat, overjoyed at seeing people he should by rights have never seen before in his young life.

"I had been wondering how to explain it all to you, but it seems you know more than us!" Nina sat back, suddenly feeling weepy. Summarising it all like that and seeing her Grandma's and Bob's reaction, it was all a bit much. "Help?" Nina added, looking like a lost deer.

"Oh, my dear, so, you don't know, do you. Or, you've forgotten, maybe." Nellie smiled, looking quite in charge and totally reassuring. "You'll interrupt me if I forget anything, won't you Bob?"

Bob nodded, with an expression much like Brent's now, kind of open mouthed and speechless looking at the little boy on the screen, realizing he really had moved between worlds. Or had he? Had they?

"Anyhow, so, we were at our own wedding, just like Kade said, and now we're back, and we've got the feathers, too, and need to decide how to deal with them. Have you got your feathers?"

Nellie had obviously covered enough to totally freak Nina and Brent out, while Kade was running around as if he had just been told it was his birthday, pulling Brent's sleeves and then Nina's, repeating, "See, I told you! I told you!" With the biggest smile on his little face.

"What, one of the hawk feathers? Yes! We've got some, I forgot all about them! The one at the hospital helped him when he wasn't coming round so well, made him stronger."

"I had to say bye bye to my Mum, she's on Earth 6 with me, but I had to say bye bye to her here, she didn't feel like staying." Kade repeated what he had said in the hospital, though this time less sadly, instead looking confident and happy about being understood.

"So, Kade, tell me something." Bob leaned forward. "Are you comfortable, about moving between worlds? You know, we've only been to Base Earth and Earth 4, but Greg told us that the multiverse is real, and you get that, do you?"

"We're old, you see." Nellie added. "Over eighty years old. It's taking us a bit getting used to all that, we've never known about this before. So, can you help us understand?"

"I can help, but not as good as Damian can, Damian is amazing, he's a Hawk Master, and he's going to teach me. He's really really cool! Pow wow! Like that!" Kade punched in the air, excited.

"Are you sure, Kade? Our friend Damian?" Brent asked, now totally bewildered. Damian, of all people, a master of sorts, really? Kade nodded vehemently, his bright blue eyes shining. "Damian is even on the Intergalactic Council in that massive Hall of Ice, it's like a ginormous castle, and only really special and clever people can see it and go in there. They can call up the Icehawks, they are like Superman!"

Bob and Nellie looked at each other. Kade had just mentioned the castle, the one they didn't understand was there, why it was there. Nellie took a deep breath. "So, let me get this straight. That 'intergalactic council', that means aliens, right, Kade?"

Nina and Brent sat looking at each other, open mouthed, they couldn't believe what they were hearing. Nina realised she was actually starting to feel sick. It was like some movie scene, but a movie she didn't particularly like. She grabbed Brent's arm.

"I want this to stop, I can't handle it, Brent."

He nodded, feeling much like the same.

"Aliens, yeah, ET's, but they're helping, they're goodies. Nothing to worry about." Kade shrugged his little shoulders, waved it off, completely unaware that Bob and Nellie didn't look exactly thrilled or in any way reassured with his news. Neither did Nina and Brent.

"Well, that'll take some getting used to." Bob took a deep breath. "So, it's happening then. Are you two okay over there, Nina? Brent, you're looking a bit pale around the gills."

Nina looked glumly into the V-screen. "If I hadn't seen the hawk in the hospital and now heard you talk like that I'd have said Kade had been watching too many cartoons, but everyone I love seems to know about this. Mum was talking about it, too, she said she'd even seen Dad. And I felt it with her, but it's gone from my head now. Maybe I can't handle it? Am I blocking something? How many others are there, how many people know all this? I'm scared. Yes, okay, I admit it, I'm scared."

"Nina, darling, we saw Greg, too. Your Dad is doing fine, he's really happy, and is working with his friend Paul on Earth 4, they both talked to us, tried to explain. Bob shouted at Paul at first, told him to stay away from Sophie, that seems funny now." Nellie laughed.

"Sophie? Who is Sophie, Grandma?"

"Sophie and her little brother Stefan live down the road from us, sweet children they are. They collected some hawk feathers, dropped by the Icehawk when he was here. They collected a small bunch of them and brought them to us, that's how we got to Earth 4. To be honest we thought it was a drug effect, nothing else. Seems like we were wrong."

Bob shook his head. "It's all pretty bizarre this, isn't it."

"Sophie and Stefan and me, we played at your wedding, didn't we!" Kade piped up. I'd like to play with them again! Stefan is my friend. I want to get a VeeCee, can we get a VeeCee?"

"They play the VeeCee on Earth 4? Cool!" Brent laughed, relieved.

"At last something I understand! I like playing VeeCee, too, we'll get one, for sure. Better than a football, isn't it?"

"Much better." Kade nodded enthusiastically. "Can I have a big one?"

The grown-ups laughed together through the V-screens, what a relief it was to talk about a simple game.

"You said Paul just then, didn't you, Grandma. That wouldn't be Paul Coll, would it?" Nina asked, already knowing the answer. Of course it would be. Her Dad was alive on some other Earth talking to anyone but her. She felt that pain of bitterness that shows in the eyes in an instant, her tone sobering the mood again.

"Sweetheart, yes, you talked to Paul yourself, and to your father, you were all there at our wedding, I saw you with my own eyes. And you will be here again, at our wedding in April, won't you?"

Nina nodded, without really understanding.

"How come I don't know or remember any of this? I would feel it, wouldn't I, if I had seen Dad?"

"But you did talk to your Dad, out loud, when you were holding onto the feather on your Mum's chest, Nina! You told me off for interrupting you, kind of shouted at me, really hostile you were, it freaked me right out! You were the only one who seemed to understand everything then, it was me who didn't get any of it! I haven't experienced anything strange at all, except for getting a kick out of holding the feather! I'm just listening to everyone going on about weird things, and I'm on the outside, watching! It's starting to cheese me off, to be honest." The more Brent voiced what had been happening the angrier he got.

"You have to breathe it in, Daddy." Kade patted him on his arm.

"I can stay with you when you want to do it and show you what to do."

Nellie and Bob nodded in agreement, touched to hear Kade call Brent 'Daddy'. "That's the difference, Brent, it needs the feather, holding it is one thing, but breathing it in is a very different thing altogether. We wouldn't have known if little Sophie hadn't told us, her and her brother sniffed it instinctively, and now they want us to tell the whole village what to do, whether we should all sniff them, hold them, or not touch them at all. Nellie said she'd make an announcement in the Shed soon, daft woman she is." Bob chuckled, half amused but much more concerned than he let on.

"That's easy!" Kade called out. "Just tell them they can all choose for themselves, see if they want to! Easy peasy!"

There was silence from the four grown-ups. And then spontaneous laughter.

"Trust a child to come up with the perfect answer." Nellie smiled into the screen. "Thank you very much, Kade, what a clever little boy you are. That's exactly what I will tell them."

Nina still looked worried. "How did you feel when you came back then, Grandma? I'm still scared. You know me, I'm even scared to get drunk, really, but this is.."

"Pretty far out?" Brent finished the sentence for her.

"Yes, far out, way too far out!" Nina could have hugged him for understanding, and felt a complete coward seeing that both a five year old and a pair of octogenarians could cope with all the craziness when she couldn't, at all.

"Maybe you'll know when you're ready, Nina, we were dithering, too. And you'll know when you're ready, too, Brent, or even if you want to be. I don't think it's good to do anything while you feel pressured." Bob was trying to comfort both of them. "It was exhausting coming back actually. At first we felt really energised, I felt like a young man again, but it's a lot to take in, and yeah, the journey between realities takes it out of you. It helps talking about it though, it helps us talking about it with you guys! And it'll be amazing seeing Mary and talking some more with her, too. Do you know how long she'll have to stay in for?"

"Maybe a day or two, for observation?" Nina replied. "We had to agree to take Kade back for a check-up, tomorrow, so maybe we can pick her and Bill up at the same time, that would be good. Shall we talk again when Mum is with us?"

"All right, Sweethearts. And Kade, I'm so glad you've found a home with Nina and Brent, they'll take good care of you." Nellie smiled warmly.

"Welcome to the family, son." Bob added. "It's a good one, it's taken me much longer than you to decide to be part of it. Clever kid."

With that everyone hung up, and took a minute to digest what had been said. Nellie and Bob hugged each other quietly in their kitchen, and Brent, Nina and Kade sat cuddled up on the sofa.

"Well, it's all pretty weird, I have no idea what to make of it, but I guess we'll have to get used to a new reality, eh?" Brent summed it up.

"And we'll be a family." Nina talked across the top of Kade's head, breathing in his lovely smell, with her girly bubble bath scent in his hair. "And we'll get you your own Superman bubble bath. Would you like that?"

Kade nodded, fiddling with his teddy, his concentration already back on the cartoons.

Chapter 32
Getting Real

"WOULD YOU LIKE to join Mary at the table for supper, Bill? Shall I walk you across? You should be able to go home tomorrow, if all is well." Luis smiled and waited for Bill's reply, who had basically been spending the day staring into space, and generally being very quiet, though his monitors told him that physically he was as fit as a fiddle.

"Home to what?" Bill replied with a dull voice, and even duller eyes. "I'd been used to living on my own, just having the company of my friends, being the cheerful village bus driver, maybe take Mary out one day, but now? It feels shit. I didn't see any other wife in any other life for me, in that brief visit of whatever that was, all I saw is that I'm with Mary already in some other place, Earth 16 or wherever, but here? What is there for me here? I'm bound to get fired, seeing I wrecked the bus and am over the hill anyhow, collect my notice chip and just become a number, like everyone else. Mary will be dreaming about Greg in a million other worlds, and little Kade and Nina and Brent are a family, too. I've got nothing. So don't look at me expecting me to be happy to be able to go home. Because I'm not, and I'm not going to pretend to be."

It was upsetting seeing the big man like that. Luis understood exactly what Bill meant and tried to think of something comforting to say, but couldn't. Had he experienced the same as all these people, he'd have to agree, it would be enough to lose one's mind, never mind getting depressed about things. "Let me take you across to Mary's anyhow, and don't you start getting her down, you hear? She's been trying hard to stay on top of all this, so be gentle, ok?" Luis was determined not to have two depressed survivors on his hands, one was quite enough.

"Well, my dear, fancy meeting you here!" Mary giggled as Bill shuffled in, looking like a miserable bear, with his hair all over the place, in a hospital gown, that was way too small on him.

"Fetching, I know." Bill did a little bow, and then pointed to her gown, which was obviously her own, all pretty, with big white polka dots on a bright pink, cerise pink they called it. He was quite proud to remember that. "So how come you've got the fancy gear then? Show-off." He grumbled, but his mood was lifted hugely by that amused twinkle in her eye. That woman had eyes, he loved them, dark brown and deep as, deep as.. well, something deep.

"Nina brought it in for me, and what are you staring at me like that for?"

"Actually, I was thinking how deep brown your eyes looked, but I couldn't think of anything deep and brown, except of, uhh, mud. Your brown eyes, as deep as mud. Does that work its charm?" He laughed now, as she showed a hint of pretend outrage.

"Come and sit down and have supper with me, Bill, I'm told the chef works wonders here! I'm hoping it won't be cold toast with a cold boiled to death egg and some limp salad or some such horrors. I'm ready to go home, aren't you? Get back to living a life, and all that?" Mary asked, surprised to see Bill's face darken again immediately. "What's wrong, Bill? Are you not well? Are you hurt?" She leaned forward to feel his arm under the fluffy sleeve.

"No, not hurt, just thinking there is nothing much out there for me, without my job, they're going to let me go for sure now."

"Well, in my book that would be the best news you could get!" Mary laughed. "We'll have time to do all sorts of other exciting things, starting maybe with baby-sitting Kade, and we could travel, go on day trips, holidays, shows, concerts, and god knows what, together!"

"Together, Mary? Are you suggesting us two, together?" Bill was surprised she was coming right out with it all like that.

"Oh, come on, Bill, we've both known it's been on the cards, right? Yes, I know, Greg is about in some other place, he always has been, he always will be, and it's really good to know that, but here, well, we have to live our lives, too, and we could do it better in each other's company, wouldn't you agree?" Mary looked at him, not caring one iota if anyone might think she was being too forward. This was their lives she was talking about, they could have died but they didn't, so what good was it wasting time? She could see Bill and her together, they could make it work. Definitely.

"Well, that's cheered me right up, I didn't think you were going to say anything like that at all, but, Mary, girl, for sure, that's just right, just right." Bill fell quiet, he had this odd sensation of wanting to burst into tears, and that really wouldn't do, wouldn't do at all. The food trays were being rolled in. Cold toast, a hard boiled egg, salad and lukewarm tea.

· · · • ● ⬤ ● • · ·

PAUL COLL SETTLED into his seat, first class, courtesy of working for a famous magazine and being able to do his own bookings online, with all the best codes to get the perfect seat. High end service with a smile by a human on-board crew of two, unlike the Serfs in the back.

He pulled up his working screen, going through his notes of what the five human senses plus all the somatic, proprioceptive and interoceptive senses could pick up on. He knew somewhere amongst them would be the answer between the correlation of wavelengths, energetic vibrations, relative physical manifestations and expressions of any kind. And, considering the necessary receptors, they might well be there, but the brain may not have received any catalysts for them to kick them into action. Or it was possible that the brain had had simply no need to activate them, until now. As soon as something appeared in the awareness of some, it would soon become common knowledge, that's how the evolution of the brain worked. Or rather all evolution, adapting to changing circumstances to the best of survival. And the brain was a master at evolution, unless it was restricted in some way, thereby stopped from working as it should.

Paul held his breath, seeing the red flag clearly in front of eyes. That was it, he knew. This was another eureka moment, but one he didn't understand the meaning of. Who or what would want to stop the evolution of the human brain? And for what purpose? What if it was really more of a race to gain the ability to travel between parallel universes first? Was that the ultimate goal, to gain complete control over all of space and time? And over all the human mind?

He started to sound like Greg, which was slightly worrying but mostly reassuring. He had to talk with Mary, probably more with her than Marcus, both of them being connected with Greg, to get to grips with what the human brain and body could really do. And then help both along. Paul typed some cryptic notes about buying vegetables and a gift for Mary, he had his own secret code, long used to hiding where he got his information from. It was safer this way.

Chapter 33
The Visitor

"**G**UYS, I NEED to make tracks now and get back home." Marcus yawned. They were back at Sabine's place, the atmosphere easier, but she still looked upset. Paul Coll would be waiting to meet him in his hotel first thing in the morning, so transport was an issue. With the atmosphere between the young couple strained as it was, nobody was going to mention the possibility of Damian staying over. Marcus felt as if he was part chaperon and part excuse. Definitely a chaperon as far as Damian was concerned, who obviously wanted to be around Sabine as much as possible, when he felt fully present anyhow. Sabine didn't seem sure of anything any more, and they were all overwhelmed.

"Ok, let's come straight out with it." Damian took a deep breath. "We're in an awkward space right now, but that's only temporary, I can feel it. Sabine, you and I need some alone time together, but I know I'm freaking you out with what's happening. So, the last thing I want is to be a nuisance to anyone, I can stay at my Mum's tonight, if one of you wouldn't mind giving me a lift back there. Or I can crash on your sofa again, Sabine, no funny business, promise. Or I can come with you now, Marcus, and stay out of your way tomorrow when you work with Paul, if that's what you want. I know I have to get to grips with what Kade said to me, and with those weird memories I'm suddenly getting. Someone help me out here?"

"Is that what it feels like? Memories?" Sabine stared at him, she was tired, but so wanted to understand. "Not like visions then, or hallucinations?"

"No, much more like memories, but living through them again, intensely. It does feel familiar, but still new to me. It's weird, because it feels, well, like a previously hidden part of me. But still me and not dangerous, more like I'm having to learn something important." He swept his arms across the air. "That all this, everything that's happening, is meant to be. Sorry, I know I'm rambling on again, trying to explain it.."

Both Sabine and Marcus had watched him intently, as he had started trembling as he spoke, but didn't seem to notice it himself.

"Damian, you're shaking? Are you cold?" Marcus asked, bewildered. Damian wasn't supposed to feel the cold, and Sabine's flat was warm enough, not overly warm, but Damian's teeth were nearly clattering now.

"Are you ill? Why are you shivering, Damian?" Sabine stood in front of him, he felt truly freezing, and was trembling under her touch.

"I don't know." Damian replied, looking down at his legs that were shaking on their own accord. "I have no idea, but yeah, I'm freezing."

"Damian, something is going on, do you mind if Sabine takes a bit of blood from you right now, another finger prick, a drop on some paper? Maybe we can see what's happening, compared to the old sample in the pouch? If that's any good at all anyway, we don't know, do we."

Marcus really had neither time nor inclination to play nursemaid to anyone. Damian feeling cold like that, maybe he had caught some virus? Then going back home to his mother's place might be the best idea for him. He looked around in the flat, the windows were closed, no draft from anywhere as far as he could tell, but wait, was he imagining it, that he'd started to feel a chill, too?

"I think I'm coming out in sympathy." Sabine rubbed her arms. "I'm starting to feel cold now, what's going on? I'll go and check the bathroom window, maybe I left it open?"

Just as she headed towards the bathroom a shadow crossed the ceiling, and Sabine cried out in shock as she felt something sweep over her hair, not unlike being swiped with a towel. She ducked down, instinctively putting her hands over her head and hid her face. Marcus sat as if frozen on the settee, and looked the handsome bird squarely in the eye. It landed on Damian's shoulder, having appeared from nowhere, a bird of prey with piercing eyes, but with a touch of human expression in them. Damian stood up, he had stopped shaking, and rather than being afraid or shocked, he seemed to grow in stature and confidence, and relaxed, with a huge smile across his face. He reached up to stroke the bird's neck, and spoke to it gently, totally in control. "Calm down, you're scaring my girlfriend, shh, shh, calm down, Cikuq Aarulik, aqumsaa, pinartuk, pinartuk, shh, shh."

Sabine, on hearing Damian's voice speaking a strange language, straightened herself slowly and turned round, cautiously, to see what was going on, to make sense of it. There Damian stood, wide legged and solid, slightly turned away from her, facing Marcus, with what she could only assume was a hawk, what with all that talk of hawk feathers and such. Her Uncle Marcus sat transfixed staring at Damian and the bird, which behaved just like a tame little budgie having his neck feathers stroked.

"Cikuq Aarulik, aqumsaa, pinartuk, pinartuk, shh, shh." Damian repeated the words, with the tenderness and affection one would use when talking to a pet, however powerful. Neither Sabine nor Marcus dared move or make a sound, not that they would have been able to anyhow, especially as right in front of their eyes the beautiful wingtips started to glisten with a sudden layer of ice, they had only just noticed. Damian started humming a tune which sounded vaguely familiar, and proceeded to hold his arm underneath the hawk's chest, as if to offer it a purchase to step on.

"Your wrist, be careful, Damian!" Sabine whispered, loud enough to make it seem more like a cry, seeing the hawk's talons and the still red and crusty skin on Damian's wrist that would simply not be strong enough to withstand them. As soon as she had said it, the hawk looked down on Damian's wrist as if it was some prey to catch, but instead of sinking its beak into it or stepping on it, he rubbed his head and neck feathers over it, making the redness fade and the scars to be replaced by perfectly normal looking healthy skin. This was some kind of magic, going on right before their very eyes, in her little flat above the bakery. None of it could possibly be real, but, it was happening. Ridiculous.

Sabine looked at Marcus who hadn't moved and probably not even blinked. He just sat there, open mouthed.

Damian spoke again. "Thank you, Ciquk Aarulik, thank you, you see, I remember your name? Pinartuk, pinartuk, asirstan, shh, shh." Damian turned to Sabine and smiled. "Seems my friend felt like visiting. Say hi to Ciquk Aarulik, it means Icehawk, in Alutiik, it's the preferred language in the Council."

Sabine stared at him, incredulous. This was definitely not the Damian she was used to, the one who only spoke English, with smatterings of tourist Spanish and a bit of school French! And her old Damian certainly didn't have a habit of birds of prey perching on his shoulder. "What did you say to him, just then? Oh, and sorry, hello, uhm, Icehawk."

"I told him to please sit down, that everything is calm, and that he did well."

"You're speaking in the old Alutiik language?" Marcus finally came back to life. "I don't believe this! That's an old Alaskan Native language, and I only know this because of Greg, I think Nina's Grandmother still speaks it! Or maybe she spoke Yup'ik, not sure." Marcus rubbed his clammy palms on his trouser legs, scared as hell as to what had just happened. There could be no scientific explanation as to how a bird of that size could just appear out of thin air! And Damian speaking in Alutiik? "Greg learned bits. He used to say it's a fascinating language, very straightforward, very guttural, and that it was only polite to learn a bit of it for when he travelled up there! He wanted to feel part of the place. I don't believe this..." Marcus seemed to have rediscovered that he was sitting on Sabine's sofa, and looked round to her, to see what she made of it all.

"So, Damian, want to explain to me how your, uhm, hawk pet got here?" Sabine knew calling the Icehawk a pet wasn't as respectful as it should have been, but not for the first time that day she felt tetchy and irritated. Damian just seemed to throw these unexpected curve balls into her life, and really, all she wanted, all she really liked was normal things, especially in her own flat. None of this was normal.

"Don't call him a pet, Sabine. I'm glad you can both see him though, not everyone can, so you must be ready."

"Ready for what?"

Marcus picked up on Sabine's irritation, and had to admit, he didn't like the sound of that either.

"Ready to travel between parallel universes, to transverse the multiverse. Pretty cool, eh?" Damian suddenly laughed out loud, making even the hawk jump on his shoulder, and look at him so crossly that Sabine had to laugh.

Suddenly it was all very funny. Hysterical even. She could feel herself getting the giggles, it was hilarious! One minute the only problem was whether to allow Damian to stay the night, and the next thing there's a blooming hawk in her living room and then she's being told she could transverse the multiverse, how funny was that? "What, no parachute? No passport? Bwahahaha!" She really got into hysterics now, her stomach cramping up and this weird laugh she was trying to suppress came out of her mouth, and every time she looked at the hawk she laughed even more. Marcus stared at her, with a crooked sort of open mouthed laugh, and Damian stood, smiling, while the hawk didn't seem very amused at all, which made it even funnier. "Oh my god, oh my god, I'm cracking up!" Sabine managed to force through in between trying to breathe, which was such hard work, how did anyone breathe with laughing so much? And then, suddenly she realised her laugh was turning into crying, and she didn't know why, her giggles turning into these sobs, and she didn't know what she felt at all, crying from deep inside her, like some kind of sudden release of something. "I - don't - know - what's - happening - to me." She sobbed, trying to get some kind of composure back, and really wished there was an off button somewhere.

Marcus got up to walk over to her, to comfort her, he had seen the change in her face, only expressing what went through his head, too, his body just not following up on it as well, but yes, he felt like laughing and crying at the same time, too. They were both hysterical, that much was obvious. He hadn't counted on the Icehawk having different ideas of its own, however. It jumped off Damian's shoulder and, with just the smallest flap of his wings landed smoothly on Sabine's shoulder who shrieked in horror, before she turned very calm and still, not unlike Damian. Damian didn't look worried at all, he just observed and nodded slightly, with no desire to interfere whatsoever. "Don't worry Sabine, Cikuq Aarulik will show you, you will see, be still, let him show you, it's safe, no harm will come to you."

Sabine didn't move, and all Marcus and Damian could see was that her blue eyes looked even bluer, her light brown hair more golden, her skin glowing, and a huge smile spreading across her face. "This feels amazing! Oh, wow! Wonderful!" Sabine exclaimed, as she saw herself walking through green fields, in the sweetest, pure air, turning round seeing Damian wave to her. A young boy and a little girl were playing next to him on a swing, the boy pushing the girl, and she realised they were her and Damian's children. She looked down at her feet and realised that her cat Domino had been walking along with her, his long grey and white fur fluffed up by a soft wind, his tail high and happy. It was like her own personal paradise, she was living her secret dreams, and it felt wonderful. It was so strange, as she could still feel herself standing in her living room, knowing that she was both the observer and the observed, and it was fine, two worlds could coexist, dual awareness was possible, not really that different to daydreaming, just more real, more physical. She saw Damian's smile, and had so much faith and trust in him, the surge of love rising for him in her heart was the purest, truest and most solid type of love she had ever felt.

So that was where he had been when he had been preoccupied, when she thought he was ignoring her earlier, but no, they had a life together already, children even, and Domino was still there, too, it was all possible, all going on at the same time! Time was just an illusion of limitation! From one angle it looked like a stick you had to travel along, end to end, but viewed from the side, you could see it all, every life, all time, at once. It was all happening at the same time, the stick held by the same hand, there was no limit how it could be turned or what side of it could be seen, it was simply another dimension. It could be a ball, an oval, a circle, any shape at all, but mostly time was something useful, a measure, a tool, no more, no less. She got it now, she saw that on Base Earth the way to look at time was like breathing air through a rubber tube, locked into manageable perimeters, totally ignoring the air outside the tube, and forgetting that it's there. The general belief and expectations were governed by the understanding of the tiniest measurements of it, and by physical mortality. How ridiculous it all was. "We are born with endless potential, so thinking we have to do everything in that endorsed limitation is such an illusion, no wonder people get confused and depressed and forever thinking there should be more to life than this, when we can all feel there is more, more of everything!" Had she spoken out loud? She looked around at her children playing, it was so heartwarming to see them giggling and playing like that, and wonderful being a mother and having a family with Damian, and at the same time she looked through the scene, like through a sheer net curtain, seeing Damian and Marcus watch her as she stood in her living room. She addressed them directly, repeating her question. "Did I say all this out loud, you two?" Only then she realised the hawk was still sitting on her shoulder, like an old friend, his weight comforting. She knew him, he was just one of the many guided messengers to teach them, and Damian was so good with them.

"You did, well, not sure if you told us ALL your secrets, but it sounds you're getting it all down amazingly well." Damian walked up to her and put his hand on her free shoulder. "The giggle turning into crying did you good, it was a sign of releasing internal barriers. We all run around with a ton of resistance to seeing what's really happening, and cause ourselves a lot of unnecessary grief. It's good to hear you talk like that and means you understand what I'm all about. Eventually we will be able to help a lot of people, together, with Marcus's help, too, of course. Nina, Brent, Mary, even Paul coming tomorrow, we are all ready, because basically, we decided to be, actively wanting something different." Damian saw Marcus frowning at him. "I just didn't know it until I woke up to it myself, I had been dreaming about making a difference almost as long as I can remember. It is here where it is needed, but we need help from all of us in the various Earth planes where we live our ideas out. We all exist everywhere, but actually in reality all our lives in the multi-universe depend on our very existence here on Base Earth."

Marcus's frown had only deepened, it was one Damian knew only too well. "You're not sure about this, are you Marcus, you're not feeling it yet?"

"That's about right. No, I'm not feeling it. Considering I have had no experiences like what you have had and Sabine just had, but you're talking sense in a quantum physics way of looking at things. You might even be talking about gaining conscious awareness of the quantum universe and if you're having a real physical experience of it, well, as a scientist I just wish I had the same experience rather than just being a bystander to progress." Marcus felt embarrassed, recognising he was as upset as Sabine had been earlier. "So, what would I need to do to experience the same? And would it be safe for me? I'm more afraid of this than I thought I would be." Marcus looked just like her Grandad when he was embarrassed, it was so endearing that Sabine walked over to him. Putting her arm under the hawk's feet, feeling his almost frozen wings, she let him step onto her arm before passing him over to step onto Marcus's shoulder. She turned to Damian, and mouthed 'Alright?'

Damian nodded. "It'll work if he's ready, but Ciquk Aarulik

didn't volunteer, so not sure what will happen there. Marcus, everyone has their own challenges, and I can't say what yours are, and which Earth life you will see. Ok?"

His words were already lost on Marcus who was busy marching with the concert band in the searing heat of Barbania, playing the Oehler clarinet his Dad had just given to him to try, and he'd been right, it played well. It was outrageously hot, what a ludicrous idea to play in the middle of the Italian summer, and the different fingering took a bit getting used to. He saw Sabine marching a couple of rows in front of him, and he knew that Yvonne would be there watching them in the shade under the gelato sign, mixing in with the locals, all their friends clapping and cheering them, well, him, mainly. She always cheered him on, calling him a clever dick for having his degrees both as a vet and in music. His Dad rated the music more, but they had a 'contract of mutual admiration' as they called it, a phrase coined one late evening over a pint or three of Hobgoblin, their favourite brew. It was good to march next to him. It was their quality time together, years of memories relived every summer, and each summer they said it might be the last time they might want to endure the summer heat, but every summer they came back anyhow. It was a family thing, and they loved moaning about it afterwards, but not as much as they loved the al fresco evening meals around the huge tables laden with glorious Italian food, surrounded by jovial company, music and wine. Family and friends and music, that's what life was all about. And his beloved animals. He loved being a vet, being useful, he felt he understood them and his furry and feathered friends understood him. Such easy non-verbal communication, no fancy terminology needed whether it was just a little hamster or a temperamental race horse. It didn't matter, for when in trouble, they all spoke the same language, needing love, safety, and of course decent food and water. And sometimes a little medical help, some medication or surgery, and that's where he came in, and at this, he was skilled.

Marcus felt himself thriving in that life. At the same time he sensed that he was sitting on Sabine's sofa, with a hawk on his shoulder he could not relate to at all. Not as a vet, but as a lonely scientist surviving mainly on intellect and ego. Marcus sat, seeing his perfect life, with tears streaming down his face, sobbing like Sabine had never seen him before. She and Damian looked at each other, aghast at the upset they witnessed in this elegant man who always seemed so much in control. The formal dark blue suit he was wearing only served to magnify his distress.

Damian lifted his hand to stop Sabine from rushing to her uncle, and began to speak in the language Sabine didn't understand "Awa'i, shh, shh, enough now, enough, be calm."

Both Marcus and the hawk responded, the bird bowing his head to stroke Marcus's cheek with his neck feathers, already dripping with the ice water that was covering nearly all of it now, and Marcus stopped sobbing, looking round, as if disorientated but relieved. "I now know what I should and could have done with my life." He said quietly. "I could have played after all, I was just afraid, listening too much to my darn stupid ego loath to making mistakes. I told myself I wouldn't be good enough."

Sabine ran to him and sat next to him, kissing him on the cheek just like she always did when she was overcome with affection for him. "But, Uncle Marcus, you ARE living it, just on another Earth, just feel it, you might have a different job to do here. Everything is okay just as it is!"

Marcus held onto her hand, nodding and trying to smile through his tears. Why had he never dared to be who he really wanted to be?

"It's time for Cikuq Aarulik to leave now, he will first turn completely into ice to purify himself, then water, then steam, then pure energy very quickly, and disappear, it is what he has to do, how it works. He is getting weaker already. He will join with the others, don't worry, but it's time to earth ourselves here now, ground ourselves properly, please do exactly as I tell you, Marcus and Sabine." Damian spoke with absolute authority, while watching the icehawk very carefully, setting him down on the floor in his sculptured beauty, still moving, but his eyes less alert somehow, half living, half frozen. A creature of wisdom.

"Kayagnaituq, Cikuq Aarulik, kayagnaituq, it's easy, icehawk, it's easy."

Damian spoke softly, while Sabine and Marcus watched, close to tears again, both of them, it was as if a new friend was dying right before them. Damian turned to them, and said as gently as he had talked with the hawk. "Now, you two, all I want you to do is concentrate on your feet on the ground, right here, you can stay sat down, Marcus, but concentrate on being back here, keep it up until I say otherwise, look at each other to keep yourselves here, together in this room, that's all it takes. Feel your feet on the floor, be present right here, now."

Sabine and Marcus reluctantly did as they were told, not really wanting to take their eyes of the bird, but not wishing to be lost in an in between state of two worlds either. This would require some practice. There was a slight draft in the air, a barely perceptible shiver of sorts that distorted the room much like a mlrage, like the reflections ahead and above the hot tarmac on a midsummer's road. That wavelike shimmering of a non-substantial substance, that tricked the viewer.

"A second of realisation how illusory our so called realities are." Marcus would recall later. The hawk had gone, leaving three glistening feathers on the floor as a parting gift. Damian stood, with his eyes closed, palms as in prayer in front of his chin, humming that song again, the one he had hummed earlier, that sounded as familiar then as it did now.

"What is that song, Damian? I'm sure I've heard it before, it's familiar." Sabine managed to ask, with Marcus nodding, he, too, wanted to know.

When he was ready, Damian opened his eyes, and looked at them with a deep kindness. "You might know it as an old John Denver song, I reckon John must have known, understood that there is more, but I don't know if there is anyone who actually knew him in person who would agree with me. The words are simple, and profound, and it's one of the few melodies the hawks can rest in, knowing all is well. It helps them home. It's called 'The Eagle and the Hawk'.

"Oh goodness, yes, I remember that tune, from the 70s maybe? John Denver died in a plane crash, didn't he? And you think he may have known all about all this? Wow!" Marcus exclaimed.

"Before my time, though I think I've heard it, yes, I'm sure I have." Sabine added.

"That's the one, yes!" Damian was pleased. "As said, it's a purely personal guess that John knew, and maybe, just maybe, decided to leave Base Earth to concentrate on a different Earth plane. But who knows. It's always a soul decision, when we 'leave', you know? We just forget what we chose before birth, and then, at the stage of dying, or rather when moving to another plane and afterwards, we remember again. We have so many lifetimes to live out with this one, in this wonderful varied crystalline multiverse until we decide to go back to the one soul state, to remain connected there and continue to create, or to come back again, as individuals with a different set of choices. Anyhow, that's the song, it'll be good for you to sing it often, it will attune you."

"So, where do the icehawk fly back to?"

"There is a mountain called Denali in Alaska, it means 'the Tall One.

I've never been there, not here on Base Earth here, no, but on Earth Four it's where the Intergalactic Council Hall of Ice is built, but even there only visible to those chosen. All selected galactic members of the universe are represented there, honouring creation itself, and peacefully working together for the common good. But, enough lessons for today. Now we need some food, to continue earthing ourselves properly. And then we should probably call it a day for today, let each of us recover. I'll go back with you tonight, Marcus, as planned, make sure you're alright. Is that ok with you, Sabine?"

Sabine stood up, looking taller and stronger, glowing with a new confident air about her and looked him squarely in the eye. They both knew they'd be a team from now on, and that they could cope with whatever this new situation would mean for them. "Absolutely, keep Marcus company, Damian. I'm fine.

Actually, I'm excited. And I recognize you now, or remember you, not sure which."

Damian shook his head, amazed. How could they know what they didn't know? But, Sabine mirrored what he felt within, total confidence. He knew who he was now, and that he could change lives for the better. That's all he had ever wished for. And he wouldn't forget it either.

Chapter 34
Thrills and Science

THE TRAIN FROM Leeds airport took Paul through the lush green Yorkshire countryside. It was good to be back. He sniffed the jet lag remedy again, drawing the serotonin, melatonin and Siberian ginseng mix deep into his nostrils, almost immediately being able to visualise the effect of the perfectly balanced combination transverse the blood brain barrier. It would hit those tiny clusters of brain cells, the suprachiasmatic and dorsomedial nuclei, their responding signals almost immediately cursing through his veins, adjusting his body and circadian rhythms to local time. Even his breathing changed in an instant, became deeper, more relaxed and open. That tiny bottle really was a gift from the gods, and he was lucky to be able to be sensitive to the immediate internal changes going on, they were subtle, but powerful.

He rolled the tiny white bottle between his fingers. Clever how the nostrils were such an easy bridge to the brain. An image of Shamans sniffing different plant extracts and powders up their noses with a spring levered tiny wooden spoon, a bit like snuff, came to mind. It would help them journey into the lower, middle and upper worlds, aided by rhythmic drumming where they could gain otherwise hidden knowledge. Why was that such a mystery still, how it all worked? That would be his next project absolutely. The more Paul thought about it the more excited he became, in all his years of research he'd been fascinated by Shamans all over the world, their knowledge and traditions almost identical across all continents, why was that, and how was that possible?

He looked around the train that would pull into York within minutes. All these passengers going about their daily lives, and nobody was really ever able to tell what world everyone was living in. There it was again, those watchwords that made him tingle now, worlds, awareness, knowledge, and lack thereof. He'd need lifetimes to figure it all out. Perhaps Greg felt another lifetime was needed, too, that he had done all he could on this plane, and moved to a more advanced one? 'No doubt about it,' he heard Greg laugh, with a resounding sense of approval and joy, Paul was convinced he was on the right track. Maybe even those hocus pocus Aquarian age beliefs, still allowed as they were too vague to be classed as religions, had something going for them after all. Good grief, he was starting to forget the rules, what was scientific and what was not. He remembered something else that Greg had said.

'Stop fighting everything with outdated logic, why limit yourself? Why? Give me one good reason why you are so afraid to grow? Grow some balls, Paul!' and they'd both laugh and he'd nod but really he had no idea how to do that, to grow, balls or not. Maybe it was time to change, to be brave and a little insane. He'd get to the hotel in one of those Serf taxis, and get a good night's sleep, and meet Marcus tomorrow. Maybe even meet Mary, too, beautiful Mary.

· · · • ● ● ● · · ·

"WELL, I'M PLEASED to say the doctor agrees, you two can go home!" Luis smiled cheerfully at Mary and Bill as they were having breakfast. The visiting doctor had passed them without much of anything to say, just looked at the monitors, nodded and mumbled something neither of them understood, but they second guessed his nod after he punched something into his records before disappearing again. Bill had called after him 'Have we passed?' but never got a reply.

"Being in a coma used to sound much more impressive." Bill complained. "Now I don't even know what story to tell. Except that I've seen you in your fluffy gown, Mary." He grinned, thoroughly pleased with his own joke.

"Will you be able to come to Yvonne's get together, you two?" Luis asked. Somehow, Mary and Bill seemed like old friends already, and it had been kind of Yvonne to invite him and Ian along.

"Wouldn't miss it for the world." Bill's grin grew even wider, as Mary looked on and smiled. "I'm going to show off with a new woman on my arm, and probably just sit there like a Billy tomcat that's got the cream."

Mary patted his knee, amused. "She better be good to you, this new woman, otherwise I might have to have a word with her."

They all laughed, enjoying the relaxed mood. Luis felt slightly uneasy that the bizarre occurrences of the past few days felt like some dream already, one that was becoming ever more difficult to remember in detail. But looking at Mary and Bill all relaxed in the pink glow of deciding to be an official item, well, perhaps none of it mattered anyhow. He and Yvonne had done well to protect their patients the best they could, and the fact they were bound by the code of confidentiality was a relief, nobody would ever know anything of the feathers, hawks, or the strange conversations that had been going on. They had double and treble checked every monitor, every recording, there was no trace of anything untoward going on at all. There was no explanation for that, either, but, again, a relief. All that mattered would be that these good people would be able to continue living normal lives, and that little Kade had a loving and secure new home. If it took forgetting what they had experienced to make sure of all that, it would be worth it. Ian had been right to say that certain sounds were inaudible to humans for a reason, maybe they should leave it at that.

"WHAT A GLORIOUS morning!" Marcus knocked on Damian's door to wake him up, and to thank him for his support since his embarrassing performance the day before. What on earth had possessed him to turn into a gibbering wreck as against both Damian and Sabine coping perfectly well? But what an experience! That hawk! Just appearing like that! And seeing another life! His life! He wanted to see more! All of it! But now what, what in the here and now? He'd have to keep his head together and simply decide that it would be a good day to meet Paul, swap what they knew, or at least some of it. The least crazy bits. And Damian would be right there, by his side. How wonderful that was, what a privilege to be in this incredible young man's company. And he'd look for a small gift to take to Yvonne's in a few days time.

He smiled at the message she had left on his iLink, talking about the get-together, making it sound like nothing but an ordinary social evening. It was very strange, the feeling he got when he looked at her message for the umpteenth time, of a happy and fizzy kind, which he didn't even try to explain away. He couldn't wait to see her. She'd be so proud to hear the way Damian had handled himself, and if his space hopper abilities were to frighten her he'd be there to comfort and reassure her. That's what he'd call Damian now, 'Space Hopper'. He laughed. A Space Hopper probably wouldn't be satisfied to play his assistant for very long. If anything it was Damian who would need an assistant, if he was going to move between worlds. Marcus had written in his journal last thing, didn't want to forget any detail of his mythical encounter with another life, but reading it again in the morning it had read like some fairy tale, or like the dreamy ramblings during a crazy night of one too many.

"So what's that Paul like then?" Damian asked between bites of toast. "Are you looking forward to meeting him?"

"I think so, yes, I don't know him really, but he's a sound writer, into it for the science rather than the glory, so all in all, yes, I think he'll have something to add to the picture. And he was a friend of

Nina's father and of Mary's, too, so that'll be interesting. Not sure what he'd make of the idea of other lives and icehawks though. Let's go easy on him, shall we?"

The welcome between the three men was a good one. They eyed each other up and saw immediately that they all had different qualities to offer. There was an edge to Damian that Paul wasn't quite sure about, but he also came across as solid and dependable and very alert, quite a combination. Damian had been introduced to him as Marcus's assistant, but Paul had the distinct feeling there was more to the young man, something he wasn't told, so he decided to be on his toes and somewhat cautious. Call it a reporter's instinct. Marcus was taken aback by how closely the picture he'd had of Paul matched the real life version. How familiar he seemed, with his ridiculously high forehead and tall lanky frame. He even managed to make Marcus, usually so in control during any new encounter, feel the closest to inferior he had felt for a long time. He was glad to have Damian with him, who seemed to know all about Paul in an instant but chose to keep his thoughts to himself, at least until they'd have a chance for a private chat later. There were some pregnant pauses and half sentences in the conversation as the three of them headed towards Marcus's car after picking Paul up from his hotel, obvious to them all that they were circling around the subject of hawks, especially in relation to the accidents. Marcus finally decided to take control once they were in the privacy of his car.

"Listen, Paul, we'll have to go past my lab, and it would be good to lay all our cards on the table in private before we get there, it would be a shame to miss out on our mutual insights. I am simply deciding to trust you, seeing we're both friends of Greg's and Mary's, it would be good to know you feel the same way? There is so much we must work on, and trust between us is essential. For Mary's sake, too, she's been through a lot. You seem strangely familiar, wouldn't you agree, Damian?"

Marcus looked at his rear view screen to watch Damian's reaction who was nodding in agreement and gave him the thumbs up. Paul nodded and swiped his iLink into the deep sea dive setting, showing it wordlessly, which only caused Marcus and Damian to burst out laughing.

"Haha, you've been doing it, too, so I take it we're all on the same side then." Damian grinned. "Good one! Though it can't be that much of a secret any more then, if everyone and his dog know about it."

"Manners, young man, manners!" Marcus laughed, and Paul was clearly amused also, the ice well and truly broken.

"I agree, let's work together. It feels good! How is Mary?" Paul asked, trying to hide his nervousness.

"She's great, I got a message from her daughter Nina earlier that her and Bill can go home today, it seems like they're an item now." Marcus laughed. "Odd how things turn out, she's been on her own since Greg died, apparently her and Bill, he's the local bus driver, have been having an eye on each other for a while. Accidents bring people together, don't they."

"Mary? And a bus driver?" Paul's question came out less casually than he'd intended, he couldn't believe what he was hearing. Mary had been married to one of the brightest scientific brains he'd known, and now she was getting it together with a bus driver? "Oh my god." Paul muttered, trying to stay calm, but he didn't feel it. He'd had so many internal conversations with Mary, about feeling sorry that he hadn't been in touch, that he had liked her way too much even after Greg had snapped her up, that she'd remained his secret crush for years, decades even, and that she was the main reason that he was here at all. And now this. He hadn't even thought of the possibility and felt sick to the stomach just thinking of it.

"Seems that's a bit of a disappointment then, am I right, Paul?" Damian had watched Paul's face grow pale, what he could make out from the back seat anyhow, and felt his pain. When had that started, that he was able to perceive another man's pain so acutely? He could see the heartbreak right there in front of his eyes, realising that Paul had probably never looked at his feelings quite enough before the mention of Bill.

Marcus threw Damian a cautionary glance through the screen,

Paul's private life was really none of their business. He could have kicked himself that he'd gossiped about Mary like that, he had been way out of order. What a fool he was turning into, it was beyond embarrassing. He'd have to get a grip in front of Yvonne at her party, especially with Paul around, who wasn't a bad sort, super smart, probably way more attractive than him, and with that deep American accent to top it all. How annoying.

"Yes, you got that right." Paul finally allowed himself to reply to Damian. "Looks like I hoped she'd be on her own still. I should have been in touch with her, I'm a fool. We go back a long way, back to our first days at university, when Mary was dropped off by her father to start her studies. It was a huge culture shock for her, Alaska to Oregon, you know? She and Greg were good together, I didn't get a look in. And I've blown it again, by the sound of it. Don't let on that I said anything, please? It'll be good to see her anyhow. And we have work to do to keep me busy." He wasn't even trying to hide his sadness.

"Hey, let's just see what's going to happen, we all make fools of ourselves in love, don't we." Marcus replied, again out of character, having to stop himself mentioning Yvonne right there and then. That really wouldn't be appropriate, considering he was talking to her son and a virtual stranger, and totally premature. Yvonne might not be interested in him one bit, after all. What was happening to him? It was time to change the subject. Some talk about feathers and ice, and different worlds would do. And Paul, well, he wasn't shocked at all. Instead, he briefly filled them in with Greg's, and now his theories of actual parallel universes, a multiverse, and search for a way in, to experience them consciously. That Greg was probably listening in to their conversation at this very moment... that they could all talk with him right now if they just found a way to bridge the gap, which was no more than a gap of consciousness, after all.

"Ha, Paul, I think we already have a lot of answers for you." Marcus was back in his element. "But for now I really want to see about the antifreeze gene in Damian's blood, figure out exactly what it's for, and what the melt water has to tell us. Fancy helping me figure out the results when I have them, Paul?"

Paul nodded enthusiastically, soaking up the male bonding he had rarely experienced in New York. He wondered if Greg himself was adding some magic to their interactions.

"And you have to promise not to dissect me in the lab as your guinea pig." Damian growled, knowing full well he would never have to worry about anything ever again, he was way ahead of those two. The hawks would be there to help him if necessary.

Marcus's lab was impressive, gleaming, he walked in with his usual air of command he showed at work, people nodded, one waved with a wink, possibly in relation to the hot holiday he'd pretended he'd been on, but nobody really looked up that much from their work, showing little interest.

"You're popular then, Marcus." Damian said under his breath. "That's a bit of an understated welcome, isn't it? Are they always like this?"

"Let's get to work." Marcus replied gruffly, embarrassed that his unpopularity had been quite so obvious.

"I get the same where I work." Paul said quietly. "We're the oddballs. Don't worry about it, pal."

The surgical knife cut through the plastic pouch with ease, releasing the foul smelling iLink and it's watery mess into a sterile steel bowl.

"Oh dear god." Damian groaned. "That's disgusting!"

"Yup, revolting." Paul pinched his nose with his fingers.

"Who would be a nurse, they are heroes, they are. Make sure you let your mother know I said so, Damian. And to tell her her son needs upping his hygiene standards." Marcus laughed, seeing Damian was truly embarrassed.

"Did that officer really expect me to put that iLink back on? No way I'm going to do that, it's gross!"

"Glad you agree, son, now, let's see what the analysis throws up. Haha, throws up, see what I did there?"

Paul and Damian both smirked, but Paul already had his eyes fixed on the monitor showing the first results of a few drops of the sample Marcus had fed into the analyser.

"Look!" Paul exclaimed. "Are you a diabetic, Damian? And those proteins, are those the ones you mentioned, Marcus? And this one, that formula there, I happen to know it, it's the same as that mountain plant, what is it, I know it, yes! It's Leontopodium alpinum! How on earth does Edelweiss get in there?"

A few further keystrokes by Marcus and the analyser spat out the strangest mix of a complex antifreeze protein bonded gene, then close to diabetic values, then a whole lot of beta-keratins, as found in beaks, feathers, hooves and horns, and, there it was, the mountain flower Edelweiss. All helpfully cross referenced on the screen.

"I was right! Edelweiss! Look! How unbelievably exciting!"

"Well, can someone please tell me what an Edelweiss does?" Damian asked.

"There is a song about it, but I'll be damned if I can even remember what it looks like, and what does it do?"

"And how much of any of it would be down to the sample being spoilt both in the pouch and contaminated in the bus itself?" Marcus added.

"You threw your iLink on the floor, didn't you? Let's see if the Edelweiss is connected to your human cells or is part of the ice water, it might have come in on that ice storm? Would that mean it had blown in from the alps? Damian, I only know it as the hardy white alpine flower, and that it's a traditional symbol for bravery, hardiness, protection, that kind of thing. Not exactly useful."

"Can your analyser pinpoint locations, Marcus? If we knew where that came from, unless it's part of Damian somehow, maybe we could tell where the ice storm came from?"

"I can put some more drops in and see what it says, specifying to look for geographical markers, sure, good idea, Paul."

Marcus realised how happy he was having these two men in his lab, brotherhood of men and all that. He carefully dropped some more of the smelly solution into a new sterile receptacle and slid it into the analyser. The screen showed 60°07′28″N / 149°26′00″W almost immediately, which was as unexpected as Paul's sudden roaring laugh. "I don't believe it, I just really do not believe it!" He looked close to getting some exuberant hysterical fit. "You know where that is, don't you?"

Damian and Marcus looked perplexed, first at each other and then again at the coordinates.

"Well, ok, it's way up North." Marcus was quite pleased to have figured that much.

"Not just North, Marcus, it's where Mary comes from!! Near enough, in that part of Alaska. In a place called Steward maybe, or thereabouts. I only know those coordinates as I remember mapping the area with Greg, when he went up there."

"And now it shows up in a bus in North Yorkshire? Come on, that can't be right, it's thousands of miles! Seeds wouldn't get carried by winds over such a distance, would they? How does it come up with that?"

Paul was in his element now. "Welcome to the world of advanced DNA technology, every place has its own fingerprint like imprint on any living substance native to it, including plant life, even soil, sand, spring water...but you know that better than me. But good grief, the water... what does it say about the water? And about the keratin from the feathers?"

Marcus swiped across a few further options on the screen, and there it was again, the same coordinates, every single time.

"Is your machine saying I'm from Alaska, too?" Damian mocked, deciding to play along. They were getting close.

"Because we know that's not true, don't we."

"Well, according to the analyser you are, or rather your blood is.... how interesting is that?"

"What do you make of it, Paul?"

"Well, he'd need the antifreeze gene more there than here, so that would make sense. And you said the Icehawk was seen over Chignik, probably the most impressive sighting, as far as we know, right? Let's research some more, connect everything we know with Alaska only, and see what we can come up with over the next few days. No wonder Greg was so fascinated with the place, it's starting to make sense, isn't it." Paul shook his head. "But it's still not giving us any answers. They are just more clues for us to figure out now, aren't they? We need more of them before we understand anything. So, what are the bits about this we do actually understand?"

Marcus breathed out an involuntary sigh of relief, grateful to concentrate on pure theory for a moment, it felt like an invitation into a comfort zone he had almost forgotten about. "I read this book a while back by an incredibly talented scientist, Professor Laura Mersini-Houghton. She believed in the existence of a multiverse as a scientific fact, way back, in 2013, or thereabouts. She understood how it works, at least to some extent, though she failed to prove it in the end. Along with other quantum scientists, I might add, who came to the same very straightforward conclusion from observing the behaviour of electrons being shot through two slits, creating the wave-particle duality. Both evidenced by the patterns the electrons make when hitting a screen once they had passed through the slits. Energy spreading in several directions, connected by invisible communication, not just one, while we only see life as a singular concept."

"Yes!" Paul got excited, he had forgotten about this, how come he had ignored it for so long? "Not just electrons, protons and neutrons and even larger, combined molecules, too! Anything that could be called a particle, or a combination thereof, I might add, nevertheless have their own wave nature and even a wavelength, relative to their momentum! And resonate in quantum terms!"

Damian looked from one to the other, secretly amused, all he had to do was concentrate his mind and let go at the same time. And he didn't need to be a scientist to realize that the momentum given to those particles in those experiments was akin to the intention he himself needed to focus on, to be able to do what he was capable of. He actually felt quite excited about it, it wasn't the talking about it, but the urge to do something! He wasn't going to argue with those two though, they were having a good time. And, didn't he only just learn this himself? Literally waking up with new knowledge? He felt like being gentle, like a parent watching kids at play. They had no idea that the day was a long way from over and he needed to conserve his energies.

"Well, you two are losing me big time, but everyone knows that governments use quantum computers to solve complicated problems, so a quantum universe has to exist, doesn't it!"

Marcus nodded, grateful and relieved that Damian joined in pretending to know nothing, rather than tell all with his much more valid actual experience. He really didn't want to be reminded of his life regrets, right now he desperately needed to be a scientist again. Damian gave him a wink as if to say he understood. What had happened the day before was private and would stay that way.

"Too right, yes, Damian. I think smelling the feathers is the thing, though, the key is the nose, the sense of smell." Paul continued, in full flow, just a touch patronisingly. "Scent messages go to conscious cortical areas. After a relay in the olfactory cortex, signals enter a way station called the thalamus, and then travel onto the frontal cortex, where identification and other related thought processes take place. Thus, odor messages go to primitive brain areas where they influence emotions and memories, and to "higher" areas where they modify conscious thought. Sorry, is that too complicated for you?"

It was pretty hard not to burst out laughing in response, even Marcus had to turn away to hide his amusement. He turned back round, knowing what to do now. "Well, yes, all true, but as you said, all this shows us something, but not everything, that's what my gut says anyhow. How about I add more of the sample to the machine, and let it work its magic over a few hours, see what else it comes up with, and we leave it be for now? We could head towards my niece's Sabine's place, meet up with her, it's a beautiful drive. We could spend a bit of time showing you the area and see what insights might bubble up just relaxing about it, have a meal out somewhere? And Damian, I want to get your mother a small gift to take to the party, you can probably help me choose something?" Marcus had tried to sound as casual as possible, but saying her name was rather disorientating, and he found himself flustering. Damian laughed and patted Marcus's shoulder, amused. "You really like my Mum, don't you! Could be worse, but remember young man, I'll be keeping my eye on you!" He laughed again. "Sorry, couldn't resist it." He grinned, and Paul fell in with the general amusement, especially as Marcus was actually blushing while he keyed in a few more software commands and got ready to leave. "Back tomorrow!" He called out to his staff in the next room who looked more relieved that he was going than anything else. They'd all be wondering who the two strangers were, but it didn't matter, they were used to him not sharing any more than he had to. Damian was pleased. Marcus had picked up exactly what needed to be done to get him where he wanted to be. He just didn't know it yet.

Chapter 35
Out of the Mouth of Babes

SABINE'S LITTLE FLAT was filled with the smell of coffee for herself and Nina, and the comforting scent of warmed almond milk with honey, Kade's favourite. The fact that Sabine had known what he would like and got some in minutes before her guests arrived showed her that her abilities were changing, she knew things now she couldn't have known. Was it really so easy to tune into other lives, minds, worlds? Just by asking questions and being open for whatever the answer would be? "So, are you going to start school here in Kirkby, Kade? After the winter celebrations?" Sabine watched him, while he was busying himself trying to wind Nina's black hair round some pencils, the newly appointed mother clearly loving every second.

"Yes, Mummy Nina said it used to be called Christmas, but I don't remember that. And that there was a man with a red suit and a big tummy and a white beard that used to give out the presents, I like that."

"'*Who*' used to give out presents, not '*that*', Kade, darling." Nina tried in vain to remain serious as that bit of education met a rolling of those big blue eyes, a big sigh, and then a bored "who" from the little man.

"You three are going to have fun, aren't you." Sabine laughed, picturing herself and Damian having fun like that one day.

"Oh, I'm loving every minute." Nina positively glowed. "It's like we've all known each other for ages."

"Well, we have, silly!" Kade shrugged his shoulders. "It's just that you don't remember and I do."

Sabine watched as Nina's smile fell, and made a mental note to ask her about that at an opportune private moment. They'd hit it off so well, and both knew they'd need each other's support. There was nobody else who had experienced anything like what they had.

"So, how are you and Damien getting on then? It must have freaked you out a bit, that he might have some goofy blood in him?" Sabine nodded, unsure how much to tell.

"It did a bit, at first. All right, a big bit. You'd think I could just have a normal boyfriend, not someone with a weirdo body chemistry. But somehow I'm okay now, we're going to be a good team. It's early days, there's a lot to learn now, for all of us."

"Maybe he's an alien or something?" Nina laughed, or rather pretended to laugh, she hadn't admitted to anyone how scared she was about everything. After all, she did love being a new Mum, and didn't want anyone to doubt that. But Mary and Bill already talked casually about life on other Earths as if that was a normal thing to talk about now, Brent and Connor had argued in the workshop about it that very morning, and even old Spencer was apparently still merrily sniffing feathers not worrying about it all. And she was getting these odd flashbacks of sorts herself, finding herself resisting them with all her might. She didn't want to know, she just wanted everything to be normal again.

Sabine felt her distress. "Let's just call Damian a bit special, Nina, I'm sure I'll have stuff to compare with Uncle Marcus, but we'll be alright, we'll adjust to anything that crops up." She burst out laughing. "Marcus sent me the blood analysis earlier, they were in the lab this morning, it's just unreal! Not so much alien, more part frog, part flower, can you imagine? Hilarious! Seriously, he seems to have Edelweiss genes in his blood. I don't think it's in the melted water, it's attached to his DNA, not the water at all. Beats me. I'll be able to call him 'flower', haha, like a proper Yorkshire woman, though he might not be so impressed.."

"I hate it! I hate it all, it scares me!" Nina finally burst out, defiant, ignoring her own rule about not discussing anything much of importance or negativity in front of Kade. "Nothing is the same any more, I just hate it. I don't understand how Damian being so different doesn't freak you out!"

"But Mummy, it's protecting him from radiation, why do you hate that?"

Kade piped up, looking genuinely puzzled. "He needs it, I think it's good."

He carried on playing with Nina's hair.

Sabine was dumbfounded. "It is, Kade? It's protecting him? How? Against what radiation?" Sabine put down the drink in front of Kade who climbed down on the floor to sip at it carefully, as if to make sure it was just right, and much to her relief he smiled and drank some more. He looked cute, sitting there cross-legged, mug in hand, and not at all like someone about to offer advanced explanations about universe hopping.

"Well, when he travels between different earths and calls the Hawks like he does, he has to stay safe and awake enough, to get through the portals, see? And the Edelweiss bits protect him against sun rays and all the space rays, against baddie spy rays, too, and he can't freeze to death either, so he's really cool. It means he can go everywhere loads of times, without getting tired out like Grandma Nellie and Grandfather Bob. They got really tired on Earth 4. I think I'll be the same as Damian, I'd like that. I want to grow strong like him."

Nina and Sabine looked at one another, lost for words. And then it hit Nina, the question that must have troubled her all along. "Is that how my Daddy died, Kade? He wasn't safe like Damian? He didn't have the Edelweiss DNA or the frog gene to help him?"

"Probably, but he's all right everywhere else, isn't he, he didn't really die, and anyhow, you said you wouldn't be afraid! If you hate it, you're probably just a scaredy cat. You said you're his daughter and you won't be afraid. So don't be, Mummy! Anyway, I'll help you."

Nina didn't know whether to laugh or to cry, he was right, that was what she'd said, that she wouldn't be afraid. And she did touch the feather after all, and she'd been okay. Nina stroked her son's head, he was right, she didn't want to be a scaredy cat.

"Boy oh boy." Sabine breathed out loudly, stunned at the intelligence of the boy. "And you want to go to school, why exactly, Kade?"

Kade rolled his eyes. "All children have to go to school, if I don't go I won't have any friends of my own age, silly. Mummy didn't like that, Mummy said I will have to have private tutors, that she wouldn't allow me to go to school, but I want to go, so I can find out who is like me. Mummy didn't like me doing lots of things, it was boring, really really boring." He drew out the word 'boring' as long as possible to underline just how boring he had found his life before. Nina took a deep breath. "Of course you can go to school, Kade, but you've really got to stop calling other people 'silly', ok? It's not nice. And stop rolling your eyes like that, too." It was all she could do to stop herself from crying now, with utter exhaustion. It was all getting a bit much, she'd had little sleep listening out for Kade, and had been torn between optimism and pessimism, between wanting to sniff the feather herself and refusing to have anything to do with it, ever. Just days ago she'd been fed up at a bus stop about the spy satcam, and now she found herself ever more worried about the future with this boy so keen on time and space traveling who seemed to know all about spy rays and things. She almost wished she could just go back to the bus stop and her normal boring, safe life.

Sabine had a different idea altogether, that came to her as suddenly as it was unwelcome. Was Kade himself the reason why his Mum died? Because she wouldn't let him go to school? Because he got bored? Was cute and irresistible Kade capable of getting rid of people he didn't approve of? Was Kade dangerous? She watched the little boy looking entirely sweet with his neat haircut and big blue eyes, but there was something seriously creepy about him. She'd keep her eye on him, even if just to protect Nina and Brent. Sabine shivered and cursed her overactive imagination, making yet another mental note to ask Damian and the Hawks about that. Just like that. Ask the Hawks. She nearly burst out laughing, her newly gained confidence about asking the Hawks anything at all did feel amazing, she could feel the excitement right in the pit of her stomach. "There they are!" Sabine would have recognized Damian's familiar knock anywhere. "Do I look all right?" She asked Nina quickly.

"You look great, silly." Nina replied, grinning, drawing an outraged look from Kade and an easy laugh from Sabine who went to meet her visitors. Nina heard the hugging and kissing between Damian and Sabine from halfway up the stairs, and in a moment the cherished little time with Sabine on her own had vanished, the three men filling Sabine's little flat in a second. Paul was taller than all of them, there were the mutual introductions and Paul's long look into Nina's eyes, telling her with how much fondness he remembered her and her parents. Holding out his hand to shake Kade's he was pleasantly surprised when the little boy ran towards him to hug his legs, apparently really happy to see him. "Hello, hello, Paul, I know you, I know you, you're Paul! Did you bring Greg, too, did you?" Kade looked at him, with big eyes full of trust. "I know you from Earth 4 best, don't I! I know him, that's Paul!" He told the open mouthed adults around him, as he sang and jumped about, clearly happy to see this man who hadn't set foot in Yorkshire for years. Nina lent forward to grab both his hands and looked into his eyes. "Greg? So you really do know my Dad, Kade, you didn't make it up? You weren't just being clever, you really do know him?"

"Yes, of course I do! Everybody knows Greg!"

Nina leant back, staring at him. "All right, I give up. Tell me all about it, too, if you want to, Paul, tell me what Kade knows. Everybody else seems to get it except for me."

Paul looked at her, sadly. "I wish I knew, Nina, I really do. I've never met this little boy in my life, I don't know him." Paul stood with rounded shoulders, shaking his head, there was nothing else he could say. Marcus felt sorry for him, it wasn't that different to his encounter with his other life just the day before. He was still recovering from it, whether in denial or not. "It's tough being confronted with things we have no idea of, isn't it."

The subdued nods from Sabine and Nina spoke volumes, everyone felt the same, out of their depth, except for Damian who stood smiling, ruffling Kade's hair, completely at ease.

"Oh well, something else to get used to then." Nina sighed, when everyone looked at her, as if she was responsible for any of Kade's behaviour as his new mother. Or as if she'd understand it at least.

"Don't ask me!" Nina replied to the unspoken assumption. "Every day is a learning day for me."

Paul was shocked by what Kade had just said. He knew Greg? And he couldn't believe how much Nina looked like her mother. She was gorgeous. That black hair, those eyes.

"Well, hey, can we all snap out of it now? Come on guys, now we all know each other, probably better than we thought, can we go out and eat as planned?" Damian shook everyone out of the strange mood. Again Marcus was impressed how calm Damian was about everything. Nothing seemed to faze him at all. Not the news about his blood sample, not his communications with the hawks, not even Kade's obvious recognition of another place. Truly remarkable. "Yes, I agree Damian. Everyone else hungry? We thought we could get something to eat in Thornton-le-Dale and show Paul the sights?" Marcus asked, more cheerfully than he felt. "We could all walk and talk and eat and have an ice cream somewhere?"

"Yes, let's do the tourist bit for Paul. Fancy coming along, Sabine? Nina? Fancy an ice cream, Kade?" Damian's question sounded more like a request than a suggestion.

Nina nodded, resigned to just do what was best for everyone. Her chewy sweets came to mind, she really could do with stocking up. That was kind of funny, it cheered her up no end. "Yes, let's go to Wardill's, and maybe go to Balderson's, to show Paul the best two places in Thornton-le-Dale.

"What's Balderson's?" Paul asked. "It sounds familiar, have I been there?"

"Oh, it's everyone's favourite cafe, I expect you must have been, years ago. They do great home cooked food and not a Serf in sight, been there since forever. You'll remember it when you see it again, I expect." Nina replied, smiling at him, she remembered him, all geeky like her Dad. It felt a bit like old times seeing him again.

"Definitely Wardill Bros!" Damian was clearly keen. "That's the shop across the square, I love it there! maybe we'd find Kade a toy in there? It's been there for generations, too, one of those charming old shops that stock everything, books and magazines and toys and gifts and the best sweets, and chocolates especially! And marzipan! I love the stuff!" Damian laughed, with Sabine adding to the suddenly joyous mood. "And we can show you the famous thatched cottage by the stream, Paul, it's all quite beautiful. I'm desperate for a bit of normality, aren't you, guys?"

The instant nodding of heads said it all.

"Actually, I'll call Brent and see whether he wants to join us, he could meet us in the cafe, would be nice wouldn't it?" Nina suggested.

Marcus was already halfway out the door. "Definitely, Nina! Do that!" He couldn't wait to get outside and get some air. Something was happening to all of them, and trying to hang on to normality was just becoming more and more difficult. He knew they all felt it. The idea of getting a little something for Yvonne in the shops was the one thing that felt normal now.

· · · • ● ● ● · · ·

LITTLE SOPHIE AND Stefan stood in front of Nellie's and Bob's door, hardly daring to knock. Nellie had said she'd make an announcement that afternoon, and Bob had requested they come and see them at lunchtime. He hadn't said what for though, and Stefan thought that they'd probably get a telling off for something.

"Let's go." Sophie whispered, hanging on to her little brother's hand and was just about to knock just as the door opened.

"What are you two hanging around out here for?" Bob laughed, looking down at the young visitors. "Come in, glad you're here!"

"I thought you're going to tell us off for something, Grandfather Bob." Stefan said quietly.

"We were a bit scared to come in." Sophie said at the same time. Bob was mortified.

"Holy mackerel, why on earth would you think that? Come in you two, Nellie wants to ask you something, and don't you ever be scared of coming to see us, you're always welcome here! Goodness. Scared of us? Don't ever be, you hear?"

Nellie walked towards them with some steaming mugs, the kitchen smelling delicious of her famous ginger, chocolate and cinnamon cookies. "Hello, you two, I've just baked a bunch of cookies to take to the Shed later, thought we'd make an occasion of it, want to try some? But only one each ok?"

It was wonderful seeing the children's relieved smile like that, helping to soothe Nellie's own jangled nerves. "Would you two mind helping me and come on the stage with me? I'm a bit nervous, you know, telling everyone what happened, I would find it easier with you standing next to us, so that people don't think of us as some old fogies with senile fantasies, you know?"

Sophie gasped in surprise. "But Grandma Nellie, everybody respects you and Grandfather Bob! You two are the wisest people here! Nobody would think anything else! But of course we'd help, wouldn't we, Stefan?" Stefan nodded his head, looking quite serious about it, he was a strange little fellow. "I'll bring something along to help Damian then, he'll be here, too, won't he. Kade told me."

"Now that is a very strange thing to say, Stefan! Do you mean to say someone else is coming to help us?"

Stefan shrugged his shoulders, and before he could say

anything, Sophie said crossly. "He always talks like that, he's so weird! I don't even know Damian, or Kade. Stefan, you're too old now for imaginary friends!"

Stefan shrugged his shoulders again, pulled his eyebrows up as if mildly irritated, zipped up his coat and muttered. "You'll see."

Sophie practically pulled him out the door to take him home.

"Honestly, that boy. He is like Kade, don't you think, Nel? He came across on the V-screen just like that when we got introduced, didn't he. So, they know each other, how interesting is that? That could only happen with them meeting at our wedding, really, couldn't it? And Damian, how on earth does he fit in with everything? Is he going to show up?"

"Unless they know each other from another Earth, not Earth 4." Nellie replied, not knowing what to think. And even less what to tell Chignik at the meeting.

"We'll have to remember that later." Bob patted her hand. "To tell people how quickly we could all learn and adapt to change if we wanted to, just like those kids do all the time."

Chapter 36
The Cafe

DAMIAN WAS GULPING down his sausages, mash and peas at Balderson's as if there was no tomorrow.

"What's wrong with you?" Sabine laughed. "Didn't you have any breakfast?"

"No breakfast?" Marcus protested. "Don't you believe it, he'll be eating me out of house and home if he carries on like that. Even Robin was upset, and that takes some doing, to upset a Serf! He didn't plan for Damian to eat so much! You're screwing up all his calculations, son."

Damian sat back, patting his belly, very nearly satisfied, already eyeing up the cakes in the glass display on the counter. "I have to go visit someone in a minute and need all the energy I can get." Damian laughed and got up to ask for the apple and almond pie with hot custard. He was in a good mood, he loved it when a plan was coming together. "You're one of the family members, aren't you? There is a family resemblance in the photos on the wall. It's a great place you've got here, I think it'll go on forever." Damian winked and grinned at the young woman at the till, feeling on top of the world. He laughed at her easy smile in response, and took the menu from her with a flourish, which she told him he could give to the American visitor as a keepsake. It showed all the family history of the cafe on the back page. Damian bounced back to the table with his massive pie and a bit of a swagger, sat down and looked at everyone to get their full attention.

"What did you just say, Damian? You've got to visit someone?" Sabine asked, frowning.

"Yup, sorry, I'm having to rush, everyone, I've got to fly off somewhere in a mo, well, I might as well tell you what's happening." Damian looked at everybody staring at him in amazement, especially Sabine who was trying not to care how flirtatious he'd been with the pretty young woman at the till. Damian grasped her hand across the table, looked at her with his best smile, and then at Nina, then at little Kade. "I'm going to go to consult with the Intergalactic Council in the Hall of Ice on Earth 4 in a moment, before seeing Nellie and Bob in Alaska tonight, just for an hour or two, help them with their announcement, so I'll be backwards and forwards quite a bit."

"You what?!"

"Haha, very funny!"

"Are you out of your mind?"

"What do you mean?"

The voices swirled all around him, his mind swirled, too. He hadn't been quite sure whether all the instructions he had received during the night had been a dream or not. So, that's why his shoulders were always itchy. It made sense now. He needed his wings. Thankfully Kade's eyes remained fixed on him, like an anchor. It helped.

"Why didn't you tell me! You're one of the Hawks, not just the Hawk Master!! I get it now! You can do it, you can be one of them, you can go anywhere!" Kade had whispered it, but loud enough for everyone at the table to hear.

"You're a Hawk?" Sabine stared at him. "You're an Icehawk, and you never told me? You bastard! Who ARE you?" Sabine felt she couldn't breathe, her chest tight as if in a vice.

"I didn't have a clue myself, Sabine, please believe me, not until I got told, last night, I thought it was a dream, and then this morning when I got so hungry, I knew it was real! I've never even met Nellie and Bob, but this morning I could feel that they are going to need me. Tonight. I could see and feel them worrying about everything. It's too much for them, they need help up there, and now I know how I can get there when the time is right. This morning I also saw that I need to travel to Earth 4, not on a pot luck journey sniffing the feather, but using my own wings and purpose, so to speak. I can't reach the Intergalactic Council here, I have to do this, and it's time." Damian sat up straight, pulling his shoulders back, confident, not caring overly much how upset he had made them. This wasn't the Damian they knew and loved.

"Well, go to your aliens then, if that's what you have to do, you might be one yourself for all I know!" Sabine really cried now, burying her face in her hands, no longer even willing to look at him.

Marcus shook his head, shocked, but more than anything sad that he couldn't help. He felt useless. He put his arm around Sabine, who was trembling with the shock. Damian, seemingly unperturbed, turned to Nina. "Your Dad knew this, too, he's helped to pave the way, Nina. I've got to help your Grandma, okay? Greg's body died when he tried too much too soon, because he didn't have the same blood as me, but his mind understood all of it and he did survive everywhere else, and he's still helping. And yes, I am one of many Icehawks, but by no means the only one. We all follow the call of the Great Spirit, as does the Intergalactic Council. We all have different tasks, I don't know mine yet. Little Kade here is waiting to be a hawk, even you, too, Nina. You didn't know you've had it in you, Nina, did you. But trust me, there was more to you wanting to cover up that spy cam in your car than you thought."

"I think that's enough now, pal." Brent felt Nina's fingers dig into his hand at such a flippant mention of her Dad's passing.

Damian, unworried, looked at everyone in turn, feeling fantastic, strong. "All will become clear in good time, I'm still learning, too. And it's okay, really, it is!" He smiled, his ego in love with his own words and with his new found power, unperturbed by Nina's and Sabine's tears streaming down their faces. Paul was aghast, this behaviour was very bad form, not at all sophisticated. If what Damian said was true then surely there would be a better way of breaking such news to loved ones than come out with it in public, in a cafe? Brent kept hold of Nina's hands, in part to comfort her, but partly because he realized he'd always known it, subconsciously up till then, that she was special, ahead somehow. He also knew that freedom needed grounding, it needed steady people around to provide a safe haven. Determination rushed through him in an instant. He would help her, and Kade, too, as husband and father, the best he could. Maybe they needed him as the solid, earthbound one? He wasn't going to fly off anywhere, he'd stay put, be a stable anchor at home for them. It felt good.

Marcus and Paul tried their best not to show how upset they both were. This was huge. Even to witness what was happening was mind-blowing, but to experience such a developmental leap in person, for real? And why Damian of all people? Why not scientists like themselves, who were most certainly able to handle the unknown better, and most of all more elegantly? To sit on the sidelines now was humbling, upsetting, exciting, frightening, all at the same time. And all their science and endless calculations would be of little use, it was almost laughable that they had thought otherwise.

Damian focused on Sabine's eyes only, willing her to understand. He had to tell them something else. "Sabine, all human beings are being prepared to travel anywhere they like, at will. Through time and space, on this earth, across universes, and no ruler, no government on Earth will be able to even see where anyone is going, let alone stop anyone. We're going into iLink free territory, at last! Isn't that just the best?" Damian laughed out loud, triumphant even. "It will take time to learn how to be truly free, but it has started! My blood already has all the qualities to get through the dimensional portals, to reassemble myself somewhere else again, and I guess I've always wanted to. It's the revolution I was looking for, but, wow! This is much better, more effective than I could have ever dreamt of! It will set us all free, you'll see! Over time anyhow! But I have to go now, sorry, it's urgent now. I need to learn from the Council, they are summoning me. I'm so excited, can't wait! I'll go out into the back patio there and disappear for a bit, I'll be back soon, promise. I love you Sabine. Don't worry, we'll be okay, we're meant to be together! Kade, pal, no shouting about it in the streets, ok? See you later, Junior Hawk Eyas!"

With that Damian got up to rush out to the deserted outside seating area with the upturned patio chairs, a hint of ice already on his jacket. He had a strange kind of walk, a definite arrogance about him. And his legs looked shorter. Nina was compelled to run after him, as was Sabine. Marcus and Brent jumped up to follow, too, only Kade and Paul remained sitting.

"You knew about this, Paul, didn't you." Little Kade stated calmly, as if talking about something entirely ordinary.

"No." Paul shook his head.

"But having met you I'm suddenly starting to know things I didn't before. I even remember seeing you and Greg in the other place, I don't know what to say. We're friends on Earth 4, too, right?"

"Right! You've got it! You and Miss Kelly sometimes help me with stuff!" Kade beamed. "He called me a junior hawk, an Eyas, did you hear that? Oh wow, I'm a fledgling hawk, and I'm going to get bigger and stronger, wait and see!"

Before Paul could even ask who Kelly was, the others walked back in through the door, looking bewildered and upset.

"Did you feel the cold?" Marcus asked Nina, who nodded her head, then shook her head, then nodded her head again. "He's gone. Just like that. I just can't believe it. I've got to call Grandma and tell her to expect Damian, or...something."

Kade climbed onto her lap to give her an unexpected cuddle. "Grandma Nellie will know what to do, she always does, just like Grandfather Bob! My friend Stefan will help. Can I have some cake now please?"

The cafe staff had no idea why the mood of the previously cheerful group of friends had changed so much, they hadn't seen the hungry one leave.

· · · • • ● • • · · ·

CONNOR AND SPENCER walked together with their shopping, happy to have bumped into each other in the bread aisle. Spencer, who was limping as always, obviously had something on his mind, so Connor made sure to slow down his pace enough for the old man. "What's up, Spenc? Something troubling you?"

"Aye, lad, it's the feathers affecting people around here in a way that's troubling me, you know. Strange stories, aren't they, that are doing the rounds. I've got one of my own, not sure what to make of it now." He shrugged his shoulders. "Anyhow, if you want to see what else they can do, you're welcome, I've still got that drawer full."

"Well, you did talk a bit strangely, about something you saw when you sniffed them, if that's what you're talking about now, Spenc? It put me off, for sure." Connor remembered.

"Well yeah, I guess." Spencer took a deep breath.

"You know that limp I've got? Well, it's all to do with that, you know. I haven't told anyone though, so keep it quiet, okay?"

Connor patted him lightly on the shoulder, he wasn't a gossip, Spencer knew that. "Trust me, mate, no worries, but what are you saying? I mean, I know you've been sniffing them, but what's that got to do with your limp? You've had that for years!"

Spencer nodded. "Three years, more or less exactly, no longer than that, mate, no longer.."

Connor could tell he needed to be gentle, Spencer was obviously upset.

"So, do you want to tell me about it then? What happened?"

"Bit of a tough one to explain, but I'll have a go. You know I ended up with the feather that was on the poor sod Greg's chest when he died. Well, I sniffed it, didn't I, instinctively, and I went on a trip of sorts, a bit like the old LSD I used to play around with in my youth. I thought it was probably a flashback of sorts. It can happen, everyone used to know about it, but I don't think it's so popular now. It was good though, and I met Julie again on that trip, the love of my life she was.

Anyhow, so there I was, on my bed at home, having sniffed that feather and having some kind of LSD trip or whatever it was with my Julie, she must still be on my mind a fair bit, otherwise why would I have conjured her up? She said hi, fell into my arms, it was so good to see her, can't tell you how good. Anyhow, we went all the way, made love right there on my bed, both older like, but it was real, I tell you, it felt real. I smelled her, felt her, kissed her, heard her laugh, looked her in the eyes, and we had the best sex, and then she told me that I should stay with her on Earth 5, she was there, and she was waiting for me, and all that. That's when I knew it wasn't real, there's no Earth 5, it's all garbage, she ain't waiting for me anywhere! I was goddam heartbroken. And then it all went crazy pretty quickly, I pushed her away and shouted 'No! You're not real!' and I swear she not only disappeared like a ghost or something, but I looked down my leg and it looked like a flipping bird's leg or something, guess it might have been a hawk's leg, but it freaked me out, I tell you, I totally lost it."

"Spencer, that's a freaking nightmare! What did you do then?"
"Well, I reached across to that big green bottle I got by my bed, as a self defence weapon of sorts, you know, one of those heavy vintage ones, thick glass and all that, and I smashed it against the edge of that old washstand, the one with the slate top, to knock the bottom off, and started hacking on my own leg. What a prat, eh, I was tripping pretty badly then, must have been, 'cause it didn't hurt, I didn't feel a thing. I saw the blood pour out of the bird's leg and thought great, I'm winning, and hacked into it some more. And then I fell asleep or something, not really sure, but I came to and was laying in a pool of blood on my bed, and my leg was killing, I was screaming in agony, I tell you."

"Hell, Spencer! I thought you had an accident at work, isn't that what you told everybody?"

"Nope, wrong, I was already retired then, remember? I told everyone I'd been drunk and fallen over onto some tools, but nah, I did that all to myself, nipped a tendon in the process, hasn't been right since." Spencer fished out a tissue and blew his nose hard. Connor couldn't be sure he wasn't crying.

"God, I don't know what to say. Is that what's happening to everyone else? Something like a bad trip?"

"I haven't a clue, if truth be told, Connor, not a clue. I was convinced that's what I'd had, but now with all what's been happening, you could say I'm confused. That bus icing over, the feathers there, poor Mary and the others, and the little kid, surely they can't have all had the same trip?"

"Nope, that wasn't a trip, Spencer, you're right, you can probably try and chop your own leg off with a bad hallucination, but you couldn't ice over a bus and end up in hospital like everyone did. And the feathers are real, aren't they. And Damian, too, that bloke is really going through it, Brent said as much, I don't think he's imagining any of it."

"Yeh, that's what I've been thinking, too, mate, precisely that."

"You know what that means then, don't you Spencer?" Connor asked cautiously, aware that Spencer might not have thought what he was thinking at all.

"What? What is it supposed to mean? It means that I've been on some stupid dumb lusty trip, and everyone else got some real thing going on that's way beyond me." Spencer looked so cross with himself, that Connor couldn't help but laugh. "No, you bright spark, it means you're one of them, you're probably the same as Damian. Don't you see? According to Brent Damian is getting to grips with other universe stuff, and you've rejected the idea out of hand. What if it was true?"

Spencer stopped and stood, staring at Connor, incredulous. "You mean what I think you mean? That there really is an Earth 5 or whatever? And that with Julie, you think..?"

"You've got it." Connor nodded. "I think you traveled to see her, probably missing her, and sniffing that feather enabled you to do it. If you hadn't been such a druggy in your misspent youth you'd might have taken to it completely differently."

"And I wouldn't have chopped into my leg like a crazy person.

That's for sure. Flipping heck... so, she's really waiting for me somewhere?"

"At a guess, yeh, I'd say so. Mary talked about Greg, she's sure he's at whatever earth she said he was, and Brent said Nina talked at her Mum's bed to her Dad, how out of it she was, it scared the living daylights out of him. Strange she can't remember it, though. Nina, that is, Mary remembers everything, so does Bill by the sounds of it, though he's been a bit quiet about everything, hasn't he."

"Yeh, he has." Spencer agreed. "It must be a bit weird for him to think Mary is with her husband still somewhere else right now, at the same time. Seriously awkward, that must be."

They had arrived at Connor's door.

"Well, I'll leave you to it. I've got to be at the workshop tomorrow, I'm standing in for Brent again. They've got to get more stuff for Kade, kids furniture and all that. They've been dropped in the deep end, good and proper, haven't they. Sleep well, mate, try and get some rest, too, eh? Who knows where you'll decide to go next." Connor laughed more easily at his own joke than Spencer did, whose head was already deep in questions and possibilities.

Unpacking the shopping in his kitchen Connor was still thinking of what Spencer had told him. He didn't find the idea of visiting any other universe attractive at all. He'd never seen the hawk, and the feathers were ok for a quick pick-up, but really, they had all gone cuckoo over them. The only thing he thought was in any way relatable, was the sample of contact rubber Damian had brought along, that was something he could handle. It looked like a good idea. He'd talk to him about it, figure out how to make more. Maybe go into business with it, he'd always dreamt of being his own boss. Well, he was fairly sure he had.

Bill and Mary had settled down in Mary's living room. Bill could still hardly believe he was there with her at all. After years of just being her jolly bus driver and the local everyone knew, to be in her place now and her being so caring and affectionate towards him was almost unbelievable. He looked around at the photos and paintings on her wall. All beautiful, interesting, cultured.

Images of her and Greg who didn't look that dissimilar to Brent, pale and freckly contrasting with the Alaskan looks of mother and daughter. Greg and Mary both in their graduation gowns, looking young and excited about their future, a class photo of all of them throwing their graduation hats up into the air. That Paul was in one of the photos, caught looking at Mary in a way that Bill didn't like one bit. Photos of Nina when she was a little strip of a girl, one of her running down the path into the sunlight, and another of her on someone's knee in a house in Alaska, surrounded by other adults, one of whom he assumed would be Nellie, Mary's mother he had heard so much about. They looked very similar.

"Who's the guy with the long hair? Handsome devil, isn't he, like out of the movies. Looks strong, too, like me, spitting image." Bill laughed, hiding how inadequate he felt. He'd always felt inadequate. Never having been blessed with good looks he had made charm, kindness and humour his trademark, he knew he was popular enough. But he had never had much luck with women, he had always been that typical best friend, their shoulder to cry on when things went wrong with their boyfriends. The proverbial 'good egg'. How he was sick of all that. He didn't want to be a good egg, he wanted to sweep Mary off her feet, he wanted to be dashing and irresistible and strong and show her how safe she'd be with him now. And he certainly didn't want that egghead from New York turning up getting in the way of that, this was a stag to stag battle, no matter that he was fat and old and didn't have a degree. He and Mary had bonded being in that coma together, he remembered seeing her on Earth 4 with her Greg, all married and loved up, and how much it hurt. But this here was the real deal, and here she said she wanted to be with him, so he'd be damned if he'd let another professor type get in the way of their happiness. He just wouldn't have it.

"You didn't listen to a word I said there, did you, Bill? About Bob? Him in the photo you're staring at as if someone had stolen your dinner?"

"Haha, sorry, my love, I was somewhere else there for a minute, true. So if that's Bob, is that the one you've been talking about marrying your mother? He's striking, he doesn't really look old, does he."

"Well, the photo is over 25 years old, so we all looked younger then, but yes, he's striking, he always was. He was well known in Chignik and beyond, you know, he saved a few people's lives."

"Really? Did he? How?"

Bill was curious, not only curious about people that had shaped Mary's past, but about people living in such a remote wild place in general, a bit like learning about history in an accessible way, not from books.

"Oh, there are many stories about him." Mary smiled, fondly remembering them and looking at the picture with her family and Bob in Alaska with obvious affection. "Like the one when a tourist boat capsized just off Chignik harbour, and he shouted for help, running along the beach shouting at the top of his voice for everyone to get the little boats out. He jumped into one himself and raced over there to get people out the freezing cold water. It's not like here, you know, it's cold enough at the North Yorkshire coast, but nothing like up there, you only have two minutes or so before you die of cold, long before you would drown. So he had to be quick, people say he ran like the wind, and made everyone do the same. All the people were saved, even those tourists who couldn't swim and had taken their life jackets off, like some idiots always did. Every single trip it was the same, the tourists would come, first all keen to learn our ways, and then get all patronising, thinking they'd know better. You should see the gear they arrived with sometimes, you know, like those fully kitted out hikers who never do more than 5 miles but have maps and brand new boots, and water bottles and glucose with them, just in case they get lost on the moors. Here the farmers laugh, well, we laughed there too, all their showing off didn't mean anything when they ended up needing to be rescued." Bob was amazed at the gritted teeth cynicism in Mary's voice, he hadn't realised she had felt like that about tourists growing up. "Well, I hear what you're saying, but surely visiting for the first time they didn't really know what was needed? Maybe they got advice about what to bring with them, you know, looked it up on the internet or something? Like when I went to Spain for the first time, and thought to buy a sombrero before I even got there, to look like a local. I looked like a right wally." Bill laughed at the memory of it, automatically. He had learned that laughing at oneself was the best remedy, always, to overcome the awkwardness of being the odd one out.

"You're right, I'm being unkind." Mary conceded. "Mocking the tourists was a bit of a sport of ours, I guess no different to people being a bit racist here, against me when I first arrived, and against Nina, too, with her mixed race looks. I'd never thought of that, really. All these silly concepts we all carry around, they're not really helpful, are they. But, anyhow," Mary continued looking back at the photo. "Bob was there, quick as a flash, pulling them out of the water, bringing them back to safety. And another time he saved an injured wolf, too, he'd been shot, but only wounded, not killed, by one of the hunters. He found him in the wounds, and carried him home. Can you imagine, carrying a wild injured wolf? He looked after him, nursed him until he was well again, and everyone wondered if the wolf would stay with him after-wards, but he didn't. Bob made sure of it, he'd walk with him for miles, every day for weeks on end, until the wolf remembered where he came from and went back to his own pack.

It was a thing Bob said a lot, we all have to remember where we come from. It feels pretty apt now, what with parallel earths and learning a new truth. Remembering where we come from. Don't you think?"

Bill felt that familiar fear of rejection restricting his throat. Did she remember that she belonged with Greg still? That she came from an academic background? That she'd be more comfortable with the kind of people she was used to, university types, scien-tists, men like - Paul? "Uhm, want to clarify that?" He frowned at Mary, whose turn it was to be surprised at his tone. There was so much they didn't know about each other still. "What I'm trying to say, Bill, is that I am from this Earth. I am fully committed to my life here, I want to live the reality here, not swim about on different planes of existence. I want to live here, with you, it's our turn now. We deserve this. Greg and I had our turn, we have a beautiful daughter, we had a beautiful life for as long as it lasted. Nina is being thrown into a life where she will have to deal with a little boy who seems to know all about living in parallel worlds. She doesn't remember what she knew with me at the hospital, rejecting the memories. But she won't have a choice, she will be dragged kicking and screaming into alternate realities, and the only way she will be willing to learn how, is to be there for little Kade and to feel close to Greg still. I do have a choice, and I choose the here and now, with you. And I'm so glad the accident happened, it brought us together, didn't it?"

Bill had listened to her, his heart lifting as she spoke. She really meant it. This gorgeous woman wasn't interested in the egghead, she didn't even hanker after living a possible life with Greg. She hadn't changed her mind, she wanted to be with him. In *their* here and now. "I like this place best myself." Bill's voice was hoarse, as he was trying to ignore the lump in his throat. "It's got you in it, and if that old friend Paul of yours gets any ideas, well, I give him a good old fashioned piece of my Yorkshire mind. You told me he fancied you in your youth, I don't forget stuff like that, you know!"

Mary laughed at Bill's half grumpy half happy face. "Oh Paul, yes, he's always carried a torch for me. Don't worry about him, I've never been interested in him, I let him down gently at uni, maybe too gently? No, Bill, you're a decent, kind and caring man who makes me laugh and who makes me feel wonderful about life again. I thank you for that. And I want to make you feel wonderful about life, too!" Mary laughed and hugged Bill around his ample frame, feeling like a teenager. It was good to remember that this life on Base Earth still held wonderful surprises as well. She had no intention of missing out on anything at all.

Chapter 37
Jacques

D AMIAN FELT HIS head resting heavily on the tabletop, his cheek cold on the hard surface, the image of Sabine's anguish raging in his mind. How long had he been asleep? Were they in the cafe still? He opened his eyes to the familiar glistening of the intricate relief carvings in the ice he was already tracing with his fingertips, like many times before. The table of the Intergalactic Council! Embarrassed, he sat up with a start, facing the almost endless table, with kind but serious eyes upon him. The Pleiadians, the Arcturians, the Hathors, the Zetas, the Quarnthians, even the Mantis Beings were all there. He was back in the Hall of Ice. It was magnificent. It felt part home, part at school.

"Welcome back, son." The dark eyes to his right smiled along with the voice, which sounded reassuringly English with a strong French accent. Confused, Damian saw that this time he was not the only human at that table. "Sorry, it seems to have been a hard journey, do I know you?" Damian was quite sure he had never met the man before. There was a movement going through the other Councillors, like a Mexican wave of a visible tremor that came across as great amusement.

"You managed to make a bunch of Intergalactic Councillors

laugh, that's a first." The stranger chuckled, his informal demeanor wrong-footing Damian even more. "I'm sorry, have we met?" Damian apologized for the second time, looking into his father's eyes. His father? The idea ripped through him like a blunt knife, painfully, he had no idea how his head would come up with such a thing. He hadn't given the father he had never met any thought at all, not for years!

"Calm yourself, Damian, you're quite right. I can read your mind, you see, we all can. My name is Jacques, by the way. And yes, I am French, but you can tell me that I don't really have an accent." The man laughed again, amused by his own joke. Damian felt like he had been punched in the stomach. This was neither expected, nor pleasant, nor fair, to present him with his past, let alone a parent he had never met in his life! In front of other members of so many universes, all watching his reaction! "You see, son, that is exactly how Sabine felt, just moments ago, when you showed off about being a hawk. In front of a whole group of people, in a public cafe."

The accusation screamed in Damian's heart, her shock and helplessness still etched on her face, it was how he had left her, had decided to leave her there. It was unforgivable, he knew that, but had he even had a choice in the matter?

"I didn't have a choice!" Damian heard his own outrage in his voice, forgetting where he was. "I was called here! With practically zero notice, and just days ago I didn't know anything about anything!" He swept his arm across the table, managing to include every single council member, his leather coat, dripping with water, looking dirty and out of place in the magnificent surroundings he had woken up in. "Did you do all that? Did you? Have I been set up like some lab rat in some great experiment? Are you all enjoying yourself? Well, if it's all the same to you I'd rather go back and have a normal life back on Base Earth, I didn't sign up for any of this!" Damian was furious, he wanted nothing more than to be back with Sabine, his mother and his friends. Thinking of Yvonne made him more angry still. "Is that what you did with Mum? Just leave her after a bit of fun, leaving her struggling to bring me up on her own?"

The fury in him rose to insane proportions he barely recognized in himself, it felt as if his whole being was dissolving in a shower of angry, red hot flames, the pressure in his head becoming almost unbearable. His hands, his arms, his body were shaking with the intense frustration he had kept under wraps for so long. Apart from Jaques's next to him, the strange faces, none of them human, nodded their multi coloured heads, gently, like flower heads in the wind, weightless, effortless, almost cheerfully. Damian thought his head was going to explode, he literally didn't know what to do. Had he been on some night out in York he might have kicked in a window somewhere or looked for someone to fight with. Here, however, even in his deepest rage, he realized there wasn't a single person or anything familiar enough to get hold of to vent his anger on, no glass to smash, no bottle to throw, not even a pillow to punch. He was the only person he could hurt with his own anger.

"Are you seeing it now? Are you finally getting it, Damian?" Jacques, his dark eyes now intense like his son's, shook Damian's arm, releasing drops and feathers on the floor around him.

"See what?! What are you talking about!?" Damian shouted back, lost in this strange world he knew and didn't know, that was safe and not safe, where he had a father and no father, his real home far far away, possibly out of reach forever. Again the amused tremor was rippling through the heads of the Council around him, even his Dad smiled now.

"Ah, now we are getting somewhere, son."

"What, what do you mean,.. Dad? Can I call you Dad?" Damian replied, suddenly weak, his anger had left him, now hanging strangely visible, floating in front of him, like a sack of suspended heat, mocking him, unreachable now. Jacques patted his arm. "We are all alone, in all universes, in places we know but don't, with people we know and don't, with dreams that might or might not come true. You can see your anger there, right in front of you? That is what has been driving you all your life, your outrage at me, your outrage at your earthly laws, your outrage at injustice, at pain, at suffering, at poverty, and that is exactly why you are here. You weren't chosen, you chose your own path towards the light, to get away from your own darkness. Enlightenment is as much a punishment as a lesson, as it is a reward, didn't you know? Definitely nothing to show off about."

Damian's head was swimming again, what was this man, who proclaimed to be his father, saying? What did all that mean? The laughing heads rocked some more, it was starting to get upsetting. "Who says I am enlightened? I'm not saying that, I've never said that!" Damian protested weakly. Jacques shook his head. "That's exactly what you have been saying, all along, thinking you know better than the sheep you derided so often, thinking they needed you to be the leader of the revolution, haven't you? Haven't you? Even now, seeing your anger as the empty bag it is, with nowhere to go, you still judge!"

Damian looked at his weakly clenched fists, shaking his head, too tired, confused and emotional to understand anything at all.

"Please tell me why I am here then, Dad? Why can I talk to hawks, and travel across universes, why am I different to the others? And what is my task now? Am I a fool? Did I do something wrong? And why didn't you stick around?" Even as Damian was asking he could feel himself drifting, through the strangest sensation of utmost care and tenderness, a love he realized, could only be felt through surrender. Was it just love that remained, when everything else was gone? Why had he never seen that?

"Ah, I can feel, you are beginning to understand." Jacques replied, kindly. "Your anger, anyone's for that matter, stands empty by itself and is only a useful energy when transformed into love. Love attracts, anger pushes away. Anger used well enables you to achieve almost anything you want. What do you really want, Damian? No need to answer now, it's for you to figure out, in good time." Jacques' expression softened. "I've been waiting for you to show up for a long time, I've been watching you, even though I have been dead on Base Earth even longer. Your beautiful mother never knew I died. You and I are very much alike, we are both here now, aren't we? We share that energy within us, that anger that we both recognize now as such a lonely and toxic state, pointlessly hanging there. It blinds you to who you really are, a being of love, and exquisite design, that is eternal and endless. We all live forever, exist on one plane and move to another, there is no limit. In my case my senseless anger made me very stupid, I drove too fast, right into a wall. It was as simple as that."

Damian stared at his father, too shocked to respond at all. Jacques smiled, he knew some lessons were harder to take than others. "Once you let go of the weight of your frustrations, consciously, you will release your will, energy, intention, into a much higher place. That is why you have come here, knowingly or not, to get our help, to learn how to become conscious and free."

This time the gentle nods of the Council members were kind in their agreement, their eyes focused on Jacques alone.

"And that, dear Damian, is what you were born to teach." He continued. "For now we're using the icehawk's appearance as a simple tool to wake people up to the fact that there is 'more'. You are no more a hawk than the icehawk that showed over Chignik Bay. It is simply an energetic tool, a vehicle, we had to think of one that fitted in, at least somewhat, with people's expectations. We could have used anything, UFO's are kind of popular. Not that we need them." Jacques laughed, as did the council members around them. "And I think the intergalactic community has done a great job helping out, don't you? They are pretty worried about us, kind of sweet, really." Jacques smiled at the murmur of appreciation that went through the ever bobbing heads that seemed to agree with every word he said. "Once you understand energy, even what it means to breathe it in, to absorb it, once you truly understand it, you can transform yourself into pretty much anything you want. That is, after all, how whole universes are created, how anything is created, simply by mastering your creative force. And we, as human co-creators, who are just beginning, are in danger of destroying our very essence before we have even begun to understand who we really are. Why? Because our imagination, instead of giving us wings, is being intentionally clipped to make us too afraid of almost anything."

Damian understood that, at last there was something he could relate to, offering enough relief he managed a smile.

"But remember, Damian, you can only teach what you needed to learn yourself, it's the same for everyone." Jacques paused. "Why wasn't I around? Because I was a vain, self-centred idiot out of control. I crashed into that wall because I gave no thought to anyone else. I blew my future on Base Earth with your mother, and my future with you. Don't make the same mistake I did." Jacques sounded rueful, his face distorting strangely, his voice turning into a distant echo already. There was that pressure in the head again, the itch in the shoulders, the cold. Damian, barely conscious now, reached out to hang on to his father's arm, but it was too late. He was alone, back where he had wanted to be more than anywhere else, in Sabine's flat, even if he had fallen into a puddle of water on her carpet.

· · · • • ● • • · ·

"I THINK YOU need to take Sabine home, Marcus." Brent whispered. "I reckon Damian pushed her too far just now."

"I think so, too!" Nina agreed. "What's he playing at? It might be all new to him, and make him feel a bit special, but wow, the way he said they were meant to be, scary! Like she didn't have a say in it at all! They've only been together for 5 minutes! Freaky, it's getting freaky. Don't you even think of pulling stunts like that with us, you hear, Kade?"

Kade giggled, whispering 'Scaredy cats!' to Paul, who wasn't quite sure whether to agree with him or not. Sabine looked awful, that much was clear, it was right to take her home. Marcus agreed, relieved that at least he could be there for her.

Sabine swiped her iLink across the door screen to her flat, barely able to stand, still feeling sick to her stomach, in desperate need of a rest, Marcus and Paul by her side. The door opened with the familiar hiss, to open to the sight of Damian crouching on the floor, collapsed and small, with his arms and legs curled under him, wet, shivering and in tears. Sabine let out a small cry, Paul just able to catch her as she reeled, with Marcus rushing ahead to pick Damian up to help him on the sofa. Marcus felt surprisingly calm. "So matey, we're back here again, eh? You seem to be fond of the place, that's a given. Are you back with us now? Or have you got to fly off again somewhere?" He tried hard to be jovial yet calm, as if he was talking to an accident victim, it didn't feel far off. Apart from that he had no idea how to be of any use at all. Marcus decided to call Yvonne.

Yvonne looked around her living room, amused that she felt the need to prepare for the get-together days in advance. But, in her defence she did have to organise things in between shifts, and she really wanted this to be a success. Tinkerbell had done well, having prepared a list of snacks of almost every description and ordered them to arrive just a couple of hours beforehand. The Serf had even presented a plan to arrange the furniture differently to create more space for everyone, it worked really well! Yvonne was recounting again who would be expected. Damian and Sabine, Marcus and Paul from America, Luis and Ian, Mary and Bill, Nina, Brent, and Kade, Old Spencer, and Connor. Fourteen people all together, herself included.

She didn't even know what she could call it, a party? They could certainly celebrate Mary and Bill being well again and an item, and Kade having found a new home so quickly. Most of all that Damian was safe and with good people, especially Sabine. Everyone had found someone, she thought, not quite daring to hope that her and Marcus would join the 'everyone'. And then there was that visitor Paul, she didn't know anything about him at all, except that he was an old friend and colleague of tragic Greg. But now that her home looked ready and welcoming, she would be able to relax and enjoy everyone's company, Damian and Marcus especially. She looked in the mirror, recognising that look in her eyes she hadn't seen in a long time, one that was looking forward to seeing a special someone. How long had it been?

Her iLink buzzed, as if on cue, it was Marcus. She laughed into the speaker, her heart beating just that bit faster. "Hey, it's you! I was just thinking of you, well, about everyone at the get-together! You are still coming, aren't you?"

"Hi, Yvonne, glad to find you in." Marcus's voice was serious enough for Yvonne's smile to drop in an instant. "Are you free to come to Sabine's place, if I give you the directions? I think Damian needs you, actually, we all do."

"Yes, I've got the night shift today, I could come now? Nothing bad has happened, has it?" Yvonne tried to sound light and carefree, but knew full well that Marcus wouldn't have called her sounding like that if they only wanted her company for the day. And she also knew he wouldn't say what was up if it was in any way strange enough to alert anyone listening in.

"Oh, he's a bit off colour, and we'd love to see you anyhow." Marcus replied as cautiously as he considered wise and gave her the directions which were simple enough.

"I'll see you in a bit then, do I need to bring anything?"

"If you've got a spare set of clothes for him, that would be good, seems he got soaked somewhere out there, Yvonne."

For some reason what had happened played out instantly in her mind. She shivered inwardly. Was this going to be another 'new reality' for them all now? Shocks of cold and wet and hawks and other surprises? And her son right at the centre of it all? That couldn't be easy for Sabine. Clothes flung in a bag, Yvonne pulled the fresh bunch of flowers she had only just bought out of the vase, grabbed some paper to wrap around the stems and put them on the backseat of her car for Sabine, they might just help cheer her up.

Marcus was doing all the right things, Sabine realized, her heart jumping at the thought, Damian needed tender loving care, not her being freaked out about something that was happening. And he looked awful. She rushed towards him. "Damian! Oh Damian! How long have you been back? Poor love, you're all wet!" Sabine hugged her rather unusual boyfriend who was looking very different without the swagger he had when he left the cafe earlier. Damian looked up at her, still in a very strange crouched position on her sofa, with tears falling from his eyes. "I'm so sorry, I am so so sorry, Sabine, I've done it all wrong, showing off in the cafe the way I did, I got carried away with myself, I know better now. And I met my Dad, I met my Dad." Damian carried on crying as if his heart had been broken.

Paul, Marcus and Sabine looked at each other, stunned, Damian's father had never been mentioned before. How and where had that happened? "What more does he have to go through?" Paul whispered to Marcus who was watching Sabine showering Damian with tender kisses on his cold lips. Marcus agreed, it really seemed too much for anyone. He couldn't wait for Yvonne to arrive.

Yvonne almost fell through the door to rush to her son, her eyes taking him in, like only a mother can, before she could even reach him. "It looks like you need taking care of, Sweetheart. Sabine, love, would you mind running a bath for him? And have you got hot chocolate in the house? It worked years ago, it should work now."

Sabine jumped up, relieved to see Yvonne, why hadn't she thought of any of it? It wasn't as if they hadn't been through it before! Damian straightened himself up and looked his mother in the eyes. "I saw Dad." His voice was croaky. "He died, did you know?"

The stunned silence in Sabine's living room seemed to go on forever until Yvonne replied, her shock apparent. "Jacques? You saw Jacques? How, I mean, when? And what do you mean, he died?"

Damian sat up some more, straightening himself up, but looking so very tired. "Mum, I arrived at the Intergalactic Council, didn't feel too good, and he was there, giving me a right ticking off. He's all right though. He said, quite rightly, that I was already beginning to show off and then told me why I was there. He told me, Mum, that he died before I was born and that you never knew. It was a self inflicted accident, he drove too fast and into a wall, he's ashamed of it. He's alive there though, and must be quite high up in the Council."

Yvonne sat down next to her son, shocked to the core. "I thought he just didn't care, he'd stopped replying to my letters after I told him about you. Goodness.." Lost in memories she sat down, interweaving her fingers with Damian's.

"He was quite proud of not having a French accent, which of course he had. Does that mean anything to you, Mum?"

"His chat up line, that's how we met." Yvonne replied, almost whispering now, not telling of their passionate night that had made time stand still. She had fallen in love with him, head over heels, and when she found out she was pregnant he was nowhere to be found. It had broken her heart, it was only Damian's arrival that had half managed to put it right again. Such a long time ago, another life.

"Do you want some privacy to talk?" Marcus offered. "I could take Paul out somewhere while you two women help Damian back on his feet?" It was the least he could do to help, he knew that, but didn't quite know how to feel about a part dead, part alive father of Damian's, who obviously knew everything about everything, unreachable in some distant place.

"That's considerate of you, yes, thank you, Marcus. Much appreciated." Yvonne gave him the sweetest smile that made him glad he had offered it. Sabine looked pleased, too, Damian looked beyond caring, Paul readily agreed. All Marcus really wanted to do was to take Yvonne into his arms, able to tell her that he could make everything all right for her, and for Damian, too. He almost wished Damian was still young enough to actually need him. How could he compete with a father in another universe who was pals with extraterrestrials or whoever those council members were?

Chapter 38
The Brooch

DAMIAN DIDN'T RESIST being fussed over. The sweet smell of hot chocolate had filled Sabine's flat, mixed with the scent of the bubble bath that was waiting for him. It was wonderful. Everything felt soft and inviting, the gentle words and touches from the two women he loved more than anything in the world, he even had fresh clothes on the chair. His Mum, his Sabine, Base Earth. So much love, so much to love. And so much to be grateful for. Never again would he take anything or anyone for granted. Not wanting to show that his eyes were filling up with tears, he bent down more deeply than necessary to take off his boots.

"I just had a thought!" Sabine sat up, with excitement in her eyes! "I think I'm realizing something! Damian, you're supposed to be refreshed and younger looking, and feel all energetic, aren't you? Through touching or sniffing the feather or being a hawk covered in feathers or whatever? So, you're not, are you? You're exhausted!"

Yvonne almost jumped up in response. "Yes! You're right, Sabine! That means something! So, what does Damian need? Another feather? What?"

Damian sat up slowly, it was true, joining his other self in another universe should double up his energies at least. "Hm, you're right, Sweetheart, what are you thinking?"

"Well, I'm thinking that meeting your Dad has obviously upset you, and I don't know if there was anything pleasant about this trip? And maybe there's a difference how you feel depending where you end up going? Like it feels good going somewhere good, and horrible if going somewhere horrible? I felt amazing when I saw us as a family, when the hawk sat on my shoulder, it must have shown! Did it?" Sabine put her hand over her mouth, she hadn't told anyone what she had seen, and how happy she had been about the vision of her and Damian as a family, with children.

Yvonne was stunned, she had no idea what Sabine was talking about. "A hawk sat on your shoulder? When? How did that come about?"

"We had a bit of an occurrence right here, Mum. Marcus was with us, too, and experienced some things of his own he didn't expect. I'd rather he'd tell you himself though." Damian could feel an idea forming in his head, though Sabine looked like she had figured it out already and was keen to continue. "It means to recover now you should go there, go where you were really happy and well, and regain strength from that! Like Mary and Bill did in hospital! It's worth a try! Can you just go, somewhere else, to get energised again? Not trying to get rid of you, honest! It's just, you need to know if that would work, don't you! You can't end up in a state like this forever and day!" Sabine laughed out loud, surprising herself how suddenly comfortable she was thinking of Damian as a time and space traveller.

"But surely you are too weak to go anywhere at all just now?" Yvonne protested, not liking the idea one bit. It was upsetting enough having to get to grips with the whole idea that Jacques had made an appearance in some other universe, let alone to see Damian weakened even more in any way. "You don't know what you will experience, you didn't expect to see your father, did you? It's all too out of control, I don't like this much. Bill, Mary and Kade, too, needed strength to survive, and received it, yes, but you just need some rest and hot chocolate, surely that's enough?" Yvonne surprised herself with her somewhat defensive response. Damian shook his head. "No, Sabine is right, Mum, I need to get strength, because I've still got to help Nina's Grandma in Alaska, whether I like it or not. I thought I was going to get instruction as to what to say from the Council, but I think the message was more about what not to say or think. I will tune in and enjoy a little bit of energising, but don't worry, I'll stay right here, mind travel will be enough for this one."

Damian smiled gently, he had just realized something new, so simple, yet so profound. Sabine and Yvonne sat back to give him a little space and watched him lay there, eyes closed, and saw first a smile and then a gentle glow appearing on his features. Within minutes he looked no longer exhausted, he simply looked like a young man resting and totally at peace.

"One day I'll go with him, see what he goes through, but I'm not ready for that yet, are you?" Sabine whispered to Yvonne, who squeezed her hand in response, shaking her head.

"No, I'm not keen either, but I guess it'll be yet another 'new reality' to get used to. It never stops, does it! I'm fed up with constantly 'new realities'! I don't fancy bumping into Jacques for starters. It would be like falling in love with a ghost, and what good is that? Are we supposed to meet everyone we've ever had a connection with again? Even people who hurt us? We'd have no peace, ever, would we!"

Sabine shook her head. "I don't know. But I do know that if we have the choice to go somewhere where we can be well and happy, we have to start practising going to better places in our minds here and now. Focusing on what we want suddenly makes more sense than before, don't you think?"

Yvonne felt the truth of it, that it would become part of her. Was it as easy as that? "That's a profound statement, Sabine. I'll have to let that sink in. We use visualisation in patient care all the time, that could be a starting point of sorts. Interesting."

"So, what will you do when you get back to New York?"

Marcus asked Paul, as they were walking round the village, heads bowed, not looking happy campers at all.

"I really have no idea. Nothing makes sense right now. Do you know, there is an old Chinese saying, 'When a man looks down he is sick, when a woman looks down she gathers strength?' Well, we must be awfully sick." Paul laughed. Marcus laughed along, not quite sure what Paul thought was so funny though. "Do you realize that we actually believed we'd be at the forefront of new discoveries and we're so far behind that it's more than embarrassing?" Paul let out another chuckle that was worryingly close to a sob.

"Tell me about it." Marcus answered dryly, not quite knowing whether to cry or to laugh either. "I miss Greg, don't you? He managed to stay in front somehow, didn't he, even in death he still seems to be in front. I offered Damian a job as my assistant, and it helped him out of a hole, but since then he's literally changed beyond all recognition, I have no idea what Sabine will make of it all, and whether he'll still even need any kind of job is another question altogether. He seems a bit of a loose cannon though, not just in the old cosy earthbound sense. I know this sounds bad." Marcus felt uneasy talking about his worries like that, but was glad to have Paul there as a sounding board. "Can you imagine someone like Damian darting about in universes, grabbing random facts to spread ideas which might after all be merely justifiable gut reactions? Is he a good or a bad example of things to come? I have no idea, no clue, have you?"

"No, but it doesn't worry me so much, he couldn't do it on his own, could he. It's obviously a learning process, just like studying or being trained for anything new, mistakes will happen, sure. But there must be more people like him, there might be a whole helpful network out there already for him. Even little Kade is pretty clued up, at barely school age! He did manage to remind me of another life somewhere, too foggy as yet for me to know what to do with it. The idea of Kade himself is perturbing, but not as worrying as the talk of extraterrestrials round a big table having their hand in things." Paul shook his head how perfectly relaxed Kade had been in the cafe, in contrast to the adults. "And, come to think of it, the ice storm accidents with the feathers have been happening all over the globe, so there might be lots of conversations like this going on all over the place." Paul paused before continuing. "But yeah, my friend, we're definitely behind. I wonder what it would take to be in front, or at least in the middle of things, rather than just being observers?"

Marcus smiled cautiously in response, not knowing whether to tell or not.

"I'd say, Damian is the man to ask after all is said and done, he's the one who knows more than any of us." He hesitated, feeling tearful just thinking of the wonderful life as a vet and a musician he had seen himself in. "I'd rather stay as I am for now, I did have an experience with Damian and the hawks, I was shown another life option, and I'm not actually sure I want to experience any more of that. It's pretty confronting to see the result of choices you said no to in the past play out in front of you." Marcus's face turned hard, and Paul realized there would be no point in asking him to elaborate. And again he felt frustrated and left out. Why was it so easy for others to experience the extraordinary? And what would his 'extraordinary' be once he did have the chance to see it?

· · • ● ⬤ ● • · ·

"LOOK AT IT, just look at it! It's paradise, isn't it?" Brent exclaimed, looking fondly at their house and garden, basked in bright sunshine, with their son running up the path. Nina squeezed his hand, her smile spreading across her face. "Just think, we wanted to move. Different timing, and we might have never met Kade, and he'd be with social services, it doesn't bear thinking about, does it."

"No, it doesn't. But you know, I haven't forgotten what Damian said earlier, that you'll be looking at universe hopping and following in goodness knows what Kade will be doing, too. And I made a decision there and then, want to hear it?"

338

Nina turned to look at her husband, she knew that voice, that was calm and determined and that usually meant he wouldn't change his mind, whether she liked it or not. She could see the love in his eyes though, which was reassuring.

"Go on then, what have you decided? I don't even know whether I want to hop anywhere at all anyhow, seeing I don't even want to move now!"

"Well, I suspect you might well want to, I think you will need to be there for Kade, probably even meet his mother, find out what he needs from us, all that. One of us has to be able to understand him and where he goes."

Nina nodded thoughtfully, she hadn't thought about it much beyond being surprised at what Damian had said to her, but it made sense. It even had an exciting ring of truth about it already, even though the very notion of following in her father's footsteps about exploring other realms had been far from her mind until now.

"Wow. You've really thought this through, haven't you!"

"Yes, I have, and I also know that it takes one very special husband and parent to cope with you two." Brent grinned at her widely. "Someone who offers straightforward earthbound stability at home. It means I want to concentrate on what we are doing here only, I need to make sure business is ticking over, and make sure that we can deal with whatever changes will come right here on terra firma. I have to be the husband and father you two will want to come home to. Otherwise I think we will get lost in a sea of endless new possibilities, you know? Probably even lose each other, each of us floating about all over the place. I won't allow us to lose each other, I'm determined to be the anchor for my pioneering family." Even as he said it Brent had that wonderful solid feeling again, he loved the idea of just making his furniture and enjoying a simple life, that's all he had ever wanted anyway, with just a little spice thrown in here and there. He'd have plenty of that, he was quite sure.

"Oh, Brent, I love you, my carrot face." Nina hugged him as hard as she could. "We'll never be bored again, will we! Everything has been happening so fast, it's been crazy!" Nina laughed happily watching Kade calling to Jester through the letterbox. "But yes, home...home is you and little genius there. Are you happy, Kade?" She called to him, filled with the sense that everything was going to be alright. Kade ran back to give his new parents a hug.

"It's really happy here, so I'll be happy, definitely! Much better than on the other earths now." He nodded vehemently, before his shiny blue eyes clouded over. "My Mum wanted to die, all the time, my Mum was sad all the time." Kade spoke quietly. "She didn't like it here, she always said she'd kill herself if it wasn't for me."

"Oh my god, why didn't you tell us, Sweetheart?" Nina hugged him again, and Brent stared at him, shocked.

"It's over now, isn't it." Kade shrugged his little shoulders.

"The accident was just right for my Mum, it's what she wanted."

"You know, I'm starting to think it was perfect for all of us." Brent nodded. "Nina and I wanted to move somewhere new, felt bored and stuck, didn't feel challenged enough. And then, when you were all in hospital, we realised we wouldn't want to move away from Mary, nor from you for that matter, we hated the idea. And now we've become your parents, and feel very, very lucky." Brent smiled warmly at the little boy and ruffled his hair.

Sabine motioned to Yvonne to follow her into her little kitchen, Damian was fast asleep, still with a smile on his face, and thankfully looking very normal indeed. "What do you think about all this, Yvonne? Will he be okay from now on? He was awful in the cafe, you didn't see him, but he was really stuck up, totally up himself, actually."

Yvonne saw that Sabine was struggling to remain positive, that she was swinging between being in love with her son and wanting to run a mile or ten. And who could blame her?

"I keep wondering, what if that crash hadn't happened?" Yvonne replied. "It was very strange timing, just when he lost his job. I'd call it coincidence, but I'm not so sure now."

"The Icehawk didn't cause the crash, Damian thinks he

did." Sabine said quietly. "He thinks the Hawk came because his wanting to get away was so strong. And because he must have been ready to learn whatever it is he's learning now. He's probably feeling pretty guilty about it, too."

Bob was going through the cupboards, trying to find something to eat. He just couldn't stop eating, and couldn't understand it, he'd been like it since he and Nellie had come back from their Earth 4 adventure. It was all a bit bizarre, trying to plan for their wedding when he felt they had been there already, it would almost be like a repeat performance and who would want that? Nellie was sitting in her chair, staring into space, fiddling with her mug of coffee that had gone cold. "That wasn't so smart of me, was it, to say there would be an announcement. The more I think about it, the dafter that sounds, what can we tell them? Maybe I should just tell them to sniff those feathers if they want to and not if they don't, like Kade said. And leave them to it, after all, that is what we did, and the children, too."

Bob nodded, triumphantly holding up a packet of cookies. "Yeah, I was thinking that, too. We could do with a bit of help though, couldn't we. Maybe something very clever and Elder-like will come to us in the next few hours?"

Bob and Nellie laughed together, it was like an exam they hadn't practiced for. How long had it been since they had felt like that?

· · · • • ● • • · ·

MARCUS RAN HIS fingertips over the little gift bag in his jacket pocket. He had nearly forgotten about the little music box he had bought for Yvonne at Wardill's, just before the fiasco at the cafe. Nina was right, that shop had everything, in an endearingly old fashioned way. Paul had picked up a pretty blue flower brooch he was tempted to give to Mary, but he knew he was just torturing himself, he'd take it back to New York with him, knowing she wouldn't really want anything from him at all. Least of all a feminine brooch, however pretty. It did feel exciting to buy a present for someone, though, even if he didn't have anyone to buy it for. Not yet anyway.

"Do you think it's safe to go back to Sabine's now?" Marcus was pretty sure that Paul was getting as restless as he was. "I don't know when Yvonne has to start work, but it might be a good idea to go and see how the three of them are doing?"

The three were all smiles as the two men came in. Damian was up, looking refreshed and determined. "Hi, Marcus, Paul, you just caught me, good. I'm ready to see Bob and Nellie now, feeling strong again. If all goes well I will remember what to say, and yes, I will be back real soon! I'm sorry I was such a jerk in the cafe, it won't happen again, you have my word." He hugged Sabine who looked completely at ease now, and walked down the stairs, to save them from having to watch him disappear again.

"Shall we call Nina and Brent and tell them what happened?" Sabine suggested. "I don't want them worrying about me any more than necessary, and I'd like them to know that Damian said sorry for being such a pain earlier."

Yvonne got up, grabbing her coat. "Yes, good idea. But I've got to get to work, I'll get a sandwich downstairs, and will leave you to it then. I'm glad it all came good in the end, though I have my doubts that Damian was really as well as he was pretending to be. He didn't look right to me, but that might be just me worrying. Would you let me know when he's back, Sabine?" Yvonne smiled warmly at her. "And thank you for everything you're doing for him, I'm glad that you two have found each other!"

"I'll walk you down to your car, Yvonne." Marcus blushed a little saying it, keen to have Yvonne's company just for himself for a few seconds.

Sabine motioned to Paul to take a seat while she swiped over her iLink to call Nina. It was the loveliest family scene appearing on her screen, Kade on Brent's lap as Nina answered, some food laid out in front of them, Kade drinking from his new drinks bottle.

"Hi, guys! Just to let you know Damian arrived back here, he was pretty weak and humble when he first got back, but he's gone off to help your Grandma now, Nina, he looked fine about it. And nowhere near as full of himself as earlier. He apologized about his behaviour earlier. I could tell he was sincere." Sabine smiled. "You guys look cosy!"

"We are, well sort of!" Nina laughed. "We're having a kind of normal abnormal conversation about school here." Nina laughed again, amused by her self-coined phrase.

"Oh, have you seen the school already, Kade?" Sabine asked, knowing he'd appreciate being talked to directly.

"Wait for it!" Brent shook his head. "He's not talking about Kirbymoorside. He's talking about Chignik. How about that then!"

Paul and Sabine both let out an exasperated sigh.

"It never stops, does it!" Paul exclaimed. "What are you up to now, Kade? Do you know the place?"

Kade looked at his parents, shaking his head. "He's doing it again, not remembering, isn't he! Why does he keep doing that?" Kade whispers had been loud enough for everyone to hear. Paul decided to test him.

"Go on then, Kade! My friend Greg, and Mary, too, told me quite a bit about Chignik in the past, so, let's see if you really know the place! Describe it to me?"

Kade rolled his eyes in an exaggerated fashion.

"Well, Grandma Nellie and Grandfather Bob and Damian and Sophie and Stefan are going to be on the stage in the Shed soon, the place with the big blue doors and try and tell everyone what they are doing, which is really funny! And all our friends will be there, Ken and Bianca from the store who always gives me a sweet, and Miss Kelly is going to be there with everyone from school, she'll get all giggly around you, like she does. You're always really giggly with her, too, not all serious like here. And she's not going to give anyone any homework today either, and she's going to wear that blue flower pin you gave her."

Kade wriggled off Brent's knees. "Oh, not sure now, that might have been on Earth 4." Kade scratched his little head. "You're all confusing me now! Anyway, Stefan is going to use the Yup'ik tool to help Damian."

"I rang Grandma to warn her that Damian is going to arrive there." Nina interjected. "I have no idea where this little man gets all this stuff from, but, hey, giving her and Bob fair warning was the least I could do. I guess they'll work it out over there?"

Sabine and her friends looked at each other, simultaneously aware that they were all perplexed but no longer afraid at all. The three laughed, surprised and relieved at the same time. "See you at Yvonne's party tomorrow!"

What none of them had noticed was that Paul had sat back, pulling out the flower brooch from its bag, staring at it, turning it over and over, trying his hardest to comprehend how it could be in two different places at the same time, or even at different times, as he was sure Kade had talked about the very same pin. And, was Kelly the woman he had bought it for all along, a complete stranger he had never even met? All he could tell was that Greg was laughing at him from somewhere. Perhaps, just maybe, he should book a flight to Alaska, just for research, of course.

Chapter 39
The Yup'ik Tool

DAMIAN FELT HIMSELF slip. He had no idea where he was, there were only vague memories of sitting with his Mum and Sabine at her flat, and having to meet someone important he just couldn't think of, and no energy to do anything about it at all. Was this what schizophrenia was like? Were schizophrenics really time, space or multiverse travellers? He was too tired to follow up on that thought, later would do. He tried to feel his body, to make out whether he was standing or lying down, but couldn't feel himself, couldn't even feel any air on his face. He was alive though and something was drawing him. He was being pulled, as if by some invisible force, there was no pain, and he gave no resistance. Was he really being pulled or was he falling into a deep sleep? Barely conscious, he didn't know. He bent his head, It was easy to do, forwards, then back, or at least he thought he did, he couldn't feel a pillow, nothing to hold his head up, his chin dropping on his chest. So he had a chin, that was reassuring. It was warm, too, that much he could figure out. None of the damp cold of being an icehawk. None of the pain in his legs that went with that, none of the numbness in his joints. He tried to feel his hands, make his fingers and thumb touch, nothing. Ah yes ! The faintest of sensations was there, his fingers or something else?

He was tired, so tired, he couldn't be sure. He felt himself sink deeper into unconsciousness. Blackness enveloped him.

Nellie and Bill had been stunned by his arrival, despite Nina's rushed warning just minutes earlier. Damian had literally fallen through their front door, collapsed on the mat, shaking. They had barely been able to drag him to the nearest chair, not strong enough to get him to the bedroom, and propped him up leaning against the kitchen table. Bill had stoked the fire some more, the young man felt cold, but there were no feathers on him, none of the hawk appearance Nina had warned them about. Damian's head had lolled around, he was fainting, they thought, but then he said 'I'm so tired' and they decided to let him sink forward and sleep, with his head on his arm.

"He's breathing well enough, Nel, what do we do now? Shall we call the doc? Or just wait?"

"I don't know, Bob, it might harm him, if we interfere with what might be a recovery of sorts? Let's leave him to sleep, he looks like he needs it."

"Yes, my gut says much the same." Bob agreed and like Nellie felt an instant warmth towards Damian, it was close to seeing their own child asleep.

"Love is the same everywhere, isn't it, the caring." Nellie whispered. "It feels the same, whatever the circumstance. I'd say he's quite a special man, wouldn't you agree?"

"He is, and so young! What a time he must have had, being thrown into different worlds from one day to the next." Bob was trying to comprehend the incomprehensible.

"It's always the young ones that lead the way, look at Nina and Brent now with Kade. I'm not sure if either of us could have adopted a child so readily, so unexpectedly, so selflessly. What can we Elders do, in any of this? Really?"

There was a knock on the door, Sophie's tell tale knock.

"Come in!" Bob called out as usual, the girl walked in, nodding her head, looking at Damian asleep at the table, not at all surprised. "Stefan said I'd find him here, that he's lost. He said it happens sometimes, in the beginning. I don't really know what he's talking about though. He understands more than me about all this, all this, - stuff!" As ever Sophie talked shyly, but couldn't control her hands from circling around trying to describe the 'stuff'. Nellie laughed, she knew exactly what Sophie meant, this 'stuff' was huge. How else could it be described than by waving one's arms about? "I'd describe all this stuff just like you Sophie, there is no better way! So, Stefan knew all about Damian being here, what else does he know? Anything you can tell us would be really helpful!"

"Well, Stefan asked me to bring this for Damian, and said it would help him." Sophie fished about in the satchel she had brought along and pulled out a small wooden item, a simple rectangular shovel, with a wooden rim and a thin rope attached underneath.

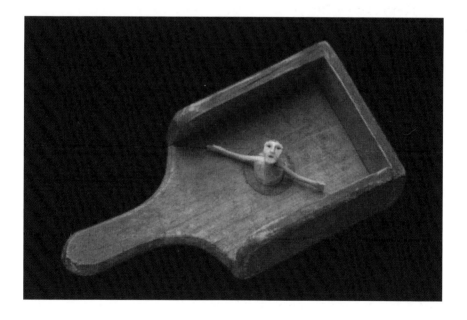

Right in the middle of the shovel an amusing effigy of half a man looked up at the user, as if he had come up through the surface, activated by the rope being pulled. Nellie and Bob recognised it immediately as an old Yu'pic Shamanic tool. It was as significant, as it was a fun thing to have. They hadn't expected anyone to possess one still, let alone anyone in Chignik.

"Goodness!" Bob exclaimed. "That's got to be two hundred years old! Do you know what it is, Sophie?"

Little Sophie handed the tool over to Bob, and cleaned her as ever steamed up glasses, shrugging her shoulders. "It's been in a box in Stefan's room for ages, not sure where it's from. I think someone might have given it to him as a present to play with?"

Both Bob and Nellie marvelled at it, they couldn't remember where or when they had seen one like it last. It was a magical little antique. Every tourist knew the Shamanic drums, but this was quite a rarity.

"Well, Sophie, it's a Shamanic tool. You know how a true Shaman is able to travel between our world and the spirit world? And between the lower, middle and upper worlds? He does that, with his mind, in trance, to fix problems on different levels for the benefit of his village, his community. And you know the old dances, showing the Shaman's crossing into the world of spirit guides? Where the Shaman emerges from a hole in the ground, that represents the portal between worlds. This is what this tool is all about, It shows the emergence, and the shovel shape is meant to show the geometry of the village dance floor, look, it's even got the walls here." Bob stroked his finger over the wooden edge. "And look how the Shaman comes up through the hole in the floor when I pull the string! Isn't it wonderful?"

Sophie giggled as the little figure emerged from the circular opening, much like a jack-in-a-box, and his moveable arms sprang open. She thought it was funny, and even funnier that Nellie looked so seriously at it.

"And that, him coming through like that, means he's coming up, in one world or another, from the one before. You see?" Nellie had completed Bob's description, but with less amusement in her voice than him.

"So, is that Damian then, popping up all over the place? Is he like a Shaman?" Sophie asked, not sure whether to be impressed or not. Most grown ups she knew seemed to prefer pills from the doctor over Shamans, whom she just knew as strange old people who held secrets nobody understood and which didn't seem that useful at all.

"It's an interesting thought, Sophie." Bob said kindly. "To be honest, I don't know. I think he can do things nobody else I've ever met is able to, but I'm not a Shaman, so maybe we should arrange a visit with one and ask him?"

Nellie had taken the tool off Bob to feel it's weight, and make the little figure come up and disappear again, it was true, it was fun. She looked across to Damian who was still sleeping right in front of them, dead to the world. How could this possibly help him? Though the meaning was obviously a match to his experience.

"I wonder what made Stefan think of it? Did he say anything else?"

Sophie shook her head, looking embarrassed again.

"No, he just said to get it to him because he'd need it. I think Stefan thought he'd know what to do with it?"

Bob looked across to Nellie who seemed comfortable but unaffected by it. It wasn't like the feather effect then. "It looks like it's just something for one person, doesn't it. Or maybe to demonstrate something? The meaning is pretty obvious, isn't it, Damian obviously does pop up like that, but apart from that, how it's supposed to help, I'm lost." Bob shook his head, Stefan was, what, eight years old? What on earth was going on with the kid. He had been the first one to pick up the feathers, too. And sniff them.

Damian stirred at the table, moving his arms, very slowly, and feeling the weight of his head on them, stretched them out across the table, and pushed himself upright, his eyes still closed, as if they were hard to open. He looked pale, Nellie noticed it first, and Sophie turned her head quickly towards Nellie, mouthing silently 'I think he's sick!' Bob was watching, too. The last time he remembered seeing anyone that exhausted was when he'd found a tourist that had lost his way in the mountains, and Bob had found him, by chance, barely able to stand. Dehydrated, cold, hungry. "I think he needs some water and some sugar, in case he's dehydrated? See if he wants it." Bob went across to fill a glass, adding a pinch of salt and spoonful of sugar to it, which he hoped would be helpful. Nellie had rushed over to Damian and touched his arm. "Hello, my dear, it's Nellie and Bob here, you've come to visit us, and we're delighted to have you! Take your time, rest as long as you want to."

Damian heard the words, though they didn't make sense, last thing he knew he had hugged his mother goodbye in Sabine's flat, after the best sleep there. Why should he be at Nellie's and Bob's now? He was so tired, so tired. He realised he was sitting on a chair, and had an overwhelming urge to lay down. A faint voice in his head told him that wasn't the thing to ask for just arriving somewhere, but he knew it was necessary, and he needed sugar, he knew that much. "I'm sorry to have to ask, have you got any sugar, something sweet I could have?"

"Good, I must have read your mind." Bob was relieved he got that much right. "I added some sugar and a pinch of salt to this glass of water, any good? And would you like some cake?"

Without replying Damian opened his eyes just long enough to see the glass Bob had put down in front of him and drank it down, barely able to swallow, gulping desperately, almost greedily. He then nodded and whispered 'Yes, please, Bob' and tried to raise himself from the chair, looking round to see any space to lay down. Sophie understood. "He wants to lie down somewhere, shall we help him to the sofa in your back room? I'll help!" With that she walked up to Damian, and lifted his heavy arm around her tiny shoulders.

"You can lean on me, I'll take you to the sofa in the next room."

If Damian hadn't looked so awful Nellie and Bob would have burst out laughing, this strip of a girl trying to support a grown man was just the cutest, funniest idea. But Damian nodded, and did get up, slowly, gingerly, and he did support himself on both the table and Sophie's shoulder. "Lead the way, Little Hawk, lead the way." Sophie's eyes widened in delighted surprise at her new name, while Nellie had taken the plate with the cake off Bob who'd rushed to Damian's left side, and the very unbalanced three made their way to the back room, until Damian could lower himself onto the sofa. Sophie was already by his feet, taking off his boots, Bob helped him out of his heavy suede coat, and laid him on his back. With Damians head well supported by a cushion on the armrest, Bob unfolded the blanket to spread over him. Nellie held out the plate to Damian. "Can you manage there, dear, can you eat like that?"

"Thanks, Nellie, yes, I'll be fine." Damian replied gratefully and ate, hungrily. He was still confused, he had absolutely no idea how he had got there, nor could he remember what he was supposed to be doing there. He did know that Sophie was one of the new Little Hawks, like many children now, just like Stefan, a bit behind Kade still, but becoming ever more powerful in their own right.

"Pull the string!" Sophie suddenly called out. "I don't know why I know, like someone just told me, but he needs the little man to come up! I just know it! He's struggling to do it himself!"

Nellie understood immediately, and reached forward, holding the toy over Damian's chest, and pulled the string. As soon as the little figure popped up, Damian gasped, as if gasping for air after a long dive underwater. He opened his eyes, staring blankly, and gulped a few more breaths down into him, trying to push himself up to a sitting position, with a huge effort.

"Damian! Oh goodness, Damian!" Nellie cried out. Bob was by his side, quick as a flash, to help him up. Sophie stared at the toy tumbling off his chest on the floor, where it landed, upright, but with the little figure turning and turning, like a wind-up toy. She was sure it glowed, not like a torch or anything like that, but that it emitted a slight glow all by itself.

"Look!" She called out, with such amazement in her voice that the three grown-ups followed her gaze, only now noticing the figure, that was circling round and round, arms outstretched. "He's dancing! It's like he's alive!"

Damian smiled upon seeing it, and reached out his hand to receive it, as Sophie picked it up gently to pass back to him. "Here you go, Damian." She whispered, handing him the toy she had so casually stuffed in her satchel earlier, recognizing it as something precious and sacred now. She felt it had maybe saved Damian's life, he looked so much better already. The little figure was still whirling, it was extraordinary. Damian took it, his eyes shining as if he was meeting an old friend, and then the memory hit him, with joy and relief. He knew why he was there, what he had to do.

"The meeting! I'm back now! I was going to support you at the Shed, Nellie and Bob. That's why I'm here, I remember now! Hello, dear Sophie, please thank Stefan for remembering the emerger tool, he must have known I'd need it. I'm still learning, obviously, aren't I. Behind every big hawk there are wonderful little hawks."

Damian laughed now, so glad to have himself back, recovering fast. Getting up to shake Bob's hand, then Nellie's, then to give them both a hearty hug, he looked a different man from just minutes earlier.

"I sure am glad you're looking better now, Damian, and thank you for coming to help." Nellie felt she could relax now, for the first time in ages, she could feel the stress and worry fall off her shoulders. Bob was relieved, too, though not quite so sure why or what to make of it all, and not overly happy to be thought of as 'needing help' either, true or not. "So, what's the plan then, Damian? You're not going to spring another surprise on us, are you? What we really wanted to do was to give everyone a bit of reassurance that everything was all right, don't know what else to say, really, except that Nellie has this way of surprising me still."

Damian nodded, he got what Bob meant, and understood his pride. He had felt the same often enough. "You've been hungrier than usual lately, haven't you, Bob, more so than Nellie, isn't that right?"

"Well, yes it is!" Nellie replied first. "He can't stop eating!"

"Thanks for that, Nel." Bob muttered in response, he'd have preferred a straight answer to his question.

"Bob, it means that you are preparing to do some more traveling to different Earths, so don't in any way assume your job is finished here. That is what you're worried about, isn't it?"

Bob didn't know what to say. Yes, of course that was what worried him, every day, but the thought of doing more universe hopping wasn't attractive at all. "I'm an old man, Damian, and yes, I still want to be useful, sure. Who doesn't? But all this 'stuff.'" He smiled at Sophie acknowledging her term for it all. "Well it's all getting a bit much, I don't see the point of it. And you still haven't answered my questions, Damian. Never mind about me, what about you? What are you doing here?"

Nellie held his hand and squeezed it slightly, she could tell Damian's appearance and offer of help had upset him. It was good to feel his squeeze back.

"I am trying to answer your question the best I can, Bob. You remember when you saved the wolf, yes?"

"How do you know about that?" Bob frowned. He didn't like that much either, the fact that this stranger knew long gone details about his past. It was a good job that he was a friend of Nina's, otherwise he'd have been tempted to show him the door. Sophie, though, had obviously taken to him, the little girl was clearly developing a crush on Damian, as her shiny wide open eyes showed. She hadn't taken them off him for a second.

"Bob, you helped the wolf recover and return to his pack, you saved him in more ways than one, didn't you. And that is what you're here for again now, to do exactly the same with your people here. You're still their hero, you know. They will listen to you and Nellie more than to anyone else."

Bob laughed. "Oh, Damian, please. As a little boy I dreamt of being the one who was going to get our land back, I pictured myself as a great hero, and you know what? It never happened? Fancy that." Bob laughed again, almost relieved now. Whoever or wherever Damian got his information from, it was far from accurate. It can't have been more than a rumour or even an educated guess. Sophie, almost reluctantly taking her eyes off Damian, couldn't believe what he was saying. "But that's not true, Grandfather Bob! Everybody knows that you saved those people from drowning, that was a real heroic thing! We all know that you're a hero, everyone in Chignik knows it, probably everyone in Alaska!" Sophie waved her arms about again, surely Bob must have known how famous he was?

Bob shook his head. He never really thought about all that anymore, he hadn't realised that anyone else still did. He was an old man, that was all. "Really? They think I'm a hero? Oh, my dear, not so heroic how I see it. A real hero would have whisked Nellie here off her feet decades ago for starters."

Damian smiled. "Be that as it may, you and Nellie are both very much needed here."

Bob shook his head. "I just don't get why the icehawk showed here? Don't tell me he is lost, too."

"No, he isn't, far from it." Damian smiled. "He showed up here partly because he was able to, the atmospheric conditions creating the aurora are perfect to turn his energy into something visible. A bonus is that his very image is so welcome here, so readily accepted. A combined effort by the other Galactic Council Members. A few of them are more comfortable in hot and dry conditions, still causing the same ice storms though, oddly enough, and some are more comfortable at sea. Many of them visit Base Earth all the time, and look for those who are ready, or want to be taught, that's why you have such randomly spread sightings, deaths, accidents."

"Causing deaths and accidents for what purpose though? It's a cruel way of going about things, isn't it?" Bob interrupted. "I understand the benefit of multiverse minds working together to affect change on Base Earth, to steer the course of events everywhere, but what good can anyone do without being present here? As anywhere else is not a creative space, if I got that right?"

Damian nodded, his hand resting easily on Sophie's shoulder, who didn't dare say anything at all in case he moved it away. She really liked listening to it all, and understood most of what the three grown-ups were saying.

"All the creation happens on Base Earth, that's correct. But the other planes need leaders, too, unencumbered by concerns here. And there are planes that are being honed as back ups, by some Galactic Council Members, and some by old leaders from Base

Earth. Abraham Lincoln is just one of them, Frederic Douglass another. Marie Curie, Maya Angelou, so many more. None of the great minds really ever stop working."

Bob fiddled with his beard, that was a lot to take in. "All right, I guess that's reassuring. But why you? What's your role in all this? It sounds a pretty well organised system to me, without needing someone who is being used as a birdman, or whatever it is you'd describe yourself as? Hope you don't mind me asking?"

Damian really laughed now, that was probably the best and boldest question anyone could ask. "My role? I'm the surprise effect, for one thing. I'm doing what Greg had wanted to do for years but in the end wasn't physically able to. I'm quite sure though he had an influence on what people and locations he recommended as suitable." Damian smiled to himself, he knew full well that Greg had very much instigated just about everything. "My appearance helps to break up concepts, to open people's mind for the greater truth that is out there, and to lead them to different planes when necessary. They can't do it on their own yet. We've been evolving so fast!"

"So," Bob interrupted. "Is this really evolution? Or something else?" He was having his doubts. "Evolution happens slowly, doesn't it. Imperceptibly. But this? This has been a crazy time! Not sure if I trust it to be a natural thing."

Damian was seriously impressed with Bob's dogged questioning, determined to give him clear answers. "Vibrational speed doesn't need the conditions of natural evolution, it's a spiritual opening up within ourselves to what more we can be, a more rounded knowledge. Or, if you like, an increased awareness of what exists already, and the icehawk you saw, the little icehawk occurrences and what is happening to all of us Novices now, we're all part of that greater awakening, a speeding up of vibration."

Nellie, who had been listening quietly until then, was shaking her head. "What good is a speeding up of vibration? I don't understand the terminology. What's vibrating?"

They were old school, they had been talking about vibes all their lives, good vibes, bad vibes, but this? This was all beyond her. Bob, too, felt out of his depth. What had he actually been trying to do with his life? He didn't know any more.

"I know how you feel, I really do."Damian watched the turmoil that suddenly showed in both the old people's faces. "You're thinking it's all too hard to understand, and that you don't need this in your life." Damian laughed. "Welcome to my world. Basically, the higher our consciousness vibrates energetically, the higher the tone of existence. Higher vibration is creative, positive, proactive, works towards betterment. Lower vibration is destructive, only answers to base instincts of survival and procreation, and it works entirely towards selfish means. Lower vibration has no interest in global awareness, none in the health of the unseen, the intangible, none in universal love, which is nevertheless equally vital to the quality of all our lives." Damian stopped, catching breath, unsure where he knew all this from, but also knew that it was right. "I guess my appearance and abilities serve to simply inspire those who emit higher vibrations already to create more imaginatively, but those of lower vibration don't need encouragement, they need showing a different reality to raise their awareness. I'm kind of hoping there will be many more of the likes of me, it feels pretty lonely right now."

Bob felt himself agreeing wholeheartedly to what Damian had said, but he was tired, he didn't mind admitting it. "Well, I don't envy you, son, but I'm asking you to leave us alone as much as possible. Nellie needs rest, this is taking its toll on her, and on me, too. I want to be able to look forward to celebrating our wedding the way we had in mind, without thinking the sky might fall down."

Damian nodded. "Yes, you're tired now, I know Bob, but I'm pretty convinced you will both surprise yourselves, Bob. Your energy will come back, I promise. A bit like mine just a few minutes ago, wait and see." Damian turned to Nellie. "And you'll be getting curious about it all again sooner than you might think, dear Nellie. Nina will be around to help you, too, though she doesn't know about it yet." Damian smiled, stroking Nellie's hand, giving her a bit of an energy boost in the process.

"You two have wonderful adventures to come yet, joyful ones, you're the wise Elders here for good reason."

Bob smiled, it was a kind thing for Damian to say.

It was time to go to the Shed, Nellie felt herself getting ready to push herself up to leave. "I don't know about curiosity, but it does feel special to witness the great change, the time of the Icehawk. I wanted to thank you for coming, Damian. I think I know what to say now. Are we all ready?" She looked at Bob who got up to get their coats and at little Sophie eager to leave now. "You can read my mind, Damian, can't you, I can tell. Is it right, what I'm planning to say?"

Damian looked tall and strong now, it was a joy to see him transformed like that. He turned to Nellie, and with utmost tenderness kissed her on the cheek. "Yes, you are. You've known all along, haven't you. And yes, we've got to go, I think the Shed is filling up already."

Nellie shook her head. "We got that message about creating with more imagination on our wedding, didn't we.. goodness, I had already forgotten."

"Me, too." Bob admitted, as the four made their way to the Shed, seeing others walk towards it, too.

Chapter 40
Joint Lives

THE SHED FILLED quickly, everyone curious what Nellie and Bob would have to say, wondering who the strange man was whose arrival nobody had noticed. The fact that he had brazenly made his way onto the wooden stage with Bob and Nellie, flanked by little Sophie and Stefan, who had run to join them seemed a bit out of order. Topping that, the stranger stuffing Nellie's baking into his mouth as if he hadn't eaten for days didn't help either. It was bad form, the villagers thought, taking an instant dislike to this greedy pale faced intruder. He didn't even wear the right shoes, a brown leather jacket that was wet through even though it hadn't been raining, the man made no sense at all. How on earth was he connected to their wonderful Elders?

Nellie raised her hand and, as was customary at the start of important meetings, began to sing the old song.

".. See us reading

... Scriptures and sacred texts

... Listening to our inner guidance

... Tasting our own Godliness

... Freeing our souls

... As we dance together

... Open and free.."

It felt good, and the stranger knew the words, so that was something at least. Nellie smiled, feeling it in her heart that it was her time to guide them. With Bob and Damian like pillars on either side of her, giving her all the love and strength she needed, she knew she would find the words.

"My friends, a long time ago there was a poet called William Butler Yeats, and one of the lines he wrote was 'I will not be clapped in a hood, nor a cage, nor alight upon a wrist.' He was talking about the spirit of the hawk as much as about the human spirit. We have all seen the Icehawk. Some of us have touched the feathers brave little Stefan and Sophie brought us, some of us have heard and experienced strange things. Bob and I have gone on a journey, and we want to tell you about it, and we want you to believe us, that this reality is not all there is, that all of us are living many, many lives in different parallel universes. And each of those universes can only exist through our imagination right here."

Unperturbed by the noisy incredulity that reverberated through the Shed Nellie continued. She told them how she and Bob had found themselves at their own wedding, how exhausting and confusing it had been, but how exhilarating, too. How it could heal and rejuvenate them to feel their energetic multiverse selves combine when holding and breathing in the feathers. "As we can only live the lives we create in our thoughts here, we will learn the consequences of both our positive and negative dreams and intentions, see them lived out across time with absolute clarity. We all create our own heaven, and our own hell. Other galactic civilisations are aware of this, and are watching us, helping us through a sense of awakening to enter the 5th dimension, and every other dimension after that." Nellie paused, and looked at all the pairs of stunned eyes locked onto hers. Nobody had ever heard her talk like this. "Yes, there is life on other planets, and yes, we all get help from other galaxies all the time. How much have we forgotten, even how to speak to our guides from the other worlds. The Icehawk we saw is one of them, and he has many well-meaning helpers here." Nellie turned to Damian and without hesitation repeated what he seemed to transmit into her mind: "This has become an unstoppable, guided movement supported by higher minds than ours, to safeguard our contribution to creation itself, and to safeguard the health and survival of this wonderful planet."

"So, what do we have to do?" Ken's voice, ringing with respect, came from the audience. Bob had watched Nellie and saw she was tired. Her speech had taken it out of her, channelling the explanations he didn't recognise as her own. She had done well, better than he could have done. He had also heard the words in his head even before she had spoken them, he knew it was right, he was shown, too. Damian winked at the children.

"Grandma Nellie is right, we saw it." Sophie responded bravely, and Stefan nodded, smiling at his mother's anxious face in the audience.

"Let me take over from here, Nellie." Bob put his hand on her shoulder, and addressed the crowd. "You heard what Nellie just said, and that is how it is. It's especially Stefan and Sophie, though, who have really moved things along, being very courageous indeed. Well done, you two, for helping us so much!"

There were a few cautious claps of applause as Bob smiled gently at the children who blushed with pride, and continued. "Please be kind to them, and proud of them. Actually, it's the children who will be able to find it easier to cope with the changes that are to come for all of us, we must give them the freedom to develop their abilities. So, Ken, that's the first thing we need to do." Bob paused to make doubly sure he had everyone's full attention, feeling Damian's power next to him. "Some people amongst us have already become part of the group of Icehawks, and part of the Intergalactic Council, a wise and protective force who will help us. Our friend Damian here is one of them, we are very privileged that he has come to visit us." Bob turned to face Damian, who looked strong and charismatic and had finally stopped eating. "Damian? Would you mind saying something?"

There was a rising murmur of amazement in the crowd as they

saw the stranger grow in stature, with a glowing energy about him. Even his wet brown leather coat looked different somehow, it was, yes, lined, rippled, and icy.

Damian stood and looked into the eyes of all of them, with kindness and determination. "Ken, and everyone, I'm sorry to drop in on you like this, uninvited." Damian nodded at Ken who felt flattered that the stranger had remembered his name. "I am just here to tell you that we will all be learning very fast. Our minds are expanding like never before. Some of you might feel that hunger for freedom already, for a change for the better for all, you might feel the itch in your shoulders that will make you want to take to the skies and fly free. If you recognize yourself hearing this you will be invited to join the intergalactic family very soon, to help spread the message of a new creative wisdom. The freedom we are all looking for can be found in other universes, on other Earth planes, parallel to this one. And, learning how to, we will create it here. Nobody will be able to stop us, nobody!"

"It's a revolution!" Miss Kelly, the teacher, burst out, laughing out loud, surprising everyone. "I knew it was going to come, this is it, it must be it! The Aquarian Age, isn't it!"

Damian laughed with her. "Yes, you're right, Kelly, you've felt it, too, haven't you! But, remember, folks! Every one of those other Earths depends on you here! So use your imagination the best you can!"

Bob joined in, feeling his own enthusiasm now. His life wasn't finished yet, not by a long shot. "I just know it! We will think bigger, faster, better than ever before and we will grow braver to become true individuals, the best we can be, with our own ideas on how to live our lives."

Damian patted Bob on the shoulder. "Good to know you and Nellie will be there to inspire everyone when I'm gone." He addressed the audience again, feeling his coat grow heavier and colder as he spoke. "In a moment you will see the way I have learned to travel. Rest assured, you will learn it, too. Anything is possible if you open your mind to your limitless potential." Damian looked around, knowing that words would not convince them, they would have to be shown. In a kinder way than he had sprung it on Sabine, whose image immediately rose in front of his mind's eye. He had to get back to her, it would be getting late there, he needed to hurry now. "Please trust us here on this stage, and remember you all saw 'The Sign' of changes to come, exactly as the old scriptures promised. They were right, and the time for change is now. You and your ancestors, together with a little help from our galactic neighbours, have created the icehawk you saw, through your dreams and imaginations. My new abilities to travel are the manifestation of who I wanted to be. And you will see your dreams come true, too, if you just allow them to be. Make them good." Damian looked around, met with mainly stunned looks, though some excitement was shining through, too. It would take time for everyone to be convinced, but it didn't matter, they were all just at the beginning. "Friends, trust your inner voices. I shall go and leave you in peace now." Damian waved to the audience who this time applauded him a little more heartily, and turned to embrace Nellie and Bob, who hugged him back like an old friend. He knelt down to hug Stefan and Sophie who gave him a kiss on his cold cheeks, with fresh tears running down her face. She hated goodbyes. Damian fixed his eyes on hers and wiped her tears away. "Don't worry, Little Hawk, you're a Queen, remember? Keep calm and strong, I'll see you again soon, thank you for everything."

Still kneeling, Damian turned and stretched his head up high, chin forward. He opened his now feathery arms wide, his coat, hair and face blending ever more into beautiful shades of glistening browns, still recognisable as Damian, but looking ever more hawk like, the air shimmering around him. There was no fear in the crowd as they watched his wings turn to ice, there was only a sense of joy and excitement as he took off, effortlessly, rising above them, elegant and beautiful. The doors sprung open, as if on cue, as he glided through them dissolving into watery invisibility. His parting gift of brown feathers floated gently down all around them.

· · · • • ● • • · · ·

SABINE TRIED TO enjoy soaking in a soothing hot bath in her flat.
She was on her own now that Marcus and Paul had decided to
call it a night and drive back to York. Yvonne had gone to work
and Nina and Kade were back home with Brent. She looked
across the bubbles at all her simple homely bits and pieces that
made her bathroom look like the seaside. A few large shells here
and there, the pale blue on the walls, and the cream wooden
floor with a beach towel to step on. The bathroom cabinet where
Uncle Marcus had left his iLink what seemed like half an eternity
ago. The piece of driftwood she'd found in Robin Hood's Bay,
now doubling up as her robe hook on the wall.

Nothing had changed, and yet everything was different now.
Her Uncle Marcus no longer just had eyes and ears for her, she
had to share him with Damian and his mother now, and she had
to share Damian with everything that was happening to him. Just
thinking of it made her eyes sting with tears.

Yvonne and Uncle Marcus were at the beginning of a perfectly
normal romance, and so were Mary and Bill. It would be all smiles
at the party, everyone happy. Neither of them growing wings or
hooves or flying off anywhere. It just wasn't fair that she got none
of the delicious benefits of a new romance, only abnormal, mainly
frightening times so far. She used to love coming home from her
job, relax, enjoy life and dream of some far off soulmate to meet
one day, with no bigger concerns than work, perfecting her music
practice and what to have for dinner. It had been an easy life, full
of hope.

Sabine held her breath, pinched her nose and lowered her
head under water, as she always did, to let everything wash over
her.

Damian's boots dripped on the mat outside of Sabine's door.
He was back. Cold, wet, starving. His brown suede jacket heavy
with damp, some feathers still stuck to it, dotted over him like a half
plucked chicken. He had no idea how long he'd been standing
there, literally, trying to find his feet again, making sure he was in

one piece, adjusting his senses. It was a relief to be able to knock on her door this time, he didn't think brazenly landing in her living room was quite the civil thing to do. His arrival skills must have progressed, that was good news. There was a hint of her bubble bath he could smell, and of the coffee Marcus liked, even on the landing Sabine's place smelled wonderful, welcoming, safe. All he really wanted was to get out of his wet clothes, have a hot shower and get into bed with Sabine and sleep. But he knew she was waiting for him in there, probably very much fed up with him, and would be looking to him for some guidance. The guidance he so sorely wanted for himself.

Sabine heard Damian's knock just as she stepped out of the bath. Her heart did something, whether skip or sink she wasn't quite sure. She hadn't really expected him any more, even Marcus and Paul had got tired waiting for him. The memory of her running up the stairs not so long ago, so eager to see him then crossed her mind, and her bitter disappointment when he wasn't there. What if he couldn't wait to see her just the same? She flung the fluffy robe round her that he knew so well, and ran to open the door for him, hesitation forgotten.

He looked amazing. Wet again, as usual, and tired, but his eyes glowing, his posture tall and straight, with a relieved smile on his face that was so good to see.

"You've still got feathers stuck on you, you daft thing!" She joked and pulled him in the flat, no longer able to hold back her need to kiss him. "Where have you been?" She mumbled as they both kissed hungrily, she slid his wet coat off his shoulders, not caring that it dropped on the floor.

"At a meeting." Damian laughed, before kissing her some more.

"Seriously! Like any ordinary bloke, I've just come back from a meeting in Alaska! That's so funny! Can that be our new line, that I'm just going to meetings?" Damian's delight at having found such a simple way of looking at things was so obvious that his laugh was infectious. Yes, somehow that would make the strangeness of his disappearances alright!

"Oh, I love that!" Sabine hugged him, she would be able to handle that, she felt sure of it, it happened to couples all the time, didn't it. Shift workers, doctors, firemen, she could just get used to having a partner with unusual working hours. It was almost ordinary. Smiling, she didn't mind thinking of the words 'partner' or 'husband', she just wanted to be with him, so much, forever and ever. Damian hugged her firmly in response, himself relieved to think he could find a way of dealing with the changes as they happened. "I love it, too, I'll be able to cope better this way, I think! Everything has happened so fast, I'm so so sorry, Sweetheart. I want to spend my life with you, have babies together, buy you kittens and puppies and have a cottage with roses round the door, the whole works!" Damian got breathless, his eyes beaming, the words almost tumbling over themselves.

"But I know everything's been so fast and weird, and I look like a plucked turkey, so don't answer now, I will ask you again, and again and again, until you're sure and hopefully say yes. Ok?"

Sabine laughed with him, excited and carefree now, she knew she'd say yes, it didn't matter when, she'd say yes anyhow when the time was right. But for now she could ask him to stay the night, have him there with her, just the two of them for a change, she so wanted him to stay. She laughed when Damian made it pretty obvious he didn't need inviting twice, both of them seeing a future far beyond the night, ready to start on the road of their life together. Unable to stop kissing her, Damian looked quite serious when he looked into her eyes. "I will always say yes to you, you know. To you, to us."

Sabine kissed him back and laughed again. "And tomorrow we go to your Mum's party as a proper couple. And we'll watch Uncle Marcus give her the music box and her being all smitten."

The bedroom door closed behind them. Nobody would disturb them now.

The next morning Nina cheerfully waved her two men off, as they were heading for some serious male bonding in the toy and cake shops in York. "Have fun, boys!"

"And you enjoy having some quiet time on your own, Huskie!"

Brent blew her a kiss through the car window and drove off, with a very excited little boy on the back seat. It took Nina all of an hour to start itching with restlessness. The house was so quiet! She laid her clothes out in readiness for Yvonne's party, turned on the music on her iLink, pushed the headphones in her ears and went outside. Looking up at the sky she couldn't help but laugh. The conditions were just about perfect.

Humming along to 'The Eagle and the Hawk', Nina felt for the fresh packet of chewy sweets in her pocket. Oh yes, she knew exactly what she would do on this sunshiny day. The sugar would come in handy.

The End

· · • • ● • • · ·

Printed in Great Britain
by Amazon

45151392R00212